REMEMBRANCE

Ripley's heart leaped at a low cry from the door where Remembrance stood, her eyes big and luminous in the faint light. He said, "Remembrance, I wanted to tell you—"

She fumbled with the strap, then suddenly dropped the bag and ran toward the door. Ripley caught her, drew her hands from the latch. "Remembrance! Look up at me." Deep joy filled him. "Remembrance! I love you!"

She turned suddenly in his arms. "I love you, Rip. I've been trying all along to think I didn't." She was crying quietly in his arms, one hand against his cheek. "When I touched that bag—I knew you'd take that bag and go away over the hill and you wouldn't be coming back."

He smoothed her hair. "But I am coming back." He caught her closer. "I've got to." Her arms tightened. "I just want to be part of you and care for what matters to you." He stroked her cheek. "This war won't last forever."

Her breath went in brokenly. "But we've got to win it first, Rip."

. . . AND REVOLUTION

This is the first book in a series of historical novels by Bruce Lancaster that brilliantly portrays the people and events of the American Revolutionary War. Watch for the forthcoming books titled *The Secret Road, Phantom Fortress,* and *Blind Journey.*

TRUMPET TO ARMS

by Bruce Lancaster

PINNACLE BOOKS NEW YORK CITY

This is a work of fiction. All the characters and events portrayed in this book are fictional, and any resemblance to real people or incidents is purely coincidental.

TRUMPET TO ARMS

A Pinnacle Books edition, published by special arrangement with Little, Brown and Company in association with The Atlantic Monthly Press.

ISBN: 0-523-00887-2

First printing, July 1976

Cover illustration by Bruce Minney

Printed in the United States of America

PINNACLE BOOKS, INC.
275 Madison Avenue
New York, N. Y. 10016

FOR MY WIFE

JESSIE PAYNE LANCASTER

From the east to the west blow the trumpet to arms!
  Through the land let the sound of it flee;
Let the far and the near all unite, with a cheer,
  In defence of our Liberty Tree.

—THOMAS PAINE, *The Liberty Tree*

FOREWORD

On the morning of April 19, 1775, a British detachment set fire to some wooden gun carriages in the town of Concord in Massachusetts. The smoke was seen by a few militia companies who were watching from a near-by hill. Thinking that the town was being burned, the companies soberly marched down to prevent, if they could, such a tragedy. To reach the town, they had to cross a bridge held by British light infantry who fired on them, took a volley in return, and then fled in inexplicable panic.

The militia kept on marching, not only into Concord, but on to Charlestown, other companies joining them en route. Many thought that Charlestown was the end of the march. It was the beginning. There would be no halt until six years later on the muddy ground about Yorktown in Virginia.

This book does not attempt to tell the story of those five years of marching. It is concerned with the strange transmutation of local militia companies from all the Colonies into the first American Army. It ends with the campaign of Trenton and Princeton, by which time a man of the period could reason that that American Army was an enduring, permanent entity, could foresee its probable survival.

Specifically, we are concerned with what happened to a few imaginary people and with one actual regiment—John Glover's Marblehead men, the Twenty-first (later the Fourteenth) Massachusetts Infantry whose military descendants are now crossing bayonets with the Japanese instead of with the Hessians.

The imaginary people may move freely within the limits of possibility and probability. In dealing with the regiment and the larger units that affected it, a good deal of care was required. Records of the time were kept most sketchily or simply not kept. Thus it is often impossible to say exactly what given units were concerned in a given action. For example, many accounts of the battle of Princeton state that Haslet's First Delaware Regiment was present, and it is known that Haslet himself was killed there; yet records show that the regiment had been disbanded some time before, owing to expired enlistments. Or records may seem to be contradictory. John Glover's Marbleheaders were in camp at Beverly at the time of Bunker Hill. How, then, may one account for the presence of two members of that regiment in the casualty lists of the battle?

In such confusion, it has been necessary to fall back on possibility and probability. Thus, if a brigade or division is known to have been in an action, it is justifiable, I think, to assume that its component regiments, unless specifically excluded, were also present.

The appearance of Marbleheaders on Knox's march with the Ticonderoga guns is entirely fictitious. But again, the records of that march are so fragmentary that I felt no hesitation in assuming the incident. For all I know, they *might* have been there, and their background and training would have made them a logical choice.

The main acknowledgement which I have to make is to my wife, who studied each line and each page of the manuscript, ever ready with helpful suggestion or stimulating comment, always encouraging.

No one can write of the first year of the Revolution without constant reference to the works of Allen French. To his writings, to his advice, and to his interest in this book I owe a great deal.

To Scott Mabon I am indebted for his interest and his high degree of editorial skill.

In collecting material and tracking down sources, I was greatly aided by Mr. Robert Haynes, Mr. Foster Palmer, and the staff of the Harvard College Library.

B. L.

LINCOLN, MASSACHUSETTS
January 1944

TRUMPET TO ARMS

PART ONE

FROM THIS HOUR, FREEDOM

I

THE marine's coat was harsh and red against the bare tree trunks as he leaned on his musket to stare up the course of Vine Brook. A wan March sun, now high above Whispering Hill, fell on his deep-set eyes, high-bridged nose, and strong chin. As he remembered the terrifying glitter of steel that he had caught at day-break along the Aberjona, his glance marked out a route over to the western ridge—a towering rock, a clump of willows, a tunnel-like cleft. The chain of cover would carry him, well hidden, across the valley. He shook himself and slithered down, his legs wobbly with fatigue. Branches struck against his brass-fronted cap and caught at the long tails of his coat. From each bit of shelter his eyes tried to pierce the tangle of trunks and stark limbs. Once he shrank back, trembling at a sudden din. Then he scowled at the crows that winged north above him, cawing.

As he started up the west slope, pain stabbed at his foot and he knew that the blister he had first noticed far back by Rag Rock had broken. He swore mechanically and ducked into a clump of firs by the crest to study the uneven road in front of him. Hunger swept over him and the woods swirled before his eyes. This seizure was stronger than the one that had gripped him before daybreak and he leaned against a tree until it passed. Then he resumed his mute questioning of the road. Just an old lumber road, but it must run on into Lexington, to the trim taverns where a shilling could end the surging weakness. No. The town, sprawling along the main highway, might flash with the same steel that had frozen him along the Aberjona.

He plunged on until he came to a stream which he knew for the Shawsheen, muttering along among black rocks. Beyond the stream lay Bedford, remote from the main roads. Few towns in eastern Massachusetts could be safer for him than Bedford.

Soon he was looking onto the prim street from a hollow between two shattered houses. Cautiously he skirted a woodpile and edged up to the small-paned windows of Increase Fox's tavern. If there were danger for him, the tavern would hold it rather than a village house.

He could see a fire on the broad hearth, a man seated at a table close by the blaze. The light was poor and the marine could make out neither cut nor color of the coat. He started to move away uncertainly. Then a scent of new-baked bread curled toward him. He gripped his musket, stepped to the broad door, and pushed it carefully open.

The man by the hearth looked up. "Hi! Inky! Here's a Lobster."

The marine felt the warmth of the room move toward him. The man had said "Lobster." He was safe for the moment. He eased himself into a chair, dimly aware of a rumble from the room beyond: "Tell him to take his trade to them as wants it."

The marine fumbled a coin onto the table. "Got to eat," he muttered. "I can pay." Then he slid forward in his chair, saved himself by gripping hard at his musket.

The man by the fire snarled: "Drunk! We'll roll him out."

The marine forced his eyes open, tried to speak. From the depths of an opal-tinted mist, the man swayed toward him, finger pointing. "No! You're Rip Mayne or I'm a Tory! Ain't you now, ain't you?"

"Yes. Mayne. Got to eat." The tones were thin, uncertain.

The man backed away. "Inky! The Lobster! It's Mel Mayne's boy!"

From an inner room Increase Fox hurried, lean and aproned. "What you talking about?" He stared. "By God, it's him all right!" His eyes flicked from the red coat to the deep-tanned face above it. Then he dove into the inner room and came back with a steaming plate, a mug. He picked up the shilling, grunting. "God damn me if I ever expected to see a Concord boy turn Lobster." He pulled a chair close to the table, the other man clattering up beside him.

Ripley Mayne snatched at the iron spoon and plunged it into the pork and beans. He was hardly aware of swallowing the first mouthful, felt his throat close against the second. Fox pushed the mug toward him. "Take a pull at that milk. You ain't been living high enough to pile into pork and beans like that."

Mayne dropped his head to avoid the stares of the men, ashamed of his hunger and his weakness. He drank the milk carefully.

Fox leaned his elbows on the table. "You know me?" The marine nodded. "And him?"

Mayne, chewing carefully on fresh bread, said: "Abner Merrill. Used to live past Blood's, out Carlisle way."

"Still do. Now what you got to tell us—me and Inky?"

Mayne sipped his milk again. The room had steadied down and a gradual warmth was creeping over him, melting the weary shakiness of arms and legs.

"Go on. We're waiting," said Fox.

"Never mind about me. What about Father?"

"Saw him up to Barrett's Mill last night," began Merrill. "He was helping—"

Fox kicked him under the table, then tapped the foul anchor on the cap's brass plate. "Where'd you get this?"

Mayne shook his head impatiently. "Father still holding the farm?"

Merrill blew out his cheeks. "Added that piece that takes in the hemlocks by Egg Rock last year. Been made head of—"

Again Fox's foot swung. "We're wasting time. Rip, what you doing in that coat?"

Mayne said tersely: "Deserting."

The men stared. Fox said: "Sure of it?"

"You don't desert from His Majesty's Marines without thinking a lot."

Merrill sucked his teeth. "Uh-huh. Seen deserters shot on Boston Common."

Mayne's eyes hardened. "They're glad to get shot by the time the guard's through with them. I know."

Fox leaned across the table. "You're deserting. That's one thing. Next is, how'd you get so's you had something to desert from? You went to England three —four years ago. What happened?"

"Ever hear of a press gang?"

Fox scowled. "Better tell the truth. Can't press for army or marines."

"They don't call it pressing. But they've got laws that say how a dozen different kinds of people can be taken. Smugglers for one."

Fox made a gesture of disgust. "Smuggler! A farmer like you!"

Mayne shook his head wearily. "It was about that stuff from my Uncle John's warehouses that I took to England to sell after he died. You knew about that.

The press picked me up. A navy press. They couldn't use me, of course. But they looked at my papers and took me to a J.P. and he damned me for a rebel and smuggler. By God, I bet I've been a better subject of the King than he has. But he just waved those Martinique invoices at me and told the press to take me away."

Merrill blinked. "But you weren't a smuggler."

Fox glared at him. "That'll make Rip feel better. Well, what then?"

"What do you think? I've been serving in dockyards and on stinking ships. I've frozen off Copenhagen and I've fried off Tangier."

Merrill nodded complacently. "Now just think of Mel Mayne's boy seeing all those places!"

Fox contemplated the deserter through half-closed eyes. "So it was true after all! Your father'd told folks about getting a letter from you—maybe more. But most thought that you'd got into trouble and he was covering you up."

Mayne stiffened. "You doubted him?"

"Easy, easy. They ain't a man about here that'd question the word of Melven Mayne. Folks nodded and said you'd taken the stuff to England to sell for the estate and no money'd ever come back—nor you, neither. So they figured that Mel'd stretched his conscience a bit and who'd blame him? Well, how'd you get back here?"

The answer was heavy with weariness and anger. "Last winter, my ship—a seventy-four—put in at Chatham. Before we could land, the bastards snapped us onto another ship that was ready to sail. No warm uniforms, no pay. You're only paid at the end of a cruise, and if you're not ashore—which we weren't—the money goes back to the Admiralty. There's eighteen months' pay I'll never get. We ended up in Halifax, the damnedest, coldest, foggiest port on God's earth. Last month we came down to Salem and as soon as my platoon was landed, I got myself lost and hit inland. I'd been planning it ever since we cleared for Halifax. One way or another, I was going to get back here."

"Are they on your trail?" asked Fox.

"Don't know. Thought I saw guns along the Aberjona this morning, but I've been keeping off the roads."

Fox and Merrill exchanged glances. Fox said: "They ain't got patrols looking for you—not this way, at least."

"How do you know?"

"We got ways. You'd have been safe on the roads."

"Maybe I'd have gone across country anyway," muttered Mayne.

Merrill gaped. "Trade soft going for hard?"

Mayne threw himself back in his chair. "You wouldn't know what I mean. You've been here right along." His fist thumped on the table. "Do you see—I was walking over New England farms. When I saw my first stone wall—"

Fox's chair rasped as he rose. "Guess I know what you mean. Seems as if you ain't had an uncommon easy time."

"Easy!" Mayne's eyes darkened. "The officers damned me for a Yankee rebel. When they found out I'd been to college, it was worse. They made me polish their buttons and their boots. They—why once off Porto Bello—" He stopped. The memory of that first flogging was too sharp in his mind.

Fox's voice was almost gentle. "What's happened has happened. Want to eat any more?"

Mayne shook his head. "Thought I could eat right down to the cellar, but I couldn't even finish this plate."

"That's the way it is," said the innkeeper. "Remember the same thing at Crown Point in '58. Well, what you going to do now?"

Mayne's fingers began ripping at the buttons of his uniform. "Get rid of all this, if you'll lend me clothes that'll get me to Concord. Then you know what I'm going to do? I'm going to harness up the biggest horse we've got and I'm going to plow for a month, steady." His voice sank. "I'm going to plow. I'm going to sow. God—it's more than three years since I turned a furrow or smelt the young shoots coming up through a Concord rain."

"Maybe they won't let you," said Fox.

"Who'll stop me?" asked Mayne, struggling with tight sleeves.

"There'll maybe be other things to do."

The soiled red jacket skated across the floor. "Not for me."

* * *

The road out of Bedford trailed away south and west. Ripley Mayne, picking his way carefully along, felt as though a tight-drawn spring within him had been released forever. A free man, he trod free ground. His body, done with tight jacket and strangling stock, began to lose its drilled stiffness, to shape itself to the loose coat and homespun breeches that Fox had lent him. Only the boots, gnawing at the open blister, were left from the past.

Half-forgotten landmarks appeared as he pushed slowly on. A blasted maple that had served as rendezvous for a long-ago hunt; a gray-black rock shouldering up among the trees by Hartwell's Brook; then, from a low ledge, a glimpse of bright water slipping through the meadows—the Concord River. Salem, the land about Whispering Hill, near Bedford, had just been stages on his route. But the river—it was an open trail that led back to his deepest roots, to the sober town and the old house at Nashawtuc Hill. He swung his stick and quickened his pace, thoughts deep in the land that lay to the west. At last, the belt of trees that had masked his view for the past mile or more ended abruptly and the Concord ridge swept up at the right. He left the road and half ran, half hobbled over plowed fields toward the slope.

When he came to the crest he had to brace himself against the sudden picture that spread out before him. At his feet, the houses huddled close against the very ridge where the first settlers, the original Mayne among them, had burrowed in 1635. Then the east-west road to Lexington and the wide, treeless marsh beyond. Slowly he took in the message of shingle and chimney, houses that had been part of his life as they had been part of the old town's. Across the road to the right, the white Meetinghouse loomed, Wright's Tavern and the milldam beyond it, the Town House and, sharp behind them, Nashawtuc Hill—his goal.

He drew a deep breath and hurried on down the south slope, crossed the road and the sweep of the sodden meadows. A stone wall loomed before him and he checked himself abruptly.

There was the old, rutted road, a second wall, and beyond it a rolling sweep of country. There was the old house, trim and solid against a far shoulder, its chimney sending out a plume of warmth against the chill sky. Below it, barn and shed spread to the west, wide doors gaping. The faint tonk-a-tonk of cow bells shimmered across the valley and a leisurely troop of cattle lounged up from the river pastures. Almost unconsciously Ripley counted them—five, seven, twelve, until the last twitching tail had vanished into the barn. Then he turned his eyes to the fields. On the east and south, furrows had already been broken. The land looked rich, well-tended. There were gaps in the stone walls that would need mending and a scrubby growth had begun to creep down from a grove that edged an upper field.

There was work to be done. Under his care, walls would grow trim again. Every field would be rid of brush and briar. It all lay waiting for him. Never again would he leave. He was part of the land and the land was part of him. He climbed over the rough stones, crossed the road and the Mayne bridge that spanned the loop of the Sudbury. With something like timidity, he stepped onto the land of his fathers. He didn't have to look for a path. There it was, under his foot, and as he followed it each rock and tree spoke to him, revived old memories.

Then the smell of cows and hay was strong in his nostrils and he peered through the barn door at the long row of swinging tails, heard the crunch-crunch of slow jaws. The light was dim, but his hand struck against a pail, a stool. He leaned his forehead against a firm flank and began to milk.

"Ripley!"

The staccato cry, almost a shout, brought him to his feet. There stood his father, tall and only a little bent, staring at him. Ripley took a step forward, hands jerking out. He felt an arm fall across his shoulder, knew that the deep-set eyes were looking into his, bright with a joy that seemed too keen to bear. Ripley cried: "Father!"

The grip about his shoulder tightened. "Rip! You're—" Melven Mayne's voice shook a little, then grew steady. A smile flicked at the corners of his firm mouth as his eyes fell on the half-full pail. "There's a lot to tell. But—the cows have got to be milked. All the hired men are at drill this evening, so you and I'll go through the herd—just the way we used to. Then we'll walk back to the house and have the whole story." He hesitated. "It—it's good to see you, Rip." Then he caught up a stool and walked off, the smocklike coat that Ripley remembered so well flicking about his stout wool stockings.

Eyes on the retreating figure, Ripley sank back on the stool and began to milk mechanically.

When the last cow had been finished, father and son hooked the heavy buckets onto shoulder yokes and carried their loads to the old stone well house, then started up the slope. Ripley, hiding his limp as best he could, felt deep contentment flooding him. The two were walking back to supper as they had walked so often in the past, as they would in the future.

His head went back as the ridge of the house showed along the hillside, the roof, and the green fanlight high in the gable. The end windows of the second floor were staring at him through their small panes, the peak of the long shed reached out toward him.

Then the wide boards of the kitchen were under his feet and he looked at the great fireplace, the oak settle beside it, at the pewter and china of the dresser that jingled to the slam of the door.

Melven Mayne said: "Old Mrs. Parr still looks after me and the house, but she left early tonight. Dinner's in the Dutch oven. We'll serve ourselves. You'll want to shave, I expect. There's hot water in the kettle."

Ripley tried to shape the words to tell something of what he felt, fumed at the New England diffidence that locked his tongue. Then he met his father's eyes and read understanding in them. He splashed hot water into a ewer and walked slowly off to his room.

The four-post bed was crisp with fresh linen and the colors of the patchwork quilt were unfaded. Floor and sill were spotless. The fire on the narrow hearth seemed newly laid. With unsteady hand he set the ewer on a small table and looked about him. The leather bindings of his books in the long, low case by the window had been oiled and their tops were free of dust. Uncertainly he opened the closet door and saw all the clothes he had not taken to England brushed and in good order. In a corner his fishing rods shone with new varnish and the trigger of his fowling piece was bright with oil. The room had been kept for him through the long months and years as though any moment might bring the touch of his hand to the latch.

He sat down on the bed, eyes far away. How often had Melven Mayne crossed that threshold to sit in the ladder-back or on the bed itself? What had his thoughts been?

Ripley shook his head, got to his feet, and stripped off the borrowed coat. He shaved carefully, then poured the rest of the hot water into a basin and soaked his blistered foot. Idly his hand went out to a small drawer in the bureau that Joe Hosmer had built for him five years ago. The smooth wood slid easily and he drew out a stack of papers—old letters, old bills. December 7, 1769—a note from one of the Wheeler girls, asking him to join in a sleigh ride to Framingham. August 10, 1771—a bill from fat young Henry Knox's London Bookstore in Boston. October 20, 1771—R. Mayne, Esq., was requested to call at the residence of the President of Harvard College. It had been about repeated absence from prayers, Ripley recalled with a wry smile.

He felt in the drawer again and found the parchment roll that testified to the fact that the President's displeasure had been fleeting. Then his eyebrows lifted. Many of the letters were unopened, had been carefully laid in his drawer against his return. He ripped apart the first white square. Winthrop Somers, a classmate, had written him, in mock seriousness, that Somers's familiarity with the alphabet and the rudiments of arithmetic had won him a post on the faculty of Yale. Later, he hoped to work his way up to a dame school but realized that he must start at the bottom. Win Somers. When had he written? The letter was headed "New Haven, in Connecticut, April 9, 1774."

Ripley flicked the letter against his chin. Where had he been on April 9, 1774? Of course—on a seventy-four off Algeciras—or was it Cape Bon in Tunis? Suddenly, the lost years began to edge into his mind. That bend in the Sudbury, which he could see from his window, recalled a stream that flowed into the Tagus, east of Lisbon. He had gone there on a rare liberty party with a young shepherd from the Grampians and a ratty little man from the stable-yards of the Bath Road. He frowned, tried to turn his mind back to Win Somers, but found that all thought was overlaid by memories of stiff files lining a gangway to receive a West India governor or a visiting admiral. Then the scene shifted to a flaming square in Jamaica through which Royal Marines, bayonets fixed, moved in a solid body through a press of yelling blacks while the night air rolled and throbbed to the beat of jungle drums off in the hills.

His father's voice, calling from the dining room, roused him. He dried his foot carefully, then threw from him the last of his borrowed clothes and began to burrow among the sleek coats hanging in the closet, among the frilled shirts, sprinkled with lavender, in the dresser. He grinned ruefully as the crisp linen slid over his scarred shoulders. Service in His Majesty's Marines had added to the solid breadth that years of farm life had given him. He started to lay out a looser, coarser shirt, a homespun jacket. Then he tossed them back. "Let them split," he thought. "By God, tonight I'm going to wear linen and broadcloth and be damned to the seams!"

Shoes, too, were a problem, but by adjusting the broad silver buckles he was able to walk out of his room without too much discomfort. He found his father in the big, low-ceilinged dining room where candlelight and firelight were soft on polished wood and silver. Ripley, covertly watching the older man saying grace, saw deeper lines than he remembered about the closed eyes, noted heavy furrows that ran from the high-bridged nose to the mouth that was precise without being prim.

After the grave "Amen," Melven Mayne's knife slid gently into a big roast. Ripley said: "I've dreamed of this. Fresh beef, roast potatoes, jelly."

"I can imagine," said his father. He indicated a fluted decanter. "Pour some of that Madeira." He talked on, eating heartily. It looked like a good year for trout. Deer were scarcer than ever, but maybe the two could find time to go up beyond the Merrimac and get a decent buck. There'd be good pickerel in Walden Pond.

Later they sat in the snug parlor where ladder-backs

curved comfortably about a fire. Melven Mayne brought churchwarden pipes and a blue tobacco jar. "Now, Rip," he said, "what about yourself?"

Ripley studied the glowing bowl of his pipe. "It's hard to think about anything just now except this tobacco. Different from the black twist I've been smoking. About myself—" He hesitated. "Well, you see—"

His father edged his chair closer. "Why not start with the last letter you sent before you were taken? You were going to see Beasley, the factor. What then?"

"Why, Beasley sent a note to the Anchor, asking me to look in the next day instead." That was how it had been. Then the walk, to kill time, through the old seaport. "And just as I was turning a corner down by the docks, people began yelling: 'The press!' "

The story tumbled out. No, the press didn't want him. But his papers! The ensign had questioned them. So had the Justice of the Peace before whom he was dragged. Invoices on goods from Martinique, from Cartagena! Hadn't those damned Colonials heard about the Navigation Acts? Convicted smugglers were available for marching regiments or His Majesty's Marines. The dockyards were calling for more men—and why? Because His Majesty must send more troops to Boston in Massachusetts. That's why. So let this smuggler fill up the draft. Plymouth Dockyard. A uniform. The ship putting to sea.

As the tale went on, Melven Mayne turned sidewise to the table, eyes on the fire. Once his pipestem snapped and he rose, found a fresh pipe, and took his place without speaking.

At last Ripley said, "That's all. They can't take me back. I tell you nothing will ever take me from here."

"I hope not. You're pretty safe, so far as marines are concerned. Troops never come this far. Random officers do dine at Wright's sometimes. But I can tell you for a fact that no troops have left Boston in more than a week. If they ever do, we'll have ample word."

"That's what Fox and Ab Merrill said. How *can* you know?"

"We'll come to that later. About your story—" Melven Mayne sighed. "I don't need to tell you that I did what I could when I had your letter. I wrote Ben Franklin in London, but all he could find out was that you had been impressed, were at sea and out of reach. It's a frightful story. Perhaps one day we can do something about it."

Ripley shook his head. "All I want is to be let alone."

"I'm glad, Rip. Now, about the town. There've been all sorts of stories about you. You may get some hard looks."

"I'll take care of them," said Ripley shortly. "Tell me what's been happening in the Province."

His father got up and began pacing about the room. "It's not easy. Just think back to the way things were going when you left. They were moving down a slope then. The slope's getting steeper all the time."

In slow sentences, Ripley learned of the growing encroachments of the Crown on what New Englanders looked upon as inherent rights of free men. The Town Meetings, the very sap and blood of New England life, were abolished. The Port of Boston was closed tight to sail or oar. A bill had been passed barring the coastal waters to New England fishermen. Almost all the Province officers were now subject to Crown appointment, not to election by the people they were supposed to serve. Then there was the matter of the powder that General Gage, in command in Boston, had seized. It had been *Province* powder. Gage had also seized Province cannon in Cambridge. Why, it was as though Colonel Pickering of the Salem militia had gone to the Tower of London and seized royal arms!

Ripley shrugged. "A lot of things are done without any shadow of right. But we'll weather all this, I guess." He trimmed the candle by his elbow. "Ab Merrill told me you'd bought the land by Egg Rock."

His father held up his hand. "We'll get to that. But I haven't finished about Province doings. No. They're more than that. They affect every colony from New Hampshire to Georgia." He spoke of the Committee of Safety, the Committees of Correspondence and Supply, that kept in touch with similar bodies in other colonies, linking districts hitherto barely aware of each other. "We've got our own Provincial Congress. So have all the others." He lowered his voice. "We're beginning to act together. Rip, it may be hard for you to believe—it is for me, sometimes—but we've actually got a Congress of the Whole—a Continental Congress."

Ripley shook ashes from his pipe. "How about the people who side with the Crown?"

His father seated himself again. "There's the sore spot. They take it badly. There's been violence against them. Not here in Concord, fortunately. But our old friend Dan Bliss had to leave town and the Lees, on the other side of Nashawtuc, are being watched pretty closely. But that's all. I wish it were so in other places. The trouble is that many of these Tories are damnably arrogant about it. They're saying that all the trouble is caused by a penniless rabble, and that the solid people are for the Crown."

"Sounds damned silly to me," said Ripley. "Sorry to hear about Dan Bliss—he had ability. And he had family and money—if that's what's meant by 'solid people.'"

"That's what they think they mean. But look at this. Dan Bliss has to run for Boston. His brother, every bit as fine a man as Dan, serves on a committee with me. No—there's no dividing line, except, of course, for Crown officers. It all might be easier if there were."

"Oh, Lord." Ripley stretched out his long legs. "What difference does it make? In a year's time it'll all be clear and Dan'll come back to Concord. What are these Congresses doing, anyway?"

"You can't see it as serious?" Melven Mayne's eyebrows lifted. "Here's one thing we've done—reorganized the militia."

"Reorganized it? Why?"

"I don't like it, but it's got to be done if we're going to do more than just talk. The militia's been sifted from top to bottom and every man who puts loyalty to Crown ahead of loyalty to human rights and decent living's been ousted. From colonels right down. We've got minute companies that'll turn out at the least warning, the regular companies, and what we call alarm companies that'll answer as a last resort—the older men, you know."

"I know. I've drilled with the militia. Once a year and every third man oozing rum." He set his pipe carefully on the small table. "Well, that won't do any harm."

"Things are moving, I tell you." Melven Mayne leaned forward. "We drill at least once a week. Last month we had joint maneuvers with the companies from Acton, Lincoln, Bedford, and Carlisle."

Ripley frowned. "That's dangerous. It's going too far. Why, ever since Massachusetts was settled, we've been snapping at England and she's been growling back at us. I can't understand all this new stuff. What's at the bottom of it?"

His father sighed. "I've walked miles over this farm trying to find the answer. I think I've got it, and it's mighty simple. We're used to governing ourselves. We think of it as a right. England's tired of our doing our own governing. She thinks it's a privilege, which she now wants to withdraw."

"But it's so simple," protested Ripley. "I don't mean your answer, but the solution. It can all be trimmed and dressed in time. As long as all hands stay set, no one'll move, there'll be a compromise and that'll be all." He looked about him contentedly. "It's good to be here. It's good to be home."

"I want you to have your eyes open in an uneasy time," said his father. "I'll—" He stopped, listening.

Out in the March night, hoofs thudded dully. Melven Mayne got up. "That'll be Bentley Stowe and Joe Ashland. They're on the Committee on Supply. Bentley's a cantankerous old fool, but he thinks right in a lot of ways." His neat queue bobbing, he left the parlor and strode to the hall.

Ripley planted himself by the fire, listening to the voices outside. Then Joseph Ashland's big frame filled the doorway, heavy face calm and judicial.

Ripley inclined his head. "Good evening, Mr. Ashland."

Ashland held out his hand. "It's good to see you back, Ripley. We'll all be glad to hear your story. Your father was telling us a little of it."

At his elbow, Bentley Stowe, lean and crowlike in rusty black, snapped: "Been a long time waiting." His hard eyes looked coldly at Ripley and his gray head barely stirred in response to Ripley's bow.

Ashland dropped his voice. "Easy, Bent, easy."

"I'm known for speaking my mind."

Melven Mayne closed the door. "Now, gentlemen, let's sit down. Pipes. Rip, just move that bowl of tobacco closer." He smiled benignly on the grave Ashland and the suspicious Stowe. "Yes, it's quite a story and in some ways it's not unconnected with things we talk about these days." His mellow voice sketched rapidly the tale of the press gangs, the long cruises. Ashland listened in silence. Stowe, his bitter mouth twisted, stared at Ripley's glossy coat until the account was ended.

"That's about right, isn't it, Rip?" asked his father.

Ripley nodded. Stowe thrust his sharp face forward. His disbelief was patent. "You're a mighty good father, Melven," he said. "Now we've got things to talk about. We're better off alone."

Ripley forced back a sudden wave of anger. After all, how would *he* have looked on such a story? And perhaps the lean, intense man was right. A current had been washing heavily through the country and its flood had not touched Ripley Mayne. Perhaps the less he heard, the better. He started to rise, then felt Ashland's hand on his arm. "Mel," said Ashland, "I'd be glad if the boy stayed."

Stowe's sallow face flushed. "How do we know he's all right? He's worn the coat."

Ripley said, "I think Mr. Stowe's right. After all, this is committee business and I'm not a member. You'll talk more freely if you're by yourselves."

He caught an odd look in Stowe's eyes as though the gaunt man felt that he had been robbed of a grievance. Ashland said: "Very well, but before you go, I've an idea that came to me while your father was talking. You've had plenty of drill, I suppose."

"Plenty," said Ripley dryly.

"Good. I'll see Jim Barrett, our colonel. He can use you."

Ripley slowly shook his head. "No. No, I guess not." He saw disappointment wither his father's face, heard Stowe exclaim in bitter satisfaction.

"Why not?" Incredulity sharpened Ashland's voice.

Ripley stared at the fire. "It's hard to explain."

Melven Mayne's voice reached earnestly toward Ashland. "I told you it was all new to him, Joe."

Ripley ran his hand over his black hair. "I said it'd be hard to explain. Father tells me you've got what you call an Army of Observation that'll turn out whenever Gage marches out of Boston in strength. One day he'll be out on a practice march. The forces'll meet. There'll be hotheads on both sides and you'll have a fight."

Ashland leaned forward. "That fight would be against the very men who stole good years from you."

"No!" said Ripley quickly. "I'd just be shooting down poor devils of soldiers or marines and I know how they live and how they came to be here."

Stowe looked coldly at him. "I'm opposed to his having anything to do with our plans. As it is, Gage knows far too much about what we do."

"Bentley!" Ashland's voice was harsh.

Ripley got up. "I can't blame Mr. Stowe, really. But I can assure all of you that I'm going to be too busy on the farm for anything like this."

Stowe's mouth set in a hard line. "So you say. But if we learn of your being in touch with the British—"

"Don't worry. I don't want *them* to get in touch with *me*. But I won't join you in fighting them."

Ashland spoke slowly. "You don't know how badly the troops have acted."

"I know what a garrison town's like. I also know what a cantankerous place Boston is."

"You mean Boston's wrong?" snapped Stowe.

"The Crown's wrong. It'll all get settled in time, though."

"But will you help us drill? Just drill?" asked Ashland earnestly.

Ripley sighed. "All right. I'll drill them if they'll take it from me."

Ashland looked relieved. "That's as much as we may ask, I think."

"I'm opposed to his having anything to do with it until we know more about him," said Stowe. "After all, he's worn the coat."

"We know him," said Ashland.

"But ain't Dan Bliss a Concord man and didn't we know him and his father and his grandfather? Dan's been sliding off toward the Crown so fast his coat-tails are smoking. Now what I say is—"

"That Rip's mighty tired and doesn't want to listen to us any longer," broke in Melven Mayne good-humoredly.

Ashland laughed. "That's the most sensible thing that has been said so far. Come to my house when you're ready, Rip."

"You won't have to wait long," said Ripley. "Good night, Mr. Ashland. Good night, Mr. Stowe." He rested a hand on his father's shoulder. "There are a lot more things that I want to talk to you about if you're not too tired when this is over."

Alone in his own room, Ripley knelt by the low window that looked out toward the Sudbury, a band of peaceful silver. The earth between him and that band was his. It lay there waiting for him.

II

DESPITE the early spring that bore a promise of rich rewards to the land and those who worked it, Ripley was aware of a growing uneasiness as March faded into April. He found it hard to fit back into his place in the quiet town. That there was deep suspicion of his past in many quarters was bad enough. But even among his old friends and classmates who welcomed him and who tried loyally to understand his holding back from the hot fever of the times, he felt uncomfortable. The years that he had spent as a marine had created an awkward gap.

As he crossed the North Bridge through a heavy flurry of April snow, he wondered morosely why he had let himself be dragooned into drilling the Concord companies. In the first place, it cost him hours of work about the farm. Then, although the men had been taking his instruction almost eagerly, there had been an undercurrent of jeering which he laid largely at the door of Bentley Stowe. That bitter man had been fulminating against Ripley, calling him the Prodigal. He hinted that the desertion was sham, that Ripley was in constant communication with Gage and Pitcairn in Boston.

Ripley shook snow from his cocked hat as he started up the slippery road that led to the muster field near Buttrick's house. He saw scurrying figures, muskets jouncing on their shoulders, on the skyline.

The snow squall died away as he reached the crest. The drill field was spattered with dark footprints and clusters of men threw snowballs, scuffled, shouted. They caught sight of Ripley and formed ragged lines. Jared Barnes, sergeant of one of the minute companies, loped up. "Ready to start? The boys are waiting."

"How about the officers?"

"Won't be here until later," said Barnes, rapping his snowy boots against a rock.

"Have you called roll?"

Barnes shouted a command. The other sergeants began rattling off the lists of names as Ripley took his place facing the lines. It *was* odd, he thought. Even without their officers, the companies stood steady, every eye to the front. Suddenly there was a shout of laughter, a rustle behind him, and a deluge of something soft and dry crackled over his head and shoulders. He spun quickly, saw a loose-jointed man, empty sack in hand, run hooting toward the stone wall that bounded the field.

Ripley looked at the snowy ground at his feet. It was covered with corn husks. Husks for the Prodigal, husks whereof the swine did eat. Slowly he forced back his anger, turned to the rocking lines of men. He deliberately stirred the husks with his foot, raised his voice: "It's a damned poor recruit who throws his rations about like this." The snickering died away, into an almost respectful hush.

Sergeant Barnes took up the ritual again. "All present or accounted for."

Ripley nodded. "Break them up into platoons. Have the sergeants put them through their facings. You watch the minute companies and I'll take the others."

For half an hour Ripley splashed about in the slush, hovering over the most awkward groups, trying to put the stilted language of the Norfolk Exercise into intelligible terms. Over and over he explained: "You're at attention, your heels four inches apart. Now—put your right heel four inches back of your left. Make a quarter turn to the right on your heels without moving them. With*out* moving them—"

One by one the officers began to drift onto the field—Colonel James Barrett, his son Nathan, the captain, Major John Buttrick, Minott, Hosmer, Miles. The companies were formed, given over to the officers while Ripley ran from one flank to the other, explaining to Charles Miles that his minute company wheeled raggedly because the men nearest the pivot were taking too long steps, urging Joe Hosmer to bark out his commands more sharply. Then he stood by Colonel Barrett and watched the long column tramp round and round the field, the sergeants yapping, "Hep-hep-hep!" while a cloud of urchins, sticks over their shoulders, scuttled delightedly after them.

Barrett cleared his throat. "Look any better to you?"

"They'll do. They've got spirit and they're trying all the time." Privately, he thought that there was too much talking in ranks, arms were not handled cleanly and footwork was ragged. Still, there was an amazing underlying seriousness and there could be no doubt that the Concord companies were formed of material that a regular officer would have given ten years of his life to train and handle.

When the drill was over, many of the men straggled away from the field, but others, in squads and platoons, stayed to work on difficult points by themselves. Ripley was buttonholed by Miles, by Hosmer, by Minott, asked to shed light on the mysteries of the hollow square, of movements from column to line. Dusk began to fall over the trampled field as Ripley scratched diagrams in the snow, draggled urchins squatting wide-eyed among the attentive officers.

Freed at last, he tramped home through the slush and changed his wet clothes. Melven Mayne was reporting to one of the Congressional Committees down at the Meetinghouse, so he dined alone, his restlessness growing. After dinner he idled about the house, picked up books, laid them down unopened. Suddenly he snatched up his cloak and hat and started for town, hoping to find some congenial stranger at Wright's, someone like that man from Woburn who, in a mournful voice, had told stories until the taproom had echoed to the shouts of his listeners.

He plodded on through the slush, crossed the milldam, and pushed open the heavy door of Wright's Tavern.

The little taproom at the right of the hall was empty, save for the tapster, a shambling bear of a man whose real name had been buried long ago under the title of Featherfoot. Ripley waved. "Brandy for me."

Featherfoot lumbered about, filled a thick glass. "That look right to you? Water?" He wiped his hands on his apron. "Kind of quiet tonight, Rip, but you ought to have been here last night. Pucket, the hired man to Buttrick's, was showing how he could move an army corps across the Assabet in ten minutes—exact. It was mighty cute."

Ripley swished his glass about. "Must have been reading the Bible."

"Huh?" Featherfoot's ponderous face wrinkled in thought.

"It's the only book I know of that tells how to walk on water."

The shambling man looked slightly shocked. "Now, Rip, I don't know's you'd ought to talk like that."

The door of the taproom burst open and a tall young man stood in the entrance, his caped shoulders nearly filling it. Piercing blue eyes fell on Ripley, high-colored cheeks wrinkled in a grin. The man bellowed. "Saved! By God, I was scared I'd have to drink alone."

The tapster beamed on him. "The same as usual, Mr. Cuyler?"

Cuyler scaled his hat onto one table, dropped his cape on another, and swung easily into the chair facing Ripley. "The same and double." He grinned at Ripley. "You're paying for this. Mine's the next." He caught eagerly at a small glass of Holland gin, drained it, then flipped it over his shoulder to gaping Featherfoot.

Ripley laughed, carried away by the ruddy man's calm assumption of welcome. He raised his glass to the other's toast as he studied him. He was sure that he had never before seen that square, clear-skinned face, that blond hair that curled so closely about the wall-shaped head. "Stranger, Mr. Cuyler?" he asked.

"Stranger than hell. Never heard of this town until two weeks ago and never saw it until last night. Speaking of strangers, do I have to bribe Atlas there back of the bar to find out who *you* are?"

"Bribe me if you like," grinned Ripley. "The name is Mayne—Ripley Mayne."

The blue eyes brightened. "Know you nearly got me into a fight here last night? Fact. Someone was calling you a spy and using a hell of a lot of adjectives. Course, *I* didn't know anything about you, but it struck me he didn't either. Just being stinking and trying to get set down as a good patriot. I've seen them before."

Ripley shrugged. "He probably meant all right, whoever he was."

Cuyler thumped the table. "The hell he did. He didn't mean anything—or so he said after I pulled his nose." He glared at Ripley over the top of his glass. "Spy. Without even seeing you, I knew that he was full of canal water. What's his idea?"

"Thanks. I've had to pull one or two noses myself," said Ripley. "About the spy business—" Briefly he sketched out his story while Cuyler's blue gaze fell unwinking on him.

When Ripley had finished, Cuyler waved to Featherfoot. "The next is mine and the one after that. Here's a New Englander that isn't scared to put two sentences together—and about himself." He took his filled glass from the tapster. "You know, I got a hundred miles into Massachusetts before I found out they knew any word except 'maybe.' "

Ripley nodded. "That's because we don't want to show off before the more backward Provinces."

"Maybe," said Cuyler.

"Learning fast, isn't he, Featherfoot?" grinned Ripley.

"Can't make me mad," said Cuyler solemnly. "My father's New York Dutch and my mother's Connecticut Yankee." He stretched out long, slim legs. "See those gams? Yankee. The rest of me's Dutch. When I was born, the midwife turned me upside down and said: 'He's Yankee,' so they decided to call me Preserved Ichabod Cuyler. Then she righted me and they saw my face and shoulders and said: 'He's Dutch.' That led to a sort of a fight, right there, between the two families. My old gentleman could yell louder than all the others put together, so head and shoulders won and I got called Joris."

"You remind me of McTavish, out Carlisle way," said Ripley. "His people had to wait a long time before they could decide whether he was Angus or Agnes, or so they say."

"Not me!" roared Cuyler. He picked up his glass, stared at it and bellowed: "Betrayed! Not a drop! Hoy! Ganymede! Gin! Brandy!"

Fresh glasses slid onto the table. Ripley said: "What's a Yorker doing up here?"

Cuyler smacked his lips over his gin. "My aged parent's on the Committee of Correspondence." He wrinkled his forehead. "Never saw such a man for committees—Committee of Supply, of Public Safety—Committee on Early Iroquois Thunder-mugs, too, I guess. Well, the chap that usually rides up here fell out a second-story window one jump ahead of a husband. So I took the job."

"What'll they do when *you* go out a window?"

"Send the husband. Say, what are the Tories doing up here?"

Ripley sighed. "Making trouble and scuttling into Boston as fast as they can."

Cuyler scratched his head. "I got a surprise when I came up here and saw the people. Down in New York, the Tories say that all the best New Englanders —" he puckered his face into an expression of extreme hauteur—"the people one would care to know —are for the Crown. Just the rabble's making the noise."

"Take a look around," said Ripley. "One Johonot's a Tory, another's against the Crown. One Saltonstall hangs around Gage at Province House and another's thick with Warren and Adams. They—" He ran his hand over his black hair. "Hell, that's what *we've* been hearing about New York. Someone wrote my father that if he could see the New York Tories, he'd realize that he was on the wrong side."

"In New York!" Cuyler flushed. "Tell your father not to read letters from just plain God-damn fools. Look at the Schuylers, the Livingstons, look at John Morin Scott, Duane, Lispenard, Jay, Roosevelt. Just tell your father that!"

"And he'll say he'll stop reading their letters if you'll stop listening to their talk."

Cuyler nodded solemnly. "And he'll be right." He stopped, cocked an ear to the outer hall where heavy footsteps mingled with the slam of the big door.

"Who's that, Featherfoot?" asked Ripley.

Featherfoot thumped out of the taproom. Ripley went behind the bar and filled up the glasses. "You'll be going back tomorrow?"

Cuyler screwed up his eyes. "Not I. Your Congress hasn't got anything to send yet." He took his glass from Ripley, drank, winked. "Besides, I found some unfinished business the first night I was here. Hey! Here's Ganymede."

"Who was it, Featherfoot?" asked Ripley.

The tapster whispered. "Officer."

Ripley was suddenly alert. "Alone?"

Featherfoot nodded. "Just him. Was to meet some others in Lexington, fell asleep in his chaise and ended up here. A bit swipey, he is."

"What regiment?"

"Fourth. King's Own. I know the uniform."

Cuyler waved his arm. "Go in and tell him to bite his foot."

"That's it," said Ripley. "And tell him to take a kick at the moon with my compliments. And more provender for us." He raised his eyebrows as a discordant roaring came from the room across the hall. "What's that row?"

Cuyler cocked his head. "Sounds almost like a song."

"Almost?" Ripley listened intently. "By God, it is. I know that one. It goes:—

> *"We be*
> *Soldiers three,*
> *Lately returned from the Low Countree."*

The old song echoed against the pine walls. Marlborough's soldiers coming back from Ypres and Passchendaele at the dawn of the century had sung it. Now it rang in a Concord taproom.

Featherfoot joined in, then slipped out in answer to a shout from the other guest. He returned grinning. "Rip, the officer of the Fourth kind of likes your voice. He says will you two go in and share a bottle with him."

Ripley looked dubious, but Cuyler scrambled up. "Share seven or seventy. This'll be fun. Can he sit up?"

"He can sit up all right," said Featherfoot. "More

he drinks the stiffer he gets. Ain't hardly a wobble left in him."

Ripley laughed. "All right. An officer of the Fourth won't know me."

The lone occupant of the dining room, blue cape huddled about him, sat rigidly at a disordered table where two candles glowed on a bottle of port. A hard, lined face turned to Ripley and Cuyler and a creaky voice said: "Not often you hear anything but damned rebel songs outside of Boston. Want you to join me. Always glad to see people from the right party."

Cuyler, eyes on the bottle, said: "Sir, there's no one righter than me and my friend."

"And when we're right, we stay right," said Ripley.

The powdered head bowed stiffly. "Does you credit, I'm sure." He waved toward the bottle. "Will you take port or will you name your pleasure?"

Cuyler grinned. "If I named my pleasure, it might take our minds off drinking. I'll have Holland's."

"Brandy for me." Ripley pulled up a chair, shoved one forward to Cuyler. "So you liked our song?"

"Best bloody song in the world." He gathered his cape closer about him, coughed. "Blast this climate. Been barking my head off all winter." He stared at Ripley, said: "Three loyal subjects of the King. May I know your names?"

Ripley nudged Cuyler under the table. "This is Concord. Let's say my friend's name is known to the New York garrison. And mine—well, being in Concord, let's say that mine is Legion."

The officer goggled bloodshot eyes at Ripley, then barked with laughter. "Legion. His name is Legion. Bloody good." He swung about in his chair. "Where's that cursed tapster? Here, you. Step faster when you serve His Majesty's uniform."

Featherfoot, wooden-faced, gravely set glasses onto the disordered cloth, rumbled out of the room. Ripley said: "We know your unit, sir, but to which of its officers are we drinking?"

"Know the uniform, do you? It's Lieutenant, Lieutenant Felton, sirs, at your service." He gazed about the room. "What the hell were we going to do? Oh —" He snapped his fingers. "Sing, by God." Head rocking he bellowed out:—

"We be
Soldiers three—"

Ripley and Cuyler joined in. Featherfoot brought more glasses as Ripley started a new song:—

"I'm sick of parading,
Through cold and wet wading,
Or standing all day to be shot in a trench.
I'm tired of marching,
Pipe-claying and starching.
How neat we must be to be shot by the French!"

Felton slapped Ripley's shoulder, shouted to Cuyler. "Damn me if your friend Mr. Legion doesn't know the old songs better than I do." He looked at Ripley as though he had difficulty in focusing his eyes. "Bloody good. Only, in the last line, it's all wrong. No bloody Frog-eater ever shot one of His Majesty's men. Did he now? Did he?"

"Not of the Fourth," shouted Ripley.

"Nor the Tenth," echoed Cuyler.

"My treat," cried Felton, thrusting his lined face across the table.

"Damn the rebels!" His voice cracked as he raised his glass. "I'm coming back here again. Tell the boys in Boston 'bout this place." Felton waved his glass. "Meant to go to Lexington. Rode right through and my horse stopped here. Intelligent animal." He emptied the last of his port into his glass, shouted for a fresh bottle. He slung a heavy arm about Ripley's shoulder. "Have you chaps in to the mess in Boston.

Have—" He stared at Ripley, underlip slightly pendulous.

"Be delighted," said Ripley.

Felton still stared at him. Slowly the mask of drunkenness cleared from his weather-beaten face. His mouth grew tight, grim. In a low, level voice he said: "I saw you flogged."

Ripley forced a laugh. "Some mistake, Lieutenant. I never served in the Fourth and—"

Felton's lips barely parted. "The Fourth be damned." He reached a veined hand to the empty chair, hidden by the tablecloth, slowly drew out his hat. Ripley stared at the brass-fronted cap, at the foul anchor that gleamed on the metal.

Cuyler sprang to his feet. "You can't—"

Felton disregarded him. "A deserter. Your time couldn't be up. I saw you flogged on the *Cumberland* off Trinidad. I'd come over from the *Essex*." His voice grew lower and harder. "You're under arrest."

Ripley's foot shot out, clamped hard against the sheathed sword that slanted down from the marine's belt. He felt the slim blade bend in its scabbard to the pressure of his boot, as Felton tugged at the hilt. Cuyler lunged across the table, caught the marine by his shoulders.

Felton tried to rise from his chair, floundered as the tug of the sword held him fast. Red with fury, he shouted: "You're resisting arrest. You're resisting one of His Majesty's officers." He began to bawl: "Landlord! The Watch! Call the Watch! In the name of the King! The Watch!"

Cuyler cried: "How about it, Rip? How about the Watch?" and stood by the door.

"Don't worry," said Ripley. Then to Felton: "Stay where you are. Steady, I say!" He forced the marine back into the chair from which he was struggling to rise. "Sit there. Now listen to me. You're in Concord. There isn't a Tory in town, so save your breath. You're going to get back into the chaise and get out of here as fast as you can. Hold still or I'll choke you. You get out of here quick—and stay out or I'll dump you in the Mill Pond. Joris, get his sword."

Cuyler's huge arms held the storming man. His big hands unbuckled the belt and the sword clattered to the floor. Ripley picked it up, shook it at Felton. "I'm going to keep this until you're out of town. Then, tomorrow, I'll send it on to Buckman's Tavern in Lexington and you can get it there."

Felton struggled, but only thrashed, helpless, in Cuyler's clutch. Ripley slipped out the door, called for Featherfoot. "Get that chaise around here quick. The officer's got important business in Boston."

Featherfoot nodded affably. "I wondered what he was screeching about. Must be mighty important business." He winked, opened a back window, and began bellowing to the stableboys. Wheels ground on the soggy road outside and Ripley stepped back into the dining room where Felton cursed and raged. "All right, Joris. We'll frog-march him out."

He caught the officer's collar. "Catch him by the breeches, Joris." They marched the raving man into the hall and out to the road, pitched him into the chaise. Ripley said: "Keep going straight and you'll end up in Boston. Try any tricks and God knows where you'll end. And don't rave about coming back with a platoon to get me. You'd need every soldier and marine in Boston and have to borrow some from London even to start looking for me." He stood aside, smacked the horse's rump with the empty leather scabbard. There was a yell of rage. The chaise bucketed wildly off down the Lexington road.

Ripley stepped back into the taproom, Cuyler at his heels. "Featherfoot," said Ripley, "put his dinner and his drinks on my score. Give me a brandy." He sat down, head resting in one hand. There'd be trouble now. Felton would report. A squad or even a platoon might come out over the Lexington road, past Meriam's corner and into the calm little town.

Across the table Cuyler looked wonderingly at him. "Jesus, Rip, you move quick when you have to."

Ripley nodded absently, drank. "And I had to. No mistake." He drummed on the table. "What the hell will I do now?"

"Do?" said Cuyler. "Just what I'm going to do."

"What's that?"

"Have a drink and another."

Featherfoot looked admiringly at Ripley. "That brandy slid out your glass like water down a flume." He placed a fresh one on the table, gave Cuyler more gin. Then he said: "You know, Rip—that ain't going to hurt you none—around here. I'll start telling a few of the boys and I guess we ain't going to hear any more spy talk about you."

"Yes—but Gage and Pitcairn are going to hear deserter talk about sunrise tomorrow."

"What of it? Ain't we got a guard up the ridge watching the roads all the time? We'll pass the word along to Lexington and Arlington."

Cuyler reached over, patted Ripley's shoulder. "You'll be all right. I'll start jogging about the country a little. I might hear something."

Ripley nodded slowly. "Guess it'll be all right. It'd take the British a month to decide to go looking for me." He ran his hands through his hair. "Kind of a shock, though."

Cuyler smiled grimly. "It'd have been a worse one if you hadn't stepped on his toad sticker." He turned to the tapster. "What'd you tell Rip he was from the Fourth for?"

The big man began to stammer. Ripley said: "Oh he was all right. The Fourth's got white facings, like the marines. Featherfoot didn't see the cap and he couldn't see the blue-and-red piping on the buttonholes. How could he, when the damned ape was huddling in his cape like a pregnant gypsy? *I* didn't see a thing and God knows I've seen enough marine uniforms." He pushed back from the table. "Well, Joris, how long are you going to be around here?"

Cuyler looked owlish. "Nothing for me to go back for just yet. The aged parent's deep in committees. Look, how about meeting here tomorrow night?"

Ripley grinned. "How about that unfinished business of yours?"

Cuyler waved expansively. "I only work on inspiration. Tomorrow night, then? I'll look for you. The first real drinker I've met since I crossed Spuyten Duyvil."

Ripley shook hands. "Tomorrow night it is." He nodded to Featherfoot and started home.

As he turned down Main Street toward the milldam and Nashawtuc Hill, he looked back over his shoulder. The windows of Wright's threw bright oblongs of light onto the Lexington road, lighting up the figure of a man who faced east, leaning on his musket. Among the gravestones beyond, a lantern flickered on vague shapes as a new relief started up the ridge, heading for the vantage point above Meriam's corner. He whistled under his breath. Some sense to that guard after all.

III

In the little room that looked down to the Sudbury, Ripley blew out his candle and crawled gratefully into bed. With his new friend Cuyler and Melven Mayne he had worked late at Reuben Brown's packing Province stores for shipment west. Once the last of the stores were gone, there'd be no pretext for Gage to march troops into Concord. The guards would be gone and life would resume its old tenor. He sighed with satisfaction as the night wind brought the creak of wheels and the rumble of heavy carts moving west out of town.

Sometime during the night he dreamed that he was on the deck of a first-rater off the coast of France. He had been told the legend of a sea-buried cathedral and, as he walked his post, he was sure that he could hear the drowned bells tolling soft and low. The dream persisted, became fused with reality. He woke, his ears filled with a distant throbbing. The bells were real. He stumbled to the window, his eyes hunting a glow in the sky. But the night was black, so he crept back into his blankets.

Once more he was awakened. More bells were ringing, booming and clanging over valleys thick with trees, wailing across bare meadows. Then far away a single musket shot echoed flatly. Through the mad voices of the bells came the distant roar of an alarm cannon.

The bells stopped suddenly and the Concord night hung calm and peaceful about the old house, the quiet stressed by the trill and quaver of frogs. He thought: "It must be a fire. A big one." The soft blanket of silence was ripped by a fresh burst of bells, more shots, and the drumming of hoofs as an unseen horse thundered over the South Bridge.

Ripley started as a hand touched his shoulder. He saw his father in tasseled nightcap and woolen robe, a shaded candle in his hand. "It's come," said Melven Mayne. "The British are out. Listen."

Out of the dark-curtained land toward town, a drum began to mutter. Melven Mayne leaned on the window sill. "They're calling out the men of Concord. Hear the bells and the guns. That's Bedford calling now. There's Lincoln. I can't hear Lexington." He drew an unsteady breath. "I guess there are a lot I can't hear, but they're calling, too. Sudbury and Watertown and Marlboro and Worcester." He started for the door. "I'll go to Wright's. They'll assemble there."

Ripley suddenly fumbled for his shoes. "Wait for me."

"I think you'd best stay here. Really—I mean it."

Ripley dropped a shoe. "All right. But let me know what's happening if you can."

"I've told you. It's come. We didn't want it." He sighed. "Sometimes I wish I were more of a praying man." The candle flickered away through the house.

When the outer door had slammed behind his father, Ripley tried to push his thoughts into calmer channels. Suddenly he made a wild gesture that sent sheets and blankets flying. "Damn it, he shouldn't go alone."

He gathered up his clothes and huddled into them. He slanted his watch toward the window. Quarter to three. Snatching up his hat he raced out of the house.

As he turned onto Main Street a heavy wagon rumbled past him, stacked high with barrels of stores, heading inland. He fumed: "Why did it have to be tonight—if it is real? Another day and we'd have had every damn thing out of here. There'd be nothing for the British to find if they did come."

Ahead of him lanterns bobbed along beside hurrying legs. On the still distant walls of Wright's, orange oblongs glowed, were cut across by hasty silhouettes, glowed clear again. Somewhere a man shouted. "I tell you Colonel Barrett's gone back to his farm!"

Ripley slackened his pace. It might be a false alarm, if Barrett had gone home.

The thick lines of men, leaning on their muskets in the dark of the Lexington road, took his crumb of comfort from him. Someone jostled Ripley, a familiar voice shouted: "What's stirring?"

There was relief in the sight of the heavy-shouldered figure. Ripley forced a laugh. "This is a hell of a time to be coming home, Joris."

"Home? I wasn't going home but those damned bells got me jumpy."

"What are they saying in Wright's?"

"How'd I know?" Cuyler swung his cape and a

faint whiff of scent reached Ripley's nostrils. "Haven't seen the place for two days."

"Come on," said Ripley. He led the way past the waiting militia, saw Joe Hosmer coming from the group of officers. "Joe! Joe! Anyone know anything?"

Hosmer stopped. "Hello, Rip." Then his voice dropped. "It's the real thing."

The chill of certainty that Ripley had been fighting settled deeper. "How do you know?"

"Why—" He looked at Cuyler. "Who's this?"

Ripley introduced the two and Hosmer went on. "It was Dr. Prescott. He'd been at the Millikens' in Lexington. Coming home, he met that man Revere from Boston." He caught Ripley's arm. "There's no mistake. Gage has ordered out the flank companies. Revere had word and was spreading the alarm."

Ripley's mind caught at a spar of hope. "Revere's no soldier. He could be wrong."

"Not this time. We knew that a lot of British officers were out tonight, pretending they were dining in Cambridge, in Lexington. They were really patrolling. They caught Revere and a man named Dawes. They caught Prescott, but he got away." He paused, then said quietly: "Better get home, Rip."

Ripley shook his head. "They wouldn't send all the flank companies out after *me*."

Cuyler caught him by the collar. "They might send some of them, though. Mr. Hosmer's right."

Hosmer coughed. "Another thing, Rip. Some people think you know all about the British—that you're waiting for them."

"You're caught between two fires, Rip," said Cuyler earnestly.

Ripley cried, "Can't the damn fools see—" He shoved his hands into his pockets. "When you're caught between two fires, the best thing to do is to sit still. Joe, I'm staying."

Cuyler and Hosmer exchanged glances. "Well,

what are you going to do besides stay, Rip?" asked the New Yorker.

Ripley turned to Hosmer. "Where's your company, Joe?"

"Most are across the pond, shifting barrels of bullets. But wait—here's something for you to do. I've got a patrol on the tip of the ridge by Meriam's, watching the Lexington road. My boys are all solid for you, and you'll know a lot better than they what anything you see or hear means. It'll keep you out of sight of Stowe and the people that yap with him."

"Rip, you'd better go home," said Cuyler.

"Joe's right," said Ripley. "If you'd use those Dutch brains, you might be able to see it too. If you see my father, Joe, tell him where I am. Come on, Joris." He started east along the Lexington road, the great wall of the ridge looming at his left, then cut up a path that led to the crest, pushing briars and branches aside.

At the east end of the ridge, a mile from the center of the town, the two halted. Ripley hailed a knot of Hosmer's men posted a few yards down the slope. "Who's that? Jake Day? Joe Hosmer sent me. I'll be up here on the crest."

Down below someone grunted in assent. Cuyler perched on a fallen birch. "Show me what to watch, Rip, and I'll turn loose the God-damnedest pair of eagle eyes east of the Catskills."

"You'll need them. Now start here—the road to Lexington's at our right and runs about east. Down at our feet's the road from Bedford that hits the Lexington road from the north at right angles by Meriam's. Meriam's house is about a hundred yards north on the Bedford road."

"They'll be coming along the road from Lexington?"

Ripley leaned his shoulders against a tree. "*If* they come. Suppose Gage had ordered an embarkation drill for tonight. A civilian sees it, sends word to Revere, and we spend the night watching for troops that may be asleep in barracks by now. Of course, if it's true, we'll—Jake, Jake Day! What orders have the companies got if the Lobsters come?"

"Orders is we're not to fire first," called Day.

Ripley slapped his thigh. "That's the sanest order Barrett could have given. They'll come into town. We'll fall back. They'll search, won't find much, and go home." It could be as easy as that. But—there were old troops in the Boston garrison, used to burning, rape, and pillage in the Low Countries. He remembered an innkeeper on the Bath Road, a retired sergeant who had set himself up out of church silver looted from Flemish towns. Ripley shivered, then sat down beside Cuyler to watch.

Hours passed. The eastern sky began to lighten. A horseman galloped east along the Lexington road. "That's Rube Brown," called Day. "He was going for news as soon as it got light."

The treetops off beyond Meriam's took on a weird shimmer, seemed to detach themselves from the dark countryside, and the Lexington road stood out sharper between its belts of stone wall. A steady wind sprang out of the west, flowed through budding trees and spilled down over the ridge. In the pasture beyond Meriam's, a dog trotted wearily on after a night of ranging the Lincoln woods.

Through the chill air a single sound beat its way, the flap and thud of hoofs. Ripley jumped to his feet. The Lexington road was quite distinct now and showed empty clear to the rise a mile east. Then a single rider topped the crest and raced on toward Concord. Reuben Brown had come back.

Day shouted to Ripley. "Hey! What shall I do now?"

"Send one of your men back to find out what Rube saw," called Ripley. There was a sound of confused argument below while the guard wrangled over who should go. At last one of them trotted off along the ridge toward Concord. The minutes dragged on. Then the runner pounded back along the ridge. "It's them. They fired on Parker's company to Lexington."

Ripley caught him by the collar. "Fired?"

The runner gulped. "Rube seen it. He seen smoke on the green and our fellers running."

"How many British? Did they have artillery? Are they pushing on here?"

"Guess they got everything," the man panted.

"What's Barrett doing back there?" snapped Ripley.

"He ain't there. He's to his farm burying cannon. The rest is arguing about what to do."

Ripley swung his arms. "Oh, God, holding a town meeting with the Lobsters only five miles off. Why don't they fall back to Buttrick's!"

From the hidden town behind them the breeze brought a faint snapping sound over the ridge, a snapping that slowly grew clearer. *Rap, rap, rap-rap-rap.* "Drums!" said Day. "Coming out of town." Now fifes threw a thin wisp of sound into the air, high and shrill. Ripley slapped his knee in exasperation. "They're coming out!" Then he felt a sort of hard gladness sweep over him. He said between his teeth: "Ball or blank, they're marching to meet it."

Fife and drum grew louder in the west as the quick notes of "Roslyn Castle" surged on along the mile that lay between the center of town and Meriam's corner. Day caught his musket by the sling. "Come on," he shouted in a cracked voice.

"Got orders to go?" cried Ripley. "No? Then stay here until you get some." Day grumbled, but settled back, feet scuffling among dead leaves.

Cuyler laughed nervously. "Damn it, here I am with the Lobsters coming and not even a rock to shy at them."

With startling suddenness the musicians stepped into sight on the road below. Then the first files of the Concord minute companies swung on in their wake, row after row of slanting muskets. The men of Concord had been called. They had answered. With them marched the Lincoln companies. There they were, stepping out along the enigma of the Lexington road—cocked hats, broad hats, smocks, sleek black coats, homespun, a faded uniform or two, relics of the old French wars. The guide across squads was ragged. Muskets slanted unevenly, but the swinging boots bit out the sharp, sure rhythm of the march. Haywards, Barretts, Buttricks, Hurds, Wheelers, Minotts, they were marching out to meet whatever the distant rise of the Lexington road might hide.

"What'll they do?" muttered Cuyler, gnawing his lips.

"Do? They can't do anything. They've got a hundred and thirty men at the most, if I've counted the files right. They ought to have ten times that number. They ought to go back."

A voice, far along the road, wailed a command, a dirgelike shout that was caught up by others. The pace of the rear files slackened, the fifes and drums, silent for the last few minutes, ripped the air again, and the four companies curled back westward toward Concord in a great loop.

Ripley felt Cuyler's hand hard on his shoulder. He shook his head impatiently. "I don't know any more than you do. They've ordered a right-about and you can guess why as well as I can. Probably they—God!"

The thin tones of the Concord fifes were drowned in a crashing whirl of music that swept up from the hidden lands beyond the rise in the Lexington road. A flood of color topped the crest, flowed steadily on. Blue coats, red coats, white coats, yellow coats, were gay in the morning sun as the fifers and drummers swung along. Behind them loomed the red bulk of the companies. Ripley felt his throat go dry as his eye measured the scant five hundred yards that separated the leading British musicians and the last drab ranks of the militia. Any moment, he thought, Concord and Lincoln companies would scatter, melt away under the oncoming menace. Then a wave of pride swept over him. Unhurried and in good order, the militia filed on past Meriam's corner and were lost to sight under the steep flank of the ridge.

Cuyler's voice, suddenly calm, said: "How about it, Rip? Patrol or in force?"

Ripley grunted. "Count the musicians. Two for every company. I'd say six, maybe seven hundred men." He shaded his eyes. "Revere was right. Light infantry and grenadiers. No marines."

The British column was close enough now to lose something of its anonymity. Suddenly the music ceased and the fifers and drummers wheeled right and left to the rear, seeking their own companies. Hayes mumbled. "Just going to keep marching like that? Right into town?"

"Watch," said Ripley. A drum snapped. Like a banner unfolding, the leading light infantry companies in their skullcaps fanned out into the fields east of Meriam's, moving with an easy gait over plowed land. Another followed it, flowing smartly from column into line. Beyond the swaying bayonets of the last light companies, a knot of mounted officers loomed, and behind the last rider a solid mass of bearskin and bright metal told of the grenadiers.

Day whinnied: "What's them fellers doing in the field?"

"Flankers—so nothing can hit the side of the column." Ripley turned to Day. "I've got no right to give orders, but you better get back. The flankers'll come right up the ridge and follow it into town." The picket of three trotted off. Ripley, brushing Cuyler's shoulder, watched the advance toward Meriam's house where the leading wave had reached the barnyard. An upper window flew up, a gray head jutted unexpectedly, and a woman's voice, faint but clear, floated up to the ridge: "Get out that medder!" One or two skullcaps turned toward the window. An infantryman waved.

Cuyler looked questioningly at Ripley. "No hurry," said Ripley.

"Those boys take awful long steps, though," said Cuyler.

Ripley turned west along the ridge path. "I just wanted to be *sure* that there weren't any marines with that batch. Come on. We'll make knots." He broke into a trot, Cuyler bouncing along behind him.

The mile-long path slipped away under their feet and the houses down below showed cold chimneys, empty yards. As the pair neared the tall liberty pole they saw an irregular straggle of men working up the slope from the road to join the shifting lines of companies that were forming on the crest. Ripley looked back over his shoulder. At the far end of the gently curving ridge, spatters of red cloth showed among the tree trunks. He nodded to Cuyler. "They've just topped the crest—the first of the flankers. Take it easy. They won't hurry."

Cuyler checked his loping stride. "If you're fooling me, Rip, I'm going to get mad. I never did like the idea of getting goosed by a bayonet. Hey—who's that yelling at you?"

Joe Hosmer ran toward them. "What's it like? Day and his crowd all tell different stories."

"About eight hundred. Grenadiers and light infantry. No cannon. No mounted men except a few officers. Flankers are coming up over the ridge now. What's Barrett going to do?"

"He's still at his farm. Buttrick's in command. I'll tell him what you said." He doubled back toward a knot of men standing in front of the companies.

Ripley frowned. "Joris, he ought to get the companies out of town—quick." He looked apprehensively at the Concord and Lincoln men, who were breaking ranks, crowding around the officers, pushing, arguing. "Let's go get 'em like Reverend Emerson says." . . . "Hey! What they do at Lexington—the Lobsters, I mean. I bet—" . . . "By God, we'll ambush 'em like we was Indians and—" . . . "What I say is, better hold a council of war. That's it, a council of war!"

Cuyler snatched a handkerchief from his pocket, swabbed his forehead with it. "Looks to me as if a few noses were going to get pulled."

"Hell," said Ripley in disgust. "Why didn't they decide on what they were going to do before they ever turned out? Look at that!" John Buttrick, long blue coat fluttering in the wind, tried to break away from the press, was swallowed up, freed himself. Then Bentley Stowe and a dozen others swarmed about him, shouting. At last Buttrick turned his back on them, walked rapidly past the companies toward Ripley.

"What are you going to do, John?" asked Ripley.

Buttrick's jaw tightened. "Make them understand that under law I'm in command until Barrett gets back. Then I'm going to march them out across the North Bridge to the muster field on my hill." He looked at Cuyler suspiciously. "Is he with you, Rip?"

Ripley introduced the two, then said: "Better get going."

"Right away. There's one thing I want of you, though. I've got to take Joe Hosmer for adjutant. Will you stay by him until we get to the field?"

Ripley whistled softly. "How about Benevolent Bentley and his lot?"

"I know. I know. They're raising hell at the idea, but you know about these things and Joe doesn't. Bentley finally said it'd be all right if you weren't armed and Joe kept an eye on you."

Ripley flushed. "Tell Bentley to go to hell. You're in command."

Buttrick scuffed his boot uneasily. "I know—but his word carries a lot of weight in town and I don't want him making trouble." He looked pleadingly at Ripley.

Cuyler nudged him. "Go ahead, Rip."

Ripley nodded. "All right, John. I'll help."

Buttrick, looking relieved, went back to the companies and presently Ripley heard his voice, sharp and uncompromising. A drum tapped, the companies shuffled into a fair line, swung into a column, "Coming, Joris?" asked Ripley.

Cuyler rubbed his broad chin. "I've got an idea, Rip. Your boys seem a little jumpy and being a New Yorker won't help me quiet them any. I'll slide down the ridge to Wright's and wait for the Lobsters." He pushed Ripley. "Sure. It'll be all right. The officers'll come into the tavern and find the God-damnedest loyalest Tory bastard they ever heard of. I'll be mad, too, the way I've been treated by your rabble." He rubbed his chin again. "Maybe it won't hurt any to have someone here in town to see what's going on."

Ripley hesitated, then said: "All right. Get word to us if you can," and ran to catch up with the column that was slipping down from the ridge opposite the Town House. To the east, there was no sign of the British and he guessed that a brief halt had been called somewhere beyond the bend in the ridge that hid the rest of the Lexington road.

The militia column swung easily along, suddenly silent. Ahead of the leading company, a few carts crowded with women and children rattled. More townspeople on foot pushed quickly along on either side of the road. He felt much easier in his mind. The regulars probably wouldn't go much farther than the center of the town, the logical place to look for stores. There were no marines in the column. He would go as far as the muster field where Buttrick would probably dismiss the companies.

He overtook Joe Hosmer, pegging stolidly along.

With deep satisfaction, he saw the head of the column file past the gray bulk of the Manse and turn sharply down the stretch that led to the North Bridge. Soon all the companies would be perched on the muster field out of harm's way. When he made the turn himself he looked south to the town across the

Manse meadows where William Emerson, the minister, was quieting a crowd of women and children. Far beyond the Manse fields, Wright's Tavern showed clear and white. The road in front of it was suddenly alive with brass and red cloth. There was a long ripple of steel as companies, coming to a halt, grounded their arms. He called to Hosmer. "See that, Joe? They'll search and then go home."

Hosmer rubbed his chin dubiously. "Maybe they'll go home."

"Have to. I saw the whole column. They've got no supply wagons with them." He turned his attention to his own people. "Better hurry them on, Joe. They're getting jammed at the bridge."

With Hosmer, he straightened out the companies, then caught up with the last files that were moving along the right fork of the road toward Buttrick's house and the muster field. As he topped a rise he looked back over his shoulder. There was a hint of panic down in the fields where Emerson was herding the women and children into the Manse.

Then scarlet and white were bright along the road beyond the gray house. Brass and steel glinted and scarlet arms swung in crisp precision. He shouted: "Joe! Joe! Keep them going. Here come the Lobsters!"

The step of the militia increased. Soon a shoulder of the hill hid the bridge road from Ripley's view. He pushed on, wondering why the British had sent troops so far out from the center of town. Then the road curved toward the crest of the hill and the brown track below was unveiled, showing the light infantry flowing along the road that led to the bridge.

Ripley shouted again: "Hurry them up, Joe! Keep them moving! I'll stay here and watch the Lobsters."

He settled himself in the shelter of a flat rock while the steady tread of the militia died away toward the muster field at the top of the hill. On the road below, the British were coming on smartly, six full companies of light infantry. As Ripley studied them, the leading three companies halted and gave ground to the left of the road. The other three pressed on past them, crossed the bridge, and filed away on the lower road that skirted the base of the hill along the near bank of the Concord River.

He sprang up from the rock and started for the muster field at a sharp trot. The lower road, now hidden, would take the three companies straight to James Barrett's farm, nearly two miles away. If John Buttrick would only dismiss the militia, the men could slip away toward Carlisle and the last chance of clash would be avoided.

He scrambled up the steep slope of the muster field and cold fear settled over him again. There were the Lincoln and Concord companies standing with grounded arms. But beyond them, other units were shuffling and dressing. There was Isaac Davis and that meant that the Acton men had come. Beyond Acton he made out Carlisle, Chelmsford, Littleton, Bedford.

Joe Hosmer called to him from the flank of the Concord minute-men. Ripley said: "Is John going to send them home?"

"Don't know. What did the Lobsters do?"

"Three companies stayed by the bridge. Three others took the road to Barrett's. Tell John for God's sake to dismiss us."

"He's going to stand by for orders. He's right."

"Stand by for trouble, that's what he's doing," growled Ripley. Then he shrugged. "I'll keep an eye on the lot by the bridge, anyway."

"Wish you would, Rip. Send word to me by the boys we've got watching if you think there's anything I ought to know."

Ripley ran to the edge of the field that looked down to the river and the bridge. The three remaining British companies had crossed over to the near side. One of them had moved a hundred yards along the lower road and now stood halted, looking up at the hill. Another, in skirmish formation, had moved up the hillside and was deployed just out of musket range, some seventy yards below the edge of the muster field. A single private stood rigid on a tall rock, watching the militia. The last company was drawn up in close formation where the roads forked on the near side of the bridge.

Ripley narrowed his eyes. There was nothing very threatening about the British so far. And they wouldn't stay very long where they were as the men seemed to have left their packs in the town. He was about to send someone back to Hosmer with this detail when a fresh company of light infantry swung down the road from the Manse and headed for the bridge. The new unit came on, tramped over the echoing bridge, filed on past the waiting men below and pressed on along the road to Barrett's.

Abruptly he turned on his heel and found Hosmer. "Nothing'll happen—for a while, anyway. Four companies have gone to Jim Barrett's to look for stores. The others are just watching us." He hesitated. "No chance of dismissal?"

Hosmer scratched his snub nose. "Guess not. Barrett's just come back from his farm." He pointed to a knot of officers in front of the Acton men. "He says we'll stay and watch. No one's to fire unless we're fired on. That's flat." He punched the turf with the butt of his fusee. "Uh—had the boys change their flints, just to give them something to do. Was that all right?"

Ripley nodded approvingly. "That's good soldiering. Not that they'll need the flints." He pointed to the motionless skirmishers, to the other companies below. As he pointed, the company down the road stirred, wheeled, and fell slowly back toward the bridge. "See?" said Ripley. "Just watching, that's all. By the way, what will the other Lobsters that went through find at Barrett's?"

"Jim says he laid all the cannon in furrows in his west field and plowed them under. They'll be hidden all right." His eyes turned toward the roofs of Concord, a mile away. "Wish I knew what was happening in town."

Ripley laughed. "I'll tell you what's happening. The officers are having a drink at Wright's. The men are betting rum rations on how soon they'll start back for Boston." He watched a single officer who strolled nonchalantly along the lower road, a fusee swinging in his hand. Probably a volunteer, Ripley thought, who had attached himself to the column to escape the boredom of Boston.

The trees off in the town seemed suddenly thicker. Ripley squinted at this. Thicker and browner. What could give that illusion? Lack of sleep? The brown climbed higher, expanded into a lazy plume of smoke that curled about the distant roofs, rose heavy and oily. His chest tightened in sudden anger. He wheeled on Hosmer, but the latter was racing off toward Barrett and Buttrick shouting: "They're burning our town! Will you stand by and let them burn our town?"

Barrett shouted: "Company commanders! To your posts!" Men spun about, doubled back to the waiting lines. Barrett roared: "Take care to wheel by twos. March!"

The long lines wheeled into column, marked time, then began to trickle off the field and onto the road that led down to the bridge, the Acton men leading. Suddenly the Acton fifer began to shrill out "Yankee Doodle," the thin notes, exultant, derisive, whipping into the spring air. Other companies took it up and the soil of Buttrick's Hill shook to the steady tread of the men of Middlesex County. Lincoln passed, Carlisle, Bedford, and last of all came the Concord alarm company, gray heads, bald heads, wigged heads high. Veined hands strained at heavy musket butts, feet that had scaled the walls of Louisburg or crept along the wooded trails about Lake George stepped out with a new surge of youth. Down below, the three British companies had fallen to the far side of the river. The lone officer whom Ripley had seen was sprinting after them, one hand clutching his hat while his cartridge box danced and banged about his hips.

A wave of desolation swept over Ripley. Clumsily armed, nearly bayonetless, the Middlesex militia was marching on a bridge held by veteran regulars. Back in the town were hundreds more alert, trained British. Why, *why* had Barrett ordered the advance? It was worse than useless. It was hopeless. Better lose a house, a barn, than bring on a massacre.

Hosmer was yelling at him, waving. He ran across the fields to catch up with the center of the column. Hosmer seized him by the arm. "For God's sake, Rip, stay with us."

"I'll stay," said Ripley tersely.

"Get on up to the head. Barrett's turned command over to Buttrick. John's up there with Robinson, the lieutenant colonel." Ripley started out at a sharp trot.

The column was veering off to the left toward the river and the narrow bridge as Ripley overtook Buttrick and Robinson. The British, now entirely on the other side of the river, were drawn up in a thick column, three companies deep. Suddenly a British officer, slim and immaculate, darted out, two privates at his heels, and began tugging at the loose planks of the bridge. One was pried loose, another. Buttrick ran on ahead of the Acton files, face red and voice outraged. "Here! Put those back! It's *our* bridge!"

The two privates looked up uncertainly, dropped their plank. Buttrick quickened his pace. "You, sir! With the epaulets. This will be a court matter!" There was a sudden scramble of feet and the three scuttled back to the red companies. A single voice across the river rasped: "Take care to charge for street firing!" Buttrick strode grimly on.

Ripley shouted: "Major! John Buttrick! Get back!"

The first shot came with stunning suddenness from the opposite bank. Ripley caught Buttrick's arm. "Fall back on Acton! That was a warning! Just a warning!"

He pointed to the ripples in the smooth river where the shot had smacked. More shots rang out from across the stream. Bullets whipped into the water or sang eerily high in air. "I told you! It's just the officers firing. They're warning us."

Grudgingly Buttrick fell back toward the Acton men, Ripley close beside him, eyes on the companies across the bridge, barely a hundred yards away. He could almost make out the faces under the brass-fronted caps—ex-farmers and townsmen from Wiltshire, from Surrey, cast in a red mold, waiting. They hadn't fired. Probably wouldn't, except at command. Only the officers out on the flanks had drawn their triggers. And those same officers, if they had any sense, would order a retirement by divisions. If Buttrick would only halt the march of the militia. He looked back at the Acton men, saw Ike Davis fingering the lock of his musket, face pale but composed. A strange hush had fallen over the scene, broken only by the crunch, crunch of the militia files.

Then the hush was ripped by a sudden shout from across the river: "Charge!" Other voices barked: "Make ready! Present!" Smoke, flame, and tearing sound rolled in a thick blanket across the head of the British column. Something struck against the back of Ripley's knees and he went down in a hard crash with Buttrick's voice bellowing above him: "Fire! For God's sake, fire!"

The smoke and the flame and the sound welled again as Ripley staggered up, staring at Ike Davis's body sprawled motionless at his feet. Another man lay beyond him. The British had fired again! Had they? The smoke drifted over him from behind, was torn with fresh smoke, flame-stabbed. Slowly his head cleared. He looked down at Davis again. Ike Davis. *He* couldn't be lying there. He had a new gun barrel that he had promised to show Ripley—

He stooped, picked up Davis's fusee, gently unslung his powder horn and cartridge box, then spun about, facing the British. The volley, Davis's death, the answering crash, had taken place so quickly that the British front rank had only just trotted off, right and left down the column to take their places in the rear. The former second rank, now exposed, were raising their pieces by precise counts. On the near side of the bridge, Buttrick was carefully reloading his musket. Behind him men were scattering on both sides along the riverbank, edging close to the bend by the bridge, muzzles toward the red mass on the other side. No one seemed to be giving orders to the militia. Ripley snatched off his hat, waved it in great sweeps. "Fan out! Hit them in the flank! Stay on this side of the bridge! Fan out!"

Then he dropped to one knee, sighted carefully at an officer who was making his way to the rear across the Manse fields, two privates at his heels. He fired. The officer spun about, stumbled, recovered himself, and ran on close by the stone wall. Across the bridge, the front rank was still going through the cumbersome ritual of loading and presenting their pieces. Any second their volley might crash among the Middlesex men.

The bank to the left and right of him erupted in a blast of smoke and flame that lurched out across the sluggish river, hung idly in the calm air. He sprang to his feet, tense, poised. Where was that British volley? The smoke cloud rolled slowly downstream, uncovering the red mass across the bridge. Ripley stared in amazement.

The head of the British column was sagging, fraying out. He could no longer see the facings of the uniforms, only red backs cut across by white belts. They were running. They were racing. Two or three red figures sprawled on the road, forgotten in the mad scramble. A few officers danced along by the fugitives, lashing out with the flats of their swords. Then they were caught up in the eddying rush.

Ripley suddenly found that he was yelling, that his

throat was aching with the effort. Behind him, men bent over two homespun figures, were jostled in the mass that poured onto the bridge, muskets high and eyes staring. He looked for Hosmer, saw him pounding over the planks close behind Buttrick and ran to overtake him. The men that he passed were grim and silent, save for an angular Lincoln farmer who pressed on muttering hoarsely: "The King's troops! We've gone and fired on the King's troops!"

He caught up with Hosmer, who panted: "Buttrick's going to take them up the hill where the road bends. Then wait and see what happens."

Ripley grunted in approval. They'd command the road to town and the road to the bridge and at the same time be out of harm's way. He looked back at the far bank. Many men were climbing the hill, making their way back to the muster field, but the bulk were streaming over the bridge, keeping very fair order and moving at an unhurried pace.

He suddenly shied like a frightened horse as he stumbled against a huddled red form, saw another beyond it. The nearest man lay flat on his back, arms wide-flung and the fresh, winy stains on his white facings turned to the sun. He looked like a decent, competent private. He'd be sentimental about women and children and probably kept a dog, now patiently waiting in a Boston barrack. It couldn't be helped. A decent man, he'd have shot down Concord men or burned Concord houses if so ordered.

Buttrick was calling for Ripley, pointing to the sharp bend in the road where the last of the fugitives were pouring back toward town. "What'll they do now?"

Ripley panted. "Beyond me. I can't see why they broke in the first place. They're regulars." A thought struck him. "How about those four companies that went on to Barrett's? They're in our rear!"

Buttrick blinked. "By God, I'd forgotten them. I'm going to post the men back of that stone wall up the hill."

"Better hurry," said Ripley. "If those four companies are coming back and hit us in the rear—"

Buttrick nodded grimly. "Wouldn't be much fun." He turned. "Come on, boys, step it out."

Back of the stone wall that faced the Manse and the now distant river, Ripley watched the militia companies file up the grassy slope—gray coats, black coats, blue coats, faded brown smocks. The units looked smaller now. Many had straggled back to Buttrick's helping the few wounded. Still, the disorganization of victory wasn't as bad as it might have been. A good two thirds of the original force had crossed the river and were swarming up the hill.

Hosmer ran up to him. "Rip, stay here, will you?"

"Right," said Ripley. "I'll—hey—look at that!"

Far beyond the Manse on the road back to Concord, the fugitive light infantry had regained some semblance of order, but were keeping up a feverish pace.

"Seem in a hurry," said Hosmer calmly.

"My God—can't you see anything?" Ripley pointed beyond the head of the light infantry. From town, an endless stream of brass and bearskin was pressing on to meet them. "Grenadiers!" snapped Ripley. "Now we'll have something to worry about." He yelled along the wall: "Look to your primings! Get ready!" Buttrick's voice roared out: "No one to fire until *I* give the word. That still holds!" Hosmer returned to the major.

Ripley slipped down back of the wall, slanted his piece over a rock, his eyes on the steady march of the grenadiers. They met the head of the light infantry, opened their ranks and let the fugitives through. Then they closed up again. "Now we'll get it," Ripley muttered. "Now—" He was on his feet, staring in astonishment. The grenadiers, five strong companies, wheeled abruptly, countermarched with rigid precision and followed the light infantry back into town. Ripley sat down abruptly. "I'll be damned!" He felt weak, shaken. He took off his hat, wiped his forehead.

Then the thought, "We've fired on the King's troops!" ran through his head as it had run along the column down by the bridge. Who had fired on the King's troops? Why, some of the militia of Middlesex County. What would happen? More troops would come to Concord. Perhaps militia from other counties would join those troops. There would be arrests— His mind grew numb trying to piece out the results of that clash. He gave up puzzling over it and turned his attention to the militia's position.

The hill was an extension of the long low ridge that ran on through Concord and out into the country in a northerly direction. The road from town lay along its foot, then turned sharply west toward the river and the North Bridge. Across the river lay the dome of Buttrick's Hill that masked the country beyond. The road itself, stretching on to the bridge, lay silent and empty, save for the two red heaps that sprawled there.

Something stirred at the far end of the bridge, a long, lean figure in indeterminate clothes. Ripley recognized the unmistakable halting gait of Sonny Graham, an awkward, dull-witted boy who did chores about town. The boy came on across the bridge, a small axe in his hand. Ripley started up. "Someone ought to send him home." Then he stared in horror. One of the red figures had stirred, half raised itself on its elbow. Sonny had jumped like a frightened rooster, had struck down with his axe. Now the boy was racing off through the meadows and the red figure lay inert.

Gradually the ghastly scene at the bridge was caught up in the unreality of the whole day. It would go on forever like this. He'd spend uncountable hours behind stone walls, watching from hilltops. There had been no beginning, would be no end.

A sudden burst of talk spattered along the wall. Buttrick, back among the trees, shouted: "Steady!"

Ripley joined Buttrick and Hosmer who were pointing down the road toward the bridge. Across the river and along the lower track that led off to Barrett's, the head of a red column appeared, stepping quickly out toward the bridge and the sharp angle where the road turned back to town. "The companies that went on to hunt at Barrett's," said Hosmer mechanically.

"What'll they do?" Buttrick turned worried eyes on Ripley.

"Can't tell yet. Better have the men ready, though."

"They're all right." Buttrick nodded toward the wall where musket barrels jutted, the men back of them watching the red snake that moved on across the bridge coming closer and closer. Suddenly Ripley snapped his fingers. "They'll let us alone."

"How do you know?"

Ripley pointed to the leading company, whose men were stepping over the two bodies that lay in the road. "When a British soldier won't stop for his own dead, he's in a hell of a hurry to get somewhere." He studied the oncoming men dispassionately. "About a hundred, say a hundred-twenty. If you move your lines down within range—"

"No!" said Buttrick abruptly.

"But you've got them cut off, you see. It's the logical move." He pointed at the empty road that led back to town. "The nearest help's a mile away."

"No," said Buttrick again. "This isn't war. They fired on us at the bridge. We fired back. That's all—unless they want to make it more. Besides, our companies are all mixed up. A lot of officers went back up my hill. There's no one to give commands."

The quick march below continued. The first company reached the bend, swung on toward the town. From the road, white faces turned, stared up at the stone wall and its bristle of barrels. Back of the wall, men watched unblinking, lips drawn back over their teeth, fingers restless on musket lock or cartridge pouch. The hush, broken only by the scuff-scuff of boots below, was oppressive.

At last the road at the foot of the ridge was empty.

There was nothing to tell of the passage of the King's troops except for the fading noise of boots and equipment off toward the town—just the noise and the two red bodies that lay on the straight brown track down by the bridge. Muskets were withdrawn from stony rests, men sank back on their heels looking about them wonderingly. A single voice murmured: "Well—what do we do now?"

Ripley looked east toward the town. The roofs were masked by the high ground, but the skyline was clear and calm. Hosmer glanced at Ripley. "What's the matter?"

Ripley pointed toward the town. "What started us down the hill back there? The smoke, wasn't it? We thought they were burning the town."

Hosmer squinted, then rubbed his nose. "By God, that's right. No sign of smoke now." He moved his feet uncertainly. "But there sure was before. I saw it."

Buttrick turned abruptly to Ripley. "Think they'll come back?"

Ripley thumped the ground with the butt of his fusee. "Damn it, I don't know. I've never seen British troops act this way before. They broke at the bridge after two ragged volleys from us. The grenadiers that came out to support them just let them through and then went back after them. The four companies that just went by didn't even stop for the dead down there." He paused, eyes on the road below. Then he set his chin. "My guess is that they won't."

Buttrick's care-worn face tightened. Then he said: "We'll have to go and find out."

Drums tapping softly, the mixed companies straggled down the hill to the road, formed into column, turned east to Concord. Once on the level, the order and steadiness that had marked the first descent to the bridge reasserted itself. Ripley waited by the edge of the road until the last squad had passed and then began to work up the column, eying the men. A few, badly shod, limped heavily and every now and then he saw flushed, feverish faces. But they all marched in silence, eyes hard and mouths set.

Up by the head of the column, Buttrick swung along rigidly. Ripley watched him. Was he going to lead the companies right over the mile of road and into town? What if a solid wall of grenadiers were waiting in the broad space by the Town House?

Following Buttrick's quick gesture, the leading files trailed away left through a gap in the low ridge. Hosmer, ranging up and down the column, raised his thick eyebrows as he came up with Ripley. "Buttrick knows what he's doing," said Ripley. "We'll have the ridge between us and the town. Better stand by for orders. Ten to one he'll halt us when we're out on the flats."

The march went on, the long column trailing out through the gap and filing onto the great meadows that lay north of ridge and town. Ripley eyed the upward sweep of land that hid the houses. What lay behind it? The ridge might mask gutted houses, paneless windows, sagging doors, and the scattered litter of a looting army. He looked up the column toward Buttrick, saw him turn, raise his hand. The column halted, a good two hundred yards north of the ridge.

Suddenly lithe figures moved against the sky along the ridge and the sun winked on brass and polished metal. Ripley cried out, pointed. The figures, in their light infantry caps, were moving *east* along the ridge, paralleling the Lexington road. He shouted again. "Major! Major Buttrick! They're hauling out! They're heading back toward Lexington!"

Buttrick trotted heavily up to him, stared at the ridge. The light infantrymen, heads turned toward the meadows, began to trickle down the northern slope. Halfway down, they checked their descent, faced east, and began working along the flank of the ridge, beating up bushes, circling about outcroppings of rock.

Ripley caught a questioning look from Buttrick. "That's one of the few things they've done today that

I can understand. They're getting out of town. There'll be more of them on the south slope and the grenadiers'll be on the Lexington road."

"You've been right so far," said Buttrick cautiously. He studied the slowly vanishing flankers. "I wish you'd take five men and follow them along the crest. Keep where I can see you and signal to me if there's anything that don't look right. I'll start the rest east along the meadows."

Ripley shook his head. "I'd better go alone. Five men might look like fifty to the Lobsters and they might come back to have a look at us."

"Please yourself," said Buttrick and moved off toward the head of the militia.

Ripley found himself running up the last few yards of the slope. What would he see from the top? There *had* been smoke, heavy smoke. Then Concord lay spread out before him. Wright's, snug in the sun; the Meetinghouse; Dr. Minott's; the Town House. For a moment it was a day like any other. A few people walked slowly in from the direction of North Bridge. A wagon or two jolted past the millpond. Old Mrs. Moulton appeared at her front door and began to sweep the steps vigorously.

Then he looked east. On both slopes and the crest, light infantry were working carefully along. Below them, on the Lexington road, more light infantry and great blocks of grenadiers were drawn up in column, motionless, faces turned to the flankers above them. The nearest company in the road was a good five hundred yards east of Ripley and the head of the column was hidden by a bend in the ridge.

Wright's front door opened and a blond, curly head peered cautiously out. Ripley waved his fusee and shouted, "Joris!" Far along the ridge, two or three light infantrymen looked about, their faces whitish discs. One of them started back toward Ripley, musket advanced. Then he turned and trotted off after his fellows.

Joris Cuyler plunged across the road and began threading his way upward among the tombstones. Ripley ran to meet him. "What's been happening? Better go and tell Buttrick."

Still panting, Cuyler looked down at the militia in the meadows. "Heard some funny things." His blue eyes were hard on Ripley. "They say your people scalped the wounded, gouged out their eyes and cut their ears off."

"Scalped? Gouged?"

"That's what they said. Six wounded."

"That's a lie!" began Ripley. Then he remembered the flash of an axe on the sunlit bridge. Rapidly he told of Sonny Graham. "And that's all. Sonny's just weak in the head and got scared. I thought you'd have more brains than to swallow something like that. I saw the whole thing, first shot to last."

Cuyler looked relieved. "Well, they believe it though." He jerked his thick shoulder toward the still-waiting grenadiers. "It's put them in a rare mood."

Ripley grunted. "And by the time they get back to barracks, they'll be saying we burned forty at the stake. Forget it. What's been happening?"

Cuyler's breath was heavy with rum. "They've got a colonel in command. His name's Smith and he's so fat the seat of his breeches drags on the ground. He's the sappiest chuff I've ever seen—doesn't know if he's in London or Albany. Oh, I meant to tell you. His second-in-command's a marine."

Ripley started. "A marine?"

Cuyler nodded violently. "Just him. All alone."

Ripley's breath whistled out in relief. "That's all right, then. What else?"

Cuyler's grin dug deeper creases in his broad cheek. "They've been buying me drinks. The marine tried to get rough with the chap who's taken Featherfoot's place today and damned if the tapster didn't whack his chops for him."

"He hit a *major*? What happened then?"

"Nothing. We had rum. That marine, Pitcairn, is a pretty good sort."

"Quit rambling. What went on?"

"Nothing, I told you. They searched a few houses. That big girl who lives next Reuben Brown's chased two grenadiers out of her house with a broom. They chucked a few barrels of stores into the millpond. That's all."

"But we saw smoke," protested Ripley. "A lot of smoke."

"Oh, that!" Cuyler waved expansively. "They were burning gun carriages in the Town House but old Mrs. Moulton asked them not to, so they put out the fire and burned the carriages out in the street. Then—"

Ripley shook Cuyler's shoulder. "You ought to have stopped on the first bottle. She *asked* them not to burn the Town House and they quit?"

Cuyler looked surprised. "Sure. Why not? There's a woman sick in one of the houses and an ensign put a guard at the door to keep search parties out."

"This is the damnedest day I've ever put in," said Ripley. "They march eight hundred men clear from Boston to search a town, and if someone yells at them to get out of a house, they go. A tapster hits a major and nothing happens. They start to burn a building and quit because an old woman asks them not to." He wiped his forehead. "All right. Do you know what they're going to do now?"

"Look at them. They don't want to play any more, so they're going home. Pitcairn got a few chaises, gave receipts for them, and chucked some wounded men into them and started them back. If it weren't for him, Smith would still be buying me drinks."

"Hear anything about more troops coming out?"

"They didn't say anything when I was around. Hi! There they go."

A drum tapped out of sight along the road. The waiting companies stirred, shouldered their muskets in a smart whirl of steel, and moved off toward Meriam's corner and Lexington.

Ripley looked down at the meadows, where the militia stood at ease. He saw Buttrick raise his arm and make a sweeping gesture in the direction of the British march. Then he set off at a trot eastward along the ridge, calling over his shoulder: "Come on, Joris. Let's see the Lobsters out of town!"

Far ahead, Ripley caught glimpses of red backs among the trees, judged that the light infantry were nearing the east point of the ridge where he and Cuyler had watched through the early morning. Below, in the meadows, the militia was marching stolidly parallel to the British but hidden from them by the high ground.

The ridge ended in a sharp knob, the same spot from which he had watched dawn come up over the Lexington road. Ripley caught hold of a young birch, swung himself to the peak, and the flat country spread out before him. He shouted: "Get up here and wave good-bye to your boozing friends, Joris!"

Cuyler scrambled up beside him and the two looked down. The grenadiers had passed Meriam's corner and were pushing east, their progress slightly delayed by the narrow bridge over Mill Brook. Beyond the head of the column, light infantry formed a screen in the northern fields and were moving steadily on. Two or three mounted officers, one very stout, had halted their horses across the little bridge and watched the oncoming sea of bearskins and red coats. To the left, the head of the militia companies, Buttrick in the lead, was just emerging onto the Bedford road about a quarter of a mile beyond the junction with the Lexington road.

"That all?" asked Cuyler, fanning himself with his hat.

"As long as we keep out of range."

"H'm—maybe we'll keep out of range, but how about the Lobsters? You didn't hear them talking in the tavern. Even a Concord man admitted that they sounded a little cross."

"Forget it. All they want to do is get home—quick."

"Maybe that's what the books say, but—" Cuyler broke off, studied the slow march of the grenadiers, then looked north at the militia companies who came on, seemingly oblivious of the British. He yelled: "Look! New boys—off there on the Bedford road. Coming this way!"

New companies, pushing on from northern towns, swung off the road, spread out, and began working rapidly toward the Meriam buildings. The militia in the meadows shouted, broke ranks, and ran to meet them. More shouts arose south of the Lexington road and thin lines of drab-hued men scurried over the marshy stretch. The last squad of grenadiers, safely across the little bridge, wheeled abruptly, raised their muskets.

Ripley found himself roaring: "Don't shoot! Don't shoot!"

Crashing smoke blotted out the sunny road below. In the fields about Meriam's, militiamen froze into immobility or pitched heavily to the ground. The smoke cloud from the bridge drifted away, crashed out again.

Ripley gripped his fusee. "I'm going to see this through. Get on back to town. Find my father and tell him that I've gone on." He dropped down the steep slope of the ridge, raced across the Bedford road and plunged into the fields. All about him, men were slipping behind trees, taking shelter back of rocks and hummocks. A single musket blasted close behind him, another flamed off to the left and the fields erupted in a stream of uneven fire that threw a heavy white blanket between the militia and the road.

Ripley shouted for Hosmer and Buttrick, but the men who lunged past him through the smoke pall were strangers. He waved to the nearest men. "Get up closer! You're seventy yards away. Get into range. Up by those last trees. Come on!"

Rough bark scored his cheek as he fired from the lee of an apple tree, aiming low into the rolling smoke that hid road and bridge. He bit open another cartridge, loaded, primed, glided closer to the stone wall that edged the road. The shouting spread far off to the left: he heard footsteps rushing away through the fields, heading east and paralleling the Lexington road.

Suddenly the fields were still and the smoke thinned. Beyond the stone wall, the British column pushed doggedly east. By the little bridge, one arm trailing over the edge, lay a big sergeant, heedless of the dead weight across his knees. Something stirred in the grass by the side of the road and a light infantryman staggered to his feet, lurched off after his fellows, bleeding fingers over his face.

Ripley straightened up. There was Meriam's stone wall which he himself had helped build, a solid, peaceful wall that had been raised to make a boundary. Now it marked a battlefield, called into being by a useless volley. He thought bitterly: "They started it. We've got to get them out of the township, out of the county." He loaded hastily and turned away from the road. Back toward the Meriam house, men were slowly getting to their feet. In the doorway a tall man called to hidden companions: "No one hit! By God, no one got hit!"

All about Ripley men were running through the fields, keeping well away from road and wall. He shouted: "Hosmer! Joe Hosmer!" A long-nosed man looked around. "Who you want?"

"Seen any Concord men?"

"Nope! We're Reading. Some Bil'ricky folks just ahead."

Ripley wove on through running men, looking for familiar faces, but companies and towns were hopelessly mingled. Even squads had broken up. There was nothing left but a leaderless swarm of armed country people rushing on, hard-eyed and silent, on the flank of the British line of march. Out of sight ahead, scattered shots echoed flatly. Ripley splashed across Mill Brook. "There's no turning back. I've got to see this through," he thought.

A voice bellowed, "Rip! Rip! I've got one!" Spanning the brook in a vast leap, Joris Cuyler thundered on, brandishing a heavy musket. Ripley slowed to a trot. "Damn you, why didn't you go back to town?"

"One of the boys at the farm got nicked in the arm and he gave me his gun and his powder. By God, I'm going to get a lick at those bastards. They started it!" He veered off toward the stone wall and the last red company that was vanishing back of a fold in the ground.

Ripley caught his arm. "Keep away from that wall. They'll have flankers out."

"You're the only one that thinks so," shouted Cuyler. "Look up there. They're edging in toward the road again."

"And they'll get snapped up. Damn it, I know march tactics. Come on with me." He started away from the road at a sharp trot. Cuyler pounded after him. "Going to let them get away? God damn it, I'll—"

"No! I'm not. But I'm not going to give them a target. We'll work way up ahead of the column and wait for it. I know a good place."

"All right, all right," grumbled Cuyler. "But how about the fellows that don't know as much as you do?"

"Hell, they won't listen but we'll give them a chance!" He waved his arm to clusters of men who were angling back toward the hidden road and the wall. "Keep clear! Get ahead of them. Make for the bluffs!" Heads turned, men hesitated and a few swung away toward Ripley and Cuyler.

Suddenly Ripley halted, hand raised. Off to the

south and out of sight, cries echoed, then a single regular volley crashed out. "I told you!" shouted Ripley. "Our people are getting back of walls and woodpiles and the flankers are spotting them like sitting birds. Keep wide until we get to the bluffs." He took up a steady lope.

When the roof of Hartwell's farm showed to the south, Ripley began to edge gradually back toward the road, leading the way through a thick maple copse. Other figures moved under the budding branches, calling: "I know a place. Cross the road and—" . . . "I'm a stranger here. Where'll I find cover?" . . . "Jake, Jake, make for Stobbs's pasture!" The copse rang on with the shouts of men from far and near.

A growing trail of men scrambling after them, Ripley and Cuyler fought their way up a steep slope, emerged on a rocky hogback that butted into the Lexington road at right angles. Ripley ran to the southern tip and looked down.

Twenty feet below him the road curved away to the left and the high ground that masked the roofs of Lexington. To the right, a quarter-mile stretch of road showed clear to the west before it lost itself in wooded turns. Cuyler whistled. "What a place!"

"This is too damned close," said Ripley. "There's higher ground by those rocks."

"The rocks? God, that's a range of forty yards, easy. We ought to get closer."

"Forty's a pretty long shot, I admit," said Ripley, "but it'll be safer." He pointed to the flank of the hogback. "That country's too steep and broken for the flankers. They'll have to fall back on the column and then fan out again when they get past this bend. If we sit up here and dangle our toes over the edge, we're damned apt to get them tickled. Back there we won't be bothered."

Ripley moved swiftly among the men who were swarming over the crest, waved them out of the danger zone. A few grumbled and one red-haired farmer growled: "I ain't taking orders from no one that ain't out of Woburn." At last, however, they were all posted in fair cover.

Ripley chose a big rock, balanced his fusee on it, while Cuyler made himself surprisingly small behind a fallen log.

Suddenly other drab figures appeared on the flat ground on the other side of the road, found cover a respectful distance from the brown track that cut under the nose of the hogback. The men about Ripley began to whoop and shout: "Hey! Where you from?" The answers came thin and clear: "Framingham!" "Marlboro!" "Harvard!"

Ripley raised himself on his elbow. "Shut up! Want to tell the Lobsters where we are?"

Cuyler nagged him. "Hell, they can't hear."

"Maybe not right now, but they're coming closer all the time. Listen!" To the right, distant, isolated shots rang out, were joined by others. The noise thickened, spread, was suddenly cut through by one solid volley, another. Smoke began to well up through trees a half mile away, drifted closer.

Suddenly in the fields at the right, a swarm of light infantry broke from a tangle of underbrush. A second line followed them. Cuyler struggled to his knees. Ripley pulled him down. "They'll have to hit onto the road. Besides, they're nearly two hundred yards away. You couldn't hit them with a cannon." Cuyler grumbled, rubbed the butt of his musket angrily. Then he bounced up again. "They've found something down there!"

The men in red were circling cautiously toward a little shed that lay half hidden among scrubby trees some twenty yards from the road. Suddenly they closed in, bayonets poised. Shouts echoed. One shot rang out, another, and smoke began to drift up through the scrub. Then there was silence and the light infantry appeared on the edge of the road, several of them carefully wiping their bayonets.

Ripley drummed his fist on the ground. "What damn fools were down there? Just asking to be snapped up." He suddenly sank lower back of his rock. "Watch out! Here it is."

Scarlet and white showed unexpectedly at the far end of the road to the right and the first of the grenadier companies appeared. Its ranks were ragged and unsteady and the men moved at a rapid gait that was nearly a trot. More companies, then light infantry came into view, lurching along, more grenadiers.

"Come on! Here's your chance!" shouted Ripley. "Don't waste your shots!" He watched the feverish progress of the red column down there on the road. One hundred yards—seventy—sixty—fifty—

Smoke and flame welled from the high ground. Under the lifting edge of the cloud, Ripley saw black-gaitered legs buckle, saw a lone bearskin spin dizzily across the road, lie rocking against a stone, its metal plate winking. He rose to his knees, reloaded, fired once more. Through the curtain of smoke grenadiers were pitching to the ground, running forward with their heads lowered as though breasting a torrent of rain. A horse reared, dashed away through the haze.

Ripley was aware of Cuyler roaring above the din, saw him stand up and fire blindly into the smoky welter. He shouted: "Come on. We'll make for Fiske's Hill in Lexington. No use staying here."

He swung about, ran along the hogback that was covered with racing men, all striking away from the road, watching for a chance to circle back and hit the head of the column again. When he was a good two hundred yards away, Ripley slipped down from the high ground. The British had broken through the belt of fire that had struck them and were actually running, heedless of a spatter of weak fire that still pursued them. Two mounted officers were ranging up and down the column, waving their arms in a vain attempt to slow the pace and bring order back to the ranks.

By a swampy patch, Ripley halted, looked back. "Joris!" he shouted. "Joris!" Running men looked incuriously at him, kept on their way. "Joris!" Ripley cupped his hands about his mouth. "Joris!"

From a clump of birches, someone waved. Ripley ran to the slender trees, saw three strangers supporting the heavy-shouldered New Yorker. "Are you hit, Joris?"

Crimson of face, Cuyler sputtered: "This isn't a wound. It's a God-damned insult." He slued his body around and pointed with his free arm to the blood that was staining the seat of his breeches. "How the hell will I explain *that?*"

Ripley slung his fusee over his shoulder. "I'll take him back. Come on, Joris."

"Take me back be damned," roared Cuyler. "Keep going and drill that light infantryman where he drilled me. You find him, now!"

"We'll take him home," said one of the men supporting Cuyler. "I got no more powder. Joe's flint won't knap and Abel's clean shut of powder, same's me."

Ripley hesitated. Cuyler stamped his foot, winced with pain. "Go on and get that light-infantry son-of-a-bitch."

Ripley looked reluctantly at Cuyler's bearers. "Keep him well away from the road. You may run into stragglers. Good luck, Joris."

He unslung his fusee and ran off toward Lexington. The delay had left Ripley almost alone in the meadows north of the road. He increased his pace and began to overtake small, straggling groups of militia who answered his questions in monosyllables. They were from Weston, from Framingham, from Marlboro, Ayer, Lancaster. One group, which had some semblance of cohesion, shouted that they were from Lexington, that the British had massacred their people on the green at sunrise. Then they swooped off toward the road, heedless of flankers, and began to fire at long range.

At last Ripley neared the crest of Fiske's Hill, where men on the skyline were waving, pointing down to the road and the town beyond. Tired legs suddenly gained new life and all about Ripley men were running, shouting. He vaulted a low gate, then stopped.

Off to the right lay the Lexington road, a long, gently sloping strip that boiled with a torrent of red and white, bearskins and skullcaps hopelessly mixed, no gaps between companies, no neat lines right and left down the flanks. Men collapsed, rolled by the side of the road, clawed themselves upright, labored on with thrown-back heads and bared teeth. Knapsacks fell from galled shoulders, dusty bearskins pitched to the road, were beaten into the dirt by grinding heels.

A short, thick-set man leaned on a long musket by Ripley's elbow. "Shouldn't a happened." He gestured and the fringes of a hunting shirt flicked. "No, sir. All wrong. Tom Gage, he was with Braddock. He'd ought to know what bush fighting means."

"You've served?" asked Ripley.

"The old wars. Ranger, I was. Nahum Sholes, from up Merrimac way. Was heading for Boston to trade some and got mixed up in this." With an odd air of detachment he hooked his thumbs in his belt and watched the tortured red column.

Ripley's jaw set as he studied the rout. There was little musketry along the flanks, but the growing panic seemed to force the flying troops faster and faster. Suddenly he said: "We've got them!"

The ranger nodded slowly. "Neighbor, you're right." He pointed at bright flecks of steel at the front and flank of the retreat. "Officers is pinking at 'em with swords. Come on!" Catlike, despite his odd bulk, Nahum Sholes glided on past Ripley, struck out at an easy lope. Other men took up the shout and set off, powder horns and pouches dancing. Ripley called: "Bear off to the flanks! Hit for the high ground beyond the Meetinghouse."

Sholes looked over his shoulder approvingly. "Neighbor, you're talking sense. Wide it is."

In a great curve the mass of militia pounded down the hill, veered well off to the right. More drab forms showed on the brow of Loring's Hill, began to trickle down toward the Green, at whose far end a thin line of bearskin caps formed raggedly, officers raving and storming behind them. Smoke jutted from near-by trees, flame stabbed out from between trim houses. The grenadiers melted, broke, joined the shattered red mass that flooded east and south down the road to Boston.

Ripley and Sholes, keeping clear of the ruck of the pursuit, swarmed up the opposite hill.

"Now let's get high as we can," called Sholes. "I like to be where I can look down at folks and know they ain't no one can look down at me." His short, bandy legs churned ahead. Suddenly he stopped, dropped to the ground. Ripley slid up beside him. "What's the matter?"

The ranger's lined face was bitter. "Look at that. Had 'em in a trap. Now someone's gone and opened it."

The road from Boston was filled with a solid column of troops in cocked hats, troops that swung steadily west toward Lexington. In the fields on both sides of the road, trim lines of flankers moved. Far down the road, more cocked hats swayed and bobbed.

The tattered companies of light infantry and grenadiers broke into a last desperate dash toward the relieving column. Men fell, struggled to their feet, caught at flying fellows, dragged at arms and legs, fighting madly to break away from the pursuit, to fling themselves into the shelter of the oncoming British ranks.

Sholes raised himself to his knees. "Well—what do you think of that?"

Dazed, Ripley shook his head. Somewhere along the morning's march, fat Smith must have taken alarm and sent word back to Gage in Boston. Now the relief had arrived at the last possible moment. Ripley shaded his eyes, studied the newcomers. Cocked hats, so far as he could see. That would mean that the line companies of the regiments to which the grenadiers and light infantry belonged had been sent out—the bulk of the Boston garrison of veterans. Back on the Lexington Green, the pursuers had halted, uncertain, looking apprehensively at the heavy red masses that had appeared so suddenly.

The Boston column halted and the fugitives poured through gaps in the ranks, fell headlong among the gaitered legs of the infantry.

Sholes made a gesture of patient resignation. "Guess that changes things some. An hour more and we'd have captured the—"

The first cannon shot came with stunning unexpectedness and a ball screeched high in air in its curving flight toward the Green. Ripley flattened himself unconsciously. "Where the hell did that come from?"

"I had it in my pocket. Where do you think?" said Sholes impatiently.

A second gun slammed. Back on the Green there was a sudden crash of boards and militia scattered from the Meetinghouse, whose walls showed a smoking rent. Sholes rubbed an unshaven chin. "Now I always did hold it was unlucky to shoot a praying house."

Ripley struggled to his knees. "The bastards! Using a church for a target!"

"We-ell," said Sholes. "Don't know's I blame 'em, seeing all them little boys with guns around it."

"How'd you like it if they blasted a hole through the church in your town?"

"Don't live in a town." He got to his feet. "Neighbor, you've served, same as me. I can tell. What do you say we do now?"

"We could stay here and see what happens. Or we could work up to the left flank of the British and take a look."

"Both good. One's soldier, one's ranger. I say, we'll prowl the flanks. You know these parts? Take the lead."

They threaded their way down a slope that hid the crowded Green and road from them, moved profanely through a swamp that wound about the base of Munroe's Hill with its red tavern. From time to time they called softly to each other as shifting red figures on the skyline caught their eyes. Other boots squelched in the morass, voices called in hushed excitement. Most of them, to judge from their curt words, had just reached the battle road after a long march from unknown towns.

At last Ripley left the swamp and worked cautiously up the hill to a rocky spot southeast of Munroe's Tavern. Behind him Sholes chuckled. "You done good," he said as he peered out over a boulder. Their circuit had brought up well in the rear of the main body and they looked out on distant red backs, cut across with white belts. The advance guard was out of sight toward the town.

"How many new ones, neighbor—what is it—Mayne? Neighbor Mayne?" asked Sholes.

"Trying to figure it out. There are some down that hollow there that we can't see. But—they're spreading out three companies deep—figure thirty-five men to a company—" He shut his eyes—"maybe eight hundred, maybe a thousand counting the advance guard. Wonder what they'll do now? Push on to Concord and burn the town or head back to Boston?"

Sholes nodded reasonably, his mangy fur cap tilting forward over his nose. "Well—they's two ways to find out. One's to go ask them. One's to squat here and wait. Seems to me squatting's a bit more sensible."

"Only thing to do, I guess." Ripley studied the waiting companies. The men were standing at ease, but keeping their formation. Over a rise of ground toward Lexington, a straining squad of blue and red gunners trundled a light field piece back toward the main body. The door of Munroe's Tavern stood wide-open and men were carrying some grenadiers inside. On the grass in front, a group of officers stood, bottles and glasses in their hands. Nothing in the whole scene indicated whether the next move would be advance or retreat.

Ripley propped his back against the boulder. "Nothing to do except watch and keep awake. I was up all night."

Sholes was sympathetic. "Liquoring?"

"No. Watching and running and marching."

"That's what you get, living in a town. Runs the guts out a man like sap out a maple. Hell, it ain't five mile from here to Concord. I couldn't sweat up an appetite on that." He unslung his greasy haversack and pulled out grayish slabs of salt meat and coarse bread. "Better vittle up with me."

The meat was musty and rank, but Ripley ate it greedily and gnawed at the moldy bread. The ranger waved away his thanks. "Hell, a neighbor's a neighbor," he growled. "Eat hearty and keep your eyes on them Lobsters. Seems to me you know more 'bout town troops'n I do, being used to forest forts and such."

The sun moved slowly down the sky as the pair studied the waiting British. Officers shuttled back and forth between the resting regiments and the broad door of the tavern. Sweating gunner's shifted the field pieces back toward the silent ranks, then trundled them off out of sight down the road to town. Sholes, his eyes never leaving the troops ahead, droned on about old ranger days. Ripley listened idly as he tried to make out the facings of a regiment that was drawn up at right angles to the rest. Then he began counting his cartridges. The dead Davis's cartouche was bigger than most. Ripley had fired five rounds, but still had thirty-seven left. He tested their wrappings to be sure that they were tight, and turned his attention back to the fields beyond Munroe's.

There was the same aimless coming and going about the tavern. At Ripley's side, Sholes had grown excited by his own talk and his voice had risen. "Rogers a great ranger? Huh! He was the greatest of 'em all—with his mouth. God damn it, he wa'n't fit to scout the same trail with Iz Putnam or Johnny Stark. He—"

Ripley sprang to his feet, a hand on the ranger's shoulder. There was a sudden tightening of the long lines of red-coated men. Then drums began to slam. The companies faced about, turning their backs on Lexington. Ripley shouted: "They're going back to Boston!"

Sholes jumped to the top of the rock. "They got to. Look what they done!"

Wood smoke began to blow across the fields and flames worked up through the roof of a house that clung to the opposite slope. Beyond it, a second house, a barn, shimmered back of a murky curtain. Ripley cried: "God damn them!"

Sholes dropped to the ground. "Ain't no use cussing about them houses. Lobsters was scared folks'd be potting at them from the windows. Get moving. This ain't no place for us."

With a last glance at the blazing roofs, Ripley ran on with Sholes. He tugged at his watch. Twenty minutes after three. Sholes roared at him to hurry and pointed backwards toward Munroe's. The light infantry, whipped into some semblance of shape, had spread out over the fields and the main column had lurched into motion. From the extreme rear, musketry broke out as the militia took up the pursuit again.

Ripley shouted to Sholes: "Make for the rocks in that field. We'll wait for the Lobsters there."

"That's sense, neighbor," said Sholes.

To Ripley the world became a succession of fields, all alike, cut by stone walls, cut by a road that was choked with a red throng at which he fired, never hearing the blast of his fusee, never feeling the kick of the butt against his shoulder. As he ran, he saw nothing clearly save Sholes's broad back bobbing on in front. When the broad shoulders were still, Ripley stopped. When they moved away, he followed. Sometimes there were houses and once his vision cleared so that he could see the sign of the Black Horse Tavern, close to the Cambridge line.

Then, hours later, he knelt, loaded, fired, loaded, fired, loaded and fired— He blinked. The sheen of water was before him. Far away, over a neck of land, a big ship was swinging broadside, its gun ports open and marines in the fighting tops. The last of the retreating mass was trailing away over a low hill toward the water and the shelter of the ship's guns. Painfully, Ripley pushed back from the wall and saw Sholes perched on a log close by, puffing contentedly at a stone-bowled pipe.

The stocky man blew out a cloud of smoke. "Knowed you'd come out of it. You been setting there snapping an empty musket for the last fifteen minutes."

Ripley scowled. "Empty? You're crazy." He plunged his hand into the cartridge box that had banged against his hip all the way from the North Bridge.

"Neighbor, you fired your last round back there to a place they called Prospect Hill. Yes, sir. By damn, you've been kneeling there going through the drill pretty as you like. You'd holler: 'Prime and load!' Then you'd twirl that gun about and fuss with your rammer. Pretty it was."

Slowly Ripley got to his knees. The scattered

houses, the low hill and the water, danced before his eyes. "By God, we've come clear to Charlestown."

Sholes tamped the bowl of his pipe complacently. "Might be. One town's about the same's the next to me."

The flank of the nearest ship spat red, veiled itself in a thundering cloud. A heavy ball wailed through the air, thudded out of sight in the distant marshes. Ripley got unsteadily to his feet. There was something wrong about the footing and he seemed to be walking off along a curving line.

Strong hands caught his shoulders and Sholes growled. "Where the hell do you think you're going?"

Ripley said: "Back to Concord. Got to get there."

The ranger sat back on his heels. "All right. Go break your God-damn neck. But have a bite of this first." He held out a silver flask. "Got it off that dead Lobster back there by Arlington," he explained.

Brandy bit at Ripley's throat, flooded his stiffening limbs. He nodded. "Good stuff. Start in a minute." He rubbed his eyes, looked toward the shoreline where men were shouting. "What are they yelling about?"

"Just making a lot of noise, wondering the same thing I am—what the hell do we do *now*?"

Sholes glanced down at Ripley, saw that he was asleep. He drank deeply himself. When his pipe was empty, he threw up a shelter of branches, raked together a deep bed of leaves, and rolled the sleeping Ripley onto it. Then he lit a small blaze, ate sparingly from his haversack as fires began to appear through the gathering dusk. One by one they flamed up, settled to a steady glow. They stretched from Charlestown Neck west and then south and east, forming an arc of living fire about the Boston peninsula. They blazed along the tidal reaches of the Charles River, in the outskirts of Cambridge, and in Roxbury across from the narrow fortified Neck that led into the city of Boston itself.

Far beyond the range of Sholes's keen eye and ear, weary men tramped through the night heading for the arc of fire, men who had been brought out of western towns and counties by the warning voice of gun and bell. From the valley of the Connecticut they came, from the woody tangles of the Berkshires, from the hill towns in the far northwest of the Province. None of the marchers knew what had happened. They only knew that something threatened all that they lived by, threatened the old liberties that their fathers and grandfathers had won for them and to which they themselves clung beyond fatigue, hunger, and the reasonable promptings of fear.

IV

It was late afternoon of the next day when Ripley and Sholes reached the bridge that led across the Sudbury to the Mayne lands. Along the hill, the roof of the old house seemed to peer down at them over the grassy shoulder, its gable windows eying Ripley as it had eyed other Maynes crossing the bridge, footsore and powder-stained.

Sholes tilted his fur cap. "Your folks had sense not to build down in all them streets and houses. Packed in so close, by God, a man wouldn't know if he was in bed with his own woman or some other feller's. Course," he added philosophically, "the other feller wouldn't know either, but that don't change the point."

Ripley clapped Sholes's back. "The Lobsters didn't get this far. Look!" He pointed to the unshattered panes. "Damn it, some of those places we passed near Arlington had me worried. Come on."

The side door of the house opened as the pair ran

up the path. Melven Mayne, gray and erect, shouted: "Rip! You're all right?"

"Now that I know that you are," said Ripley while his father patted his shoulder. "And this is Nahum Sholes. He looked after me."

"Ain't needed much looking after. I been following him today cause I'd made up my mind to stop a spell with you folks. Leastways until I'd kind of smelled out what was going to happen."

Melven Mayne accepted the travel-stained trapper. "Of course! Rip, we'll have to forage for ourselves, because Mrs. Parr's in the town helping get it back into shape. But there's a roast and I'll bring up rum."

Sholes's eyes glowed. "Now I been telling myself all along that they'd be rum!"

Melven Mayne held the door open. "In with you. You'll find another visitor who may surprise you."

On a low cot by the window lay Joris Cuyler, flat on his belly, his blond hair crinkly as ever and his pink face wrinkled in a grin. "Your father picked me out of a cart by Wright's and brought me here."

The older man chuckled. "He bawled for rum and told me not to worry about you."

Cuyler waved his hand. "Nothing to worry about. Every time the Lobsters saw that black head of yours they thought it was a crow perched on a stone wall."

"What do you suppose they took your rump for, you chuff? Look, Joris, this is Nahum Sholes. He knows all about gunshot wounds. He'll fix you up."

"No need," said Cuyler. "Your father brought Dr. Minott in and the damned sawbones said I was all right. Didn't ask my opinion about it." He rolled slightly, winced. "A Lobster shot at me and missed, so I turned the other cheek and—well, hell, what happened to you?"

"Ran a long way and got damned hungry," said Ripley.

"And thirsty," said Sholes, his eyes on a row of

black bottles. He rubbed his hands as Melven Mayne set a great roast, vegetables, bread, and pudding on the center table. Plates and glasses were quickly filled, Sholes smacking his lips over the first taste of West India rum.

"Just what did happen beyond Meriam's corner, Rip?" asked his father.

Rip drank with deep satisfaction. "Doesn't seem to me that I remember much about it."

Sholes waved his knife. "This was kind of a battle. And the only folks that knows about a battle is them as wasn't there. I'd been lotting on your telling *me*."

Melven Mayne shook his head. "No one knows very much. We know that Smith came to Concord with about seven hundred men. He retreated and Earl Percy met him at Lexington with about a thousand more. Then our militia chased both lots right back to Charlestown. That's about all we know."

Sholes poured more rum lovingly. "Anyone know what we done to them?"

"Too early for that. It does seem that they lost more than two for our one. But that's a guess."

Sholes eyed the older man somberly over the top of his glass. "Got *two* hit for one of ours?"

Cuyler smiled grimly. "That'll teach the Lobsters."

Sholes bounced in his chair. "And by God it'll teach me never again, so help me, to soldier with a bunch of ham-fisted, wall-eyed clod punchers. Why —" he thumped the table—"that road was lined end to end with muskets and there was the Lobsters marching along it. God damn it, if I'd had fifty rangers with me, I'd a had the Lobsters licking salt out my cap in an hour and never lost a man! Marksmen! Why, a blind squaw seven month gone'd a shot better than the militia!"

Ripley pushed the bottle toward Sholes. "Drink up and cheer up. What do you expect from the militia? We're farmers, not hunters. We have to go fifty miles for deer and it's close to a hundred years since we've had to think about Indians. Why *should* our men be good shots? Besides, powder's been too scarce for target practice."

"Was our shooting so bad, Rip?" asked his father.

"Sholes may think so. But by British standards it was wonderful. By tomorrow they'll be saying we sent picked marksmen out against them."

Cuyler raised himself cautiously on his elbows. "What are you going to do now?"

Ripley pushed away his plate. "Take the chaise and go back to Cambridge and find something to join. Billy Heath's sorting out what's left of our regiments and sending word for the boys who dropped out along the road to come back and report."

Melven Mayne drew a deep breath. "I knew you'd take your part, Rip. For the whole thing, whatever it may be, as well as for yesterday. I'm glad."

Ripley got up. "It's grown into something a lot bigger than just the militia of one town, than just a town fight. It'll spread."

Sholes reached for a bottle. "Maybe you're right. Neighbor, I guess I'll crowd you a bit in that chaise."

"I—I hate to leave you alone with the farm, Father," said Ripley.

"That's all right. I made up my mind last night to lease it. I was sure you'd stay with the troops. I'm to fill Olin's place in the Massachusetts Congress and shan't be around much." He got up, slowly. "I'd looked forward to the spring and summer, Rip. Can't be helped. I'll see to the chaise for you. Stable the horse at Bradish's in Harvard Square." He turned to Joris. "Mr. Cuyler, the house is yours, of course, for as long as you want to stay."

Cuyler flounced angrily on his cot. "Thanks, Mr. Mayne. It won't be long. As soon as this tail of mine heals, I'll hit for New York. If I can't find a regiment to join, by God I'll raise one of my own and enlist in it."

Ripley laughed. "Keep your mind on your fat bottom. Now I'm going to throw a few things into a game bag to take with me. Have a stirrup cup poured for me when I come back."

The sun had set behind a wall of sullen black clouds as Ripley and Sholes climbed into the chaise. Melven Mayne laid his hand on the dashboard. "We've said about all there is to say, Rip. You've a twenty-mile drive. Now God bless you both." He gripped Ripley's arm and was gone.

Ripley let the horse pick its way down the slope and turned to look back at the house. The wide front door was just closing on the tall form of his father. He shook the reins as the chaise turned onto the road. Sholes grunted: "Maybe setting in to rain."

Ripley looked off to the southeast where clouds were gathering thicker and thicker, clouds that caught a faint glow as they mirrored the great curve of campfires.

PART TWO

JOHN GLOVER

Night after night the great curve of fire glowed about Boston from Charlestown on the north to Roxbury on the west. Within the curve were anger, frustration, a hint of panic. Without was chaos.

By day and by night, new formations streamed in from remote parts of the Province. Then units from Connecticut appeared, from New Hampshire, from Rhode Island. Some were solid and well-equipped. Others were as unprepared as those who had followed the battle road from Concord to Charlestown on the nineteenth of April.

The pattern of the siege of Boston began to emerge. The Provincial Congress realized the hopelessness of the militia organization and abolished it in one bold move. In its place was authorized a Massachusetts army to serve for eight months. In varying degrees, the other Provinces followed suit. So, under the very eyes of Gage and the beleaguered British, one army was dissolved, another formed to take its place.

Chaos increased. The King's health was still drunk as regiments were brought into being, only to be broken up again by order of Congress. Eager men trailed for months from camp to camp, looking for a unit that they could join. Officers schemed for rank, contractors squabbled over profits; self-seekers, civil and military, hampered every effort. Often men would not serve under officers from other towns, other counties than their own. At times the curved line that hemmed in Gage's veterans was stretched painfully thin. But always just enough men could be found to meet an emergency, to serve a few more days, to hold together the cadre of a growing regiment.

And the siege went on.

I

RIPLEY wrinkled his nose and walked faster as the May sun drew out fetid exhalations from Cambridge Common. Here at the north end, the huts were dirty and ramshackle, the spaces between them littered with rotting vegetables and old bones. A few men lounged in the doorways, yawning and seemingly oblivious of the human and animal offal that lay about. Then cleaner air came to him as he passed into a section of neat tents where streets were well swept and screened latrines told of careful discipline.

He cleared the Common and entered the graveyard that spread out beyond the stumpy tower of Christ Church. Nahum Sholes, in his wanderings from regiment to regiment, often pitched camp among the headstones and Ripley looked for the economical spread of canvas that would show that the old ranger was in residence. He found the canvas neatly rolled close by the fence and cursed irritably. Sholes could have been of little help to him in his present difficulties but it would have lightened his sense of depression to have talked things over with the stocky man. Noon tolled from a bell in the Harvard Yard. At least, he could go to Bradish's Blue Anchor for a good meal.

Harvard Square was buzzing with life under the elms that fringed it. The weeks that had passed since the first wild rallying of the town companies had brought out a spattering of uniforms that showed bright against the drab of civiliandom. Most of the wearers were officers who had provided their equipment out of their own pockets but there were an increasing number of the new jackets, brown faced with red, that Massachusetts was beginning to issue. A file of men from the Connecticut Weathersfield company, smart in blue and red, swung down toward the Charles River and a few Rhode Island gunners aired their odd, twisted skullcaps by the fence that girdled Harvard Yard.

Ripley scowled at a blue and white officer who rode through the Square. "Damn it, everyone else seems to *belong* to something," he muttered. His discontent deepened as he went down Boylston Street, and pushed into Bradish's where a noontime crowd ate in a clatter of china and cutlery. Brandish himself, fat and leather-aproned, stood inside the door. "Prime steaks today, Mr. Mayne," he said.

Ripley looked about the room where brown shoulders, gray shoulders, black shoulders, blue shoulders, dipped and rose over high-piled plates. "Can you give me a table by myself?" he asked.

Bradish stretched on tiptoe. "H'm. Have to wait, I guess, unless you want to sit with that feller in blue at the back of the room."

"It'll have to do," said Ripley resignedly. He wedged carefully on past the crowded chair backs. "Is this place taken?" he asked.

A neatly powdered head inclined gravely. "At your service, sir."

Ripley sat down, noticed that his neighbor was dressed in well-cut civilian blue, that his frills and ruffles were immaculate. Then he forgot about him, watched the carts and the squads of men that moved in unending lines down Boylston Street. He ate his steak and greens absently and helped himself to rum from the black bottle on the table. As he filled his glass he was aware of his neighbor's eye resting quizzically on him. "I'm afraid I've not given you much company in exchange for this seat," said Ripley.

The stranger smiled slowly as he filled a curved, porcelain pipe. "It is not always that one wishes to talk." His voice was oddly modulated.

"Then I trust I didn't break into your thoughts."

"Not at all. I am a well of garrulity at all times. But I judged you to be not recipient. Why, then, should I intrude?"

Ripley looked more closely at his neighbor, saw a face rather wide at the cheekbones, a little pointed at the chin. Somehow he didn't look Cambridge and his speech had more than a trace of foreign accent. His "judged" had almost been "chutched," "intrude" was "intrute." The stranger looked up at the rows of bright pewter mugs on the wall and puffed at his pipe. "Naturally, the first question one asks these days is 'What is your regiment?' If not that, 'What do you sell to General Ward?' "

Ripley frowned. "I haven't a regiment, nor anything to sell."

The stranger said calmly: "Then indeed are you odd."

"You'll find plenty like me. I've been in two regiments that were disbanded. Then I had a captaincy in Nixon's. Just an hour ago I heard that Congress has reduced the strength of the companies. That left too many officers. As the junior captain, I was turned loose again."

"Ah. The reduction. Yes. A pity that it leaves you at the wind's end, but it was necessary. For myself, I was glad when I heard of it, for the hundred-, the seventy-man companies were not—how should I say

—wieldy. I may tell you, too, that there will be further slight changes."

Ripley started to speak, but the other cut in. "You are thinking that I, a foreigner, seem to know much of Province doings. But are we not all foreigners, we white people here?"

"Oh yes, I suppose so," said Ripley, fighting back a feeling of impatience. He eyed the man again, wondering what could have brought that manner and that accent to Bradish's in Cambridge. He said: "If I may ask a question, what are you selling to our army?"

"To our army? Nothing, although in my time I have dealt in many things. I was born in Denmark. An uncle brought me to the West Indies. Trading, I came to Boston. In Boston I stayed."

Ripley raised his eyebrows. "What brings you to Cambridge, if you're not dealing with the army?"

"Ah, I did not say that I do not deal with the army. I do. Having been trained in Denmark as a soldier, I offered my services."

Ripley felt a wave of dislike creeping over him. It was a bad sign if foreign adventurers were coming into the army. This was a private fight and no outsider should feather his nest over it. "Do you think they'll take you?" he asked.

The Dane smoothed his frilled shirt. "As to that, it is arranged. When I heard the news of the nineteenth, I asked my friend Dr. Warren—a neighbor of mine in Boston—where I might be of some use. He would have it that I take a regiment but for that a Danish cornetship hardly qualified. Hence I act as adjutant to Colonel Gerrish's regiment."

Ripley tried to hide his unbelief. The Dane smiled to himself and tamped stringy tobacco into the bowl of his pipe. "May I tell you, once more, what is in your mind? You are of the old stock. You resent that I, who never tasted baked beans or pumpkin pie until I was older than you are now, should have wormed my way into your Provincial army. I am right?"

Ripley flushed. "No. Of course not. I didn't mean—"

The Dane held up his hand. "Believe me, I can understand. You think it is only *your* fight? Listen to me, my friend. I came to Boston from the Indies in '72. I've been living there ever since. Why? I might have traded better out of St. Croix or out of Fünen in Denmark. But in Boston I found a spirit stirring that suited me. At first, I own, I thought your Adams, your Hancock, your Warren, were just vaporing. I found that they weren't, that they were speaking for free men, not just in Massachusetts, but everywhere. I began to go to the Green Dragon. I listened to speeches and I ceased to be a foreigner. I began to think: 'This the Crown may not do to *us.*' Or, 'This *we* may not tolerate.' Soon I had lived all the years from 1620 on. They were part of me. For myself, when I heard of the Concord fight, I slipped out of my house, evaded Gage's sentries, and quit the town. Let Gage confiscate house and goods. My feet are set on the path I have chosen."

Ripley studied the man. "It strikes me that I've been more than a little offensive."

The other looked surprised. "Not at all. In your place, I should have been far more incredulous."

Ripley nodded. "The idea of a man who wasn't born here fighting for Massachusetts—"

"No!" The Dane cut in quickly. "I do *not* fight for Massachusetts and that is a thought which we must get rid of. You others, you are too close to the event. You see this matter as rolling up over Boston Bay. But it is everywhere. A right lost to Massachusetts is one lost to North Carolina, where I have been, or to New York. Men say that your Sam Adams has roused the country. It was roused without him. This fight concerns all. Up at the College I hear the good Heath or fat Ward talk about the Massachusetts army, the Rhode Island army, and I break into a cold sweat."

Ripley said slowly: "Perhaps we are too close, as

you say. But it *is* hard not to think of Rhode Islanders, say, as a separate lot that have come up to help us finish up the mess that started last month."

Blandly the Dane smiled. "It's against all reason, isn't it, to think otherwise?" Then he burst out, "I tell you, that thought frightens me. Take this, for an example. Some very sapient madmen have just taken Fort Ticonderoga from the Crown and what has happened? The Congress of all the Provinces down in Philadelphia is in a flurry. What shall be done with the fort? It was taken by men from the Hampshire Grants, from Massachusetts and Connecticut. And it is located in New York! A scandal!" He slapped the table. "They argue now, 'To whom does it belong?' Some are even suggesting handing it back to the Crown to avoid bickering! Belong! It belongs to all the colonies and yet they debate while a hundred heavy guns rot up there, guns enough to blow Gage and his men out of Boston in a day's time—if those guns were here."

Ripley drew a deep breath. "You're right. We've *got* to think like that. Of course, this has all happened so suddenly that we don't get a perspective yet. And, too, you must keep in mind local feeling."

The Dane gestured impatiently. "I do not forget that feeling. We have it. But we have something else besides. You still think of the little town companies sitting about Boston, fretting lest Middlesex County be put aside for Essex, Massachusetts for New Hampshire! We have a siege here, as real as any siege of Prince Eugene's or Marlborough's or Turenne's, and such a siege you may not carry out by towns and counties. The localism must stop, I tell you. Soon we must have a New Hampshire colonel leading Maryland troops, a Massachusetts platoon embedded in a Virginia regiment, brigade staffs that include the whole country from the Grants to Georgia." He drew a thick watch from his fob, stared at it. "I warned you that I was garrulous. It is myself that I should have warned. The hands have raced. Do you go up by the Yard?"

As they turned up Boylston Street, Ripley said, "You've given me a lot of new ideas. I wish you'd give me some about finding a regiment."

The Dane shrugged, ran his stick along the palings of the Yard. "My free advice would be to go down to Delaware and talk to Caesar Rodney. But it is too soon for that. Have you had experience?"

Ripley went through his well-worn speech. At last the Dane nodded. "Now this war of ours, it is not a war of generals yet. The Duke of Marlborough or Condé could do little better than does poor sick old Artemas Ward. Nor yet is it a war of colonels. No, as I see it, it is a war of junior officers, of sergeants."

"I don't care about rank. I want to get it over with and go back to the farm," said Ripley.

"No doubt. It is often easier to be a private. But you have no right to be one." He paused by the gate between Massachusetts and Harvard Halls, his cane tapping a stone hitching post. "Gerrish? Prescott? Ha! A thought leaps to the mind. I take it that you are free? You shall come with me. The one man out of the whole army whom *you* should meet is in Cambridge today. I'll present you and—" He threw back his head, laughed heartily. "For more than an hour we talk and we do not name ourselves, one to the other."

"I'm Ripley Mayne, of Concord."

The Dane raised a finger to the brim of his cocked hat. "Christian Febiger—at your service."

They walked to the far end of the Common where the Dane led the way down Linnaean Street and turned up a short path bordered with budding roses. The green door opened to his rap and a neat old woman ducked her mobcap to him. "Not gone back I hope, Mrs. Moresby?"

"That he ain't, Mr. Febinjer. Ain't even hollered for his horse." She beamed and vanished into the depths of the house as Ripley and the Dane entered. "Better wait here," said Febiger as he strode to a door at the end of the hall, calling: "John? I'm coming alongside with a cargo for you."

A deep voice answered: "Kit! By God, get through that door before I drag you over the threshold. I've been wondering about you!" The door closed, shut out all sound save a buzz of voices that lasted some five minutes. Then it opened again and Febiger, smiling serenely, stepped out. "I leave you in his hands. Colonel John Glover is a very old friend of mine. I'll be glad to learn how you fare with him. A good day to you, Mr. Mayne." He touched his hat and sauntered out, humming to himself.

Ripley tapped on the white door. A voice boomed: "Come in!"

The man who sprang up from behind the deal table was short, broad-shouldered. His reddish hair was neatly clubbed, his blue eyes deep-set and twinkling, his nose tiptilted, his mouth and chin firm. He waved an arm toward a chair as Ripley quickly took in the tailless blue jacket with its leather buttons and the full white trousers. "Mr. Mayne. Glad to see you. Tell me about yourself. Kit Febiger's been here so long that he's no better than any other New Englander. He just said I might find you possibly useful in some respects." He slammed his elbows on the table. "Out with it. Who are you? What have you done?"

Ripley sketched out his brief history, restless under the unwavering scrutiny of the colonel who nodded energetically from time to time, thrust out sudden questions, called for quick restatements. At last Ripley concluded. "—So I'm out in the rain once more and getting damned sick of it."

Glover swung himself about in his chair, looking out on the neat kitchen garden in the rear of the house. Then he spun back. "Know anything about us?"

"Only that you're the Twenty-first Massachusetts and come from Marblehead."

Glover's big hands folded on the table and his chin jutted forward. "We're a marine regiment and we do the damnedest things. I'm telling off some companies now to serve on ships and make themselves objectionable to the British. Others have got to dig. Some are going to come down here from our Beverly quarters and cruise about the Charles and the Bay and stir up all the hell they can. Do you see any way that you can fit in with a lot of fishermen turned soldier? Honestly, do you?"

"I told you how I felt about the sea," said Ripley.

A hand waved, thumped back onto the table. "It's your idea of it, that's all. Look at me. I started as a shoemaker and to this day I hate the smell of leather so I'd almost rather go barefoot. But I can still build a damned fine pair of boots if I have to." He got up, paced about with short, quick steps. "I can say 'Damn my memories and damn yours.' I can use you. No, I don't want you on the sea with Broughton and Selman. I don't want you digging." He whirled about, faced Ripley. "You've got to teach us about boats."

Ripley laughed in amazement. "Teach Marbleheaders about boats?"

"That's what I said." He jumped back into his chair, shoved a map of Boston Harbor at Ripley. "See that? We'll have to cross that water some day. My men'll ferry the army, then get ashore and fight like bull seals in mating time. Do you see your job?"

"Not yet."

Glover rumpled his hair. "There isn't a man in my regiment that can't take a dory clear to the Grand Banks and back through the damnedest hell-bending storm that ever blew. Any man can run a skiff through a fog and over a reef that'd rip the guts out of the devil. But—" he slapped the table—"that won't get an army to Boston. You've been a marine. They go ashore in fair weather and foul, don't they?"

"Yes, but they don't do the rowing. The navy does."

Glover swept the papers into a heap. "We can row boats, sail them. But we've got to learn to fill them and empty them. We've got, by God, to be able to haul boats along with our teeth when they're full of troops, get the troops out of the boats, go back for more, then scramble ashore and fight like hell. It'll take a whole line of boats and that line's got to work like a clock. Six, eight men at the oars, the rest on benches. The boat grounds. Then what happens?"

"Easy," said Ripley. "Sailors up-oars. Bow man jumps ashore. Even-numbered men get out to port, odd to starboard. Middle files go right up the center and over the bow, muskets high, powder high."

Glover nodded violently. "That's it. You've done it. You *know*. Every one of my men was born in a boat in the heart of a gale, but if I tried to send twenty across the Charles, they'd scramble like lobsters in a pot, trying to land. Those boats have got to empty smooth as pouring alewives out of a bucket, got to get away without fouling the others coming up behind, go back and get more men." He shoved away from the table. "Can you show us?"

"If the men'll learn from me."

Glover stabbed the air with a thick forefinger. "You'll find this out about the Twenty-first. They'll do anything for a man that knows his job, even if he only wears a smock. They'll hoot a mess of ignorance wrapped up in gold braid." He paused, looked hard at Ripley. "Kit tells me you had a captaincy in Nixon's. Now I know that a lot of officers have gone home rather than sign on at a lower rank than the one they held before. They say it's a point of honor. How about you?"

"I'd take a lieutenancy," said Ripley.

"By God, that's lucky," said Glover. "I want my men to prove themselves before they begin to move up in the boat. I'd like to start you off as a private in the rear rank of Speakman's company, but you've got to have some authority if you're going to teach." He leaned his chin on a thick fist. "I've got a sergeancy vacant."

"I'll take it," said Ripley tersely.

Glover's face broke into a boyish grin. "You'd have

gone in as a private, too, wouldn't you? Now I've got business that'll keep me here another day. Some damned land sharks are squalling patriotism and trying to sell us paper-soled boots and wormy beef. I've given myself twelve hours more to gaff them and bring them alongside. Meet me at headquarters at Beverly day after tomorrow at noon sharp. We understand each other? Rank and pay of sergeant—if you ever get paid. All I can guarantee is plenty of hard work, hard knocks, and hard fighting."

"Nice to be sure of something," said Ripley.

"No Glover ever broke his bond," said the colonel grimly. "Now—two more things. We're in uniform. We don't take pride in rags and tatters the way some people seem to. You'll draw one from the quartermaster in Beverly. Wear it all the time and remember every second that it's the working clothes of the Twenty-first Massachusetts Infantry."

"I'll manage," said Ripley.

"Second thing. Get ink, paper, pens. Draw me up regulations for embarking and disembarking troops from—" he ticked off the items on his quick-moving fingers—"from whaleboats; from scows; from gundalows; from longboats; from jolly boats; from snows and schooners. Then add any kind of boat I haven't named. I want diagrams. I want to be able to see where every last man'll sit, how he'll get into the boat, get out of it."

"I guess I can do that."

"And have it for me when you come to Beverly."

"Beverly? That means—"

"That means day after tomorrow—complete," snapped Glover. "I may add that I keep discipline in my regiment. I light into anyone that breaks it like a nor'easter whooping past Cape Ann." He snatched up his pen, began to write furiously. "That's all. Good day."

Ripley left the Linnaean Street house in a daze. "By

God, this is going to be a regiment! And what a colonel! He's kind of a bull seal himself!"

He went back across the Common, his high spirits ebbing a little as he saw vacant spaces that had been full that morning—spaces that had held men who had suddenly drifted back to their homes through some fancied slight or failure to obtain recognition, or dislike of their officers. He felt rather better when, crossing the street by Christ Church, he met a column of weary men whose captain, hollow-eyed with fatigue, asked directions to headquarters, adding that he and his men had marched down from the New Hampshire border without a break.

In the graveyard, Ripley found Sholes squatting like a woodchuck over a neat fire. The stocky man waved and whooped. "Hey, Rip! Got something! Go see Colonel Mason and tell him I sent you. Him and me's going to get on fine. He's to Prospect Hill. And listen! Four new gals have come to that little house down by the river. Seen one of them standing in the window nekkid as a flayed skunk. Provost can't touch 'em 'cause they're out of bounds."

Ripley squatted beside him. "You're worse than Cuyler—wherever he may be. Have you really signed up with Mason?"

"Well—" Sholes threaded a bit of salt meat onto a skewer. "I did and I ain't. Meaning that I ain't put my right name to the rolls so if something better turns up, like finding a colonel that's freer with the rum, I can go talk to him easy in the conscience."

Ripley laughed. "That'll be all right. Now listen." He told Sholes of Glover and his regiment. The ranger listened patiently, then shook his head. "It just ain't going to suit. I told you once I wasn't scared of a thing that walked this earth, but them big boats don't walk. I'll take a canoe through the whitest water you can find. But them others! I got put on a sloop up to Champlain and retched until I'd sucked the soles of my feet clear up into my gullet."

Ripley laughed. "We won't be on any big boats."

"That Glover'll have some God-damn big black boats. I know he will," said Sholes fearfully. "No, you better come along of Mason and me."

"Look here, Nahum, I'd been counting on your coming. We stuck together through the nineteenth and we've looked after each other in Cambridge."

Sholes squashed out his mangy cap. "And I'd been seeing you all bedded down in Mason's. What the hell you so stubborn about? Glover ain't no better'n Mason. I've heard about him. His men dress up in soldier suits like them little boys from Weathersfield."

Ripley slapped the ranger's broad shoulders. "Keep thinking about it. There'll be a place for you if I know anything about John Glover. See you later, Nahum."

Sholes waved his arms. "Hi! Where you going? I ain't through persuading you yet. Set down here again!"

Ripley shook his head. "Got some work to do for Glover." He left the graveyard with Sholes's protests still echoing in his ears.

The search for drawing materials was not an easy one. Many of the little shops that he remembered from college days had closed up and others showed sparsely furnished shelves. He finally found pens and ink in a nondescript booth presided over by a bold-eyed woman who reminded him of the drunken, shrieking boatloads that used to put out from the English ports when a seventy-four dropped anchor. She tried to engage him in conversation, then reluctantly admitted that while she had no paper, he might find some at Crackbone, the flax teaser's, beyond the Yard. The reek of coarse scent in his nostrils, Ripley went dubiously to Crackbone's and, in that least likely of all places, found great sheets of fine imported paper.

As he stepped out once more into the dying light, a voice from somewhere above him crashed out. "Think that's Dutch, do you? Ought to see my uncle, Henricus

Bogardus Diddleback! How's that for Dutch? And that isn't all. He lives in Womelsdorf!"

Ripley nearly dropped his parcels. "Joris!" he shouted.

A window in the second floor slammed up and Cuyler popped his head out. Then the window banged shut and boots pounded on hollow stairs. A door at the end of the house flew open and Cuyler dashed at Ripley, thumping his back and roaring out questions.

Ripley guarded his parcels with one hand and shook Cuyler's collar with the other. "You Dutch zany! Why the hell didn't you let me know you were here?" He shook him again. "Now shut up and get down to Bradish's as fast as you can. There's brandy that needs drinking."

"Bradish's be damned!" Cuyler butted Ripley toward the door. "Up those stairs." He jammed his way past Ripley shouting: "Piety! Piety! Look what I got!" His boot jarred a door open. "Here he is. Don't have to go out looking for him. Ripley Mayne. Rip, this is Piety Gore! Found her in Worcester. She said she wanted to see the army and I told her it was no place for a girl to be alone and she agreed."

Dragged over the threshold, Ripley recovered his balance and bowed to the prim, almost severe-looking girl who stood holding a lighted candle. Then she smiled and all sense of primness vanished. Cuyler waved his arms. "Sit down at the table, Rip. Piety, you sit across from him." He dove at a cupboard by the head of the wide bed and snatched out bottles and glasses, then plumped himself into a chair beside the girl.

Ripley tossed his hat onto the floor and wiped his forehead. "You'll have to be quiet while you're pouring those drinks, at least. Now for God's sake tell me what New York troops are doing up here. The last time I heard from you you'd gone into MacDougall's regiment down there."

Cuyler waved all questions aside. "Take that glass

and don't introduce trivia. My throat's as dry as Great-aunt Bywanck's oven. Piety, my chit, drink that and don't interrupt. Now here's to us and the King and every damned one of the thirteen colonies. How's your father, Rip, and what have you been doing to disgrace his gray hairs?" He drained his glass, filled it again, kissed Piety, and beamed on the world in general.

Ripley smiled across the table at the girl. Her smile seemed to envelop him in secret, intimate invitation. "You won't mind, Piety, if Joris and I go back into ancient history? We've got a lot to talk about."

She shook her head in silence, watching Ripley through half-closed eyes. Cuyler coughed. "Look here, I knew you two'd like each other, but, by God, it's got to be like brother and sister or I'll go back to MacDougall." He filled the girl's glass and held it to her lips. "What's the war like up here? What are the Lobsters doing? I've come clear from New York to find out and all you do is chatter."

"Never mind the war," said Ripley. "I asked about you and New York troops."

Cuyler's eyes bulged. "New York? What's that got to do with me? I'm the best Connecticut man that ever sanded brown sugar. Didn't my mother come from Ridgefield? Isn't it my town as well as hers?" He thumped his glass on the table and launched into a profane account of his doings. Piety, her head contentedly on his shoulder, listened and drank at an astounding rate.

Cuyler, it appeared, after joining MacDougall found little chance of action, so the big Dutchman calmly crossed over into Connecticut and argued and stormed his way into an ensigncy in Sanford's regiment. "That's why I'm here. Sanford's on his way with the rest of the regiment. Soon as I saw he knew the way, I lit out ahead of him. I got to Worcester and had about made up my mind to spend the night right there when I saw a stage leaving for Boston with Piety in it and thought I'd save time by jumping in.

And when I got to Cambridge and found these quarters, damned if there wasn't Piety."

"Amazing," said Ripley. He found it hard to keep his eyes off the girl from Worcester. She certainly had very little on under her bodice and wide skirt and, despite her slimness, was distractingly rounded.

Cuyler coughed again, then slapped the table. "We'll dine together, right here. Piety, my treasure, you know where the money is. Slip out and tell that woman down the street to send us food in plural quantities. Plural as hell. I want beef the color of a Lobster's coat and a pumpkin pie you could use for a cartwheel, and anything else you see. And four more bottles of rum. What for you, Rip?"

"I'll eat what you do, but—" he looked at the open cupboard—"why more rum?"

Cuyler screwed up his eyes. "You don't know little Piety. She put away a whole pint by herself between two and four this afternoon. Into your cape, my little brandy barrel, and tell that hag red beef and old rum."

Piety, prim-faced again, threw a scarlet-lined cape about her shoulders in a graceful sweep. "You'll still be here—Rip?"

"I'm not so sure," shouted Cuyler. "Know why Gage is in trouble in Boston? Because he's trying to do two things at once—fight a war and govern a town. Take him as an object lesson."

The door closed behind the slim girl and Cuyler winked at Ripley. "Look here—there's an empty room back of this one. I've seen some damned pretty girls around town. Just the four of us?"

Ripley sipped his rum. "In principle—yes. In practice no. Now don't interrupt. Frankly, these wenches about town remind me too much of my time in the marines, so—"

Cuyler held up his hand, nodded slowly. "Forget it. Now tell me about this damned war."

"Nothing to tell. Gage sits over there and doesn't do a thing. Hasn't even seized Dorchester Heights or

Charlestown. If we had any guns we could blow him out of the harbor. He's fretting like an eel in a frying pan. The Tories tried to organize a corps but they couldn't agree on any point, so they're blaming Gage for their own footlessness. He and his army are living on stockfish because he's blockaded tight. He's waiting for London instructions that'll probably flay him alive for losing so many men on the nineteenth. By God, I'll wager he's wishing that he'd gone into the Church instead of the army."

"Wait till he hears I'm up here," said Cuyler.

Ripley filled his own glass and Cuyler's. "If you're that important, better let Artemas Ward know. He's no better off than Gage. One day he's got nine thousand men, the next day four thousand. He's got to fight a lot of stinking snakes that are playing for rank or trying to make money out of the army. And since you keep asking me, I'll tell you that I've managed to get a sergeantcy in the best damned regiment in the army. If you were only Massachusetts, I might be able to talk Glover into signing you on as rear-rank private."

Cuyler scratched his head. "Let me see—Old Aunt Flukicker's second cousin married someone from Pittsfield."

Ripley smiled grimly. "You'd have to do better than that to please the old bull seal that's running the Twenty-first." He launched into a long account of his talk with Glover.

Cuyler listened carefully, then sighed. "Maybe I'll dig up that ninth cousin in Pittsfield. Honestly, Rip, Sanford's a good man and maybe he'll make a good regiment out of what he's got, but—I don't know—Glover sounds like something mighty solid." He laughed, slapped Ripley's shoulder. "Anyway, I'm up here where things are happening and I don't have to wait nine weeks to find out whether Gage has hanged you yet or not."

The door swung open and Piety, stiff and forbidding, came in, followed by a greasy boy who staggered under a vast tray. He tiptoed across the room, laid platters and plates on the round table while the girl watched him coldly. He said "Thank you, miss," in a hoarse whisper as she thrust a sixpence at him.

As the door closed, Piety cried "Hi!" slung her cape onto the bed and spun about the room in a wild pirouette, her wide skirts standing out about her and showing a generous expanse of white skin above her stocking tops. She ended up in the chair beside Cuyler and flung an arm about his neck. "Why didn't you tell me there was a provost guard, you ninny? I saw them march two girls off down the street."

"There, there," Cuyler clucked soothingly and filled her glass. "When you put on your cape and your leg-of-mutton face, you've got nothing to worry about." He rubbed his hands. "Look at that beef! Open a fresh bottle, Piety. I'll tend to the meat if you'll serve the greens, Rip." He picked up a carving knife, humming happily.

She made a face. "Rip, he started to sing coming through Framingham and the hog reeve tried to take him to the pound. Sweetheart, my glass is empty again."

The talk flowed on, noisy and uninterrupted. Cuyler boomed about improbable Dutch relatives and their doings. Ripley told of happenings about Boston while Piety, in seeming contentment, ate placidly and consumed rum in endless draughts. The greasy boy, apron more bedraggled than ever, came in for the trays and dishes and still they talked. At last Piety yawned, rose from the table, curled up on the bed like a tired kitten, and fell asleep at once.

Ripley raised his eyebrows. Cuyler grinned. "She'll sleep an hour or so and a cannon wouldn't wake her. Then she'll bounce up and start in wringing the neck of the first bottle she sees."

Ripley pursed his lips. "Never saw anyone like her. When she smiles, she makes you feel as if you were right in bed with her."

"Doesn't she!" said Cuyler eagerly. "That's the first thing I noticed about her in the stage."

Ripley gathered up his parcels. "I'm off for Bradish's. Got a room there."

"Hell," said Cuyler. "Don't go on my account. She won't wake for a while."

"All right. I've some work to do. Can I use your table?"

"For anything licit. Use any damn thing you want. The place is yours. The ajax is out in the back yard and you have to wear pattens to get through the mud to it."

Ripley spread paper on the table and began to sketch the outline of a whaleboat as seen from above. Cuyler watched in silence. Then he said, "What's that meant to be? A potato?"

"It might appear so to you, my good man."

"It will to Glover. Give me that pencil." The lines began to flow smooth and sure from the lead. "A whaleboat goes like this. I ought to know. Uncle Cornelis-zoon ten Bronk used to own most of the New York waterfront."

Ripley drew in his breath. "Put on full sail, Joris. Mark off the benches so I can write in three numbers to a bench. By God, you've cut my work in half." He picked up a quill and began to write: "The Whaleboat. Article One. The Manner in Which to Embark from Shingle." As he wrote, he whistled softly. He had found his regiment, his colonel. Now Cuyler was back in Cambridge.

II

At Beverly, close by Marblehead, Ripley found himself in an utterly different world. In the blue and white ranks of the Twenty-first Massachusetts Infantry, he moved among Glovers and Ornes and Gerrys, Brimblecomes, Sedgebards, and Trefrys—brief-worded men whose quick motions differed vastly from the slower town and farm folk of his youth. Their talk smacked of gales off the Grand Banks and they rarely turned their eyes or thoughts inland. Even their accent was different and he had to attune his ear to men who said "hort" for "heart," "borr'l" for "barrel," and "torred for "tarred." And, bred to the sea, not a man of them could swim.

Sergeant's knot on his shoulder, he worked long and hard in the tidal flats about Beverly through the growing heat of May and early June. Under his direction, the hard-bitten boatmen deftly handled heavy craft while he drilled them in the landing technique of the Royal Marines. "Each man's got to remember his number. Now! When she grounds! Threes and fours right up the middle of the boat. Twos, fives, and sixes, trim ship. Damn it, don't scramble like a school of porpoises. Oarsmen! Back water and do it over again!"

Day after day the companies sweated as they sprang onto the marshy shore where indignant fiddler crabs scuttled away and clamshells crunched under heavy boots. Day after day, men were herded into the boats, landed over and over until they could spill out in sure rhythm, each man in his place with musket high and cartridge box in his teeth.

The men were hard to handle at first. But when they found that Ripley knew his work, they began to vie with each other. They questioned his every statement and kept him working late each night in preparation for the next day's ordeal. Increasingly sure of himself, Ripley started night landings and hailed with delight a gale that turned the estuary into a churning caldron of waves. He drove the drenched men ashore to meet an imaginary attack. They cursed, stumbled on through the dark, and, when Ripley dismissed them, seized the boats for another hour of unscheduled drill.

One afternoon toward the middle of June, while Ripley was supervising the loading of boats under theoretical fire, Cuyler appeared on the dunes riding a great gray horse. Ripley shouted: "Hello, you oaf! Deserting again?"

Cuyler whooped: "They told me in Beverly that I'd find you curled up in a lobster pot." He thudded onto the sand and sat on a rock that was crackly with dry seaweed. "What's all this? Children of Israel crossing the Red Sea?" His blue eyes widened as a triple file of infantry moved down the sand, slid evenly into a broad barge that pushed out into open water as another took its place. "I'll be damned!" he muttered.

"That's what I tried to explain to you when I was in Cambridge last week. You were so busy explaining to me some of Piety's finer points that you didn't listen," laughed Ripley. Then he raced down the beach shouting: "Sergeant Grenda! Don't let your men crowd. You're under fire." He came back panting.

Cuyler rubbed his broad chin, eyes still on the boats. "By God, you're *doing* something. In Cambridge we just stand morning prayers, dig and drink. Get on with your work. I want to watch." All through the long afternoon he sat on the dunes, broad pink face glowing and eyes solemn. At last Ripley dismissed the men and grinned down at Cuyler. "How do you like it?"

"You've got a regiment, Rip."

Ripley pulled him to his feet. "Forget about Cambridge. You and I are going into Beverly to eat." They walked along the shell road to town, the horse clopping on resignedly behind them. Cuyler complained dismally. "Not a damned thing to do in Cambridge. Hardly any drill. Not enough powder for target practice. The men keep drifting home and so do the officers. Hard to blame them. They say they're more use to the country on their farms than on their tails. God knows what would happen if Gage ever stuck his woodchuck face out of Boston."

"It'll shake down in time," said Ripley as they

walked along a trim street of houses whose green shutters were clear against silvery shingles. "See that swinging sign up there by the corner? It's the Capstan and means rations for us, sea rations."

In the low-ceiled dining room, Cuyler brightened a little as bowls of steamed clams, basins of melted butter, and cups of broth were heaped on the table. "This is worth the ride from Cambridge," he mumbled as he stripped the tender clams from their shells and sopped them in butter.

"Why didn't you bring Piety?" asked Ripley as he sipped the hot broth.

Cuyler clattered clam shells about. "Thought I told you. I wanted to do something for the army so I let her go."

"Meaning you'd have more time to soldier if she weren't around?"

"N-no." Cuyler shook his head slowly. "Wasn't just that. You see, I let her go to that bat-faced contractor who sells sanded powder to the army. She's living with him off Brattle Street and as he's pretty old and frail, it's my guess he won't sell powder much longer, knowing Piety. So I feel I've done something for the army." He looked up from his clams as a private in blue and white paused by the table.

"Something for me, Cash?" asked Ripley.

"Adjutant says report to the colonel at once."

"And I wanted more of those soft biscuits with beach-plum jam. Hold the table, Joris. I'll be back as soon as I can."

As he left the Capstan and walked on through the town he wondered what the peppery colonel could want of him. It might be about the new plans for transferring men from barge to barge in midstream that Ripley had drawn up a few days before. He shrugged. He'd learn soon enough.

Before the newly built hut at the edge of the town sunburned sentries, trim in blue and white, stood guard at the door. Ripley nodded to them. "To see

Colonel Glover," he said and was passed on into the hut where two aides sat stiffly on benches, softly cursing the breathless air. As Ripley gave his name, a voice boomed from an inner room. "That Mayne? Sergeant Mayne? Tell him to get in here as quick as God'll let him. Maybe quicker!"

An aide opened the door, closed it behind Ripley, who saluted the colonel. "You sent for me, sir?"

Glover's gingery head lifted quickly from a mass of papers. "I did." His blue eyes were steady, probing. "Know that an inspector from headquarters was here yesterday? Major Reece?"

"Yes, sir."

"How'd you know it?"

"He came out where we were working, sir."

Glover snatched up a sheaf of papers. "He certainly sailed across your bows. Know what he says in here?" He shook the papers at Ripley.

"No, sir."

"Damn it, you ought to be able to guess! He says that your men were—what does he call it?—'inept in handling boats.' He says that you were damned obstinate when he tried to set you right and that when he took command and gave proper orders your men were so clumsy that they were a disgrace to the army. What have you got to say to that?"

"I can't contradict a major, sir."

"Learned that, have you?" Glover jumped to his feet, leaned against the rough window sill. "What did happen out there?"

"The major came by while I was giving the men embarkation drill, sir. He watched and then told me I was doing it all wrong. He tried to show me what he called the right way and three boats capsized."

"What made them?"

"Er—I don't think the men understood his orders."

"Did they ever capsize doing it your way?"

"At first."

Glover slid down from the window sill, began pacing about the room, his stock and linen crisp and neat as ever despite the baking heat. "Now I told you that I'd be watching you, didn't I? Well, I have been and the first thing I noticed was this." He spun about on his heels, pointed a stubby forefinger at Ripley. "The trouble with most of you men from the colleges is that you're too far away to get along with the others. You may be right beside them, but you're miles away. You don't touch them." He took a quick step to the table, caught up Reece's report. "Says here that you shouldn't be given a *squad* to command. I agree with him. So I'm taking this back." His hand shot out, stripped the sergeant's badge from Ripley's shoulder.

Ripley started to speak, conscious of icy waves sweeping over him, waves that left him feeling empty, shaken.

Glover went on. "I've got a good reason for what I'm doing. You know that, don't you?"

Ripley managed to say: "I must assume that, sir."

"Assume be damned. You've got to know it." He stuffed the epaulet into his pocket. "You're no more use to me as a sergeant. Understand?"

"Yes, sir," said Ripley numbly.

"Good." Glover began to pace again. "After regimental prayers tomorrow, you'll report here—to me. Is that clear?"

"Yes, sir."

"You'll report to me prepared to take your oath—as ensign." He perched on the edge of the table, booted feet swinging.

"*Ensign,* sir?" The dead air of the room took on new life.

"You've done good work," Glover went on. "I saw you take my officers and put them through your drill. You had majors and captains standing belly-deep in water. They obeyed you, a sergeant, the way the men did." He grinned. "Forget what I said about college men. You're an exception. Scared you, did I?

You ought to have known better. You handled that inspector damned well. I've got men who'd have said 'Yes, sir' to him and gone on doing what he told them, knowing it was wrong."

"My duties, sir?" asked Ripley.

"Same and more of them. You'll be assigned to staff." Glover threw himself back in his chair and snatched up his pen. "Damn it, can't you see I'm busy? Don't thank me. Report tomorrow, after prayers." He began to write furiously, grinning to himself.

Oblivious of the rain that had begun to smash down with savage fury to the accompaniment of broad sheets of lightning, Ripley ran back to the Capstan and flung open the door. Cuyler looked up from a fresh bowl of clams. "So your sins caught up with you?" he said, wagging his head. "When's the court-martial to be?"

Ripley stepped to the bar and seized a bottle of rum. "Court-martial be damned, Joris." The bottle banged on the table. "Push aside that manger of yours. Give me your glass. You're going to drink to the health of Ensign Mayne of the Twenty-first Massachusetts Infantry!"

III

William Beggs, acting adjutant of the Twenty-first, looked sourly at Ripley. "The whole damn thing's crazier than anything a horse mackerel could think up."

Ripley paced eagerly up and down the little orderly room, rapping his knuckles against the rough furniture. "Crazy? It's the sanest thing that's been done since the Pilgrims landed." He turned on Beggs. "Can't you see? We've got thirteen colonies mixed up in this and so far only four are fighting. Now the Congress of the Thirteen, if you want to call it that, has *adopted* the army of the siege."

Beggs flicked the leather buttons of his coat. "And what does that mean? It means *we'll* be doing all the fighting while a lot of Virginia planters and New York merchants sit on their fat tails."

Ripley shrugged. "I used to think so—until I talked to Febiger. Anyway, the thing's done. They've authorized a Continental Army of five thousand to serve around New York and one of fifteen to serve here. You watch. You'll see Virginians in the Harvard Yard before the end of the summer."

"And we'll pay them and feed them," growled Beggs.

"Haven't you read the bulletin? Supported by *all* the Provinces."

Beggs groaned. "Now what the hell does Philadelphia care about Lobsters in Boston? What does Albany or Charleston? I'm scared, I tell you. We've got a great spirit around here. As soon as we let outsiders into the fight, we'll damned well kill that spirit."

Ripley said dryly, "And to think that just today you were snarling at one of the companies that wouldn't take a man in because his family'd moved out of Marblehead two years ago. They called him a foreigner."

"That's different."

"Different?" Ripley's voice rose. "Look here, if we treat this as a Massachusetts war, the other colonies'll sit back and say: 'That's fine. Hope you win.'" He thumped the window sill. "No. This is an American war that just happened to start here. We're all in it. We—" He stared out the window. "Stand by for action. Here's the old Bull Seal himself."

Glover whirled in through the door. "Get out orders to move. The whole regiment. At once. Notify Colonel Gerry and Major Johonot—all company commanders. Mayne, you help him. Have the papers ready for my signature by ten tonight. Leave the date blank."

Beggs blinked. "The date blank?"

"That's what I said. I haven't been a soldier very long but I've learned this. There's no use carrying out an order you've just received. It's too late. What you've got to do is carry out the orders that are two beyond the ones you haven't got yet. Listen. Gage came out of Boston yesterday. They fought most of the day around Charlestown. I've just heard. No. I don't know how it came out. But I can tell you this —before long an aide'll come pounding in here saying that Ward wants us in Cambridge. When he does, I want the regiment to have everything shipshape so all we'll have to do is slip our cable." He flew to the window as hoofs clattered out in the street. "Maybe this is word from Ward now. No, damn it, that's no aide. Now you two set sail."

The door shook and then burst open and Cuyler, eyes wild, lunged into the room. "Rip. I've got to—" He saw Glover, straightened up. "I've got a letter for you, sir." He dug in his torn jacket and held out a white square. Glover raised his eyebrows and stepped to the window. Cuyler stood panting, heedless of Ripley.

Glover's head jerked back. "You were at the battle?" He stuffed the letter in his pocket and straddled a chair. "Sit down. I've got to hear before I finish the letter. What happened?"

Cuyler drew a ragged cuff across his forehead and moistened his lips. "We went out with Iz Putnam to dig the night of the sixteenth. He made us dig on that low hill on the peninsula, Breed's. We dug all night and then more men came up and dug up on Bunker's Hill, the higher one back of Breed's. Late in the morning the Lobsters came across. Thousands of them. In barges. They had two frigates bombarding us. Then the infantry attacked." He moistened his lips again. Glover shifted his feet nervously and Ripley leaned forward over the table, eyes on Cuyler.

"They came on in line. We held our fire until we could count their gaiter buttons. Then—then, well, we fired. It was awful. They ran, I tell you. They tried it again, right against the works on Breed's, and the same thing happened. They went over like red tenpins. A grenadier sergeant ten yards in front of me tried to crawl up toward us. He was holding his guts with one hand and loading with the other. I saw him. He—"

Glover crossed quickly to him, patted his shoulder. "Easy on the stern oar, boy. It's all over."

Cuyler drew a deep breath and his voice grew steadier for a moment. "They all ran back to the beaches. Damn it, our men had been cold as ice. The Lobsters came on again and all of a sudden we stopped firing. No more powder. They had bayonets and they got in among us and we fell back. I heard four shots from our side. Four. But we weren't running—yet." He jumped to his feet. "By God, we didn't. Some damned fool had left a lot of men up on the top of Bunker's Hill without orders. Regiments and regiments. They'd been watching. They kept right on watching. And then that Dane, Febiger of Gerrish's, rallied a lot of them and threw them right down across the Lobster columns. I saw him. He had on a white coat with red facings and he just kept walking about, shoving his men this way and that until the last powderless man was off the hill. Then he came all by himself, swinging his fusee like a walking stick and whistling. Oh damn! Oh God damn it! One gill of powder per man! Just one gill and the Lobsters would be there yet—lying in the orchards or on the beaches. They were done. They staggered when they walked and their hands shook so they couldn't load." His breath quivered.

"What happened then?" asked Glover sharply.

"N-nothing. We'd all fallen back to the mainland

and the Lobsters didn't—couldn't follow." He threw up his hands. "One gill of powder. And we found fresh regiments wandering about on the mainland not knowing where to go! Scammon marched his men back and forth all day and got a different order every hour. Now the Lobsters have got Charlestown and the hills."

Glover reached into a cupboard and brought out a rum bottle. "Have a drink and get your breath. So they've got Breed's and Bunker's, have they? Lose many men, the Lobsters?"

Cuyler nodded over his glass. "Lay in heaps. I saw one company of a good forty men and three officers change to ten men and no officers in one volley."

Glover drummed on the table. "Guess it would be good business to sell Gage some more hills at that price." He frowned suddenly. "What brought you over here anyway?"

Still drinking, Cuyler mumbled, "Letter." Glover pulled it from his pocket and grunted in surprise. "Didn't recognize the handwriting. Kit Febiger." He read on in silence. Then he said: "Sure Sanford's is broken up?"

"Men started home today. Won't serve under the new major from Pomfret."

Glover looked at Ripley. "I've seen you with—ah—Cuyler. Know anything about him?"

"He was with me on the nineteenth until he was wounded, sir. I can tell you another thing about him. He drew those plans of embarkation drill. Also, he's got an amazing eye for country. I've ridden around here with him. He can look at the way the land lies and tell you just where two roads will meet or where a stream will flow into another."

Glover got up and paced about. "So you want to come with us."

"That's what I told Febiger," said Cuyler.

Glover walked to the window. "You're a New Yorker. We've only got four men in the whole regiment who don't come right out of Marblehead." He turned to Cuyler. "Makes it kind of difficult, doesn't it?"

"Yes, sir," said Cuyler in a low voice.

Glover waved the sheet at him. "What I'd like to do is take you and throw you right into Speakman's company as private."

"That's all right," said Cuyler eagerly.

"No it isn't." He referred to the letter again. "Febiger tells me a lot more than you did. That you joined him in covering the retreat. He says further—let me see—oh, yes—'behaved with conspicuous courage, gallantry, and resourcefulness.' Kit Febiger's not a loose talker. With that record, I couldn't do less than an ensigncy—and I haven't got one. Want to wait for a vacancy?"

"I'll wait," said Cuyler.

"Hope it won't be long," said Glover. "I can use you. We may be fighting around New York one day and your value'll double." He paused, then went on slowly. "Ye-e-es, we're apt to be fighting most anywhere, now that we've got a new commander in chief."

"A what?" said Ripley.

"Heard from Elbridge Gerry. His name's Washington—George Washington."

Begg's mouth tightened. "From Connecticut, I'll bet."

"No. Virginia."

Beggs laughed sourly. "I told you. You'll see Massachusetts troops doing the dirty work while Virginians and Georgians and Jersey men—"

Glover sprang from his chair with such violence that it skidded across the floor. "By God, no man in the Twenty-first's going to talk like that. We've signed on for a cruise that'd rip the heart out of a steel ship and we're going to make port. We're going to see regiments wrecked because men scramble for high jobs. But not this regiment. We're going to see regiments break up like a bark on a reef because men don't like their officers, because they get homesick, because they don't get rationed the way they think they ought to. But not this regiment. We're going to see regiments steer off their course because they don't like the way the men from Pennsylvania or Delaware talk or spit or tie their pigtails. But not this regiment. And any man who doesn't understand that better chuck his dunnage on the dock and jump over the side after it, because he'll be no hand for *this* cruise."

Beggs slowly got up, unfastened the lieutenant's knot from his shoulder, tossed it onto the table and walked from the room. Glover glared after him. Then he whirled back to Cuyler. "He's gone. Your wait's over. I'll post Jennison for Beggs's lieutenancy. You'll be ensign in place of Jennison. Assigned to Blackler's company. Duties start right away helping Mayne with those orders I told him about. Take your oath at morning prayer tomorrow. I'll square the commission with the Massachusetts Congress." He snatched up his big hat, clapped it on his head. "Papers ready for my signature at ten. That's all." He slammed out through the door.

Ripley jumped to his feet. "The old Bull Seal! By God, Joris, you're with us. Do you understand that, you dunderheaded Dutchman? With us."

Cuyler blinked, then snatched up the bottle that Glover had left and drank deeply. He hurled the cork across the room and kicked out his heels. "A regiment! By God, I've got a real regiment at last and a real colonel!"

Four days later Ripley stood at the end of the Cambridge Common and watched the road that led in from the north. Afternoon sun, slanting down through the elms, cast dappled patches over the brown stretch that wound away across the fields. Then, far off, metal twinkled and there was movement under the trees, a thick rustle of drums and the soaring of fifes. Movement grew more distinct, became a living ribbon of blue and white as the high voices of the fifes whipped up into the swinging notes of "Yankee Doodle."

Ripley vaulted into the saddle and awaited the approach of the column. He could report to the peppery Glover that everything was ready: regimental headquarters established in the fine old Vassall house on Brattle Street; space for the sailcloth tents of the companies in the vacant land beyond; rations waiting for the quartermaster to draw them.

The music swept higher and higher and people came running from the distant college, from the houses beyond the Common. Soon Ripley could see the deep drums swaying as the drummers beat out the rhythm of the march. The musicians were abreast of him, then Lee's company, Courtis's, Bacon's, Blackler's with Cuyler grinning from its flank, Grant's, Orne's. Shoulders bent by a lifetime of oar and sail, the Marbleheaders were marching into the old college town.

PART THREE

GUNS OF THE SIEGE

After the slaughter on the slopes of Breed's Hill and Bunker's, Gage withdrew the bulk of his forces to Boston, where he remained passive. From top to bottom. his army had undergone a shock from which, perhaps, it never recovered and one which may have affected its actions to the end of the war. Nearly 2300 men had marched over the slippery June grasses to the attack. Gage reported their losses as 1054. A British officer wrote, "Some had only eight or nine men a Company left; some only three, four, or five."

Of the possible 2800 Provincials engaged, less than 500 figured in casualty lists and, as the British were unduly shaken by their losses, so were the Americans overelated. Both sides suffered throughout the war because of this faulty perspective, the Americans as much as the British.

The new commander in chief, George Washington, arrived in state during July and took up quarters in the Vassall house, which Glover vacated. The army watched him, found him cold, unapproachable, and given to aristocratic pretensions. He offended deeply by trying to set up an officer caste, an act which, oddly enough, was resented by officers as well as men. There were resignations from the commissioned ranks on the part of those who would not submit to such elevation over their neighbors.

The army watched him and slowly began to find in him unswerving devotion, a rocklike integrity, and a profound sense of justice. He was, they decided, a moderate man at heart, and they gave themselves over to his guidance as they settled back to the dull routine of the siege.

I

THROUGH the long, hot summer of 1775, Glover's Marbleheaders sweltered about Cambridge. Ripley and Cuyler made elaborate plans for amphibious descents on British posts at night and submitted them to their colonel, who approved energetically and forwarded them to higher authorities. Word came back that there was not enough powder to waste on the off chance of bringing back a prisoner or two, or spiking a twelve-pounder. Ripley cursed and fell back on an unending round of drill.

His boats butted their noses into the steep banks of the Charles far up by Watertown, rocked and bobbed on the placid waters of Fresh Pond. Twice he managed to borrow field pieces from the slow-growing train of artillery and his men, born with ropes in their hands, contrived fearsome tackle that slid the clumsy guns from shore to boat and back again. Other units of the army came to stare at the novel drill, and the Marbleheaders, startled from their absorption, stared back at strange levies from Pennsylvania, Virginia, and Maryland, gaunt silent men in hunting shirts who balanced long rifles on bony shoulders. Once or twice Ripley looked up from his work to see a knot of horsemen watching him, caught a hint of blue and buff as the commander in chief surveyed the work in silence.

Now and again, drill was broken by tours of monotonous duty along the Charles where the Twenty-first studied the silent Boston shore and sniffed hungrily the east wind that brought them the tang of their beloved sea and its salt marshes. Once, immaculate in a new uniform, Ripley superintended a special guard that lined the drive to the Vassall house each time that the big Virginian started out on one of his endless rounds of inspection. He caught a glint of cold approval in the commander's eye as it fell on the trim blue and white ranks, rigidly at attention.

"You see," he explained to Cuyler over rum afterwards, "you see, Joris, there's no sense in the other regiments raising a stew if the Twenty-first *is* always getting picked for Washington's guard. It's not the uniform alone. It's the men. It took me a long time to find out why this crowd's the best disciplined in the army. It's because they've been at sea since they could walk. They've always been part of a crew and they know what it means to work together. Take a farmer. Take a lawyer. He's worked alone all his life. But these men from the coast—they learned long ago that every man's got to do his job—or else there's trouble. So whether it's taking in sail off the Grand Banks or turning out a guard for Washington, they fall into it naturally. And we don't have deserters. Why? Because you don't quit a ship during a cruise, and we've all signed on this one for the rest of the year."

Cuyler drank slowly. "Maybe. But when this cruise is over? This eight months' cruise?"

Ripley drew in his breath. "That's what sets me shivering. Maybe it's what Gage is waiting for." He banged his glass on the table. "No. Damn it, they'll stick. Somehow or other you'll see an army right here, staring at Gage, on January 2, 1776. In the meantime—"

"In the meantime it's your turn to buy," said Cuyler.

September rode in on the wings of a gale that drenched the camps and whipped the trees along the river. In the midst of wind and rain, Glover's men made Cambridge ring to a wild celebration that echoed under dripping eaves and along streaming roads. The companies of Broughton and Selman, spirited away from Cambridge in a cloud of rumor, had suddenly been heard from. They had put to sea and captured His Majesty's ship *Unity*, laden with precious supplies, and now their shore-bound comrades stamped and whooped and drank in tribute to them.

The storms cleared and Ripley stood with Cuyler to watch a long column file north out of Cambridge. It was made up of men from many regiments, but in the van marched riflemen from the backwoods of Virginia and Pennsylvania, the long thrums of their hunting shirts swinging and their deadly rifles resting easily in scarred hands. Morgan and his riflemen; Return Meigs, Thayer, Topham with the Massachusetts men; Enos and his solid files from Connecticut.

Cuyler tapped Ripley's shoulder. "Don't feel so bad about it. Maybe they'll never get beyond Newburyport."

"Maybe," said Ripley. The men were tramping off on a long trail that would take them up into Maine, along the shaggy banks of the Kennebec and the Chaudière and on to the St. Lawrence. Christian Febiger, now riding past as adjutant to Benedict Arnold, had begged Glover to let Ripley go with the expedition, but the colonel had been adamant and now Ripley watched the smooth flow of the companies whose thoughts were on the rocky bastions of Quebec. Massachusetts, Connecticut, Pennsylvania, and Virginia—all marching to a common goal from which no one

Province or district would benefit. An American undertaking.

Someone whooped from the ranks and Ripley waved to Nahum Sholes, who plodded happily on, his legs moving in the old ranger swing and his thick nose already snuffing white water and heavy pine. Then the last of the column was gone. Ripley said abruptly, "Come on, Joris. Let's go. God, but I wish I was with them!" He felt increased distaste for the boredom of the siege and the tedium of drill. Arnold, Febiger, and the rest were swinging off on a trail that might become immortal, while he—

Then he caught sight of a familiar gingery head on the steps of of the new headquarters, saw a clean-moving company in blue and white that was stepping off on its way to twenty-four hours of guard duty about Washington. "Look good, don't they, Rip?" said Cuyler.

Ripley watched the compact files swing off toward Brattle Street. He laughed suddenly. "Damn Quebec! This is where I belong, Joris."

* * *

October slipped down from the north, stained the great escarpment of the Berkshires with scarlet and amber and gold, crept on across Massachusetts. The old, worn ridge that sheltered Concord flared with color. The hills about Boston and the Cambridge flats were ablaze with turning leaves. The army huddled its worn clothes about it, began to burrow into tighter shelters. One night a messenger thundered into Cambridge with the news that a British force, landing from warships, had burned Falmouth in Maine, that the same armada was heading down the coast toward other port towns. The peppery Glover at once called in all scattered parties and when the anticipated orders came, the Twenty-first took the road back to Beverly.

The fall rolled on, dull and uneventful. By hundreds, men of all regiments made tentative preparations to return home at the end of the year. In Beverly, between interminable spells of watching the gray toss of the ocean for the British flotilla that never came, Ripley occupied his mind by drawing up precise regulations to cover the embarkation and debarkation of troops. He spent hours on wind-swept beaches and spits, watching such men as he could wheedle from Glover as they went through the careful routines that he had devised.

One December night, when a belated touch of Indian summer had crept down along the coast, he sat with Cuyler in the Capstan drinking French brandy that had somehow slipped up from the West Indies. "I'm worried, Joris," he said, scowling at his glass. "When I went to Cambridge with dispatches the other day I heard for a fact that we haven't got fifteen hundred men signed up in the whole army."

Cuyler nodded, his broad face unusually grave. "I was at a dinner last night. There were twenty people there—army people, I mean—and only half of them were sure about signing up. You see, Rip, there are a lot of things that are making people jumpy. How's a man with a family going to live and keep his family alive by squatting back of a breastwork and watching the Boston shore? Then people are wondering how long this is going on—and how far. If the Crown's going to give in, why what's the use of tying yourself up for another year? If the Crown isn't going to give in—"

"I'm betting it isn't," said Ripley tersely.

"So am I—and what then? Then a lot of people still don't like mixing the Provinces. And a lot of people don't like being issued coats that you can poke a finger through and boots that fall apart in the first mile of march."

"You ought to come to Cambridge with me next time I go. We're sort of away from the army here. You'll see mass meetings around Prospect Hill with people debating whether or not they'll stay. I tell you, since the smallpox broke out in the camps there, you hear a lot more taking the negative."

Cuyler shook his head. "I don't have to go to Cambridge. I can watch my own company. I'm getting to know them, and I can tell you exactly how many men'll fall in at reveille tomorrow. But I can't even make a guess about how many'll be there on January first—and that's not such a hell of a distance away."

Ripley rumpled his dark hair. "I keep telling myself we're worrying for nothing. We stuck through those days after the nineteenth. We lasted through Bunker Hill. We've disbanded one army, siege or no siege, and formed another. Actually, we've done it twice because we started right up from the keel when Washington came here. We've reorganized under Gage's nose and damned if we won't do the same thing under Howe's."

"Sure. Sure," said Cuyler eagerly. "That's what I keep telling myself. But—"

"I know—*but*," said Ripley. "Damned if we won't last through. We've got to last through. Now let's get it. I'm taking your company tomorrow after sunset. You're going to come down through the sand dunes and get into the tippiest craft I've been able to find. No lanterns. No talking."

Cuyler whistled. "You're making it too easy. Why not tie our hands behind our backs?"

"I would—if it'd help. I'm going to have these companies so that they'll be able—say in six weeks' time—" His voice trailed away.

"Uh-huh," said Cuyler. "In six weeks' time."

* * *

A strong wind from the northwest whipped down over the low hills back of Beverly, set the bare trees rocking and moaning, hissed through the tight ranks of the Twenty-first as it stood drawn up three deep in review formation on the empty stretches above the town. Ripley, posted at the flank of Blackler's company, shivered and tucked his bare hands under his arms. Out in front of the regiment, the fifers and drummers were furtively blowing on their hands. Cuyler, at Ripley's left, muttered, "Hell of a happy New Year we're having." Someone in the ranks growled: "Ain't nothing to a nor'easter off the Banks." Blackler, at the head of the company, half turned his head: "Steady between decks. It won't be much longer."

Ripley exchanged glances with Cuyler, whose face was growing purple in the wind. Not much longer? Out of the corner of his eye he could see bundles dotting the ground at the men's feet—personal belongings brought along by men who were not re-enlisting. And how many other bundles might lie hidden in inns and houses, or back at the camp beyond the dunes? He rubbed his hands, taking care to keep the icy barrel of the fusee away from his bare fingers. Out of the corner of his mouth he said to Cuyler: "What the hell's keeping Glover? He's never done this before. Another five minutes and I bet the companies'll break up under their own weight."

Cuyler shivered. "I'm so damned stiff I couldn't run if someone held a mug of hot rum out to me. Hi! Something's going to happen!"

Out in front of the regiment, the drum major, a tall, heavy-faced man, suddenly raised his baton, dropped it. The drummers whirled their sticks and began beating a quick, vibrant flourish, the flams and flamadiddles snapping through the icy air like pistol volleys. Commands rapped along the front of the regiment.

Then, somewhere behind Ripley, feet pounded rhythmically on the frozen road and Colonel Glover walked swiftly past the flank of the regiment, Johonot, now lieutenant colonel, and Major Lee at his heels. Behind them a gray-haired man limped, carrying a long staff whose upper half was wrapped in canvas.

The drums were silent. Glover, the wind whipping at his face, spun about toward the waiting lines, a vast cape billowing about his trim blue and white. He threw back his head and his voice slashed through the wind: "Order—firelocks!" Musket butts thumped to the hard street. "Stand at ease!"

A low murmur of relief rippled along the companies as men huddled their hands under their arms, shifted their feet.

Glover went on. "The Twenty-first Massachusetts Infantry is hereby declared mustered out, its term of enlistment having expired at midnight last night, December 31, 1775." He raised his head and his voice rang stronger. "Those of you who have signed enlistment papers for the year 1776 will be sworn in as the Fourteenth Massachusetts. I'll be glad if those of the old regiment who have talked with me will break ranks and return to their homes—now!"

Ripley heard a vague stir behind him, heard Glover shout: "Yes, you. That's right. I know about you—and you—and you. Orne Wilson, you break ranks. You've no right to stay here and you know it. You, too, Jack Derby. I had a letter from your wife this morning and you're going home if I have to carry you there." From the rear ranks of Courtis's company a thickset man blundered out past Ripley, hesitated, then stood white-faced by a low fence, his mouth working.

"You—in Captain Speakman's!" Glover blared out. "Have you talked to me? Then get back in ranks until I dismiss you. Where's Nate Cash? It won't do you any good to hide. You can't be spared at home, so—"

In twos and threes men ran eagerly from the ranks or slouched dejectedly away to linger wistfully on the fringes of the regiment as the colonel called their names. Cuyler muttered: "Does he know the whole regiment?"

"They'd burn him for a witch over in Salem," said Ripley. "He's kept the regiment together, fitted out ships, fought for supplies, and still managed to find time to talk to men he thought ought to go home. Look! Here comes something special!"

With a quick flourish Glover whipped a paper from

his pocket. "About the enlistments for the Fourteenth—our new number. I'm not urging a man to stay who doesn't stay out of his own free will. Pressed men are no good in *this* regiment. But before you take the oath—or decide not to—you've got to hear this. It came in just as I left headquarters and maybe it'll help make up the minds of those men who've been thinking that the Crown's going to say it's all been a mistake and let's moor alongside each other." The paper flapped and rattled in the wind. "It's a speech to Parliament by His Majesty King George the Third. It's long, so I'll just tell you three things he says that are mighty important to all of us. First he says we're in open rebellion and are trying to set up an empire of our own. Second—and clap your deadlights on this—he orders an increase in the Royal Navy and the army. I don't need to tell you what the increase is for. Third—and I think from now on we'll give over drinking the King's health in the regiment—third, he's having a hard time getting Englishmen to fight against us so—" he paused, threw back his head—"so he's going to hire Germans and Russians to come over here and do it for him. Germans—and Russians. That's the answer to reconciliation talk." He crammed the paper hastily back in his pocket. "That's all. I'm not going to make any speech. The King's done it for me." He snatched off his hat. "We'll take the oath of allegiance right here. Those who refuse to take it had better break ranks in a hurry." His right arm flew up. "Raise your right hands and say after me: 'I do hereby solemnly vow that I will—' "

Ripley, his hand raised high, heard the colonel's deepening voice roll out the words, felt his own lips moving as though through their own volition . . . " 'in the armies of the United Provinces . . . defend their rights and their shores . . . so help me God!' "

The responses from the ranks, low and muted, hummed on, ended in a staccato crash. Glover clapped his hat back on his head. "I now declare you to be formally enrolled in the Fourteenth Massachusetts Infantry, to serve therein for a period of one year, reckoned from midnight, December 31, 1775."

Ripley drew a deep breath, stole a glance over his shoulder. There were scattering gaps in the ranks, gaps that had not been there when the recital of the oath had begun. But the regiment stood solid, an entity, despite the withdrawals.

Another quick gesture from Glover caught his eye and the gray-haired man whom he'd noticed before limped stiffly between Johonot and Lee. The colonel's voice snapped out: "Maybe you've been wondering what John Trefry was doing here. You ought to know that he's got a right to be wherever Marblehead men fall in under arms. He was first on the walls of Louisburg. That's one reason. Another is that he's brought you something. We've never had a proper flag to march under. We've got one now. You'll fight under it. It's been raised all along the lines facing Boston today. John Trefry, you carried one flag up the glacis of Louisburg. Today you'll carry another at the head of the Fourteenth Massachusetts as it marches back to quarters."

Trefry, his face set like a mask, dipped the pole toward Glover, whose quick hands seized the canvas sheath. A hush fell over the fields and the slap-slap of the waves out in the bay was sharp and clear. Then a flash of bright color cut through the dull winter light. Trefry slowly raised the pole and a broad flag, red and white stripes bold, was caught by the wind, whipped out into a vivid canopy above him, the Union Jack showing small and dark in the upper corner by the staff.

Something closed about Ripley's throat. His fusee shook and his fingers ached as he gripped it harder, eyes on the flowing banner. Glover's voice cut through to him. "Fourteenth Massachusetts! Our flag!" His hat swept off. "Thirteen stripes. God bless the Thirteen United Provinces!"

A ragged cheer broke out, died away. Ripley knelt, one in a long line of kneeling men, bareheaded. Then he was on his feet and the drums were rustling and banging and Glover's voice was crashing out: "Wheel to the right! By companies! March!"

The thick line broke into column, wound away toward the streets of Beverly, the bright new flag dancing over the steady swing of the cocked hats. The drums banged on. Fifes bit into the wind:—

Yankee doodle came to town,
A-riding on a pony,
Stuck a feather in his hat—

Ripley's feet seemed weightless as they rapped into the sweep of the march that wove its way up into the swaying, fluttering folds of the new flag.

Yankee doodle dandy,
Yankee doodle keep it up—

There was a scurry of feet from an alley on the right. Men in blue and white charged across the street and edged their way back into the ranks. By a hitching post, one of the men whom Glover had singled out leaned against it, sad eyes on the limping color bearer. Fife and drum raved on through the high notes. Behind the music, cocked hats and bright bayonets surged along in the wake of the striped banner as the Fourteenth Massachusetts, born of an idea that had survived stalemate and confusion and treachery, set out on its road. And people crowding along both sides of the street, crowding between the great merchants' houses and the low-roofed shops, bared their heads to the solid column and the flag that rode high in the van.

II

STUMBLING over the frozen ruts of the road, Ripley clutched his cape tighter about him and ran toward the snug hut that he and Cuyler shared. As he slammed the door behind him, the big New Yorker looked up from the clay and stick fireplace with a shout. "So you didn't desert! How was Concord? Did you bow to your father for me?"

Ripley threw his cape onto his bunk and pushed Cuyler away from the fire. "Bowed twice. He's in fine spirits. Concord was the same as ever. Featherfoot sent you his respects. I went sleigh-riding with the Buttrick girls and the Wheelers. Have you kept out of mischief during my leave?"

"You don't need all the fire. Just let me have this edge here. Mischief? Hell, I've been so bored I've been driven to rolling dice, right hand against my left. Listen—there's a rumor going around that that Englishman, Lee, is going to take Washington's place. Hear anything about it?"

Ripley held out his hands to the blaze. "Lee? I doubt it. When I came through Cambridge, the big buck Virginian was still at the Vassall house and Lee was out at his quarters at Hobgoblin Hall in Medford. Here's something that's true, though. Father heard from Philadelphia that they're debating about hiring French or German troops—sort of a ready-made army —and letting us go home. They figure it may be cheaper in life and money."

Cuyler's eyes bulged. "Hire a bunch of foreigners to do *our* fighting?"

Ripley laughed. "Cool down, Joris. I know how it hit you. When Father told me I let out a screech that you could have heard clear off on Punkatasset Hill. He says there isn't a chance of its passing."

Cuyler exhaled noisily. "You had me scared for a minute. I've never liked seeing those two ex-Lobsters, Lee and Gates, throwing in with us. I thought maybe they'd be sort of an entering wedge, something that'd ease in a lot more foreigners."

"Don't worry. I wish you could have seen Cambridge. There's something different in the air. You get an idea of solidity. Of course there are still desertions and supplies are damned hard to get. But we look more and more like a going concern."

A knock sounded on the door.

Ripley called over his shoulder. "Come in." A muffled guard said: "Colonel's looking for you, sir."

Ripley groaned. "Oh God, what now?" He hurried to Glover's quarters where he found the colonel in deep conversation with Major Lee. "Here I am, sir," said Ripley.

Glover threw back his head. "No. You're not. Tell him where he is, Lee."

His long face unsmiling, Lee unrolled a map of the Province. "M'm, Marlboro, Shrewsbury, Worcester." He looked at Ripley. "You're just getting near Leicester."

Glover thumped the table. "In fact, you're cursing Dead Horse Hill enough to melt the snow on Mount Wachusett."

Ripely shifted his feet. "I'm afraid I don't understand."

Glover swung up from the table. "Either you're there or your colonel's a damned liar."

Ripley grinned. "I can see the church in Leicester right now."

"That's it." Glover began to tramp up and down the room. "Wondering how you got there?"

"Some," said Ripley.

"Show him, Lee."

Lee handed him a sheet of paper. "Read that."

Ripley unfolded the sheet. "In camp at Beverly. January 5, 1776. In compliance with your Excellency's . . . have the honor to inform you that Ensign R. Mayne . . . in accordance with your Excellency's orders dated . . . has proceeded with one sergeant and five privates . . ." He looked up. "Dated the fifth, sir? *Has* proceeded?"

"Here's what happened," said Glover. "Those orders should have reached us on the fourth and you should have started on the fifth. But someone left them sitting about in Vassall House and we only just got them. Now, we could sit back and say the orders were delayed and let you get away tomorrow. But not in this regiment. You're going to get out of here quicker than frosted hell and make up the time that some haddock-head in Cambridge lost. Understand?"

"Everything—except what I'm going to do with the detail, sir."

Lee and Glover exchanged glances. "You're going to do plenty. And I want to tell you this—it's about the most important job that any regiment in the army's been called on to do." He stood in front of the fire, feet wide apart. "You've heard people talking about all the guns up at Ticonderoga, haven't you? You knew that Henry Knox had been sent to bring them down? Of course you did. Well, it's taken him long enough, what with thaws so he couldn't get his sledges moving and having trouble with the New Yorkers he hired and their oxen. In a day or two, he'll be getting close to Springfield. Know where that is? All right. You ought to meet him there. If you don't, keep right on going west until you sight him. He'll have been over some mighty tough hills and worse roads. He'll still have tough ones to face. See where you come in?"

Ripley whistled. "By God, it'll be great to use oxen again!"

"Use whales if you want. What Washington's worried about is this. The New Yorkers are from the lake country. They're used to snagging barges and bateaux over cliffs and running them down waterfalls, oxcarts and all. But the New Yorkers probably won't stay with him as soon as he crosses the border. He'll replace them with Massachusetts farmers that have never done anything except snake rocks out of their fields. What he'll need is men that can handle weights and block and tackle, men that can take a yard of silk thread and a rake handle and haul Brant Rock clear to the Berkshires. Now, you can take any sergeant you want—"

"I'll choose Grenda of Blackler's," said Ripley. "And another thing that struck me. The orders call for one ensign. Can't we make that two?"

Glover's thick eyebrows bristled. "Why, in God's name?"

"You say that Knox has got New York teamsters that'll want to turn back at the border. Maybe there'll be some delay in getting Massachusetts men to take their places."

"Well?"

"Seems to me it would be a good idea to have someone along who can make the New Yorkers stay on until the last minute." He paused. "Someone who knows New Yorkers."

Glover's eyes snapped. "Ha! Trying to get a berth for your Dutch friend, are you?"

"He'd be good at it," said Ripley.

Glover swept an arm toward Lee. "Change the damned orders. You ought to have thought of Cuyler. I ought to have." He whipped out his watch. "You've got exactly fifteen minutes to get ready. You and Cuyler'll draw saddle horses. The detail'll travel by cart. It's all loaded and waiting. Find Cuyler, dust him off, and go to Hut G, where you'll meet your detail. I'll have Grenda warned and he'll join you there."

Ripley, cold and fatigue forgotten, raced back to the cabin, wrenched open the door, and snatched up his haversack. "Cram everything you own into that grease bag of yours, Joris! We're casting off."

Cuyler's blue eyes widened. "Casting off?"

"Special duty. You and I. Get moving and don't ask questions." He buckled the last strap of his haversack, seized Cuyler's and began stuffing shirts, mufflers, and stockings into it.

"You're serious?" stammered Cuyler.

"No, you oaf. I'm just doing this to keep warm. Roll up those blankets." He slung his own pack over his shoulders. "Finish up your stuff and join me at Hut G. If you take more than three minutes, you'll have Glover opening up his gun ports and blasting at you." He banged out through the door.

In Hut G he found Hans Grenda, the sergeant, waiting patiently in the cold stuffiness. He nodded briskly. "Know what this is about, Sergeant?"

Grenda shook his head.

"I'll tell you when the detail reports. Got your equipment? Good."

Ripley watched the sergeant as he tested the roll of his blankets and remembered how he had been inclined to slight the man when he had first joined the regiment. It had seemed strange that such a man, narrow-chested and stoop-shouldered, with a skin so weather-beaten that it always looked unshaven, had come to wear a sergeant's knot. Then he had found that the spare frame was tireless, hands and brain deft, and tongue slow to move. He had come to rely on him more and more, had seen him prove himself many times over.

The flimsy door opened and Cuyler tramped in, laden, his blue eyes still clouded with wonder. Then one by one the rest of the detail reported, weather-scarred men whose lives had been spent beating up the coast or out to the Grand Banks in smack, yawl, or schooner. They stood before Ripley, loose-limbed and tight-mouthed—Joel Brimblecome, Abel Cash,

Ralph Truman, Obed Orne—and answered his quick questions in monosyllables.

"That's four," said Ripley. "Where's the fifth?"

The door jarred again and a man barely five feet high bounced in. "This the one?" said Ripley, taking in the wizened face, the pop-eyes, and the jutting chin and nose that reached toward each other.

"It's me." The man tapped his blue chest. "Adam Gragg, and I'm a half-pint of ginegar."

Ripley blinked. "Of what?"

"Ginegar. Equal parts ginger and vinegar. Kind of like the colonel." He gave a sudden leap in the air, caught the low rafter with one hand, and drew himself up so that his prominent eyes stared down at Ripley over the edge of the timber.

Ripley nodded. Glover must have had a good reason for choosing this undersized gnome. "Get your equipment," he said.

"Got it. It's on me." Gragg dropped to the floor.

"Got your rations?"

"They're in me. They're a-laying in my stomach and a-nourishing of me," said Gragg complacently.

Ripley hunched his shoulders into a blue cloak, picked up his hat. "The colonel's chosen us for a job that's going to be tough. We're heading inland as far as Springfield, maybe deeper. Anyone ever been that way?"

Grenda gave his tight smile. "Ain't a man here that's been fifteen mile inland in his life."

Ripley nodded. "You're going to see plenty of dry land. Colonel Knox is working over the road with a lot of guns. The going's bad. He'll need ropes and men who know how to use them. That's what we're going to do—use them. Any questions?"

"Heard we was going back on the water," said Brimblecome, his voice thick with disappointment.

"This may be the quickest way of getting back there for good," said Ripley. "Is that all? We start now. There's a wagon outside loaded with tools and ropes. You'll ride in it. Come on, Joris. You and I've got beasts waiting for us."

Mounted on a solid-limbed roan that stubbed along beside Joris's black, Ripley rode out of Beverly in the clear cold of the night, the loaded cart jolting and rattling behind him. Cuyler flounced and shifted in his saddle, ruffled his cloak about him. Then he grunted: "That was a hell of a fine explanation you gave about what we're going to do. I haven't got a wonder left in me, except about where we're going and why."

"That's fine. You'll have nothing to think about and that'll keep you out of trouble."

"Is it true about Knox?"

"It's what Glover told me, Joris. Knox is somewhere between here and Ticonderoga. He's got sixty guns of all calibers. He's got powder and flints. But mostly cannon. They're on sledges and he's got a lot of thick-headed New Yorkers driving thick-headed oxen."

"Know his route?"

"It was on the orders he showed me. Let me see—Half Moon, Albany, Kinderhook, Claverack, Nobletown, Great Barrington, and then on to Springfield."

Cuyler whistled.

Ripley nodded. "Just what I thought. Dead winter, a road that'd shake the gizzards out of a sea lion, and a young Boston bookseller running the whole show."

"We're supposed to meet him near Springfield? Hell, we'll be lucky if we sight him east of the Taconics." Cuyler pushed his hat over his eyes. "Guns. H'm. Coming this way. If I weren't a New Englander and a Marbleheader I might go so far as to say some folks might call this middling important."

"And I wouldn't go so far's to say you were dead wrong," said Ripley. "It means—by God, it means Dorchester Heights!"

"And then Howe'll *have* to come out and we'll have another Bunker Hill—"

"With the cannon on our side and *one* man commanding—not just clumps of infantry all doing what each one thinks best."

"Jesus!" said Cuyler softly. "How'd I come to get picked for the job?"

"Glover thought we'd need an interpreter for Knox's New York teamsters." He clucked to his horse. "Come on. Let's step the beasts out. First stop's Watertown. We'll let the cart catch up with us."

They trotted off along the white road. Behind them the cart clattered on, most of the men curled up in their blankets while the Punch-like face of Adam Gragg seemed to hang over the side-boards like some disembodied spirit.

III

THE LITTLE cortege made an early start from Watertown and Ripley, as they rolled on, felt that he was seeing a new Massachusetts, a new America. Strange cities and stranger islands had unrolled before him during the years of his servitude, but of his own country he had seen little beyond the narrow arc about Massachusetts Bay. Now each step of the broad-backed roan drew him away from the flatlands and stumpy hills of the coastal regions, carried him into the long bastions of rolling ridges that tumbled away west, heavy with pine and rock, like the endless combers of the open sea. Towns and villages that had been familiar names to him, but names only, now appeared on the horizon, closed about him and his party, turned them loose on the open road again.

Framingham and its white houses. Then Southboro and the rising sweep of the Troublesome Meadows; Marlboro where the Old Bay Path, older than all history, struggled up a long ridge, swept down the other side to rest in a level stretch before the laboring ascent ahead; ridge-girt Quinsigamond, lying like a curving blade of silver, seven-hilled Worcester seen through a dazzle of sunset which stained the mighty scarps and counter-scarps where Paxton and Rutland perched.

It was from these ridges and these valleys that the men of the nineteenth had come, roused by bell and by gun and by hoof, following an idea through town and forest and swamp until they came to the Lexington road and the great arc of fires that rimmed Boston. White house, yellow house by church or common, lost farm by sluggish stream, idle mill by ice-draped dam, low-eaved inn along the Old Bay Path—in some way they seemed to define more clearly for him the army that lay in the flatlands now far to the east. He put his feeling into halting words to Cuyler, who nodded in silent understanding.

As the bitter days rolled slowly by, Ripley began to worry. At each halt he asked news of Knox and the guns, but was always met with blank ignorance. Rare sleighs from the west were stopped, questioned in vain. Beyond Palmer he growled to Cuyler: "Damn it, we *know* that he got as far as the Taconics. What the devil's happened to him?"

Cuyler shrugged. "Can't lose eighty yoke of oxen on the road. Hell, the column'd stretch from the Timp to Rensselaerwyck and loop four times around old Van Hooven's Vly. Quit worrying. You're scowling so hard that even the icicles on your hat are wrinkled."

"It's plenty to worry about. We've found one spy—Dr. Church. Suppose someone like him had forged Knox's name to the letter telling about the guns?"

"What good would that do?"

Ripley flicked ice from his horse's bit. "Don't you see? Washington's only got about three thousand men around Cambridge. Howe's got about eleven thousand. Word of the guns got about in camp and men began to come back. Now—if the guns don't come—if another Church has been making trouble—we'll be lucky to find a corporal's guard around Cambridge when we get back. Wonder what the detail thinks about it?"

He checked his horse until the cart was abreast of him. The men were huddled down against the wind, save Adam Gragg, who blandly exposed to the keen wind a face marvelously swollen by an aching tooth. Broken talk came to Ripley over the slow crunch of the wheels. ". . . And damn me if I ever sign for an inland cruise again. Air just ain't got no smell to it." . . . "Near ungutted myself trying to get a whiff of a tidal marsh afore I remembered there wa'n't such around here." . . . "And I mind her rig just as plain's if we'd raised her tops'ls off the Roaring Bulls yesterday."

Ripley clucked to his horse. At least the men weren't worrying.

Two days more brought them into a towering chaos of hills that made even the homesick Marbleheaders stare in wonder. Cuyler, feet swinging clear of the stirrups, began to crow. "By God, I knew there was something in the air. That wind's blowing right off the Hudson."

"It's not that bad," said Ripley. "Probably just a dead deer that a thaw's got to up there in the woods. Look here. Unless my maps are wrong, we'll be sighting Great Barrington by sundown. I'm going ahead to hail the Committee and see about quarters and rations. If you don't see me along the road, push on until you reach the Town House." He touched his horse with his switch and trotted on.

There was little glass left in the house across the Housatonic that the Committee assigned to Ripley. He pushed the warped door aside and prowled restlessly from room to empty room. At least the roof was tight, the fireplaces seemed clean, and the woodpile in the rear would do for a regiment. He stabled his horse in a rickety shed and walked down to the road, peering east for a sign of Cuyler and the wagon. Then he saw a single horseman trotting toward him.

He jumped out into the road as he saw Grenda's spare form bobbing unhappily in Cuyler's saddle. He held up his hand. "Cast anchor, Hans! What's the matter? Where's Cuyler?"

Grenda, handling the reins like tiller lines, dragged the horse to a walk and dropped to the snow, standing wide. "The cart. The port wheel astern foundered."

"What?" said Ripley. "Oh, the nigh hind wheel. How far down the road is it?"

"Mile or so," said Grenda, chafing the insides of his thighs and looking malevolently at the horse. "Brimblecome and Gragg, they're putting a kind of jury rig onto it and Mr. Cuyler's holding up the stern. He sent me on to find you."

Ripley caught the reins. "I'll go on back unless you want to."

Grenda limped away quickly. "I'd sooner sit in a dory off the Banks in a nor'easter with a cod line freezing to my hands than pilot that God-damn animal another cable length," he said with feeling. "This our berth? I'll go in and get a fire started."

Ripley swung the horse about and, at the end of a half-mile, saw the cart weaving slowly and erratically toward him. He trotted to meet it. A stout sapling had been fearsomely lashed so its thick end trailed on the ground in the rear and the other rested on the front axle. At the tail of the cart, Cuyler set his shoulders against the trunk to check its swaying. Ripley shouted: "All right, Joris. Not much farther to go."

Cuyler straightened up, sighed ponderously. "I thought we were done for back there." He wiped his forehead. "I remember seeing a picture of a Hindu snake charmer once, but he was clumsy as a Dutch *vrouw* compared to these sculpin eaters of ours. They can make a rope climb a tree and then haul the tree up after it."

"Good job," said Ripley, eying the web of knots and coils that held the trunk in position. "See that shed off there? Get your rig up to it and I'll run my skilled eye over the wreck. Turn the detail loose in that house with the smoking chimney and join me at the shed."

When the cart had been unloaded, Ripley studied the wheel, frowning over the worn axle box, muttering as he ran a finger along a splintery felloe. Then Cuyler's shadow fell across the door. Ripley looked up. "The man who'd let an axle box get into this shape isn't deserving of Christian burial."

Cuyler looked at him in mock wonder. "My, you must have to know an awful lot to be a farmer, Mr. Mayne."

Ripley swaggered. "Set a plowshare, tooth a harrow, translate Horace, drill a battalion, geld a pig. We Maynes are versatile as hell. And that's what I've got to be right now. We can't go on with this rig of Gragg's." He got to his feet. "Damn it, I'll have to go back to town and find a wheelwright." He looked down from the little hill to the stone bridge across the Housatonic and the white town that spread out beyond it.

"I'll go," said Cuyler.

Ripley shook his head, eyes on the western rampart of hills that loomed beyond the town and its white spire. "I've talked with the Committee here. They're shy as spring woodchucks and you'd scare them back into their holes."

"Did they know anything about Knox?"

"They never heard of him. I don't think they ever heard of cannon before. If more than two people come into town, they think it's an Indian raid and get out their bows and arrows." He walked stiffly off to drag out his saddle and bridle. Then he studied the hill at his feet. By swinging through a pinewood he could save the big bend in the road and drop right down into the town. He listened to his horse contentedly crumping at its oats and made up his mind.

The old path, snow-filled, wound along the crest of the hill through tangles of wild raspberry bushes, burrowed through stands of fir and dipped into rocky hollows where hidden ice made the footing treacherous. The light was fading fast and twice Ripley had to climb onto high rocks to be sure of his bearing. At last, in semi-twilight, he swung to the right and began to work down a long hillside that led into the town, the course of the path zigzagging from one clump of firs to another, bending around great stone outcroppings and occasionally dropping straight down across open fields.

Halfway down the slope he suddenly found ice under his boots, skated wildly on, caught himself by a fir tree that momentarily checked him, then whirled madly around the shoulder of a looming rock. He waved his arms trying to get his balance. Something swished in the dusk behind him, there was a muffled shriek. A solid body, hurtling through the air, struck him just back of the knees. His feet shot out from under him. A hand caught at his shoulder as he spun and spun down the slope to come to a smothering halt in a drift of soft snow. He tried to struggle to his feet, but a weight pressed him down. He shouted "Damnation!" as a boot rapped against his shin.

At last he worked himself free and struggled to a kneeling position. He wiped snow from his eyes, gasped: "Well, I'll be a steaming sea pig!" Opposite him in the snowbank a girl stared at him, white-stockinged legs stretched out before her, elbows deep in the drift. Then Ripley caught up his hat from the ground and bowed elaborately over it. "Ensign Mayne of the Fourteenth. At your service!"

Unexpectedly the girl began to laugh. "Remembrance Morse, sir. At yours." There was a piquant huskiness in her voice. Then she started, hands flying to her disordered skirts, to the tumbled shawl about her head.

Ripley scrambled to his feet and held out his hands. "Allow me."

She drew her feet under her in a deft movement. "I'll manage, thanks." She tried to rise, staggered. He caught her elbow and steadied her. "Are you hurt?"

She shook her head. "I'm all right. Just—just seem to have done something to my ankle." She put out a hand and leaned against an elm trunk while she held one foot, shod in stout country leather, out before her.

Ripley looked at her with growing interest. She was tall, slim, with high, round breasts, and she held her head proudly.

Cautiously she set her foot on the ground, then lifted it quickly. "It'll go away in a minute."

"Maybe," said Ripley. "But I shan't." He tried to make out her profile against the snowy background. "You live around here?"

Still flexing her ankle, she said, "I won't get lost or fall down again, if that's what you're afraid of."

Ripley laughed. "Afraid? I'm utterly fearless and I'm going to see you right to your door."

She shook her head. "In the first place I'm not going there. In the second, I'm quite all right."

"You know better about that than I. If you're sure you're all right—" He put out his hand quickly as she took a tentative step forward.

She looked up at him and then laughed. "I hate to contradict myself. But I *am* going there."

"I thought so." Ripley felt a sudden pleasure in her change of mind. "Just lean on my arm and tell me how to steer."

"I'd like to ask what on earth a man in uniform is doing sliding down Sage's upper pasture on a winter evening, but I've got to show you the smoothest way down."

He moved carefully along while Remembrance Morse hopped nimbly beside him, favoring her right ankle. By a big rock, they turned down the hill again and found a beaten path that led to a covered well. Suddenly the girl stumbled and stood leaning against Ripley.

He steadied her with an arm about her shoulders. "Take all the time you want. Did you hurt it again?"

"N-no. I caught myself just in time."

Ripley studied the path, black against the snow. Then he nodded. "As you said, just in time." He slipped his arm farther about her shoulders, caught her under the knees with the other. "You twist that ankle once more and some kind old gentleman's going to come along with a knife and slice it right off."

She kicked out once, then relaxed in his arms. "I suppose it's sensible. Keep in back of those two houses and then turn in at that side gate by the big elm."

"Ahead on the port bow. Comfortable? Then here we go." She was easy to carry and the faint scent of her hair came to him through the shawl. Almost unconsciously he slowed his pace. Looking out of the corner of his eyes he could make out her face more clearly. The forehead high and smooth, the eyes deep-set. Her nose was finely arched. He looked at her mouth and closed his eyes quickly. He shook his head and plodded on, increasingly aware of the lithe figure in his arms.

He tried to forget about the nearness of her face, the stream of hair that spilled over his shoulder.

At last she said, "You're very kind, Mr. Mayne. Now here's the gate. There's no latch. Just kick it open."

He carried her up the path to a side door. Her sound foot moved in the dark, struck a ringing blow against the panel. The door swung slowly open and an immensely tall man with spectacles pushed up on his forehead looked out.

"Here I am, Father," she said.

A high-held candle burned steadily and the tall man said, quite unperturbed, "So I see. Bring her in, young man. Bring her in."

Taken aback by the cool acceptance of himself and his burden, Ripley stepped into a narrow hall, then through a door where old oak gleamed in the candle-light and a broad mirror reflected the sheen of mahogany, the leather backs of hundreds of books. The tall man said mournfully, "Put her there on the little sofa by the fire. Now, what was it?"

Ripley set her carefully on the green-brocaded piece, thinking that the final tightness of her arms, the weight of her body in his grasp, were like a good-night embrace. He shook off the thought. "She hurt her ankle," he said to the father. "You'll want to look at it. Take the heel like this—" he cupped his hand—"and turn it a little, left and right. If it's just a sprain, you won't feel any grating."

The dark, mournful face looked down at Ripley. "Oh," said the man uncertainly. "Hold it like this to find out if it's a sprain? Is that right?" Then he rumbled in his throat. "Well, it's not the way I learned when I took my degree at Edinburgh thirty years ago, and seeing that it's my own daughter I'll stick to the old ways—with your kind permission."

Ripley studied her in the candlelight that showed him deep brown eyes and hair of an intense black. He sat slowly down in a ladder-back by the fire. "By God, she's beautiful!" he thought.

At last the tall man rose slowly, his long-tailed green coat flapping about his buff breeches. "Sprain," he said. "Not a bad one. We'll get a poultice on it. Now, Mr.—Mr.—"

"Mayne," said Remembrance. "We introduced ourselves in the middle of a snowdrift." She looked across the room. "That was right, wasn't it?"

"Ripley—Ripley Mayne."

The tall man bowed. "I'm your debtor and it's not a new experience. Ever since she could walk, that daughter of mine's been falling into millponds, getting into runaway teams, picking up rattlesnakes and being carried out to sea in leaky boats." He cleared his throat, bowed stiffly. "My father had a malicious instinct which he mistook for a sense of humor and gave me my maternal grandfather's name—Remorse. Remorse Morse, Doctor of Medicine." He looked closer at Ripley. "Oh—I didn't notice that you were in clown clothes."

Ripley rose quickly. "And I was not aware that I was in a Tory house."

"Neither was I," said Dr. Morse, lined face more mournful than ever. "Red or blue or brown or just a cockade, it's all a rary-show. *Homo sapiens.* Bah! *Homo soi-disant sapiens!*" He pointed a long finger at Ripley. "Do you know what happened to me? For ten years I'd worked with Apthorp and Beekman and Lispenard and Livingston and Delancey trying to build a hospital in New York. In '71 we got our charter from the King. Last year we laid the last brick, had the wards ready for patients. Look at it now." He let his hand drop by his side. "Falling to pieces—and just those walls and the people who built them would have made New York a place where people would have been freed of the ills that come to them through no fault of their own. Ten, twenty years' work that would have spread to every city. Now it's snuffed out because half the fools in the Provinces want to play Caesar and the other half want to play Brutus."

Ripley said coldly, "You'd have had a fine hospital with a Board subject to London and a staff appointed from there. You'd work your ten years and then have to step down because someone in London's bought a degree for his son and shipped him out here to a berth he can't find in England."

Remembrance clapped her hands. "That's what I've been telling you, Father. Go on, Mr. Mayne!"

Her father turned to Ripley. "How, sir, does that differ from a Board that's run by vote-stealing demagogues who'll supplant me with a Mohawk Valley horse doctor?" He shook his head angrily. "I moved out of New York. I moved out of Connecticut. If this crack-brained war keeps on following me, I'll move to Canada and doctor Abenaki squaws."

The corners of Remembrance's mouth twitched. "You've left out the part about the human race being so stupid that it's a mercy to encourage patients to die instead of trying to cure them."

"It would be a boon to humanity—if there were such a thing. It—" He stopped suddenly, then ruffled his daughter's dark hair. "It would have served you right if Mr. Mayne had left you up in the snow. I haven't heard yet just what idiocy you'd performed this time. What was it, Mr. Mayne?"

Ripley said: "Why—I don't know exactly. I was coming down the hill . . ."

Remembrance laughed. "And I was behind him and missed my footing and smashed into him like an Indian toboggan. That's all. It was perfectly natural. What I want to know is just why a man in uniform should be sliding down Sage's hill."

"Again, perfectly natural," smiled Ripley. "I'm with a detail of men from Marblehead and we're looking for eighty oxteams and an artillery colonel."

Morse opened a tall cabinet by the fireplace. "Odd how simple things do become when just a word or two's said about them. Remembrance, I'm prescribing some Madeira for your ankle. Mr. Mayne, I take it that you'd like brandy?"

"Thanks. And a wheelwright if you've one hidden about here," said Ripley.

"An odd taste," said the doctor, filling the glasses. "Brandy you're welcome to. As to the wheelwright, I've got one but you can't have him."

"I've got to have him," said Ripley. "If I delay on the road, Colonel Glover'll keelhaul me."

"And if you bother him tonight, I'll tie you to a tree and open all your veins. The wright—he's Joe Sage and you slid down his hill just now—is recovering from a flux. You'll see him tomorrow at the earliest, although I doubt if he's got oxteams and artillery colonels in his woodshed."

"He's an enterprising man," said Remembrance, looking at Ripley over the top of her glass. "He might have. But you'll do well to wait until tomorrow to see him."

"Is he the only one in town?" asked Ripley.

"The only one between here and Claverack," said Remembrance. "It's a long walk there and you'd better stay and wait until Father says you can see Sage. His house is just two doors east of us."

"We're supposed to get on and help with those guns!" said Ripley. "If you only knew how the army needs—"

"What both armies need is a good, sound visitation of the plague," rumbled Dr. Morse.

"I don't know about the Lobsters, but we've had our share of plagues and one more or less wouldn't make much difference." He rose, bowed to Remembrance. "If we're not gone by tomorrow evening, may I look by and inquire about the ankle?"

She smiled up at him and her hand was smooth and slim in his. "You're very daring, considering our meeting. But I'd be glad to see you."

Her father opened the door. "Don't be surprised if you find her treed by a bull back in the orchard. Good night and thank you."

As Ripley made his way back to the detail and the little house, he began casting about in his mind for alternative plans in case Sage the wheelwright took too long over the repairs. Then, to his surprise, he found that his impatience was ebbing. He would do all that was humanly possible to hurry matters along. If there should be further delay—well, then, he would be able to hear that husky voice again, to watch the play of expression about Remembrance Morse's soft lips and smooth cheeks, to meet the direct look of those brown eyes.

Before sunrise the next morning, Ripley was awakened by Gragg, his swollen face bound up in a wildly purple handkerchief. "Time to change watch," mumbled the Punch-like man.

Ripley groaned, then sat up suddenly and jabbed

Cuyler's blankets with his foot. "Wh'matter?" mumbled Cuyler.

"Listen, ever know a girl in New York name Morse?"

"Lemme 'lone. Not my watch."

"In New York. Morse—her father's a doctor."

Cuyler stirred, rubbed his eyes. "Morse?"

"Looks like a thin bloodhound that's got tired of scratching fleas."

Cuyler blinked. "Bloodhound? Oh—I know. Never met him, but the aged parent did. Sawbones. I was supposed to go to his house but when I heard his name and his daughter's, I got scared. Remembrance and Remorse. Sounded too much like waking up after a hard night. Had a place out beyond Abraham Mortier's. What you want to know for?"

"Just wondered."

Cuyler flounced back among his blankets. "And you woke me up out of a sound sleep just for that? Wish to hell you'd do your wondering at Christian hours."

IV

BY NOON of that day, Ripley stood on a sharp hill west of the town and through a glass watched the road that climbed west toward the New York border. Behind him, Grenda tended a small fire in the shelter of a flat rock. The sergeant looked up to ask: "'Bout time for me to stand watch?"

"Another half hour, Hans. Damn it, one old woman and two rabbits on that road in three hours' watching. Guess it won't matter if Sage does take all day as he threatened." He turned toward the fire, then looked in surprise as he saw Remembrance Morse walking cautiously up the path. He ran to meet her. "I'm beginning to believe what your father said. You're supposed to be in bed with your foot in a splint or something."

"Supposed by whom?" she laughed as she tossed back a bright shawl from her high-piled hair. "I'm just obeying orders. Father told me to walk around to keep the ankle limber. It's a pet notion of his and it's doing me good. Give me your arm for the rest of the climb and tell me what on earth you're doing up here."

He adjusted his step to hers. "Looking for the eighty yoke of oxen I told you about. We've been here since dawn."

"We?" she said, dark eyebrows arching.

"Just the two of—" He looked at the hilltop, at the blazing fire by the flat rock and at a fresh set of footprints that led off down the hill, heedless of path or trail. "We *were* here, anyway. Come over by the fire."

"How did you happen to find this hill? It's one of my favorite climbs." She perched on the flat rock and waved her hand at the sunlit expanse of snowy fields that lay at the foot, at the dark, wooded ridge beyond.

"I wanted the nearest place where I could see farthest and this was it," he laughed. "I didn't know I was trespassing." He picked up his glass, stared at the road winding up the opposite ridge.

She cocked her head. "Are they so important, the sledges?"

"What's on them is important—if it gets to the right place at the right time."

She said suddenly, "Tell me about it."

"About what?"

"About the sledges—about the army."

He laughed shortly. "Nothing to tell about it. Just a lot of—"

She cut in quickly. "That's one point where Father and I don't agree. If I were a man I'd join Washington so fast that he'd think I was a whole regiment all by myself. Go on. Tell me what it's like over there."

He said slowly, "Well, there's not much to tell. Cambridge is a queer place these days. Lots of people have moved out to make room for the troops. The college has been moved to Concord so none of the faculty families are around. I don't know, except in a few cases, what the girls up there *are* doing. They—"

Her full lips set. "Look here. A-r-m-y. That's what I want to hear about."

"Not much interesting in that."

"Isn't there? After all, it's my country as much as yours. I'm an American, just as you are. How do people feel, what are they saying? Are they discouraged? Will they hold together? What's happened to them—really happened, I mean, not just what we read in gazettes and things."

Ripley looked at her curiously. Her eyes were serious, grave. "I see," he said. "You know, I've seldom had a chance to look at the thing as a whole. It all started that day the British came out to Concord and ever since John Buttrick marched the companies down to the bridge—why, things have been happening." He tried to sort out his thoughts, found them flowing into words.

The companies had come out. They had stayed out. They had become regiments, had almost imperceptibly changed from local, to provincial, to national units. He told of the uncertainty that gnawed at men, of regiments breaking up, of men going home in disgust, of companies that mustered fifty men at daybreak and five at sundown. He spoke of the white-coated Dane who had weaned him away from his own local feeling; told about Bunker's Hill; sketched the melting away of the army at the first of the year, its slow reorganizing.

She nodded slowly when he had finished. "I think I begin to see. There's something—something that's bigger than doubt and hunger and cold and treachery and death that holds them there—holds them so that no matter what happens there are always enough to keep that curve of fires you spoke about going."

"First hand, I can't speak for the rest of the country. But it takes a lot to get a New Englander excited enough to lift his musket down from over the fireplace. No matter what happens, I know—I tell you I *know* that the idea that turned the men out in the first place is strong enough to keep most of them there."

Cheek resting in her hand, she studied him gravely. "You told me that a lot of men went into the army just for rank. That's what would frighten me, if I were a man—not knowing enough for what I was doing. What showed you that you were fit to give orders to other men?"

"A press gang," said Ripley grimly. He told briefly of his service with the Royal Marines, spoke of his own confusion of mind when he finally deserted and made his way home.

Her eyes turned toward the western ridge and the empty road that climbed it. Then she said: "I like that. In your case it was the idea that brought you out—not a feeling of revenge, not just a chance to shoot at men wearing your old coat."

"Why would it be revenge? I didn't have anything against them. I knew them too well. Even now I have to tell myself that I can't think about *them*—only the way they're being used and what will happen if they're used successfully."

She said suddenly, "Give me your glass," got to her feet and stared at the road that wound down from the opposite ridge. He sprang up beside her. "What is it?"

She shook her head impatiently. "There's a bare patch—just on the crest of that ridge—between two stretches of pine." She thrust the glass at him.

He clapped it to his eye, swept the lens up the white slope, found the road, followed it to the first belt of pines, the next—

In the circle of the lens something stirred along the road, moved slowly, steadily on.

Ripley's hand began to shake. Eyes still on the road, he thrust the glass at Remembrance. "Oxen! And a sledge! Look, there's something else moving there—back of that first yoke! The guns! Guns for the siege!"

Remembrance, steadying herself with one hand on his shoulder, was hopping up and down crying that she had caught a flash of metal as the sun touched the distant crest.

Footsteps crunched in the snow behind them and he heard Grenda's tight voice: "Sighted their mast-heads."

Ripley spun about, caught Grenda by the arm. "Get back into town! To the wheelwright's. Get the cart on the road. Get the detail out. Tell Cuyler to meet me where the road dips down there. Bring my horse along!"

Grenda nodded silently and slipped about with his rolling gait down the path that led back to the town. Remembrance cried out: "More! Coming into sight." She held the glass to her eye and tried to focus on the road while she jumped up and down.

Ripley shouted: "What's the road like below here?"

"It dips right down again into a deep hollow. You can't see it from here. There's a little bridge, and a swamp."

"That's where we'll work!" He took a last look at the western ridge, then ran off down the path.

Her voice followed him. "Where are you going?"

He halted. "Back to town."

"Not without me! I saw them first and if you think I'm going to sit up on that hill and gape—" She caught up with him, rested her hand on his arm. "It won't do you any good to hurry because your sergeant only just went back. And besides I know the path and any-way—"

Ripley laughed. "Come ahead. I'll appoint you aide

with appropriate rank, pay, and emoluments. Is that all right?"

They started down the path, Ripley going ahead, while Remembrance, steadying herself with a hand on his shoulder, called out to him to turn to the right, to swing along past some boulders, to avoid a steep stretch.

At last they stood on the road, flushed and panting. She said: "Why don't you wait here for them?"

"No. I've got a better idea. I'm going ahead to look at the hill. When the cart comes up, tell them where I am and make them hurry. Tell them to have their gear where they can get at it."

She nodded, then said: "Will they listen to me?"

He grinned. "I'm not worrying about that. Just tell them what I said. I'll see you in town later." He waved and started off down the rutted road at a trot.

The way lay through rolling country, slight dips following gentle rises. As he ran, he studied the land on either side, noting a pine where a rope could be fastened, a clear, level space where teams could turn easily. "Now where the devil's that steep stretch she told about? A pony could haul a twenty-four-pounder along this bit. She couldn't have meant that little slope back there. She—"

He stopped. The ground fell away to the west in a killing grade and the road wound down it in a rutted zigzag, occasional boulders and heavy roots showing dark through the snow. He whistled softly. "This is it. God's bright face, how'll we do it?" He half ran, half skidded down a mile of wretched road, ended up in a deep pocket at the bottom where a shaky log bridge spanned a marshy stretch. Beyond the bridge, the road climbed again, vanished among pines and rocky shoulders. He grunted: "She called this a hill? By God, it's like the side of a house."

He made his way, stumbling and panting, back up the slope. As he swung himself up by a young birch near the top he heard Cuyler's voice: "Shall we go on?" Then came Remembrance's low, husky tones: "No. This is the best place you'll find."

Ripley scrambled up over gray, icy rocks. He saw Cuyler pulling in beside the cart and talking earnestly to Remembrance, who held the reins on the rough seat. Gragg's swollen face leered over her shoulder and the rest of the detail trotted in the snow beside the cart.

Ripley held up his hand. "Get that cart off the road! Quick! Tip it over on its side. Stack the rations and tools where they'll be safe. Grenda, I want you to stay up here with Brimblecome and Cash. Start rigging a block and tackle to that big pine." Cuyler swung down from his horse. "Joris, I want you halfway down with Gragg and Truman and Orne. Tell them to have plenty of heavy rope and all the tools they'll need. Understand?"

Cuyler grinned. "Had them divided just that way before we started out."

"Good work." He caught the bridle of his horse, vaulted into the saddle. "Ride down with me and I'll show you where I want you. Tell your men to keep going until they sight you."

They started down the wicked grade, their horses picking their way carefully and snorting in fear.

Cuyler said: "Who's the girl?"

"I asked you this morning about Dr. Morse. That's his daughter."

"Ho!" said Cuyler. "She hailed us from the side of the road and began spouting orders like a brigadier." He rubbed his nose. "By God, now that I stop to think of it, we all bit our knuckles and said 'Yes, ma'am.' 'No, ma'am!' "

"You didn't ask her who she was?"

"Rip, when she said you'd sighted the guns it sort of chased everything else out of my head. Damned if I can tell you now whether she's pretty or not."

"She is." Ripley reined in. "Here's where I want you

—just by this bend. There's a good straight run right down to the bridge from here and—"

Cuyler threw himself from the saddle. "Hey! You're right. I can run ropes from here—there's a good level space—start a fire over by those rocks." He ran about under the trees like a heavy-shouldered hound, testing the footing, kicking at underbrush, turning to stare down the slope toward the distant bridge. Then he shouted, "Bring on those damned guns!"

Ripley waved his hand and urged his horse down the road to the bridge, started up the other side, worked his way to a long, steady slope that stretched away to the west.

Somewhere up ahead a man shouted. Runners creaked. Then the road straightened and a yoke of oxen, horns and shoulders swaying with derisive slowness, wove a deliberate pattern along the white track toward Ripley. He could see the lift and dip of the yokes, a stumpy figure trudging listlessly by them. Things began to take on identity: a white blaze on the face of the nigh ox; the sawn-off horns of its mate; a red muffler about the throat of the driver; a long Biblical goad whose butt trailed in the snow.

Ripley stood in his stirrups, disappointment lining his face. Eighteen-, twenty-four-pounders? The rough sledge held nothing but six squat coehorns. Coehorns! Little, stumpy, short-ranged mortars. He shouted to the driver: "Who's in command here?"

The driver swung his goad across the noses of the oxen and the heavy beasts lurched to a halt. The next team, fifty yards in the rear, halted too. "Keep on going," snapped Ripley. "I'm just asking who's in command."

The driver spat. "Ain't anyone but me in charge of this yoke. They're mine."

"Who'd you get orders from?"

"Never took what you'd call orders from anyone. Just come out because the Committee to Schaghticoke said we was needed."

"Where are the big guns?"

"Ain't none bigger'n these. Just a lot of little pebble-flippers." He prodded his yoke into slow action.

Ripley rode on, swearing under his breath. "Nothing but coehorns? And where the hell am I going to find Knox?" He peered at the next sledge, saw three three-inch mortars lashed to it, gaping throats yawning at the sky. The next was loaded down with pigs of lead and its driver answered Ripley in surly grunts that told him nothing.

"Damn it," thought Ripley, "this is getting worse." Then he saw a rough cabin at the left of the road where a lone saddle horse stamped and shifted in the snow. He shouted, "Ahoy, the cabin!" and rode toward the flimsy door.

The door flew open with a crash and a vast figure, cloaked and hatted, filled the space. "Who the hell are you? Got word for us? I'm Major Crafts."

"Ensign Mayne. Reporting to Colonel Knox. Detail from Glover's regiment."

A mammoth hand shot out. "Get down off that damned horse and tell me about it. I'll do till Henery gets here."

Ripley followed the huge man into the cabin and held his hands out before a small fire. "I've got another ensign, a sergeant, and five men strung out along the damnedest hill you ever saw."

Crafts's heavy features darkened. "What the hell for? Do you expect to row us up the hill? Sounds like one of Gates's bright English ideas, sending seamen to us."

Ripley said stiffly, "We've got block and tackle rigged. I've got men who know how to use them."

Crafts sat down on a bench. "*That* was never Gates's idea."

"It was General Washington's and Colonel Glover's."

The major looked keenly at Ripley. "It's a good one. Say, you're no Marbleheader. How'd Glover get hold of you?"

"I'm from Concord. I went with him because I'd had marine training."

"Ho! Kind of a God-damned seagoing farmer!" He grinned. "Didn't mean to snap your head off. But if you'd been with us— A barge with guns sank in Lake George. We broke through the ice crossing the Hudson. We've had thaws that took the last flake of snow off the roads and mired the sledges. The men are ready to quit and the oxen are about dead." He slapped the bench. "I don't know how we got this far. Swear I don't. Why the hell didn't someone think of this sooner? We might have had some of the guns in Boston by now." He buried his head in his hands. "I'd about given up."

Ripley said: "I can't see why you had trouble. Those coehorns aren't much of a load."

Crafts jumped to his feet. "Coehorns be damned!" He lunged at the door, banged it open, and pointed to an approaching sledge. "Call *that* a coehorn?"

Ripley stared at a vast bulk of black metal. "That a coehorn?" shouted Crafts again.

Ripley rubbed his chin. "If it is, I'll eat it. It's a good eighteen-pounder. The drivers told me they had nothing but coehorns."

Crafts abolished the drivers with a gesture. "What's the road like up ahead?"

"Bad. But it can be done if the drivers know how to handle their yokes."

"They don't. Not for this sort of work."

"How far'll they go before you halt them?"

"Henery's heading them for three old houses beyond Great Barrington."

"*Beyond* Great Barrington? In the dark?"

"That's his idea. Send them over the worst hills when it's too dark for them to see what's ahead and get scared."

Fresh hoofbeats sounded outside. "You there, Tom?"

Crafts shot through the door, shouting, reappeared

in a moment with a tall, very fat man about Ripley's age. "Here he is, Henery!" cried the major.

Knox, stamping snow from his boots, smiled pleasantly. "The major's been telling me about you. Damn it, we can use you and your men." He studied Ripley for a moment. "I've seen you somewhere before."

"I used to come to your shop. You sold me Caesar's *Commentaries* and *Tacitus*."

Knox sat heavily on the bench. "Caesar and *Tacitus*, eh? The old London Bookstore." He sighed. "Well, we've got to forget about it and about fine bindings now. How's recruiting coming?"

"Slow, I'm afraid. The Massachusetts and New Hampshire militia have had to come back to man the lines."

The fat man pried himself to his feet. "They need a tonic and, by God, we've got it for them. Tom, those oxen have got to keep going day and night even if it kills them."

Crafts smiled darkly. "Mayne and his sea monkeys'll help us. Where are you off to now?"

"Great Barrington. Maybe I'll push right on for Springfield. I'll leave word with the committee. Now look here, Mayne, you can be a great help to us. We're broken up into divisions and some of them are ten miles or more apart. How've you planned to handle us?"

"Camp by the worst hills and wait until the last sledge is past."

"Suppose we get bogged down again after we've passed you?"

"Send word back and I'll find a way to spare a man or two for you."

Knox nodded. "You've another officer with you. How is he?"

"He can keep men working when they're asleep on their feet and make them like it. And he'll work harder than any of them."

Knox smiled somberly. "He'll have to. He'll have to be able to make corpses work before this job's done."

"He'll do that, too," said Ripley.

"Tom, I'm feeling better about this," said Knox, picking up his hat. "I'm off. You'd better take a cast back toward the rear and hurry up that next division. Good-bye, Mayne, I'll have an eye on you. Drop into my shop after the war and I'll show you some nice bindings." He nodded and strode out into the snow, Crafts following him.

Ripley mounted and rode back toward the bridge, overtaking a great twenty-four-pounder, two more eighteens. The drivers had halted their oxen and were muttering together, watching the fading light with surly apprehension. Ripley called: "What's the matter? Get your teams going."

A bony man in a long coat silently pointed down the road with his goad. Other sledges up ahead had halted. Ripley spurred his horse and trotted on until he came to the bridge. On the other side of the marsh the first load of coehorns stood in the middle of the road, the driver waving his arms while Adam Gragg glared at him, chin and nose jutting beyond mis-shapen cheeks.

Ripley swung out of the saddle. "What's the matter?" he snapped.

The driver ran to him. "This God-damn fool wants me to go up that hill! Look at it!" He threw down his goad. "I'm taking my yoke and I'm going home."

Gragg's apelike arms swept the driver off his feet and pitched him into a snowbank. Then the little man ambled back and faced the oxen. "Cast off!" he hooted. The oxen blinked in slow contentment. "Cast off! Whoosh! Whee!" The oxen shifted their feet and sighed deeply. Gragg looked sadly at Ripley. "Guess I got to pry that froach out of the snow and use him. Them beasts is anchored."

The driver, snow-covered, staggered to his feet and lunged back to the road. Ripley snapped, "Grab him and keep him quiet, Gragg." Then he picked up the goad and prodded the nigh ox. The animal and its mate stirred and began to plod on. There was a scuffle and feet crunched through the snow as the driver broke away from Gragg, roaring: "What you doing, using my oxen?"

Ripley called, "Steady, Gragg. I'll handle him."

"By God, I know my rights," raged the man. "I'm going home."

"Go ahead."

"I'm taking my team."

"Want another snow bath?"

The man was nearly crying with rage and cold. "I'll get you jailed!"

Ripley caught his arm. "Do you know where these guns are going? To the army. You've never seen it, but I have. Have you ever tried to drive a mad bull with a broken stick? That's what the army's got to do—until the guns get there. They're facing the whole British force with nothing but old muskets and a few bayonets. And what the hell are you doing? Bellowing for fear you'll sweat a pound or two off your yoke. You might as well be a Tory or—"

The man snatched the goad. "Guess another mile or two ain't going to hurt them. G'long, you!"

Ripley retrieved his horse and rode slowly up the hill. There seemed little to do at the first ascent. The sledges with the coehorns and the lead took it slowly but without much trouble. The mortars made heavier going of it but finally topped the crest. Then, halfway up, four pairs of horns showed against the snow. With maddening slowness they came on, lost headway, gained it, then stopped.

Ripley threw his reins over a branch and dismounted. The four oxen stood blowing and shivering while their driver, a stoop-shouldered man, kicked ineffectually at the clotted snow, pushed with one hand against the rear of the sledge.

"What's the matter?" shouted Ripley.

The man looked up. "Just too much for them." He pointed to the twenty-four-pounder inert on the sledge.

"Four oxen? They ought to do it with their feet tied."

"Too much. Might's well unhitch and go home."

"Give me that goad." Ripley snatched it from him, called to the oxen, who looked at him in mild surprise, then settled into the yoke and began to creep forward. He watched the curves of the road, worked the team as carefully as he could, taking advantage of each bend to lessen the grade. Then he heard a wild shout and Cuyler charged down the hill toward him, waving wildly. The sledge, well to the side of the road, began to slip, heading for a snowbank. Ripley yelled to the oxen, tried to work them more to the center of the road, but the sledge still swung toward the deep snow.

There was a sudden thud. The sledge shivered, its outer runner hanging over a steep drop where Cuyler lunged with a thick pole. Ripley dropped the goad, ran to the sledge. Cuyler's pole, rammed under the runner, had tilted it just enough to check the side-slip. "Good work, Joris," shouted Ripley. "Now, ropes!"

Cuyler vanished into the woods. Gragg, appearing mysteriously, plunged after him. Ripley prodded the oxen, but the tilt of the sledge had buried the forward runners deep in the snow and each tug drove them farther into the crust. Cuyler ran out from the trees, something clanking and rattling in his hands. He roared: "Clear, Gragg? Then come ahead!"

"Fast, or she'll slip again!" shouted Ripley.

Gragg scuttled out of the woods and knelt by the runners. Cuyler held a small block through which Gragg drove a rope. "Got the block hooked on?" panted Cuyler. Then he darted back to the woods, the rope trailing after him. Suddenly Gragg threw his arms wide. "Cast off!" he screeched.

Ripley studied the ropes that ran, black against the snow, from sledge to tree to sledge. The hitch was complete. The oxen leaned into the yoke, shivered, advanced one cautious step, another. The sledge stirred. Its front runners stirred, lifted slowly clear of the ruts, settled back on the road, and the sledge swung free. Gragg howled again and Ripley checked the yoke. The little man unhooked the block and ran for the woods, the rope swishing after him. Ripley handed the goad to the driver. "Take them along."

Cuyler lumbered out of the woods, and Ripley slapped his shoulder. "I thought we were gone then. Where are the rest of your men?"

"Farther up the hill, fixing blocks at a bad spot."

Ripley unhitched his horse. "I'm heading along. Back soon."

At the crest a small fire burned among the firs close by the cart. Grenda was stolidly watching Brimblecome and Cash cast an elaborate hitch loose from a big sledge. "All right, Hans?"

"So far," said Grenda tersely. "Better go over to the galley unless you fed down below."

Ripley left his horse at the edge of the road and walked toward the fire's glow. A small two-wheeled cart stood close to his own and shadowy figures moved in the light of the flames. One of them looked up as his steps crackled in the undergrowth. A husky voice said: "Just in time for fresh coffee and some hot soup."

Ripley put his hands on his hips. "Well—I'm—didn't I tell Grenda to see that you got back to town?"

Dark hair bent over a steaming pot, Remembrance shook her head. "You probably meant to."

"Meant to? I'm sure I told him. Look here, you've been here since early afternoon. Better climb on the next oxcart."

She held out a mug to him. "Drink that."

Ripley took the mug, sniffing happily as the hot steam rose. Then he said: "There's one with a light load coming up now. There'll be room for you. Good Lord, your father'll be calling out the minute company. You go morrising off in the morning and—"

"And come morrising back in the afternoon. Now I've just got this coffee boiling and there'll be men shouting for it."

"But do you know what time it is?"

"Somewhere between six and eight and that's close enough for me. No. Don't argue. I did go back to town on one of the horses. Then I went to the Committee and told them what was happening up here and begged a cart and supplies and got Mrs. Weale over by that big kettle to come along with me and we're going to stay until there are no more men or no more supplies. And don't worry about Father. He sent the coffee. He said that with so many loons on the road he'd be bound to get a cadaver or two and wanted to be sure that he only got well-nourished ones."

Ripley finished his coffee and watched the play of light on her hair and face as the fire flared up. Then he said: "You mean that you're going to stay out here?"

She dropped the long ladle into the kettle. "If it'll help move one gun one yard up this hill, I'll stay until my hair turns gray and see that there's hot food for every soldier and teamster between here and the Hudson. And if you think I need a guard or anything, you just don't know your own men."

Ripley nodded slowly. "I see. This'll have to go into the log. I've never seen a girl who'd—" But she moved away toward the bent woman at the other fire and began filing small wooden bowls. He watched her tall, slight figure, now dim in the shadows, now standing out clearly as the fire ebbed and rose. He thought: "No, I've never seen a girl like her before. I wish—well, anyway, she'll be here as long as there's a gun on the road." The thought sent warm comfort through him.

Suddenly Gragg tore wildly through the woods and floundered to a halt. He tilted his head back and hooked his mouth open. "Mwook! Mwook 'at. 'Eller 'ook a 'isel an'—" He stooped, spat blood into the snow, pried his mouth open again.

Little by little, Ripley gathered that Gragg had found a driver with a chisel, had held the edge against his tooth while the man banged the handle with a mallet. Delighted, the little man quacked on.

Ripley groaned. "You damned fool. I'd forgotten about that tooth. You ought to be lying by the fire. Go back up there and get some—" But Gragg had caught sight of Grenda and went galloping off, holding his mouth open and bellowing.

Evening deepened into night and still the slow procession wound up the hill. Sledges jammed their runners into snowbanks. Oxen gave up on steep grades. A load of gun flints overturned. But at each check, swift-moving Marbleheaders appeared with rope and tackle and stumpy mortar or lumbering twenty-fours were hauled out of danger and set back on the road again. On the lower slope Cuyler shouted, sang, heaved at terrific weights, stormed at sullen drivers, coaxed, laughed, threatened, and sang again. Ripley, ranging up and down the road, shouted: "Lean on that yoke! They need that gun, I tell you. Damn your molasses feet. Get them into that yoke. That gun's going to Dorchester Heights. More oxen for the eighteen-pounder. Five, six yoke!"

The night turned into a blur of snow and darkness and utter exhaustion. Once the block hitched to a sledge pulled loose and sent a ton of metal roaring down the road to bury itself in a snowbank while the oxen, pulling against empty air, pitched kicking to the ground. When the yoke had been straightened out, Ripley found that an ox had broken its leg. Sick at the agony of the fine beast, Ripley slammed a maul against its forehead and had the carcass dragged off the road. Then he turned his attention to the matter of dragging out the buried gun, a task that was accomplished only after Brimblecome and Gragg, the latter still spitting blood, had appeared from the night and cunningly slung blocks and ropes.

Again, a big twenty-four lay on its motionless

sledge, blocking the road. "What's wrong?" asked Ripley.

Grenda, snow-plastered, looked up. "It's begun to settle. If we had wind or tide to help us—" He shrugged. Ripley studied the frost-coated barrel. There must be some way— He wrenched his horse about, galloped to the crest. "Get that sledge with the barrels off the road. And the one beyond it. Unhitch those yokes. Damn it, don't argue. Get out of the way. Cash! Stand by with those ropes." He assembled eight oxen in a slow-moving string, hitched the last to the end of the rope that ran from the big pine down the mired gun. Then he prodded the lead ox, started the string down the slope parallel to the road. The long rope lifted, tightened, whined through the block. There was a flutter of action about the stranded sledge. It stirred, began to move slowly on. Ripley ducked his head, plodded down the long slope, his world narrowed to the white stretch about him and the lumbering feet of the oxen that hesitated, wavered, but never quite stopped.

An unmeasured time later, he leaned against a tree at the top of the hill, blinking stiffened eyelids and drinking hot soup while his men packed the kettles and bowls that Remembrance and Mrs. Weale had brought. He said: "Sure it was Major Crafts?"

Tired but still cheerful, Remembrance nodded. "He said to tell you that there'd be no more sledges on the road until tomorrow."

"That's good," mumbled Ripley. "Oh—ah—I meant to ask about your ankle."

Firelight glinted on her white teeth as she laughed. "You did ask me. That time the big mortar went by. The one the men called 'The Old Sow.' "

The hot soup was reviving him. He watched the play of firelight on her rounded arms, the easy grace of her slim neck as she turned. "You've done a mighty big piece of work."

She blew out her cheeks. "It'll win the war. Oh—I

meant to tell you. I saw you looking at our books. I tucked a copy of Chaucer into your haversack there in the cart. Grenda showed me which one."

"Chaucer?" Ripley set down his bowl. "I haven't read Chaucer for years. I'm going to enjoy that—so much that I'll probably forget to thank you. How did you know that I'd like Chaucer?"

"Oh—just the way you looked at our books," she said. "I was brought up on him. I love 'The Wife of Bath.'" Ripley raised his eyebrows. She went on: "I know most girls wouldn't admit it, but they like it, too. I'm saying good-night now. I'll be out in the morning before more guns come." She waved a soot-stained hand and walked off through the trees. Ripley watched the graceful sway of her hips. Warmth and light seemed to drift out of the woods with her, leaving him to the cold and dark and weariness of the night.

V

For three days more the detail stayed on the hill while sledges drawn by oxen or by horses fought their slow way east. The Marbleheaders slept in shifts as the road was rarely empty. Under a cold noon sun, under a full moon, blocks creaked and ropes hissed as great masses of metal were tugged up, up to the last level stretch. Twice Knox, fat and cheerful, rode by shouting encouragement. The huge Crafts appeared, stormed and roared among recalcitrant oxteams, rode off east again.

Ripley, ranging up and down the steep pitch of the hill, rigged up elaborate hitches with Grenda or Cash, settled wrangles among teamsters, snatched goads from unwilling hands and drove lumbering teams that had refused to move for their owners. Lower down,

Cuyler and Gragg and Orne flung themselves on stubborn loads, improvised capstans, hammered at broken runners, the Marbleheaders working in silence while Cuyler roared: "They've got to go through! God damn it, keep them moving!"

And always at the crest of the hill bright fires burned and kettles steamed under Remembrance's tireless care, and weary men tramped through the snow for coffee, for soup, for stew. Others from the town joined her, tended the fires, brought supplies of their own to eke out the rations drawn from the Committee.

Then, on a late afternoon when the westering sun was staining the ridges, Ripley felt a weary surprise as he saw Cuyler lumbering up the road, Gragg, Truman, and Orne trudging on at his heels. "What's the matter, Joris?" he called, his voice flat with fatigue.

Cuyler held out his hands, palms down. "That's all."

"All?"

"All. Everything. *Omnis*. Where's Grenda and the others?"

"Had a call this morning and sent them on. There's trouble about fifteen miles up ahead. Crafts came back."

Cuyler sank to a flat rock and wiped his forehead. "Well, by God, we've done it."

"Get on your feet, you ox butcher. Done it? Hell, we've only begun. Get the cart loaded and snake it on east as fast as you can go. I've got to sign more receipts for the Committee. I'll catch up with you."

The cart was wrestled upright, the horses hitched in. Ripley went to the fires, saw old men and women stacking kettles and pots onto carts, hand sleds. Day and night they had kept the fires going, had served hot food to the men on the road. Now their work was over and they looked tired, irritable. Ripley spoke to a fat woman who was grumbling as she scoured the inside of a small pot with sand.

"Where's Miss Morse?"

"Gone back to town. Now how I'm ever going to get this pot clean after boiling it day and night for a lot of Yorkers—Just trouble. Nothing but trouble."

Ripley felt sudden irritation, then choked it back. "I just want to thank all of you for the work you've done for us. It made a bad job mighty easy."

People looked at him uncertainly, almost sheepishly. Then a thin old man mumbled: "Well, seems like *some*one had to do it. Hey! Samanthy. Careful how you tie that skillet on. It's the one I brought to Springfield eight-ten year ago." One by one the carts and sleds trailed out of the woods and headed toward the town.

Cuyler shouted: "Here we go, Rip! All hands aboard. By God, I'm feeling good! Hills be damned! Mountains are what I want!" The cart bumped away east.

Ripley saddled his horse. "Damn it, why did Remembrance drift off like that? I wanted to see her." He climbed into the saddle and let his horse follow the rutted track. When he reached the Town House he found the Committee armed with detailed lists of supplies furnished. With a smothered oath he sat down with three lean gray men and went over each sheet, which showed not what the armed forces had demanded but what civilian authority had allowed them to have. After a long wrangle involving a missing sack of potatoes that was finally unearthed in the cellar of the Town House, Ripley signed innumerable sheets and stumped out to his horse, every muscle aching. As he mounted painfully he looked at the few people astir in the streets of the village.

"She might at least have said good-bye." He gathered the reins, swung the horse's clumsy head about. "Well, if she won't, guess I won't, either." And, having made this resolve, he rode straight to the house of Remorse Morse.

The doctor's saturnine face appeared at the door in

answer to his knock. "Thought you might be looking by," he said.

"I just wanted to thank your daughter for everything she did," said Ripley.

The door swung wider. "Come right in. I've been telling her that she worked hard. I further pointed out to her that a June bug scrambling in a bucket of molasses does too and with probably as beneficial results." He led the way to the oak and mahogany room where Ripley had carried the girl on his first night in town.

Remembrance looked up from the green sofa. She was pale but her smile was ready as ever. "This completes a cycle. I begin with one sprain and end up with another."

Ripley drew a chair forward. "Why didn't you let me know?"

"You were lugging a twenty-four on your back. I told one of the women to let you know. Then I got on a sledge and rode back to town in state."

"They never told me. Is it the same one?"

Her father said: "It is. Not that that makes any difference. If she had a third, she'd try to break it." He scowled at her. "At least you won't be flibbertigibbeting around for a while. Good-bye, Mayne. I've got to patch up two broken-legged teamsters so they can engage again to move Birnam wood to Dunsinane or whatever it is they think they're doing." He walked mournfully out of the room.

Ripley hitched his chair closer. "I really haven't had a chance to thank you—for everything."

She colored slightly. "We're the ones who ought to be doing any thanking. You're bringing the guns for every one of us."

"Ho! Of course. It was pure selfishness that kept you all out there. My men don't think so. Hans Grenda said you might have been a Marblehead girl, keeping a fire going on a beach for a ship aground offshore."

Her eyes shone with pleasure. "That's worth a dozen sprains. I felt that I was *doing* something."

"You were," said Ripley emphatically. "And we're going to miss you. There are a lot of hills between here and Boston and we'll all be looking for a fire with you tending it on the top of each one."

She stirred impatiently. "I'd give so much to be able to see the last sledge go down the last hill. And you'll be shepherding them right through to the end. Then what will you do? Your colonel ought to give you some time with your family after this."

Ripley shook his head. "Father's with the Massachusetts Congress most of the time. My mother died when I was about five. So I've just got the regiment."

"I'm sorry. You see, I know what it means. I lost my mother three years ago when there was so much fever in New York. Father was so busy looking after other people that she wouldn't admit she was sick until it was too late. She would have liked you and what you're doing. And she would have thought of kettles on the hill long before I did." She paused, then went on, "You'll go back to your regiment. Tell me about it. What's your colonel like?"

"I'd like to hear more about your mother," said Ripley.

"Some day I'll write you about her," said Remembrance. "Just now I want to know what you're going back to."

Ripley hesitated, then plunged into an account of John Glover, how he could put on a guard mount that even Frederick the Great couldn't find fault with; the next moment, he'd be going into the huts of the men, sitting and talking to them, calling them by their first names while they called him John—finding out about their troubles, helping them when he could, because Marbleheaders looked after each other afloat or ashore and rank only counted on duty. "He's giving up an awful lot," Ripley concluded, "to be colonel of the Fourteenth. He's had to give up all his businesses and he's got a big family besides. I've heard that he's found the seas pretty rough lately. But he won't give up. He can't, I tell you. He made that regiment."

She looked gravely at him. "You talk about Glover just the way Grenda and the others do. When Mr. Cuyler told me that you'd been at Harvard and wanted to spend the rest of your life farming, I thought it was funny that you should be with Glover and his boatmen. Now I see that you belong there."

"And take Joris," said Ripley. "He's New York Dutch and went to King's College and God knows how *he* wants to spend the rest of his life. You knew he was King's, didn't you?"

She smiled quietly. "Indeed I did. In fact he invited me to come down to the first graduation ceremonies after the war."

"He did!" cried Ripley. "Look here, I'm senior to Cuyler and I'm inviting you to come to Cambridge instead."

"I'd like to accept—both," said Remembrance.

"You'd like Harvard better. June in the Yard and flowers all around and the red brick showing through the trees. I'd take you into Hollis and show you my old room. I went in there last month and they still haven't put down new boards in the passage where I rolled a red-hot cannon ball in '71. We used them to heat the rooms in winter. There isn't much to the ceremonies and they're pretty dull but—"

She laughed. "I'm there already and enjoying myself." Her soft eyes darkened. "It must be sad, though. Troops in the Yard and the old buildings and nothing of the college going on."

"Wait until the war's over," said Ripley. "Harvard's weathered some bad storms in the past and she'll weather this." He watched a shaft of sunlight play across her hair. He said suddenly, "I wish there were more guns coming. Look at that sun. It means that I've got to join the detail and I'll be riding away from Great Barrington."

She smiled. "I'm sorry too. But we mustn't forget that those guns have still got a lot of hills ahead of them and that you're looking after them."

He rose reluctantly. "Yes. I guess so. And this means good-bye. I'm going to write you, you know."

She held out her hand. "I hope you will. I'll write back, wretched as the posts are these days."

He left the house quickly, still feeling her smooth palm resting in his. As he mounted and rode away, her picture was clear in his mind—not bound to the green sofa, but standing in the bow of a sloop that headed into a stiff wind, with her head thrown proudly back and her hair blowing out behind her and the breeze molding her clothes to her, a spendid, living figurehead.

* * *

Day in and day out, the Marblehead detail worked on, waited in the cold and the wind at the crest of each bad hill, shifting their feet in the snow and watching the pitch and toss of horns on the white road far below. The pattern of the march each day unrolled its slow course, flowed on to the next ridge, the next, through the black and red glory of sunset, through the lifting sweep of cold dawn.

The Connecticut lay before them and Ripley, for once, turned command of the column over to Cuyler and watched him fall like a whirlwind on the New York teamsters, who, homesick, had begun to unhitch their teams and head them back to the Hudson. Roaring and bellowing, cursing and storming in a weird mixture of Dutch and English, the heavy-shouldered man harangued, argued, pleaded. As the stars began to fade out the sledges started into cautious motion east and Cuyler, exhausted, panted to him that they would see the guns across the plain and across the river to Springfield but beyond that they would not stir.

Ripley nodded. "That'll be all right, Joris. Put Grenda in charge of the second group and don't look for me until you see me." He mounted and rode over the snowy plain, pounded into Springfield and laid siege to the Committee. Men he must have, men and oxen. The Committee listened, told Ripley to wait until they could see just how much the countryside could spare. Ripley pounded the table in the Town House, shouted that the countryside could spare anything except time, that the guns must go through. In the midst of his storming, Colonel Knox heaved his fat form through the door and into the meeting, backed Ripley up, showed a letter from Washington expressing fear that even now the guns might be too late. The Committee adjourned and began scouring the country. The long artillery train moved across the river and into Springfield. The New Yorkers were thanked, paid off, and slow-spoken farmers from the Connecticut Valley began to drive their lurching teams into the great square where the guns were parked.

Ripley drew a deep breath, counted the incoming teams and spent a whole night with Cuyler and Grenda over a map, planning the next moves of the detail. As they broke up their meeting in a gray dawn, rain began to patter on the roof of their house and Cuyler, stamping out into the slush that was turning roads and path into muddy ribbons impassable for runners, shook his big fists at the sky and yelled with rage. Ripley calmed him down and set Grenda and the others to overhauling tackle while he himself kept one eye on the sky and his face to the wind.

Then the thaw broke and the long train took its eternal course east. Palmer lay behind them, and Spencer. At Leicester they heard the bad news from Canada. The expedition wrecked, Montgomery killed and Arnold wounded. Ripley wondered about Febiger the Dane, about Sholes and hundreds of others who had marched out of Cambridge in the warm sun of early fall, hundreds who made up the now shattered forces so far to the north.

There was an easy passage through Worcester as the road skirted the bases of its swooping hills, trouble at the north end of Lake Quinsigamond where the shaky bridge threatened to collapse under the weight of the twenty-fours and doomed the column to a night on the road. Near Marlboro, a heavy sledge tipped over and for hours Ripley and Cuyler worked to extricate the screaming man pinned under the runners, only to see him die as the crushing weight finally yielded.

Day and night blurred into a series of bone-cracking heavings, of rebellious masses that slid the wrong way, of oxen whose hoofs cracked to the quick. Beyond Marlboro, Ripley lost Truman, whose arm snapped and shriveled as it was caught in the bight of a swift-running rope. There were night camps and day camps. There were freezing hours spent near a swamp where four sledges bogged down with their precious ordnance, but always the column lurched on. In brief snatches of sleep, Ripley dreamed that tatters of the army of the siege came pelting past him, dreamed that the guns were sliding out toward Roxbury and a waiting line of red uniforms. Waking, he routed out teamsters, routed out his own detail, shouting: "Get them through! They're going through. The boys are waiting for them!" Cuyler was everywhere, crawling over guns, under the hoofs of oxen, swarming up trees and casting rope ends down to Grenda or Gragg or Orne. Waking or sleeping, Ripley heard the calm voice of Knox insisting that the guns must go on, that he had pledged his word to General Washington that the train would be delivered.

"By God, Rip, that fat bookseller's a man!" panted Cuyler as he wriggled out from under a sledge at the crest of a hill. "Never had much to do with books outside of King's, but from now on I'm going to pay a hell of a lot of attention to folios and quartos!"

"So'm I," said Ripley, looking at the hitch. "Clear?

Grenda? Gragg? Cast off! Come on, Joris. Now for the next one."

Then on a frosty morning, following a thaw that threatened sledge and runner, Ripley and Cuyler gazed in silence from the hills of Framingham down to the plain that rolled on to Boston and the army of the siege. Cuyler, his voice oddly hoarse, shouted to the lines beyond the dim horizon: "Hang on, damn it! We're coming!"

Ripley's throat tightened and he felt a stinging mist in his eyes. The men of Concord and Lexington and Billerica, the men of Boston and Newburyport and Worcester and Marlboro, the men of Massachusetts, the men of New England, the men of America, could take heart. The guns for the siege were coming, coming to strengthen the lines that were held by men, by muskets, and by an idea.

Three days later, in watery sunlight, Ripley and Cuyler splashed down the soggy road that led into Beverly. They rode past the Capstan and Cuyler's mouth curved dolefully. Then the two stood in the orderly room of the Fourteenth where Captain Speakman, on duty for the day, stared at them in wonder and vanished into Glover's quarters. There was a sudden shout from within and Glover catapulted out, blue eyes snapping. "Well? What's your story? Where are the guns?"

Ripley drew out the carefully kept log. "The guns are at Framingham, sir. There's our report."

Glover snatched the shabby book, tucked it in his pocket. He snapped one arm through Ripley's, the other through Cuyler's, and dragged them into his room, kicking the door shut behind him. "Now out with it. Did you have trouble? How'd the men do? Where's Knox? How many guns are there? Damn it, don't stand there and stutter." He dropped their arms and began to tramp up and down the room.

Ripley cleared his throat. "Not much to report, sir. We met the guns west of Great Barrington. We rigged tackle whenever they got stuck. Now they're at Framingham and the job's done. Every man stood to his duty."

Glover whirled about. "Ha! You met the guns. You rigged tackle. They're at Framingham. That's a seamanlike report. Anyone hurt?"

"Truman, sir. Arm burned off in the bight of a rope. We left him with a doctor in Marlboro. And one teamster was killed."

"Killed? Bad. Damned bad. And Truman's arm! By God, the Congress'll do something handsome for him. I'll write Elbridge Gerry and Azor Orne tonight." He looked keenly at the pair. "You've been through rough weather, haven't you? Well, you're in port now. I don't care what you do tonight, but if you're not at regimental prayers tomorrow morning, I'll keelhaul you, because I'll be reading out some orders that'll concern you both. I'm making Hans Grenda an ensign and if he refuses rank again, I'll cut him up for lobster bait." He snatched up the log. "Got some reading to do. That's all. Good night, *Lieutenant* Mayne. Good night, *Lieutenant* Cuyler."

Out in the slush, Cuyler stared at Ripley. "Lieutenants! Do you think he meant it?"

Ripley pulled his cape about him. "Ever know the old Bull Seal to say anything he *didn't* mean?"

Cuyler's ruddy face broke into a grin. He bowed with mock solemnity. "Lieutenant Mayne, shall we stroll forth among the lesser species and swim in combers of rum at the Capstan?"

Ripley pushed him. "Get on down there, you mad Dutchman. I'll be with you in half an hour."

"And waste good drinking time?"

"No waste, Joris. I've got a letter to write." He waved Cuyler on and ran off through the slush.

PART FOUR

THE MARBLEHEADERS

For a month the guns lay in the Framingham mud as the two armies watched each other wearily. Day after bleak day, British and Tories and Patriots looked out on the encircling arc about Boston, at the naked bulk of Dorchester Heights. Then one morning they stared. The Heights were crowned with Knox's guns, whose muzzles threatened all the shipping in the harbor, threatened Castle Island, threatened the very rear of the British lines on Boston Neck.

Howe studied the new works, then attempted to mount a waterborne attack. A storm broke up this last stroke and Howe, not caring to face entrenched Americans again, with guns at their backs, suddenly marched his troops onto their transports, the Tories following in a drab, spiritless stream. On a sunny March day the harbor was white with sail and the great fleet stood out to sea, lingered about Nantasket Roads and then set a course north to Halifax.

Before the last redcoat had filed on board, the army that had been looped about the city for nearly a year flowed over the Neck and on into Boston. Long lines of citizens, wan and gray from the famine of the siege, stared and wept and stared again as the ragged regiments marched on down the Neck and past Boston Common.

The British gone, Washington weighed probabilities, made up his mind, and moved his army to New York, leaving a few regiments to watch for a possible British return. Among those left behind was the Fourteenth Massachusetts Infantry.

I

JUNE crept up the coast in a burst of blossoms, trailed on into July, and the Fourteenth still fretted in the salt winds that blew fitfully about Beverly. Late one afternoon assembly was sounded and the regiment fell in under arms. The ranks listened in silence as John Glover, face pale and eyes snapping, read out a long document which began: "When, in the course of human events, it becomes necessary for one people to dissolve the political bonds which have connected them with another—" It came from the Continental Congress in Philadelphia and was dated July 4, 1776. There was some cheering as the companies broke up, but most of the men tramped back to their quarters quiet and thoughtful. A few muttered that the step was too radical and drifted off to their homes.

The next day saw another assembly and the ranks whooped and yelled as the lieutenant colonel, Gabriel Johonot, announced tersely that the British fleet and army that had been attacking Charleston in South Carolina had been decisively beaten off. Speculation and rejoicing slowly died away and the Fourteenth settled back into its dull routine. Squads and companies spent weary hours patrolling beach and headland, watching for Howe's fleet, listening to every tag and rumor that drifted up from New York.

On a tour of inspection of the posts that stretched far up toward the great curve of Cape Ann, Ripley found Cuyler on a sodden beach angrily flapping his hat at high-whining mosquitoes. "Why'd you have to pick a time after sundown to look in on me. I've got things laid out so perfectly here that if Frederick the Great could see them, he'd make me a field marshal out of hand. You won't be able to understand a thing about them in this light."

"That's lucky for you," said Ripley. "If I could see enough to tell the old Bull Seal what you were really doing, he'd stuff you into a lobster pot and sink you off the Neck. Any other complaints?"

Cuyler fumed. "A cartload. One is, why the hell do we stay up here stewing, turning out the regiment every time an old woman sees a seal break water and takes him for an invasion fleet?"

Ripley slid from his saddle and stretched. "We're not missing anything by being here. Major Lee showed me a letter from his cousin in Prescott's. They don't do anything but dig. They're wearing out their uniforms and their boots and can't get new ones. I'd just as soon be up here, for the present."

"But I tell you, Howe's going to hit New York. The old Bull Seal says so. And we won't be there."

Ripley flipped sand at him. "You're right about Howe. But you're wrong about us. The first time Washington gets wind of a redcoat two hundred miles offshore, Glover'll get another one of his ideas and start us marching down there a week before orders come." He swung back into the saddle. "Well, I can't waste my time with junior company officers. I'll have some rum for you at the Capstan when I get back to town."

Cuyler groaned as Ripley gathered the reins. "And

I won't be back for another two days. Tell Glover that we're keeping a good watch. Up to sunset I'd seen seven crabs, a dead seagull, and two girls bathing in that little cove up there. That's my report."

Ripley started his horse. "Where'd you find a cove with bathing girls in New York? I'll tell Glover you've got no complaints and want to spend the rest of the war right here." Then he called over his shoulder. "Forgot to tell you. I stuck two bottles of rum in that shelter of yours."

Cuyler's bellow of delight rang in his ears as he started on his hour's ride back to Beverly. His mind was full of Remembrance as his horse clopped on.

A letter had come from her that morning. Closing his eyes, he could still see her full figure, tall and supple, bending over the kettles, recapture the huskiness of her voice. Why couldn't he have stayed longer in the western town? Her letters, allowing for the indifferent posts, had been amazingly regular, and seemed to glow with the intimacy of warm friendship. Once or twice, he had tried to put rather more than that into his replies. His tone was not answered, but there was no sign of displeasure. He began to wonder if, with the summer waning, Glover might not look with favor on a request for a furlough. He could picture himself riding into the little white town, could see Remembrance standing in the doorway, her lips parted in surprise and—he hoped—pleasure.

His horse shied violently, rocked him in the saddle as a dark shape dashed out onto the road. A hoarse voice bellowed: "Jesus Christ! Watch out! A squaw with the French itch'd ride a cleaner trail than that."

Ripley swung down from the saddle. "By God! Nahum! Where the devil did you come from?"

Sholes bellowed again. "Rip! I knowed I'd pick up your trace if I kept on going, but I ain't lotted on getting rid down. Where you think I come from? From the jail to Cambridge!"

Ripley slapped the old ranger's thick shoulders. "Damn it, man, you're supposed to be in Canada."

"Not by me, I ain't. I stuck right down the St. Lawrence with Arnold. Last month I got careless and let a Frenchy pitch lead at me and when I found they was taking me to a hospital I lit out. Figured I'd be safer in the woods. Then I come home, looking for you."

"Hold on, Nahum. That makes you a deserter."

"The hospital'd a made me a corp. I seen them before. Treated myself with moss and gum and, by God, right now I could march into a bear's jaws and come out with the teeth. Like in jail—"

"Why'd they pick you up?"

"Still a few soldiers to Cambridge and they called me a deserter. I hadn't fed, so I let myself get locked up till after feeding time and then got out easy as a snake going over a log. Look, Rip, all the way through the woods I been thinking I might maybe after all get one of them blue and white soldier suits, so long's I don't have to get into no boat. Think Glover'd take me?"

Ripley smiled. "He could use you, Nahum. But he's death on deserters. You re-enlisted in January."

Sholes roared. "Who says I re-enlisted? I was too damn busy fighting."

Ripley shook him. "You damned old fool. You're no more of a deserter than I am. You come on to headquarters with me, if you're serious. It's only about a mile from here."

"Guess I am serious, Rip. Course, it was kind of like old ranger days up there and the boys called me Mutton-lip, just like they used to. Hey! Ever tell you how I come to get that name? They was this girl up above Number Four and she— Look, Rip. You'll keep me out them boats?"

"You come on and talk to the old Bull Seal. Damn it, Nahum, it's good to have you back."

Two nights later, Ripley dozed fitfully in the hut

that was breathless with July heat. On the opposite bunk, Cuyler, back from outpost duty, snored lustily, oblivious of mosquitoes and the dead weight of the air. Ripley awoke, cursed the night, the winged pests and Cuyler, tried to sleep again. Suddenly he sat upright.

In the breathless air outside, hoofs drummed into the little town. Lights began to flare in the headquarters hut. Doors slammed and running feet ground along oyster-shell paths. Then a voice boomed, "Now! Now! Get them out on the road. Quicker than frosted hell!"

Ripley swung his feet to the floor, punched the sleeping Cuyler. "Up, animal. All hands on deck. The old Bull Seal's yelling like a conch in the fog."

Cuyler was on his feet in a single movement. "My haversack! There it is! Out my way. By God, I've made a vow that Blackler's company'll be the first to fall in. If I find a buckle loose on any of my men five minutes from now, I'll stuff his boots with sea urchins."

Ripley exulted. "Who was laughing at me for keeping packed up all the time? By God, Joris, it's come! We're going somewhere."

In the pale glimmer of false dawn, the Fourteenth fell in, was dismissed for an early mess, re-formed. A drum tapped and one by one the companies swung into column and stepped out on the long road that led west.

At first, marching in the darkness, Ripley was aware only of the steady beat of boots on the soft ground, and the creak and swish of equipment. Then the sun began to touch the treetops and the column took shape. The day wore on. The long blue mass halted, re-formed, moved on again, the men marching at ease. In the late afternoon, a drum beat the call for attention. Cuyler, plodding on beside Ripley, puffed: "Attention! What mighty brain ordered that? This isn't a parade."

Ripley craned his neck. "Cambridge already. Joris, we've been making knots."

The drum beat again. Cuyler dropped back to his place on the flank of Blackler's company. Then just ahead of Ripley the guard spaced wider on either side of the standard bearer. There was a sudden burst of color and the same flag that Glover had saluted for the first time on New Year's Day, 1776, floated high over bright bayonets as the Fourteenth came once again into the old college town. The irregular beat of boots became a steady, swinging cadence as the massed drums roared out, deep-toned. Fifes scaled high into the air, riding up on the first notes of "Yankee Doodle." Far down the street, heads bobbed at the windows of the college buildings and people ran shouting across the Common. A shrill voice yelled: "It's the Fourteenth!"

Now Ripley was abreast of the Common and the edge of the Yard showed at his left. Sight and sound seemed to lift him onto planes that he had never touched before. Bare, pit-scarred Common, mellow brick of the college—he had known them before. They had been part of his life. Now he was swinging past them, part of an American regiment, action-bound, with its new flag swaying bright against the sky, with its fifes and drums rolling out the defiant challenge of the dersive song that the men of the siege had turned into a hymn. Holden Chapel, Hollis, Harvard, Massachusetts, the yellow blur of the end of Wadsworth —their walls gave back the shriek of fife and the slam of drum and the beat-beat of the blue and white regiment from Marblehead.

Past, present, and future were flowing by under that flag as the tanned boatmen stepped off on their journey to fight beside men from the Maryland shore, the mountains of Pennsylvania, and the dagger-shaped island of Manhattan.

Then the tread of the regiment echoed against the houses of Boylston Street. The planks of the great bridge were underfoot, hollow and resounding. Beat, beat, beat, through the dust that rose from the opposite shore, the men from the coast breasted the miles that lay before them. Miles on the long road that led to the waiting American army that had lived through the first year of its test, an army that was fighting for no new lands, for no loot, for no plunder; an army that was fighting for nothing tangible, yet for something that embraced everything, was everything, was greater than everything—the idea of the freedom and the dignity of man.

II

Some days in advance of the regiment, Ripley and Cuyler rode past shabby guards in country clothes and crossed the Spuyten Duyvil at the King's Bridge that linked Manhattan with the mainland. Ripley drew a long breath as he looked for the first time on the towering palisades of the Hudson, stark in the light of the late afternoon. Cuyler stood in his stirrups and crowed with delight as well-remembered landmarks began to stand out. He pointed, waved, gesticulated in a steady flood of reminiscence.

At last Ripley leaned over and slapped his shoulder. "Look here, the old Bull Seal won't give a damn if you did catch a watersnake in that brook when you were eight. He wants to know where the brook runs and if we can land or embark at its mouth. And you'll have to have a damned good map to show him when he rides down with the regiment."

Cuyler grew calmer and the two spent the remaining hours of daylight trotting down little cart paths that led to the Harlem River, noting possible moorings, low, hidden cliffs. At nightfall the New Yorker rode into the yard of a gray stone farmhouse and a bent old woman looked cautiously out, then burst into a flood of English and Dutch to which Cuyler replied vociferously.

There they spent the night and at dawn rode out again, south down the island in the shadow of the great rampart of rock that hid the broad Hudson. Then the rampart ended in a wide plain where Harlem Village lay, began again and ran on down the island. Ripley and Cuyler forced their horses through a rocky defile that the latter called McGowan's Pass, from which the road slanted east. To the west, across a wild tangle of wasteland, another road showed. Horn's Hook, Turtle Bay, Kip's Bay, and the rising mass of Long Island; gray stone farmhouses, brick farmhouses; steep roofs and high, stepped gables; occasional great estates and pillared façades showing through parklike grounds—the narrowing island spread its panorama before them.

Under the climbing sun, the countryside began to come to life and they passed long strings of carts headed down the Post Road. Trickles of infantry on detail were met, named themselves in answer to Ripley's hail: Hand's Pennsylvanians in hunting shirts; Haslets' blue and red files from Delaware; more shirted men who drawled that they were Smallwood's Marylanders.

"It's a real American army, Joris," said Ripley, turning in his saddle to look after a party of New Jerseymen. "Makes me feel the same way I did in April of '75 when we saw the companies from other towns joining ours—the same only bigger."

"Something big's going to happen in a minute," said Cuyler. "See that house on the hill? It's Murray's. When we top the crest I'll show you something."

The horses moved steadily up a slope where a windmill turned lazily. They passed a spreading brick house and Cuyler stood in his stirrups. Then he spurred his mount and shouted, "Here we go." His horse shot on down the slope.

"Hold on, you idiot," called Ripley. "What's the matter?"

Cuyler headed his horse toward a high-shouldered stone house, step-gabled, that stood in a smooth hollow where apple trees framed a vista of the East River beyond a still pool, a formal garden. He swung off the road, jumped a low fence, and pelted on over smooth turf.

Leaping fences, swinging among apple trees, spanning a brook, Ripley finally caught up with the New Yorker, who was thudding to the ground by a high white stoop.

The half-door flew open and a little gnome of a man, long queue bobbing, bounced out onto the stoop, flung his arms about Cuyler, patted him on the back and tried to drag him into the house. Cuyler shouted: "Hold on, Father. Here's Rip Mayne, the man who led the press gang that took me up in New England!"

The elder Cuyler ran down the steps with sparrow-like briskness, shook Ripley's hand violently, dropped it, ran back and patted his son's shoulder again. "Come right in, both of you," he cried in an odd chirpy voice. He caught Ripley's elbow, tugged him up the steps. "Right into the river room, Joris. We shall have brandy." He clattered on into a broad, beamed room whose casements looked through an orchard to the East River. "Chairs! Anything that's comfortable! So you're Mayne! What's that boy of mine been doing?"

Ripley sat by a heavy carved *kas* and laughed. "Nothing much, Mr. Cuyler, except make a good name for himself in a very exacting regiment."

Erect before the delft-tiled fireplace, the birdlike man wheeled about, knees stiff and feet wide apart. "He has, has he? Do you know he's a deserter? There's a reward for bringing him back."

Cuyler grinned at Ripley. "Make him believe we're really on duty or he'll turn me in and claim the reward."

The old man tugged at a bellpull. "I would, sir. I

would at a moment's notice. He's still carried on the rolls of Alec MacDougall's regiment." He tugged again. "Where's that brandy?" A bent Negro shuffled in with a decanter and glasses. "Ha! Here we are. Serve it round, Bogardus, serve it round. Yes, sir. If you're deserting again, I'll give you up and spend the whole reward on brandy and drink every drop of it right in front of you. Bogardus, keep that brandy moving or it'll evaporate." He seized a glass, then called: "Sit still, sir," as Cuyler started to get up.

"The brandy'll keep. I'm going up to find Mother and the girls, though why they haven't fluttered down with all this din you've been making over your son's homecoming is more than I can see."

"Drink up and stop chattering. Your health, Mr. Mayne. The reason your mother and the girls haven't come down is because I've packed them off to Philadelphia. New York's no place for women these days and what else could I do except send them off with my only son consorting with loose characters in the New England woods? Get on with your story, Mr. Mayne."

Ripley told of the reconnaissance mission on which the careful Glover had sent them, doing his best to magnify Joris's part in it and to bring out other feats that had established the New Yorker among the Marbleheaders. Head cocked on one side, the old man paced up and down the hearth with stiff-kneed steps, his pointed face flowing with pride whenever his back was turned toward his son. When Ripley had finished, the father spun about and shook a thin finger at Joris. "Can't think what that man Glover's thinking about, giving you responsibility. He's just fishing for trouble and so are you. Ha! Hrrmph! So he made him full lieutenant when he came back with the guns, Mayne? Damn it, that was the least he could have— Ha! Your glass is empty. You're a military man. What do you think of things here?"

"Haven't had a chance to see much except the north

half of the island yet. If you don't mind my saying so, I'm in the dark about your sending Mrs. Cuyler and your daughters to Philadelphia."

The elder Cuyler thumped down into a vast, carved armchair that had "Gerardus Cuyler—1665" across its top. "I'm worried. People around here call me a pessimist, but I've got eyes, even if they are civilian ones. Damnation, I'm worried!"

Ripley studied the birdlike man, then said slowly, "You've seen something that you can't get out of your mind. Is it something that I can see?"

The father bounced up from his chair. "You can. See here, now. We'll all go into the city. Right now. We— Oh, damn it, no, we can't. Young John Jay's coming up from Kissam's office with some legal papers. I've got to go over them."

"I'll stay and help you," said Joris.

Ripley set down his glass and rose. "If you've got business to attend to you won't want me around. I'll go now if you'll tell me where."

Joris Cuyler nodded solemnly over his glass. "Rip's slow to move, Father, because he's a New Englander. You'll have to get used to him."

His father spun about. "If I could get used to you, I could get used to a camel with porcupine's quills. Mr. Mayne, you've got ideas and you aren't afraid to act on them. Come see me after the war and we'll do some business together. About the city. Go down to the Province Arms—it's right along Broadway past Trinity Church. Climb up into the cupola and you'll have a better view of lower New York than the angel Gabriel could ask for. Go up there and look until your eyes pop out. Then come back here and I'll ask you two questions." He tugged at the bellpull. "Bogardus, have the boys saddle up either Desperation or Ferocity for Mr. Mayne. He'll ride to town. Sir, I shall value your opinion."

Leaving the two Cuylers huddled over thick ledgers, Ripley rode out of the apple orchard and on to the junction of the Post Road and Bloomingdale Road.

Past the junction, he found a chain of forts that had been thrown clear across the lower end of the island from Corlaer's Hook to the Hudson. The city rose before him and he clattered on through straight, narrow streets where great mansions sat crowded by blacksmith shops, ironmongers, jewelers, butchers, ship chandlers, liquor dealers. Then he saw the tower of Trinity and beyond it a long building whose white cupola shone in the sun.

Ripley spoke to a liveried Negro by the broad door. The Negro looked surprised and showed him the stairs. On the second floor, Ripley opened a door, climbed again, and stood on the dusty platform of the cupola.

The mile-long city that covered the lower tip of the island lay spread before him, a welter of roofs pierced by church spires. The east shoreline was broken by endless wharves where masts swayed slowly to the tide. On the west the coast seemed empty. Ripley thought: "Joris's aged parent knows something. I can see about everything Glover wants to find out about the lower island. Let me see—on the east we can embark anywhere. West—west the shoreline's too steep. That means cliffs and deep water. We'll ride along it to be sure, but I'd say we'd never be able to handle green men from it. H'm. Good docks. Good roads leading down to them. Now what the devil makes the old gentleman so damned pessimistic?"

He studied the west shoreline and the new works, facing the Hudson, that scarred the summer green beyond the city limits. There, on rising ground and surrounded by star-shaped works, was the red brick of the New York Hospital that Dr. Morse had worked and fought for only to see his efforts killed by the war. North of it a big house shouldered above the trees and barely seen figures rode up a winding drive toward it—the Mortier house, where Washington had set up headquarters. He turned his attention back to the east, looked across the river at the hills about Brooklyn where fresh-turned earth showed ragged and raw about the new forts.

Then he looked south across the harbor. Governor's Island in the foreground and in the distance the dim outline of Staten Island. As he squinted his eyes at the hazy shore, white flecks showed against the dark of the land, moved slowly across his vision. He rested his arms on the rail of the cupola, deep lines forming about his mouth. This was what old Cuyler had sent him up to see. White flecks—sails. Two frigates at least, a ship of the line, a long string of transports.

He saw them move calmly about the north end of Staten Island. He closed his eyes, saw them coming up the East River, cutting between the American army on Long Island and its Manhattan base. He saw more ships passing up the Hudson, saw troops landing, perhaps in the strange depression between the ridges above McGowan's pass in the north, saw them land, as a feint, on Long Island itself.

What could oppose them? The American army, alone and unsupported, faced the British army and the British navy. His knuckles began to ache and he stared at them in surprise, not realizing how hard he had been gripping the rail. He looked down into the streets and saw people moving calmly about as though there were not a fleet of sixty-odd sail hovering off Staten Island. He turned and went stiffly down the steep stairs, claimed his horse, and jogged slowly back to the Cuyler house, eyes on the road.

When he entered the bright river room, as old Cuyler had called it, father and son looked up from their work. "See anything?" snapped the elder.

"A lot Glover'll want to know." He sat down heavily. "Can you tell me how in the devil's name Washington thinks he can fight with a big river between him and his base and another in his rear? God, it made me sick, just looking at it."

Joris smiled grimly. "You saw the big map at Glover's."

"That's not like seeing the real thing. Those ships! They can hit us in three different places at once. Washington must be—"

"In command of a national army, subject to Congress," said old Cuyler tersely. "Some people are afraid if we give up New York without a fight, it'll discourage the whole country. Have any special thoughts up in your perch, Mayne?"

Ripley rubbed his forehead. "A lot. Here's one. We made a big noise about the news of the whole Lobster army getting chased out of Charleston down in the Carolinas."

"June," said the elder Cuyler, nodding vigorously. "I set jereboams of brandy in the middle of Broadway myself."

"We should have gone into mourning," said Ripley dryly. "Do you realize that all the troops the Lobsters brought back from Charleston have been added to the force that Howe has over there on Staten? I know that. Heard an aide say so as I was leaving Province Arms. Don't you see that this is one time when we lose by one of our own victories? A drawn battle or a dawdling siege would have been a thousand times better than a win for us."

Joris confided to his father, "Rip'll always cure the crim-crams for you, no matter how bad they are."

The elder Cuyler said, "As a military man, how does the whole business look to you?"

"Bad," said Ripley.

"That means 'desperate' in New England talk," said Joris.

"That was one of the things I wanted to know," said the old man. "What else did you think about up there?"

Ripley slapped the table. "That we'll weather it, by God!"

Old Cuyler rose. "That's the other thing I wanted to

know. You've answered my two questions. Here comes Jay up the path now. Bogardus, load the table with all the wine it'll hold. Then move up another table. Time to think of food, gentlemen, and if Jay as much as mentions business while we eat. I shall throttle him with my own hands."

* * *

For two more days, Ripley patrolled the waterfront of New York until it became as familiar to him as the rocks of Nashawtuc Hill. Whitehall Slip and its now useless ferry to Staten Island, Coenties Slip and a straight run across the East River, Cruger's Wharf, Murray's, Beekman's. With Cuyler at his elbow he studied the stretch that ran along Dock Street from Fraunce's Tavern to Coenties Slip where Dutch and English names elbowed each other on heavy signboards: Brinckerhoff, Van Dam, Clarkson, Sebring, Abeel, Bywanck, Duyckinck, Gray, Livingston.

He came to know lower Broadway with the great house of the Royal Collector of Customs, of John Watts, Speaker of the Assembly, of Livingston, the Supreme Court Justice, of the van Cortlands. Hip-roofed English house and step-gabled Dutch, he felt that he knew them as he knew the sober fanlighted houses of his own Concord.

As he and Cuyler walked from wharf to wharf, they noted how the streets ran down to them, saw where hurrying columns of men might be jammed in the dark, where blind alleys branched off in a misleading tangle.

Then they rode up the west bank, out of the city and past the new works that looked down on the Hudson.

Each night they returned to the gray stone house where Joris worked with the blackest of ink on tough paper while Ripley read off sheaves of notes to be copied onto the growing map and the elder Cuyler strutted and pivoted about on the hearth, face alight with pride.

On the morning of the third day Ripley mounted his horse in front of the old gray house while the elder Cuyler embraced his son fiercely and then almost flung him bodily into the saddle. "Don't waste any more time!" he cried, small hands waving. "Get back to your regiment where you belong. You'll probably be tried at a drumhead as it is. And when you come down the island again, there'll always be a plate and a bottle and a bed waiting for both of you! There'll— damn my soul and eyes, what's that!"

Ripley and Joris swung about in their saddles, ears cocked to the north. It was faint at first, just a scratch of sound in the calm air. Then it hardened, cut on through the sunrise. Somewhere out of sight massed fifes and drums were rolling out the notes of "Yankee Doodle." The sound grew nearer and nearer.

Along the old Post Road where it curved down from Murray Hill marched a heavy blue column, bayonets glinting in the sun. Ripley shouted: "It's the Fourteenth!"

Old Cuyler began to hop up and down on his thin legs. "What? What? Are you sure? Bogardus! The wildest horse in the stable. I'm going to ride into New York with my boy's regiment!"

Another huge, champing horse was brought out and the three headed past the ornamental pool and the nodding roses. The long blue column was closer as they came onto the public way. The music had stopped but the men swung along with a free rhythmic stride.

Ripley felt a sudden lift as he began to recognize faces in his regiment. Captain Courtis and the first company, Grant's men, Orne's, Bond's. Then a knot of horsemen showed in the gap between Bond's and Swasey's and Ripley shouted to Cuyler as he caught sight of the familiar gingery-headed man on the bay horse.

Glover threw up his hand, swung his horse to the side of the road, Johonot and Lee following him as the column tramped on past. "You've found out what I want? Cuyler, that map you drew before you left couldn't have been better. Could have steered a course by it in the dead of night. Mayne, I want you two to see me and Johonot and Lee as soon as we come alongside."

Ripley saluted while Cuyler, flushing with pleasure, introduced his father. Glover touched his big hat. "Your servant, sir. Got any more boys like this one? I'll sign them on for any cruise I take."

Old Cuyler, stiff with pride, shook his head. "One was enough. I'd aged forty years before he'd aged ten. Colonel, my house and grounds are at your disposal. I'll be honored, sir."

"You're very kind. But we're sailing under orders. I'm to set up headquarters at a place called Hazenclever's Farm. Anyone know where that is? Guides were supposed to have met us in Harlem but they must have slipped their cable."

The two Cuylers looked dubiously at one another. Then Ripley said, "The southernmost house in Greenwich Village. It's just north of that new line of works they finished yesterday."

Glover grinned suddenly. "Then you can guide this New Yorker there and we'll follow." He bowed courteously to the elder Cuyler. "I'd be glad of your company, sir. There'll be a lot that you can tell me as we ride along."

The mounted party galloped up to the head of the regiment and fell in behind the musicians. The column wound away down the Post Road and then struck west along a narrow way that led between high bushes and saplings where the summer wind tossed and ruffled bright leaves.

Ripley, riding beside the sardonic Lee, asked: "Sure that's right about Hazenclever's?"

Lee smiled grimly. "I could never have invented a name like that."

Ripley stirred uneasily in his saddle. "We ought to be over on Long Island. Hazenclever's means that we'll just sit and watch the Hudson and there's no chance of a landing there. Not this far down the island, at least. No, we ought to be across the river or at least on the east shore here."

"You don't argue with the harbormaster about anchorage."

Ripley shook his head, dissatisfied. He had not been over to Brooklyn but he sensed an air of uncertainty in the details he'd seen about Whitehall and Coenties or the Fly Market. Organization seemed to be loose and the long summer of digging about Brooklyn had ruined so many uniforms that some units looked as unmilitary and unsure as had the men of the nineteenth. The trim, tight Marbleheaders would have produced a fine effect on Long Island.

Then the Hudson shone before them and the regiment, marching at ease, began to comment professionally on the wind squalls that swept down the broad stream. The houses of Greenwich Village blotted out the view for a moment and Ripley trotted up beside Glover. "This lane to the left for Hazenclever's, sir." He pointed to a snug brick farmhouse whose mounting gables baked in the sun.

Glover stood in his stirrups. "Someone there waiting for us. Someone—hell and death! They seem to have turned out a regiment to welcome us. Halt the column!"

The fields beyond the house were swarming with men, some in tattered uniforms, some in worn civilian clothes. In Hazenclever's broad doorway, a slim young man picked his teeth and languidly watched the approach of the Marbleheaders, road-worn but trim.

Major Lee swung his horse out of the column and trotted ahead. The languid young man looked up, still plying his toothpick. "This Hazenclever's?" Lee's voice rolled back to the column. "Ready for Colonel Glover?"

The young man looked surprised. "No. It's been reserved for us." He adjusted the sash that hung about his green velvet coat. "Been here two days."

"Well, you'll have to leave, I'm afraid. We're the Fourteenth and—"

"We're ten Bronck's Fourth New York. Quarters are ours." He jumped aside as a fat, red-faced man in a brown and blue coat came to the door. "Yankees, Colonel. They want our quarters."

Ten Bronck began to sputter. "We've got orders—in writing—to come here and—"

"So have we," said Lee.

"But I'm here. Damned if I'm going to—"

There was a sudden flurry as the rest of the riders came up to the door. The elder Cuyler scrambled down from his horse and flew at the fat colonel. "Ike ten Bronck! Do you mean to stand there and tell me that you won't make room for John Glover and his regiment? I used to fish with your father by Martje David's Vly and now I see a son of his disgracing the name of New York." He waved his arms. "Get your men out of here. Run them over the cliffs! Drown them. I'm meeting with the Committee tonight and—"

Ten Bronck fingered his lapels uncertainly. "Didn't see you at first, Mr. Cuyler. But I got my orders." His obstinate chin set. "Got orders same as he has. I'm here first—"

Hoofs pounded down the road that led south toward the city and a young aide in a faded sash galloped up shouting: "The Fourteenth! Is this the Fourteenth?"

Glover swung his horse out on the road. "It's supposed to be, young man."

The round-faced aide panted. "But you ain't supposed to be here. You're supposed to be at the hospital. Major Tilghman ain't going to like it when he hears you're traipsing up here."

Glover said to ten Bronck: "I'd like to see your orders." He followed the fat man into the house, then came out, nodding to himself. "They're in order, Johonot." He turned to the aide. "How in God's name am I going to know if we're expected in the hospital?"

"I've got it in writing!" The aide burrowed in a tight pocket and brought out a crumpled sheet.

Glover took it, stared hard at the flowing script. Then he smoothed out the sheet and slipped it into his jacket. "So far's I can make out, orders come out of any quarter the wind can blow from. My first came from Nathanael Greene over on Long Island. These for ten Bronck's are signed by Iz Putnam and the last are issued by Tilghman in the name of Washington. Set a course for the hospital, Lee."

Along a baking road that ran behind lines of fresh works by the Hudson, then through leafy tunnels where the air hung close and heavy, the sweating men of the Fourteenth marched. Joris Cuyler pulled his horse alongside Ripley's and mopped his steaming face. "My God, what sappy work! Ever think that we may have to move across the river with orders like those coming in?"

"Trying to get it out of my head." Ripley looked off to the left where the roof of the Mortier house showed above the trees. "That big Virginian's got to take a turkey wing and sweep some of the chaff off his hearth if we're going to have a chance around here."

Cuyler nodded solemnly. "He needs the aged parent to help him. Did you see how he went after ten Bronck? If that damned aide hadn't come along just then, he'd have chased him out of the place and we'd be sitting in the shade opening up the rum I've got in my saddlebags."

A breath of cooler air blew down the green funnel of trees under which the regiment marched. Cuyler crowed: "Home at last! There we are, Rip."

The trees fell away at the end of the lane and the city of New York appeared beyond the head of the column. The elder Cuyler waved to Glover and set out at a gallop toward a red brick building whose white dome crowned a gentle rise at the head of Broadway. A thick wall of sod, higher than the head of a mounted man, surrounded the neat grounds and a wide deep ditch ran at its foot.

Cuyler chuckled. "We're in luck. Big, cool rooms, our own works right in the yard."

The column trailed in through a sally port while old Cuyler waved and shouted from the high white stoop. "Bring them on, Colonel! And if any chuffs try to oust you, they'll have me to deal with." He whirled away into the building, reappeared at a second-story window. "Empty as a cornhusk!" he crowed. "You'll have as much room as a field mouse in a jereboam!" Then he was on the stoop once more, scrambling onto his horse. "Jereboam! Gives me an idea. I'll send a few of brandy over to you. This instant!" He snatched at Glover's hand. "Proud to have my boy in this regiment. Just one look at it made me ten years younger." He shot away down the drive shouting instructions to his son and to Ripley.

The regiment filed away into the wide grounds and began to pitch sailcloth tents in the shelter of the empty works. Cuyler went racing off to find Blackler's company while Ripley tramped after Glover, Johonot, and Lee into the cool hall of the hospital.

Glover flung open a door, peered into a big room where a long table and a few chairs were the only furniture. "Must be their countinghouse. Gentlemen, we'll drop anchor right here and listen to what Mayne has to say. Cuyler'll be along in a minute."

Ripley spread Cuyler's fine maps on the dusty table, began to explain the principal features of the lower island. Cuyler, still wiping his forehead, clumped in and five heads bent over the maps.

At the end of an hour, Glover pushed back from the

table. "Gentlemen, I must say I don't like it. I don't like this—" he put a thick thumb on the waterfronts—"I don't like splitting the army on two sides of this river. I don't like what we've seen of the way orders travel. I don't like anything."

Lee rested his elbows on the table. "What are you proposing?"

Glover jumped up. "I don't like any of it. But then I don't like war. However, I'm in the war and I'm going to stay in it. I'm here and I'm going to stay here. Johonot, I'm going to ride to the Mortier house back there and report to Washington. Better come with me. Lee, get the captains together and go over those maps with them." He turned to Ripley and Cuyler. "You two, for the rest of the day, sleep or get drunk or find a pretty barmaid. You've saved us about a week's work and a month's worry and you're free until sundown." He walked out of the door with his quick step, shouting: "Bring my horse alongside!"

Cuyler found a cool corner. "Rip, you can have all my rum and all my women until sundown. I'm going to sleep."

Ripley left him snoring gently in a long corridor and walked on through the hospital. The wards were empty and bare of furniture but they were clean and airy with big fireplaces. Remembrance had told him how her father had planned each brick and plank of the long rooms, had ridden over others who held out for the old small-windowed wards, shouting: "Light and air! We've been smothering patients long enough. Sun! Wind!" Now the morose doctor's dream would house a regiment of infantry, perhaps more. Its grounds were cut up by trenches and hemmed in by walls. In the angles that faced the Hudson, twelve-pounders thrust their black snouts and the empty wards echoed to the tread of a lieutenant of a Massachusetts regiment. It was easy to understand Dr. Morse's fury, Ripley thought as he leaned on a stone sill. He sighed. Remembrance must have had his letter telling of the regiment's move days ago.

III

THE August weather held clear and hot. The Marbleheaders clung to their sailcloth shelters on the hospital grounds, from which they marched out in reliefs to watch the empty stretches of the Hudson from the high works. Through a scorching noon, Ripley walked along the rear of the lines where Blackler's company, with Moses Brown's, stood watch. A voice hailed him from a cunningly propped sailcloth shelter and Cuyler's face, sunburned and with peeling nose, looked out. "Been at Mortier's? Any news?"

"Lobsters are still hanging off Staten Island, if that's what you mean." He waved a white packet. "Here's real news, though. Got a letter from Great Barrington."

"Ho!" shouted Cuyler. "So you're burrowing off like a cony to read it in your lair, are you? If undue influence hadn't got you onto staff, you'd be trying to read it sitting in this red-hot hob with the sweat dripping off your nose."

Ripley grinned. "If I get five minutes to myself I'll be lucky. I've got home mail for Glover and a stack of army orders. You'll be napping in the shade while I beetle around New York in the sun!" He waved the packet again and cut down through a shady lane that led into the hospital grounds. Remembrance had answered promptly. He had only dared take time to break the seal and look at the first lines, but the warm tones of the opening words had flooded him with pleasure.

He entered the hospital through the back door and put the stack of papers on the table of the big orderly room. Glover evidently had not returned so Ripley, with a thrill of joy, spread out Remembrance's letter. His smile deepened as his eyes moved slowly over the sheet. ". . . Had your note telling me about the Fourteenth leaving Beverly, so you must be in New York now. Somehow, I like to think of your being closer, even if only a little. I've thought so much of the days when you were here and our talks in the house and on the hills. I've thought of them when your letters came in and when they didn't. If things stay quiet down there and Colonel Glover will spare you, please don't forget about your furlough plans. You could reach here quite simply and . . ."

Ripley raised his head and stuffed the letter into his pocket. Out in the anteroom, voices began to buzz, then grew stronger. He recognized the tones of Gabriel Johonot. ". . . Now some people might think that I was urging this because I wanted command in your place."

Then Glover's voice, oddly flat and tired, broke in. "No, no, Gabe. Not you."

Ripley started. He couldn't leave without passing through the anteroom.

"Then I'll say it again, John," went on Johonot. "You've got no right to stay here. You've got no right in the army. Your oldest's not more than twelve and, damn it, you can't have them on charity—town charity."

"I know." The tones were flatter than ever. "But I've signed for the cruise."

"You signed for a cruise, years ago, with Mrs. Glover. How about that?"

"How about the regiment?"

"How about your family on charity? I'd help if I could. So'd Lee. So'd anyone in the regiment. But we're not rich men now. You go back, start trading again. Then maybe in a year or two if this is still going on, you'll come back to us. If I'm in command,

I'll step down any time you get within hailing distance. John—you've got to."

Almost inaudibly came the reply. "I don't know. I just don't know. Giving orders to others is easy. Giving them to yourself's another thing."

"There's only one order you can give yourself and more I can't say." Johonot paused, then resumed, voice formal. "Any further instructions, Colonel, about the work parties?" A door slammed and the voices died away.

Ripley suddenly realized that his hands were damp and shaky. Those rumors, heard long ago, from Beggs and others, were true, horribly true. The Fourteenth without Glover? Johonot was an able man but Glover had raised the regiment, trained it.

The door creaked and Glover walked slowly from the anteroom. His face was grayish and his eyes dull. He asked: "Anything for me, Mayne?" and his shoulders sagged as he dropped into a chair.

"Just—just this," stammered Ripley. Then he burst out: "Colonel! I've been eavesdropping. I couldn't help it."

A tired hand lifted. "It's all right. It doesn't matter."

"I ought to have banged a door or something. I— Look here, Colonel, I'm not a Marbleheader and you don't know me the way you know the others. But I've still half interest in my farm. Cuyler'll help. I'll see him soon's he comes off duty."

The gingery head shook. "I appreciate that, Mayne. I swear I do. But—it wouldn't help. This is war. If anything happened to me, what I'd borrowed'd fall back on my family, sink them deeper."

"But this wouldn't be a case of a loan. It—"

"Not to you. I know that. But to me. I don't know what to do. Maybe I'm choosing the easiest course, staying here as colonel." He lifted his head slightly. "You say I don't know you. I do. And that's why I'm talking now, not as colonel to lieutenant, but as one Massachusetts man to another. Yes, maybe it's easier

—for me. The regiment? Bah! It doesn't need me. It can sail itself. Discipline? The men have had it all their lives on ships. Standing guard? It's like standing watch at sea. Fighting? I've never fought. Johonot, Lee, Blackler, Courtis, could do as well as I, maybe better."

"I'd heard rumors, sir, but I never knew it was so bad."

"You thought of my businesses? I had plenty. *Had.* But you can't trade and dicker and still run a regiment, not the way it ought to be run. My wife writes she'll manage as long as the war lasts. She will. But have I got the right to let her? And the children. How about them? Maybe I'm worth more to the country keeping things moving in Marblehead than trying to steer a regiment that doesn't need steering." He sat silent for a few minutes, staring at the empty fireplace. Then he said: "I've got to do it. I nearly did when we started to march down here. Now I've got to." He rose, then sat down quickly. "No. I can't do it. Not in cold blood. You know about forms. Draw up my resignation. I'll sign it." He pushed a quill, a lead inkstand, toward Ripley, then got up and locked the door.

Ripley picked up the pen, dropped it. His throat felt oddly tight as he said: "No. I can't write it, either. You're the regiment and the regiment's you." He jumped up. "My God, Colonel, can't you see it falling to pieces with you gone? Can't you see—"

"Would you care to draw up a petition to the town of Marblehead asking that John Glover's family be treated as public wards?"

Ripley sat down dully, his mind refusing to grasp the fact that the peppery little man to whom he had first talked in Cambridge over a year ago was to vanish from the scene. He said, in a carefully controlled voice, "There are the orders from Mortier's. And a post from home."

Glover's hand reached out mechanically for the

packet from headquarters, touched it, then slowly shifted to the thick, folded paper from Marblehead. He broke the seal, the parcel from Washington lying unheeded at his elbow.

Ripley set his teeth and began to write. "To His Excellency, General George Washington, at Army Headquarters at the House of Abraham Mortier, Esq. Sir: I have the honor to inform Your Excellency that—"

A low cry from the colonel made Ripley look up. Glover, eyes on the letter he was reading, held out one hand. Then he rose slowly, muttered: "Not yet! Not yet!" He got up, walked slowly to the window. "We'll make port yet."

"Make port?" Ripley's voice was eager.

Still looking out the window, Glover said almost to himself: "My brother Jonathan. Disposed of property I'd held worthless." He threw back his head, faced Ripley. "Tear that up. I'll hold the tiller to the end of this action, anyway. My keel's in deep water for a few more leagues and by God I'll hold the course until I'm in shoal water again." He stepped briskly to the table. "Where are those orders? Get things sorted out. All captains are reporting here in an hour for a council." He broke open the packet from Washington, riffled through the papers. "Here. See to this. About latrines. Here's an order we've carried out already. Acknowledge. This says we're getting the flints I want. Have an ensign and five men go down to Coenties to draw them."

Ripley, bent over his work, drew a deep breath of relief. The old Bull Seal would not leave the herd.

IV

All through the hot morning of the twenty-seventh of August, there had been muffled firing from Long Island, small arms and artillery. As Ripley stood in the angle of the lines that faced the Hudson, he was reminded of the sounds that had drifted to him from distant sections of the battle road on April 19, 1775. There was nothing to see from the Hudson lines. The green spine that ran down toward the tip of the island cut off all view and the harbor beyond was shrouded in a dancing haze that even hid Governor's Island.

It was hard to keep the men's heads turned toward the empty Hudson, and weather-beaten faces unconsciously swung about to stare at the belt of trees that cut off the drumming eastern world. Ripley forced himself to study the flatlands of the Jersey shore and the turtle head of Paulus Hook that baked in the sun, unreal and dim beyond the shimmer of the river.

Sometime after noon, Cuyler puffed his way along the redoubt, his face shining with excitement. "Rip—got a rumor. Washington's left the Mortier house. He's gone across to Long Island. We've captured Howe in a coach and four and—"

"And we chased them into Gravesend Bay as soon as they landed. And here's another rumor—half our men have run away and half have deserted. There hasn't been any fighting and Howe and Iz Putnam are having a parley over some brandy."

Cuyler sighed. "I suppose. Damn it, why can't we *know* something? I can't sit still."

"I feel pretty safe, Joris. I've seen the plans of the forts over there. They're good. We've got guns. Maybe it'll be Bunker Hill with a different ending. Hi! Here comes the relief."

Cuyler wrinkled his nose. "Militia! Simeon Carey's men from Fellows's Brigade. Massachusetts militia."

"Scares me, too, mixing militia and line regiments. The militia hasn't been together long enough to be any good. They're only out for thirty days or so. Come on, let's get the relief over."

Ripley turned the section of line over to an anxious-looking farmer from Plymouth and started back to quarters with his men. Their uniforms were beginning to show signs of heavy wear but the tightness and solidity of the ranks was still evident. He watched Blackler's company file past with Adam Gragg and Nahum Sholes bringing up the rear, the ex-ranger still looking a little lost in the indefinable salt tang that hovered about the Marbleheaders.

At the hospital the men were dismissed and other companies came filing in through the sally port of the hospital works, relieved from other sections of the Hudson line, Instead of seeking the shade of their tents, they gathered at the Broadway end of the grounds and stood with their ears cocked to the east. It might be merely a shift of the wind, but the sound of firing was only faintly audible.

Inside the big hospital with its cool corridors, no one had word of events on Long Island. No messengers came down from the Mortier house and no aides galloped up Broadway. Toward the middle of the afternoon, the elder Cuyler came stamping in. He said that he could see the heights about Brooklyn and Wallabout Bay but had been able to make out no signs of activity that told him anything. He stared at a map on Ripley's wall and then went shouting through the corridors for his son.

Ripley drew up a report of his first tour of duty on the Hudson lines, slipped it into a pigeonhole, and wandered about the corridors. Glover appeared once, listened frowning from the stoop, and plunged back into the cool of the building. Major Lee, coming out with an armful of papers, shook his head in answer to Ripley's inquiry about news.

The shadows outside began to lengthen. Ripley sought the cubicle where Gragg had rigged up a hammock for him, and pulled a copy of *Tom Jones* from his pack. He'd forget about the uncertainty for an hour or two and lose himself in the adventures of Tom, Thwackum, Blifil, Alworthy, and the fair Sophia. He opened the book at random. "It was Mr. Western's custom, every afternoon as soon as he was drunk, to hear his daughter play on the harpsichord." He chuckled, turned down a corner of the page to show Cuyler. He read on. The book grew heavy in his hands and his eye-lids drooped.

Suddenly he sat up, wide-awake. Out in the grounds a drum was beating the assembly. Boots pounded along the corridor and a hoarse voice shouted, "Lieutenant Mayne! The colonel wants Lieutenant Mayne!"

The book clattered to the floor as Ripley swung to his feet, settling his stock and buttoning his short jacket. He ran down the broad corridor while companies of the Fourteenth fell in rapidly on the trampled grass outside and harsh tones began to rattle through a roll call.

A door slammed behind him and he recognized Glover's quick tread. "There you are, Mayne!" The colonel struggled into his coat. "It's just gone six. I'll give you ten minutes to scrape up as many men as you want—within reason—and go down to the docks. The regiment'll follow in embarkation order as soon as it's dark and I want you to leave one of your men at every spot where the route you take swings away from the main streets." He caught a questioning look in Ripley's eye. "No! Haven't got orders. Didn't I tell you back in Beverly that you've got to be ready to obey the order that's two beyond the one you haven't got yet? It's because no one's sent for us that I figure we'll be needed like grease for a creaky wellsweep!

And I don't want to know which dock you're going to. Find the best with the most boats and drop anchor there. Don't listen to any orders. Remember how it was when we came to Hazenclever's. Now cast off!"

Ripley ran out onto the grounds where the regiment was standing at ease, found Major Lee in charge and told him Glover's orders. Lee nodded in silence. Ripley made for Blackler's company. "Sorry, but I've got to have Cuyler and Brimblecome and Cash and Orne. Likewise Sholes and Gragg. Don't worry. They'll come back to you in plenty of time."

Blackler shrugged and called off the names. Cuyler, a wide grin splitting his face, asked, "What's this? Going after more guns?"

"Yes, but you won't have oxen," Ripley answered. He added to himself, "And you won't have anyone making hot soup for you, either." He lined the men up and explained the work in hand. Then he marched them out of the grassy sally port while curious heads looked after them from other companies.

There was aimless activity along Broadway where apprentices were putting up shutters on shop and warehouse windows. Anxious-faced men rode peering through the dusk, and files of infantry in poor order drifted down toward the wharves, drifted dully back. Supplies and equipment were stacked in random heaps in the side streets, unguarded.

Leaving men posted at each corner, Ripley turned down Wall Street, again at Broad Street, always making for the wharves. As he came down onto the waterfront with the remains of his detail, clouds of men rose from the ground, ran toward him shouting questions. Ripley waved them away and stared across at the heights above Brooklyn, inscrutable in the dying light. There was no smoke haze, and the forts were silent. The whole scene looked as it had looked to him on other evenings.

Along the New York side, clusters of sloops, galleys, gundalows, and pettiaugers rocked to the tide while men lounged on their decks. Ripley halted the detail. "Joris, you'll stay with me. Gragg and Sholes, head upstream and find out everything you can about those boats. Are they under orders? Who's in command? Are they seaworthy? Things like that. Orne, you hit downstream and do the same. Keep in touch with me. I won't be far."

While his men prowled about the docks, Ripley tried to find someone in command, someone with authority, but the same haphazard air hung over the waterfront that had struck him in the town.

One lean sallow man said he guessed he was in charge, scratched his head, said he guessed his orders only applied to Delaware troops and he didn't know where they were.

Dusk was thick as he came back to Coenties Slip. Cuyler clumped up and said that he'd found a space by a warehouse where the whole regiment could form and maneuver. One by one the detail crept up, muttered the same tale of uncertainty. The boats were privately owned. They were army boats. They belonged to ferry companies. They didn't belong to anyone. And, repeated over and over, no one was in charge of them and no one had orders.

Time slipped by. Lights began to tremble across on the heights and chains of fires glowed in the great loop of Wallabout Bay. Cuyler, yawning by a bollard, said: "Think old Bull Seal's changed his mind?"

Ripley shook his head. "Never knew him to—" He straightened up. The dull mutter of the streets behind him was cut by a rhythmic tramp. A voice roared: "Fourteenth! Wheel to the left."

Ripley and Cuyler sprang to their feet and the detail lined up behind them. A dark blur showed up Broad Street, feet beat stronger, and the Marblehead regiment swung down onto the waterfront, ranks firm and bayonets aslant. The lost men and the idlers began to stir, crowded gaping about.

Hoofs slapped along the column. Glover's roar beat

against the warehouse front. "Mayne! You there?" There was a sound in the dark as the colonel's feet hit the ground and he roared on. "Horse? Horse? I don't want a horse any more unless it's a sea horse. Take that beast back. Mayne!"

Ripley ran up and reported. Glover wiped his forehead. "No orders yet. We'll wait another half hour and then by God we'll seize everything that can float and get over somehow."

Up Broad Street a voice bawled, "What regiment's that? What regiment?"

The halted files grunted in disgust. Someone called, "The Bass Rocks Bashi-Bazouks! Who the hell do you think?"

An unseen horse pulled up and a squeaky voice piped: "Who said that? Who said that? God damn the militia. I want the Fourteenth!"

Glover shouted: "Silence between decks!" He darted off in the dark. "This is the Fourteenth. What do you want?"

The hidden voice wailed: "You're not supposed to be here. You're supposed to be in your camp."

"Ho! Am I? What am I supposed to be doing there?"

"Waiting for orders. Major! Major! They're here! It's most irregular."

Lanterns began to flash along the docks and an excited voice shouted: "You, Fourteenth! Come right down here by platoons. Don't hurry. I'll show you how! Can't have men falling into the water."

"My God!" groaned Cuyler. "He'll show us how!"

A small shape darted down the docks. "Who's that giving orders?"

"You speak when you're spoken to. I'm Major Glenn, in charge of embarkation. Who the hell are you—?"

"John Glover, commanding the Fourteenth. Out of the way." Glover's voice boomed. "Prepare to embark by companies! Mr. Mayne, you'll take charge with Mr. Cuyler."

Anxiety, fear, fatigue, ebbed away from Ripley as

he saw the marching files divide neatly, trickle away into the flatboats, and seat themselves, while a sergeant in each boat gave crisp orders to the New York ferrymen. One barge pushed out, another, and still the files came on. Ripley, holding his lantern high, felt grim satisfaction as the men headed toward him, split, trailed off to right and left. The long hot hours on the Beverly beaches, along the Charles, were justifying themselves.

Then Cuyler shouted, "That's the last company. By God, Rip, three of those barges got loaded and into the stream in less than a minute."

Ripley lifted his lantern again. There was no trace of blue and white along the waterfront. He pushed Cuyler into Blackler's barge that was just shoving off from the dock, heard a low mutter as a sergeant called roll, a detail on which Ripley had long ago insisted.

The barge swung into the current and began to edge slightly upstream, following the string of lanterns that marked other moving craft. The secret highlands to the east showed harder, black against the black sky, guarding their answer to the unspoken question that strained up from the laden boats: "What of the American army?"

The current lapped harder against Ripley's barge, shoved its nose around. Then a dull halo of light glowed from the Heights. At least, the army was still there, hanging onto the peninsula that jutted from Wallabout Bay south to Gowanus Creek. The men on the benches, slowly losing the spell of the march through the dark and the lantern-lit embarkation, began to mutter. ". . . And I ain't felt what you'd call right till we got that whiff of marsh up the Sound marching in that day." . . . "It ain't so. You don't alter course until you raise the Roaring Bulls." . . . "—Had caught a seal and hadn't more'n started to flense him when—"

Then there were more lights along the shore, a swelling hum of voices, and Ripley lurched as the boat brought up alongside a frail wharf. He sprang ashore, called: "Prepare to disembark!" The center files rose, picked their careful way forward. Boots echoed on the planks. Then the starboard files followed, the port and the whole company formed swiftly, tramped off to join the earlier arrivals by a lantern-marked rock.

There were other figures on the beach beside the Fourteenth. Back of the wavering lantern light, dim forms moved, shifted, and there was a babble of confused speech. "No. I *don't* know where our regiment is. First thing I knew them damned Germans were in our rear and flank. Then—" . . . "Joe! Joe! Who's seen Joe?" . . . "I tried to get to him, sir, by the milldam back there but the Scotch cut him off and—" . . . "We got butchered. I seen them Germans hold a wounded man and run him through! I ain't—" . . . "Let's steal a boat and get home. God, let's steal a boat!" . . . "No, sir. All I can tell is they got around in our rear."

The words, the quick accents of panic, sent a deep chill through Ripley as he ran to the solid ranks of the Marbleheaders. He saw Cuyler's face in the glint of a lantern, calm and smiling as he muttered words of encouragement to the men of Blackler's company. "Seen Glover, Joris?" he asked.

"Up beyond the right company. Say, Grenda's growling because you took the rest of the Knox chaps and left him out."

"Couldn't leave Blacker with no officers." He ran on past the rear of the company.

Grenda's pique at being left out of a piece of work somehow cheered him in its contrast to the slackness back in New York and the confusion and panic along Wallabout Bay. Those men on the beach were badly shaken, but couldn't be taken too seriously. At least, the bulk of the army was still up on the heights. Green men must have seen a temporary setback and been unnerved by it.

He saw a lantern up beyond the right company.

Then another lantern flickered, shone on the legs of a slim hunter, and a strong voice called: "What regiment is that?"

A small shape moved toward the light. "Fourteenth Continental, General."

From the ranks Ripley caught a murmur—"By God, it's the old Virginia Grampus himself."

Washington's voice, sharp in the dark, rapped out. "The what? The Fourteenth? It can't be!" More hoofs clopped on the wet sand and a lantern, held high, shone down on the tight features of the colonel. "Glover! How'd you get here? I only sent the order—"

"I know. My boys happened to be round Coenties and we got the order sort of early, sir."

A grim chuckle sounded. "That's all right." He called to an aide who materialized out of the darkness. "Guide the Fourteenth to the left. They'll join on by Fort Putnam. You're ready to march, Glover?"

"When you say, General."

To muffled commands the Marbleheaders swung into column and began a slow, black climb that took them through the dark streets of Brooklyn village, then up a steep ridge that was foul with mud. There was nothing to see save the dull flare of the fires along the distant crest of the ridge but all along the way Ripley moved through a broken drift of men hurrying toward the beaches and the wharves. Unwittingly they brought news to the Fourteenth of the day's fight, spread it in panting sentences, in shaken, scattered words: a thousand or more men lost; three generals captured; colonels, lieutenant colonels, majors, from Pennsylvania, from New York; the swift-moving men from Maryland; the trim Delaware regiments flung away in a last desperate stand that ended in death and rout.

Through it all, the Marbleheaders moved on steadily, lowering their heads and setting their shoulders as though they were nosing into a nor'easter off the Grand Banks or a tearing gale by Norman's Woe.

Then they had topped the crest and the companies turned left past massive works that rose high into the night. Trampled grass succeeded turf walls, and bayonets and muskets filed away into a shallow redoubt.

Ripley found Glover with Johonot and Lee in a small bay at the rear of the redoubt. A lantern glowed on a torn map over which hands moved. The Colonel looked up. "Mayne? Don't need you. Better berth with Blackler's so I'll know where to find you."

Ripley fumbled on through the dark until he heard Cuyler laughing with the stoop-shouldered Grenda.

"Got to give me garret space for a while, Joris," said Ripley. "What's orders?"

"Hang on here and watch. Blackler's back there with Courtis."

"Watch? What, in God's name?"

He peered over the parapet. Night had shrouded all landmarks and there was no way of telling how far or how close were the lines of fires to the south and east, fires that flickered and glowed. Once or twice Ripley thought that he could see men passing between him and the light, but it might have been nothing more than the rise and fall of the flames. Cuyler joined him. "There they are, Rip."

"That's what I've been thinking. Feels damned odd, doesn't it?"

"Not like watching them at Breed's or Bunker's," Cuyler muttered.

"Stand by," said Ripley. "Here's someone coming along the parapet!"

A lantern danced and winked, threw light downward on two pairs of legs, one long and high-booted, the other short and quick-stepping. A strong voice was saying: ". . . And I'm afraid I'll have to spread you out more to the left until Magaw and Shee get here. I tell you, Glover, our left was in the air until you came up."

The lantern bobbed away along the parapet. Someone in the dark said: "It's that Grampus again. Gets around, don't he?"

Cuyler muttered, "They never cheer him, but he makes them feel better, just being around."

"Just the way he takes me. Wonder where he's going with the old Bull Seal. I'm going to get some sleep. Wake me when you want a relief." Ripley rolled up in his blankets in an angle of the redoubt. Five minutes later Cuyler was shaking him. "Washington says you've slept long enough. Get on your feet."

Ripley, snatching up his blankets, was aware that men were falling into a single line back of the redoubt. He made a hasty pack. "What's the matter, Joris?"

"We're moving up front."

Blackler appeared at his right. "Hear that, Mayne? We've got to relieve some New York and Connecticut militia. They've got an outpost about a hundred yards in front. I'm sending Grenda and Cuyler *and* half the company. You better go down and have a look. Glover may want to know what it's like."

The half company started out through a narrow trench that wound away from the redoubt. The air was stifling in the deep cut and Ripley panted as he worked his way along beside the column. Then fresher air was in his face and he knew that he was in the open again. He heard Cuyler hail: "Hello, the post. Why the hell didn't you challenge?" His voice suddenly dropped. "Rip! Get up here!"

Ripley ran on, snatching a lantern from one of the men, and caught up with Cuyler. The light fell on a long line of trench that stretched away to the right and left. It was empty, save for a broken musket that lay on the trampled fire step.

"Been raided by the Lobsters," said Cuyler.

"Maybe." Ripley turned. "Halt the relief. Pass the word back for Nahum Sholes."

The old woodsman came trotting out into the main trench and began a minute inspection of the earth, crawling about the floor, the fire step, on hands and knees. Then he rose. "They pulled foot."

"Sure?"

"Them feet marks ain't lying—not to me."

"When?"

Sholes's thick hands felt along the ground. "Not long after sundown. Wa'n't no fight. Just pulled, that's all."

Joris stirred briskly. "Bring the relief on. Sholes, you work to the right and Brimblecome to the left. Find out how far this trench runs. Grenda, better send back word to Blackler about this as soon as they get back."

The two men slid off through the dark along the mystery of the trench. Presently they were back, reporting that there was a stretch of a good fifty yards on either side of the right-angled junction with the communication trench. Grenda slid off back to the main lines. Cuyler rubbed his chin. "One hundred yards of works to hold and twenty men to do it with. Maybe they'll send another company out. Maybe Blackler'll send us the rest of ours." But Grenda returned with the news that not a man could be spared. Cuyler would hold the line with the men he had, and Ripley was to stay with him.

"Good!" said Cuyler. "Let's take a look around."

They spaced the men economically along the parapet that was formed of earth-filled gabions. Beyond that there was little to do. Ripley leaned on the earth wall and stared out into the night, muttering to Cuyler and Grenda. "This place, so far as I can see, isn't so important, but—"

"So far as we can see," said Grenda.

"But," said Cuyler. "That *but's* the big point. If people have been hauling out here, they may have been hauling out all along the line." The three fell silent. At that very moment, red columns might be creeping up on other abandoned works, might be feeling their way forward along the very beaches below them. Cuyler sighed. "Go get your sleep, Rip. I'll wake you if anything happens. Hans, you get some sleep, too. We'll all stand watch through the day."

Shortly after midnight, Ripley relieved Cuyler and resumed his staring into the night that was slowly filling with sounds. Somewhere off behind the line of British fires he caught the creak of wheels. Once he heard a distant challenge as a British guard was relieved and a fresh one posted. A new wind, stirring among the trees, set him peering through the dark, tense with alarm.

Then the sky in the east began to pale, and with the first fading of the night heavy drops of rain fell. The men swore and wrapped old cloths about the locks of their muskets. Ripley woke Cuyler and Grenda and with them drank rum sparingly and gnawed at cold salt pork. Out in front there was nothing to see in the wet day. About three hundred yards in front of the trench, whose nakedness was now horribly apparent, a thick belt of trees masked the British lines.

Toward noon, Ripley went back to report to Blackler and got orders to return to the post. Through the long, wet afternoon he and Cuyler watched the belt of trees, fascinated. Suddenly Ripley started. "Something's moving down there. See? Where that brook turns and goes down among the trees."

Cuyler swept raindrops from his face and stared. "Men. Rip! By God they're in blue! They're digging. Listen!"

The east wind, driving stronger, brought the sharp clink of metal against stone. "Blue," muttered Ripley. "Blue—God in a thunderhead, Joris, they're Germans!" He stared at the wet tree trunks. Once a man in a miter-shaped helmet that glistened in the rain stepped into the open, ducked back among the trees.

"What's it mean, Rip?" asked Cuyler.

Ripley began to pace up and down the muddy floor of the trench, his sodden uniform dripping, and tried to reason out probabilities. Howe had won a battle the day before. There could be no doubt about that. Why hadn't he followed it up? His men, unlike those of Bunker Hill, had been fresh enough. He had thousands of them. Why? Why?

He suddenly turned to Cuyler. "Joris, can you speak German?"

Cuyler, his eyes on the woods, shook his head. "Only bush Dutch and not much of that."

"I can," said Grenda.

Ripley looked at him. "German? Real German?"

"Grenda ain't what you'd call a Marblehead name. My folks came down from the German settlement up in Maine before I was born. But we always talked German at home."

"We're going out."

Cuyler jumped down from the fire step. "By God, I've either got to move or get drunk. Of course we'll go."

"Not you, Joris. You're in command here."

"But—"

"You can't leave the post without an officer in charge. If Grenda doesn't go, there's no point in going. I'm in charge of nothing so there's no reason why I can't."

Cuyler banged the butt of his fusee on the ground. "Damn it, I suppose you're right."

"Hans, we'll take three men with us," said Ripley. "Sholes, of course. This'll be old work for him. Who else?"

"Cash and Gragg."

"Gragg? My God!"

"He acts kind of crazy when he ain't working, but you saw him with the guns last winter."

Ripley called Gragg, Sholes, and Cash, the latter a tall, sad-faced man who rarely spoke and never tired. "Nahum, I'm in command but you're the leader. We're going down to the woods and see what the Germans are up to."

Sholes licked his lips. "Easy as drinking pigeon

milk. We ain't taking muskets. Just knives. All you fish boys got 'em, ain't you?"

Gragg brightened. "For gutting cod." He clapped a long blade between his teeth and nodded happily.

"All right," said Sholes. "No hats. Nothing that'll swish or catch in the bushes."

"Good," said Ripley. "What's your course?"

"Soon's its real dark we'll go out to the brook that runs parallel to us. It bends at right angles and goes smack down to the woods."

The night was thick when Sholes led them from the redoubt. Ripley, crouching in the bed of the stream, followed on through the water whose chatter and gurgle, mingling with the beat of the rain, shut out all other sounds. Close by the woods, Sholes slid from the water and glided off to the left, belly flat to the ground. Ripley slipped after him, laid a hand on one of the ranger's heels as agreed, felt his own foot caught in Grenda's hand.

Trying to copy Sholes's snakelike progress, Ripley squirmed on after him, followed, as he slid off to the left, the blur of his hand in the darkness pointing to the ground. He put out his own hand, felt fresh earth, and sensed that his guide was following a line of unfinished earthworks. The crawling line dipped deeper into the woods, swung out, dipped again as the fresh scar in the earth wound its geometrical way along.

Suddenly Sholes stopped. Ahead and to the left, Ripley saw a dull glow. He pressed close to the wet ground, every nerve alert. Once he thought he heard footsteps, braced himself, then found that he was listening to the drip of the rain. Sholes resumed his course, working in a wide circle toward the group of men crowned with miterlike caps who huddled about a fire in a lean-to. Soon Ripley could hear their voices, strange and guttural, and signaled Sholes to stop by tugging at his foot. Behind him he knew that Grenda had raised himself slightly, listening. Five minutes passed, ten. Ripley could see the Germans, knees huddled to their chests, filling long pipes. Once they sprang to their feet as a stiff figure stalked in among them, spoke roughly, walked away again.

Then a single voice began to sing:—

"Ein' feste Burg ist unser Gott!"

A deep-swelling chorus picked up the next line, filling the woods with rich resonance. Even through his tenseness, Ripley felt a sense of wonder. Here were men from a Rhine province, singing German hymns in the Long Island woods, while beyond their vision, Marbleheaders listened—largely because his own townsmen had resolved, on a warm April morning, that British troops should not destroy the white houses at the foot of the Concord ridge.

He felt a tap on his heel, pressed Sholes's, and the slow progress continued, bearing back toward the trench and the rest of the Marbleheaders. Twice Sholes halted, raised himself on his elbow.

Ripley's heart changed from a quick beat to a powerful hammering as Sholes kicked three times—the danger signal that meant scatter and every man for himself. He repeated the motion, then counted ten. The darkness in front of him no longer moved. He stirred his foot cautiously, found no one behind him.

He lay listening, wondering what could have startled Sholes into giving the alarm, but he could only hear the beat of his own pulses. He tried to get his bearings but even the trees seemed swallowed up in the night and the rain. Panic gripped him. He was lost. The Marbleheaders, at sea almost from birth, could smell their way through the blackest night so far as the points of the compass lay. Sholes, from a lifetime in the woods, moved as easily as by day. As for himself—

He dropped his head, froze like a rabbit. The regular beat of boots sounded somewhere behind him. A man coughed, spit. The steps came nearer, began to die away again, going at right angles to his course. He got to his feet, ran on through the night. Then he sprawled at full length, cursing the root that had tripped him. But roots do not shout sharp orders, do not flash lanterns. He was hauled to his feet and a dark lantern glared in his eyes. He tried to wrench free, found his arms securely held from behind. The dark lantern flashed again and he saw a hard-faced swarthy man studying him. Senses returned, he covertly noted the bearskin cap with its black metal plate, the blue facings on the red coat. The Fifth. One of the line companies, for there was no match box on the cross belt. The officer, an ensign by his shoulder knot, motioned to one of the men to release Ripley. The man held the lantern while the ensign ruffled a small notebook. The other soldier held a bayonet point between Ripley's shoulders. The ensign said: "What regiment?"

"South Carolina militia," said Ripley.

The officer laughed. "You don't speak like a Carolinian. I've served there. What regiment?"

"Try guessing."

"They'll do that at headquarters. So damned few of you chaps are in uniforms that they'll probably stuff you and put you up somewhere. What were you doing?"

"Out walking."

The officer scratched his head, the bearskin tilting over his nose. "We'll find out, you know." He stowed away his notebook. "What I can't see is why Darby's patrol didn't nobble you. They were just ahead of us." He picked up his fusee, balanced it in his hands, and the two guards stepped aside.

Ripley's brain began to hum with excitement. "That patrol? They're over there." He jerked his head sharply back. In that instant, three bearskin heads turned to his motion. He snatched the ensign's fusee by muzzle and stock, drove it hard into its owner's face, left his feet in a wild spring, hit the ground beyond the prostrate officer and rolled upright.

In the dizzying whirl of returning to his feet, Ripley saw the lantern flash on steel, saw one of the guards lunge at him with his bayonet, miss. The other sprang across the writhing body of the officer, poised, then threw up his arms, his musket clattering to the ground. From the shadows a stocky form dashed out, snatched up the musket, fired at the second guard, shouting: "By platoons—charge!"

The soldier raced off shouting: "Turn out the guard! They're attacking in force!"

A vast hand closed about Ripley's arm. "Get going. They'll be tumbling out like whores to market day."

Ripley matched the ranger's pace. "Where'd you come from, Nahum?" he gasped.

"Ain't picked up your trail after we scattered so I come back to see. It's all right to run now. We're a hundred yards from where they patrol. I hollered enough to make them think I had a battalion with me."

"How did you manage? When I got to my feet that first guard was down in a heap."

"That was me. Throwed a knife soon's I seen you move. Here's the parapet."

Ripley shouted, "The post! Coming in. Me and Sholes!"

Gragg's gnarled face popped over the wall, vanished. Ripley swung himself into the trench where Cuyler seized him. "My God, Rip, don't do that again! Christ in the Catskills, you had me scared!"

Someone said: "All right? Sure you're all right?"

"Where's my hat? Hans, Nahum, come on. We're going to see old Bull Seal."

They stumbled back through the streaming night and Ripley, with a wry smile as he remembered the infinite ceremony attached to addressing rank in the British service, shook the sleeping colonel. Glover bounced up, wide-awake at once. "Yes? What is it?"

Ripley reported briefly. Glover sprang to his feet

and paced energetically up and down, his sodden cape swinging about him. "Digging a parallel and connecting works, were they?"

"That's the way it felt, sir."

"Sure of the direction?"

Sholes said: "Like to be that sure of salvation."

Glover turned to Grenda. "And it was the von Mirbach regiment you listened to? You didn't hear more than Mayne reported?"

"Only that they ain't figuring on moving against us right away. They talked about a siege. They said, too, they ain't killed many of our men. Just took prisoners. Said we killed a lot of British."

Glover whirled about. "That's the realest news I've heard since I dropped anchor here. It means they'll dig in and try to blast us out. No more Breed's Hill for them. And our Virginia friend's going to know about this quicker than frosted hell."

"What'll he do?" asked Ripley.

Glover smiled for the first time. "If I knew, maybe I'd be in his place. Get back now. You've done a good piece of work. Damn few people think at all, let alone thinking for themselves the way all of you did."

The three hurried away through the rain that was driving across the heights of Brooklyn in unceasing fury. Sholes chuckled: "I'm minded of the time I got to get called Mutton-lip. Ever hear about it? They was this girl swimming in a creek, see? Well, she—" He fumbled in his belt. "My knife! Where's my knife?" He ran off through the dark shouting: "Adam Gragg! You got my other knife!"

V

THE RAIN carried on through the rest of the night, into the morning. Clothes were like sodden corpse wrappings that lay icy about shoulders, numbed arms into helplessness, and made walking a shade more agonizing than standing still. From the parapet that was gradually melting into a gluey mass, Ripley watched the slow life down among the trees, three hundred yards away and well out of range. Once a small party of Germans crept out of the woods, worked their way along, and were met by draggled English, vanished with them among the trees. Twice Blackler inspected the redoubt.

Ripley looked back at the broad sweep of the East River. Little by little those works among the trees would creep forward, by sap and by parallel, all along the line. Closer and closer. What then?

He muttered his throughts to Cuyler and Grenda, who stood miserably in the mud of the trench. "Right up to us?" said Cuyler. "Damned if I don't hope they will. These works aren't so bad."

"I know," said Ripley wearily. "The works are all right. But Blackler said when Little's men came up last night they found that men they were supposed to relieve weren't there. And the men who were supposed to take over from Hitchcock's Rhode Islanders never showed over the skyline. Hitchcock's still holding where he was, I suppose."

Grenda growled, "I put to sea once with a crew that ain't ever worked together before and wasn't sure it wanted to work anyway." He jerked his shoulder toward Fort Putnam. "Guess this is kind of like that cruise."

Cuyler shook a sheet of water from his hat, clapped it back on his blond curls. "Washington's got word of what you found out—about the works down there. He'll be doing something about it. Maybe attack and break them up."

Ripley's eyes turned back toward the river that lay between the army and distant New York. "Maybe—" He broke off, jumped to the parapet, shielding his eyes against the rain.

"What is it?" asked Cuyler.

"Come up here, both of you, and tell me what *you* think."

They scrambled up beside him, their eyes following his outstretched arm. Far up the East River a slow procession of barges moved south. At the end of Blackwell's Island, the sails of six pettiaugers showed small but clear. Off Kip's Bay, a cluster of whaleboats nosed their way downstream.

"What do you think of that?" said Ripley.

"H'm," said Grenda.

"So do I," said Ripley.

Cuyler waved his arms. "For God's sake stop talking New England! What is it?"

"More coming," said Grenda. "Working out beyond Newtown Creek. Cuyler, you just wait and see."

Noon faded palely into afternoon and the strange parade still went on. The three watched, and their eyes followed each group of boats downstream, and when they looked upriver again more broad noses and drenched sails showed.

When three sharp-prowed sloops dropped anchor off Coenties Slip, Ripley jumped down from the parapet. "Joris, you've heard Glover say always to get ready for the order that's two beyond the one you haven't got yet?"

"Uh-huh," grumbled Cuyler, still studying the river.

"That's just what we're going to do right now. What do you think Washington's got all those boats for? To take you fishing?"

Cuyler dropped to the trench, face red. "By God, I've got it now. Rip, you're right." He roared: "All hands! Get your stuff together. If you can cram down any more salt pork you'd better because it may be a hell of a while before you eat again. And don't expect to be able to undo your packs until five days after Gabriel blows the last trump. The old Bull Seal's got a job for us."

The last strap had been buckled, the last clammy

mouthful of cold pork choked down by the time the anxious-faced Pennsylvania sergeant from Magaw's brought a relief down the communication trench. Cuyler shouted, "Fall in!" and started his men back toward the main works through the muck of the narrow trench.

They found the Fourteenth shuffling and splashing into line beyond the main redoubt that was filled with Magaw's and Shee's Pennsylvanians. Glover, swinging along through the wet dusk, was talking explosively to Johonot. "That's all we know. Report at the ferry. All the other regiments are to fall in under arms at seven. Chart your own course from that."

By the wharves and beaches where stacks of bales and barrels loomed wet and ghostly in the dying light the regiment halted, formed into line. Glover faced them, threw back his head.

"Marbleheaders! You've got to quit being soldiers for a while." His voice snapped with unwonted excitement. "You're boatmen until I tell you not to be. You've got to be better boatmen than you ever thought God Almighty could be." He pointed at the river. "You've got to take those boats across to New York. You've got to unload, get them back here quicker than frosted hell. Understand? *Got* to. If a ship loses a mast, build a new one out of water if you have to. If you spring a leak, rip off a piece of your hide, cut off your fingers and use them for nails. If you hit a rock, drag loose with your teeth. No matter what happens, the craft you're in goes across. *Goes—across!*" He shook his clenched fists. "This job's the most important one you've ever done and if a single man fails in anything, by God, he'd better not show his face around Marblehead again."

He paused. Ripley, tingling with apprehension and excitement, felt the tenseness of the men about him. Glover went on: "You've got to handle every kind of craft from a dory to a sloop. When it comes to rowing, I want every man that's ever slid past a customs boat on a dark night to be at the oars. I want those oars muffled. Holler and shout along the beaches as much as you want, but when you're afloat, the river's got to be so quiet you can hear a haddock scratching himself against a rock ten fathoms down. That's all. Mayne, report to me."

The regiment broke for the docks. Men shouted: "Let me get my hands on that tiller!" . . . "Old crew of the *Annabelle* this way!" . . . "Men who sailed under Pedrick, take the first pettiauger!" . . . "Old hands of the *Rose of Cape Ann*, stand by!"

Ripley fought his way to Glover, found him talking to Cuyler. "Now, you two," snapped the colonel. "You know what's happening?"

"We're leaving," said Ripley tersely.

"Right, but the army doesn't know it. The men think they're being relieved by fresh troops from New York. They've got to keep on thinking so. Then they won't be so scared of getting left behind. Here's your job." He beat his fist into his palm. "Maybe they won't be scared as they might be, but they'll still be scared. They'll come pounding down to the beaches jumpy as fish in a net and twice as hard to handle. They've got to be gaffed into the boats, quickly, quietly, in order. You two've got to go through that embarkation drill of yours, handling men that are cold and wet and hungry and scared worse than they've ever been in their lives. They won't know what you're trying to do with them. All they'll be thinking of is to get into a boat as quick as they can. How about it?"

"We'll do it," said Ripley. "Let me pick twenty men, that's all."

Glover laughed grimly. "I can't spare a soul from the boats. You'll have to take a scratch lot, militia, stragglers, slightly wounded men. You'll find them over back of that hut waiting for you. They'll be from every Province you ever heard of and a lot you never dreamed about. And they'll *have* to do. You've got a free hand from General MacDougall, who's in command of the embarkation. Use any means—*any*—to keep things smooth."

"That's a wide range," said Cuyler.

"That's a wide river," said Glover. "Now get busy. Find your men. If there's any trouble with New Yorkers, it'll be Cuyler's job to soothe them. Good luck." He vanished into the darkness.

Behind the tottery hut, Ripley and Cuyler stared in wonder at the men assigned them. There were a few uniforms in the triple ranks. The rest seemed spiritless, sodden scarecrows. Hasty questions showed that they were from Virginia, New York, Delaware, Massachusetts. Ripley said, "Lot of New Yorkers, here. Talk to them, Joris."

Cuyler held up a lantern and began to grin. "We've got a tough job to do and I guess you can do it. A lot of tired regiments are crossing to New York for a rest. A lot of abram-shams'll try to crowd in. We've got to stop that or there'll be a bad jam. When you get an order, it's got to be obeyed—quick. Now listen to what Lieutenant Mayne's got to say."

Ripley explained the embarkation plans rapidly. Then he faced the fifty men to the right, marched them to the junction of the main road and the paths from the heights. From the darkness a stocky figure glided up. "It's me, Rip. Mutton-lip. Glover figured I was too good for them boats so he sent me here to help. What'll I do?"

Ripley shouted in relief. "The old drill. Look to the rear files. Worry at their heels if they scatter. Thank God we've got one man that knows his job here."

Ripley halted his men in a column, three abreast, facing the dark heights, the rear rank standing on the very planks of the main dock. A lantern bobbed along and Glover boomed, "How's the wind setting?"

"We're waiting."

"All right. Past seven. The first companies ought to be along any moment . . ." The glossy flank of a horse loomed close in the dark, someone called: "What's this force?"

Glover snapped, "Embarkation guard, General Washington. My orders."

"Good! Good!" The horse and rider melted away into the night and Glover's lantern moved off toward the water.

Cuyler muttered to Ripley, "Every time I look around, there's that Virginia buck popping up out of the mud or riding down a cliff."

"Steady! All hands!" snapped Ripley.

From the darkness of the heights came the broken beat of marching men; a lantern swayed and bobbed closer and closer. Ripley moved out in advance of his men. "What regiment?"

"Drake's New York militia!" The light came on.

"Yours, Joris," said Ripley.

Cuyler, suddenly alert and efficient, barked, "Halt that column."

A wailing protest sifted through the night. "We *ain't* going back. Don't stop for no one. Get him out the way—"

Cuyler shouted to the embarkation guard: "Upon the center! Wheel to the right and left. March!" The right and left files fanned out, formed a great "T" on the center file, barring the road. The oncoming column slowed down. "Who's in command?" called Cuyler.

A vague voice said: "I am."

"All right. The boats are waiting. March your men by files down through my column. Keep your formation. You'll find an officer on the wharf who'll embark you."

"Good," said Ripley in a low tone. He rapped out an order to the guard, who shuffled awkwardly back into three wide-spaced files, Sholes yapping and shoving at them. Hesitantly at first, then more steadily under Cuyler's urging, Drake's men passed on, were neatly split by the motionless guard. Then their boots pounded on the dock. Ripley leaned an arm on Cuyler's shoulder. "That's one out of the way."

Cuyler stiffened. "Oh by God, look what's coming. Rip—I think the aged parent's only son'd be a lot happier edging up to a pious flask of rum. Stand by for squalls!"

The night up on the heights was shot through with waving lights. A confused murmur swept down toward the river, mingled with a heavy drumming of boots. Ripley hailed, but the stirring darkness gave back no answer. The murmur rose to a muffled roar, spread out through the rain. Ripley stepped back toward his men, shouting a command. The guard moved into its "T."

"Here we are," said Cuyler suddenly, his voice calm and level.

The night before them was filled with a tangled mass of men, hatless, weaponless, plunging along through the mud. Ripley shouted: "Halt that column."

Wild voices spattered out: "We're getting left behind!" . . . "The British is coming!" . . . "Where's them boats?" . . . "Out my way, you bastard!"

Then the faint glint of Ripley's bayonets reached the leaderless mob of stragglers. The fugitives slowed, halted uncertainly, spread out in a wide pool. Cuyler yelled: "Damn it, what regiment?"

A voice up the slope shouted: "Gay's Connecticut. Selden's behind us. We're held up. Can't get through this mess ahead of us."

Ripley cupped his hands about his mouth. "Fix bayonets and force your way through the crowd. It's orders!"

The mob shifted back and forth, began to give way. A line of lowered bayonets appeared, moving uncertainly. A panting man broke clear and ran to Ripley. "What the hell is all this?"

"You from Gay's? Bring on your men. Pass them through my files. They'll find out what to do on the wharves."

The officer, his face puckered with fatigue and worry, clawed at his chin. "We're only militia. Guess we wouldn't know how."

Ripley shouted: "Joris! With me!" He ran to the head of the oncoming company where men in smocks, men in shirtsleeves, drenched and shivering, strained their eyes with a terrible yearning toward the river and its boats. They halted obediently to Ripley's commands as Cuyler ran down the flanks. "Right, Joris?" Ripley held his fusee across the first three men of the front rank, nodded to the fourth. "Get going. Right ahead. Next man. Next man—"

Along the flanks, Cuyler pushed and shoved. One by one the shrunken companies passed on, were followed by Selden's. Then the last of the Connecticut men were aboard. Ripley turned to the leaderless mob that began to sway forward. "If you want to cross, get back to your companies. Unattached men'll be the last to go. Come on, Joris."

He and Cuyler fell back to the guard. Then hoarse shouts crashed out: "They ain't many of them." . . . "Chuck them out the way!" A stone struck Ripley's leg. Another stone whizzed and one of the guards yelped shrilly. Ripley looked at Cuyler. "Got to do it, Joris."

Cuyler shouted: "Raise firelocks! Aim! Fire!"

A ragged volley crashed out, and in the flash of the muzzles the mob could be seen falling back while the balls whined harmlessly over their heads to pitch into empty ground above.

"That's done it," muttered Ripley. "But if they try it again, we'll *have* to fire right into them. Ready for the next!"

The night flowed on in an endless succession of marching men who halted, heads bowed to the rain, passed steadily or raggedly through the bayonets and onto the boats. Some men staggered with fatigue, others quivered with panic, eyes feverish and staring. Bandaged men limped sullenly past, mouths tight. So they went, regiment after regiment, brigade after brigade, while over them the heights loomed, masked in silence and mystery, a mystery that might flare red at any second and send cannon balls crashing down on crowded beach and crowded dock.

Then tragedy drew nearer as word came to Ripley from the docks that the wind had died away, leaving the evacuation dependent on oars alone. Ripley and Cuyler exchanged glances. "Slow the whole thing up," said Ripley. "Send them through a company at a time."

"Jesus!" muttered Cuyler. "We'll never get more than half the army off."

"Probably. And we'll be with the half that's left, so we've got nothing to worry about. Take this first lot, Joris."

Massachusetts, New York, Maryland—the men came on and were fed grudgingly to the barges and whaleboats. The mob of stragglers grew stronger and bolder and twice Ripley's men prepared to fire into the mass, only to see it fade back at the last moment.

Then a sudden, steady breeze swept along the beaches and men shouted from the docks to hurry the embarkation, that sail could be used once more.

The docks rang incessantly as eager companies and regiments poured on. There was one terrible moment when Mifflin's brigade, sent down through mistaken instructions, had to be ordered back to the heights. With the river at their very feet, the brigade heard the order in silence. Ripley formed his guard more compactly, dreading a rush. Then the brigade stirred, countermarched, and began its slow climb away from safety back to the lines that, unknowing, it had left open to the British. Regiment by regiment they vanished—Magaw's Pennsylvanians and Shee's, Israel Hutchinson's men from Massachusetts, Paul Sargent's, Andrew Ward's Connecticut files.

A murmur ran along the dark waterfront. Cuyler muttered, "I'll be damned."

"We've got *some* discipline left, anyway," said Ripley. "Here comes Haslet's Delaware crowd. They'll give no trouble."

The endless stream went on. Gradually a fresher smell crept into the air and the rain seemed to be thinning out. Ripley touched Cuyler's elbow and pointed up. A gray line was forming above the black masses of the heights.

Cuyler's jaw dropped. "Daylight coming. We've still got whole brigades up there."

Sholes slid up beside Ripley. "Looks like God's trying to make it easy for the Lobsters. What'd happen if we got a few cannon balls on them cattle on the beach?"

Ripley nodded. "If that happens, Joris, you take half the guard and charge to the left. I'll cover the right."

Sholes chuckled. "What'll happen to us then?"

"Won't matter much," said Ripley.

"No. Come to think of it, don't suppose it will. Tell you one thing, though. We still got the high ground up there. And I tell you another. The Lobsters is looking west and it won't be light there for a hell of a time."

"Guess not," said Ripley. He stared up at the gray line of the heights. Then he rubbed his eyes to clear his vision. The hut close by looked blurred to him. He threw back his head. The graying crest was clear as ever. Only near-by objects looked blurred.

He pounded his hand down on Cuyler's shoulder. "Fog! By God, a real hell-bender of a fog rolling in from the sea!"

Cuyler jumped high in air. "That's done it. Sholes, get up to that bend in the road. People'll be losing their way if this thickens. I know these East River fogs. Look at that, Rip! Can't see the end of the wharf. Those men off there look as if they were wading in dirty wool. That's done it! That's done it!"

An hour later the two stood on the edge of the main wharf and watched the last of Mifflin's brigade stow away on pettiauger, sloop, ketch, or barge, then vanish in the fog toward Manhattan.

"Joris, it's gone. The whole damned army's gone and the Lobsters none the wiser."

"Look down here," whispered Cuyler, pointing to a barge that rocked close by the edge of the wharf. Four horses stood in it. In the stern, Glover sat beside a tall, cloaked man who called to the boatmen, in Virginia accents, to push off. "There he goes," said Cuyler. "About the last man off Long Island. There's a commander for you. Two thousand men or two hundred thousand, *he's* in command."

A stumpy rowboat bumped at the end of the wharf and Grenda's lean face appeared. "Better get aboard, you two, unless you want to join Howe." They jumped into the boat. "Want me to take an oar?" said Ripley.

"Hell, no. This ain't been much. Water's like a millpond. We loaded right down to the waterline and never shipped a drop. When the strays came down—well, they were just like a school of alewives. We'd let them pour into the boats and when a boat was full we'd just crack the next man on the head and push off." He pulled easily at the oars. "No—had a mighty easy night. Not that you've got complaints to enter in the log. Just standing around watching the boys going aboard."

"No," said Cuyler, rubbing his chin. "Guess we've seen harder nights, Hans."

Ripley settled back in the stern. Three or four boats showed aft in the mist, bringing the last of Glover's Marblehead boatmen home from their night's work. Beyond the last boat, the curtain of fog hung thick. Ripley whirled about in his seat. The musket shot still echoed faintly. Orange stabbed through the gray curtain, far away. There was a deeper flash, a muffled roar, and a sullen splash in the water. He shuddered. Except for the fog, those shots might be falling on men crammed on the beaches, stumbling down the heights.

Then he heard a sudden slapping of small waves in

the dense bank to his left. A canoe shot toward the boat, skimming swiftly toward the hidden New York shore. Ripley shouted: "Mutton-lip! Gragg!"

In the stern, Sholes waved a paddle. "Look what we got, Rip!" He reached to the bottom of the canoe, held something up.

"What is it?" shouted Cuyler.

"A hand."

"Hand? What the hell?"

Gragg wagged his head in the bow. "Found it back there on the beach."

"Good God, get rid of it," yelled Ripley.

Sholes pointed into the canoe with his paddle. "Can't. It's hitched on. The wounded feller's right here. Me and Adam, we went up the road and found a lot of wounded fellers and herded them down to the boats. This one got kind of left behind, so we threw him into the canoe we'd found and damned if he ain't right on his way back to New York." He flicked his paddle and sent a shower of drops over Gragg. "God damn it, are you going to sleep? Lean on that wood." The canoe vanished in the fog.

"Do those loons know where to go?" asked Ripley of Grenda.

"Sure. Falling in at the Bowling Green at the foot of Broadway. Stand by with that painter. We'll go ashore here by the stone steps."

They skirted the cannon-studded walls of the Whitehall battery, threaded their way through a street of high-shouldered houses whose windows were broken or boarded up. The street was littered with abandoned stores. Muskets lay rusting in puddles; tents, their binding ropes trailing, were troughs of canvas into which rain splashed monotonously. A derelict cart, one wheel crumpled against a wall, spilled sodden meal onto the cobbled street. A handful of men, wild-eyed and unshaven, trickled out of an alley. Ripley hailed them but they began to run, looking furtively back.

Then at the end of the street a solid line of men, muskets grounded, were drawn up by an iron-fenced green. Cuyler burst out: "By God, don't they look good!" Ripley broke into a trot, shouting. The litter and tangle of the streets, the forgotten equipment, had nothing to do with this alert, competent line of men in blue and white, nor with the short figure who faced it, hands tight behind his back.

The three scurried to their places behind Blackler's company as Major Lee faced Glover and reported: "All present or accounted for, sir."

Glover's voice boomed out in the air. "I'm not going to make any speech. But I'll tell you that what you've done's made John Glover mighty proud to be a Marbleheader. I've heard a lot of talk, standing here, about no orders coming to us. They haven't. That doesn't mean we're forgotten. The man that's skippering our ship isn't a forgetter. He's probably figured that some regiments need orders all the time. Others don't. We're going to march back to the hospital. You've got rations there. Eat them. You've got the building, and you've got tents. Sleep in them, because God knows when you'll get a chance to eat or sleep again. Major Lee'll march you back. I'm going to headquarters to report." Johonot at his side, he hurried on past the green into Broadway.

Commands snapped out, and the Fourteenth Regiment marched up Broadway through a silent city. On Broadway itself, in the side streets, was the same evidence of panic, and wherever he looked Ripley saw knots of furtive men creeping away, heading north, heading west. "Looking for their units," said Grenda.

"And scared as hell they may find them," muttered Cuyler. "God's teeth, are we the *only* regiment left?"

Ripley shrugged. "You'll see stragglers with any army," he said. He tried to shut from his mind the memory of the disorganized waterfront, the jettisoned equipment, the men who slunk away from the line of march.

By the front of the column, an abandoned drum lay in the gutter. A man broke from the ranks, picked it up, and began to tap out the rhythm of "Yankee Doodle." Shoulders straightened and heads began to sway. Through the silent streets, through the silent city, the drum tapped on. Here and there scattered men stopped, caught for a moment by the infectious cadence. Then they hunched their shoulders and slipped away, eyes on the ground. Ripley growled, "The bastards. The damned, gutless rabbits. They'll wreck us yet." Then he threw back his head. "No, by God, they can't. The States'll hold together. Somehow they will. They've got to."

PART FIVE

HIS MAJESTY'S SERVICES

By crossing the East River with almost no casualties to men or matériel, Washington had partially canceled the loss of the first formal battle of the Revolution. But he still clung to the island of Manhattan, seemingly blind to the ever-present threat of British and Hessians who now held the dominating heights of Brooklyn. Nor did he seem to be aware of the powerful British fleet which might close in on Manhattan from three sides. He broke his force into three great divisions and stationed one under Putnam about the Battery, a second under Spencer halfway up the island, and a third under Heath around the King's Bridge at the northern end.

The army, one third of which was composed of short-term militia, was shaken by the past and deeply disturbed about the future. Men still relied on George Washington as a man. Many began to doubt him as a soldier and a dull hope grew that his place might be taken by Charles Lee, professional adventurer.

Across on Long Island, Sir William Howe studied the Manhattan shoreline, wrote reports to England, studied Manhattan again. But his army remained on Long Island and the fleet, under his brother Lord Richard Howe, hung off the shores of Staten Island.

I

THE pitiless rains that had washed August out of the year 1776 had broken and a warm September flooded the island of Manhattan. In the welcome sunlight of dying summer, Ripley spread his equipment to dry on the grassy walls of the hospital works, listening idly as the two Cuylers wrangled over the probable cause of British inactivity since the retreat from Long Island. Joris turned to Ripley. "Haven't they got to refit just as we have? Didn't they have as many killed as we did? Just about?"

Ripley turned a sodden blanket to the sun. "So we hear. But they didn't lose the prisoners that we did. They didn't have their organization broken up. I agree with your father, Joris. Howe's still jumpy from the effects of Bunker's and Breed's. But wait. Did you see those frigates sailing up the East River this morning? Things'll begin to happen."

"And here we are to have them happen to," snapped the elder Cuyler. "Joris, I've a good mind to turn Tory and put you on Howe's staff. Your notions of strategy'd win the war for Washington in a week.

No less. Ha! What's this?" A sergeant from the orderly room ran across the grass calling for Ripley.

"Oh God—just as I had these getting nice and cooked," sighed Ripley. "The old Bull Seal wants me." He headed for the front of the cupola'd building where pigeons wheeled and turned in the sun.

Glover looked up from a thick pack of papers as Ripley came in. "Ho! Sit down." He folded his hands, fixed Ripley with his keen blue eyes. "I'm leaving."

"Leaving, sir?" Ripley was aghast. The army needed every proved officer it had.

"Leaving the regiment. I've just been to Mortier's house. Washington's given me George Clinton's brigade. Ordered me to take it. I'll be acting brigadier."

Ripley burst out, "They should have done it before. Some of the brigadier generals I've seen— Sorry, sir."

"That's all right. As I said, he's not making me a general. I'll keep my rank as colonel. This is still my regiment. Gabriel Johonot'll command it. He'll have no second in command because I'm taking Lee as brigade major. I'm taking you."

Ripley hesitated. Glover went on, "Hate to lose the Fourteenth? How do you think I feel about it? That's not the point. Of course, it's not something that I can really *order* you to do. You can stay right on here with Johonot. And I'll tell you this, too. If you stay, you'll get a company. I recommended you and Johonot wants you." He leaned back in his chair. "Yes, you'll be a full captain. Come with me and I'll guarantee you'll hold your present rank and no more."

Ripley thought of losing the swinging ranks of the hard-bitten Marbleheaders, losing the warm companionship of Cuyler, of Grenda, Blackler, a dozen others, of losing touch again with the strange Sholes and his stranger inseparable Gragg, losing all the men with whom he had battled and fought up the steep hills of Massachusetts with Knox and the guns. Then he looked at the little man who had brought the regiment into being. "I'd like to come with you, sir."

Glover grinned. "Would you? Good boy. I'll tell you something else, then. You won't have to leave the Fourteenth. You'll have the status of brigade aide. You'll be like sort of a painter mooring me to the regiment. I'll assign your duties and before a week's out you'll probably be wishing that you were carrying a musket in the ranks. Here's the brigade—" he ticked the names off on his fingers—"Joe Reed's regiment, mine, Bill Shepherd's, and Loammi Baldwin's. All Massachusetts and all Continental, signed to serve right to the end of the year. I'm to take over command tomorrow—that's the fourth. You come to me and I'll give you the damnedest list of things to do and to find out that you ever saw in your life. I'll want to know the markings of every buoy, shoal, reef, and anchorage in the brigade. Come to me at one sharp."

Ripley got up, looked at the little gingery-haired colonel. "I'm mighty proud that you want me, sir."

Glover's eyes twinkled. "Selfishness. I'm not much of a soldier and when anyone asks me military questions, I'll be able to say: 'Oh, Mayne knows all about that.' You'd better, too." His face grew graver. "There's another matter. You and I talked not long ago—more than I've talked to anyone else in the regiment. I've got to stay, now that Washington thinks I can do a bigger job for him. I'm writing my brother Jonathan. He's offered to see to my family decently if what I've got doesn't last. I'm accepting. I've got to. So, until the campaign's over or Washington says I won't do—" He snatched up papers, began to riffle through them. "Well—I guess we'll be seeing something of each other."

As Ripley came down the steps of the hospital he saw that the men had gathered in the grounds. Somehow the news of Glover's step had leaked out. Then Sholes burst out of the throng. "Rip! Is it true?"

Ripley nodded. Sholes sprang to the lower step and held his musket over his head. "Hey, boys. The old

Bull Seal's been made a acting jigadier brindle. Ain't you got a cheer for him?"

A shattering roar broke out from the massed ranks. "Again!" bellowed Sholes. The shouts pounded against the red brick.

Suddenly a window flew up. The cheers reached a thundering depth, then died away. Glover leaned his hands on the sill and Ripley could see that his face was working. He threw back his head. "I'm not much at making a speech. All I can say is—" His voice seemed to break. He recovered himself. "All I can say is, God bless you, damn it!" He slammed down the window, drew a curtain across the glass.

There was a hush over the crowded grounds. Then a single voice said: "Spoke like a seaman, that was." There was a murmur of assent. "'Twas fittin', I say." Slowly the press broke up and the men returned to their canvas shelters.

Old Cuyler, who had joined the throng with his son, thumped his stick on the ground. "*Only* a brigade! I shall write to the Congress about it. I shall write to Washington. You two don't know it, but I was down at the wharves and saw the army come in. The man's a genius, a damnable inestimable boon to humanity. Brigade! Where the devil's our national honor?"

Joris's mouth sagged. "Mean he's leaving us, Rip?"

"Not far. We're in his brigade. Johonot commands the regiment."

"But what'll happen?"

"You know the Bull Seal as well as I do. What I'm wondering about is not what has happened to us. It's what's *not* happening to Howe over there on Long Island."

The elder Cuyler struck his stick against the steps. "I view it all with the profoundest apprehension. Sniveling incompetence in the upper ranks of the army and they only make my son's colonel a brigadier —an acting one at that. We shall see. We shall see."

September slipped calmly on. The American army

reorganized as best it could. Howe seemed immobile across on Long Island although his brother Richard Howe's ships began to work farther and farther up the East River. The Fourteenth stayed on in the shadow of the hospital. Then on the night of the thirteenth they were routed out in a pouring rain to ferry heavy baggage and most of the army's sick over to the New Jersey shore. The regiment wondered, wondered still more as it loaded its own baggage onto boats for transport across the Hudson. The task completed, they were suddenly formed on the very docks and marched north along the island, breaking their progress at Martje David's Vly, the strange depression in the stony spine of the island at Harlem. The next day they headed north again, finally halting at the King's Bridge and Spuyten Duyvil.

Ripley, shuttling between brigade and regiment, was as much mystified as the men of the Fourteenth whom he found lying in the meadows beyond the Post Road. As he turned into the field, Cuyler sprang up from the shade of a clump of bushes. "What's the news, Rip?"

Ripley dismounted. "Hoped you could tell me. You never hear anything at Staff."

"Is it true that we've got nothing south of Harlem?"

"Wish it were, Joris. Putnam's still down by the Battery with a lot of men. Spencer's in force around Kip's Bay."

Cuyler dropped his voice. "I hear that Howe's brought his whole fleet up the East River."

"Heard that too. Maybe it's so." Ripley suddenly raised himself on his elbow. From the east and south a muffled thudding of heavy guns broke out, swelled into a steady roar. His ears called up forgotten sounds. "There's your answer, Joris. By God, it's a ship's broadside. Howe's hitting around Kip's Bay just as sure as corn sprouts!" He scrambled to his feet. "Stand by for squalls, Joris. The old Bull Seal's with General Heath down in those buildings by the King's Bridge. I'd better find him and see what he wants. He won't wait once the guns really get going. Then I'll come back and join you."

He swung into the saddle and galloped off to the low stone houses about the bridge over Spuyten Duyvil. As he pulled up in front of Heath's quarters, the half-door flew open and Glover darted out into the sunshine, saw Ripley and threw up his hand. "You'll stay right here. Those guns sound damned ugly. I'm starting the brigade off toward Harlem but we may be coming back this way in a hurry. Wait for one hour and if you don't hear from me by then, hit down the Post Road till you find me or Johonot. Understand?"

"You mean—I don't—don't go with the Fourteenth?"

"You stay right here until an hour passes or until you see me. That's all." He vaulted into his saddle and tore off down the road, Major Lee at his heels.

Reluctantly Ripley dismounted. Down in the fields a drum was tapping and men were getting to their feet. Shouts of command drifted faintly to him through the still air. The Fourteenth was forming. Beyond it, Baldwin's Twenty-sixth, Reed's Thirteenth, Shepherd's Third were stirring. Then lines formed into columns and the brigade marched south down the old Post Road toward the muffled roaring of the guns.

The morning wore on, worse than the hot hours of listening to the sound of battle across on Long Island the month before. Ripley paced up and down among the stone buildings. It seemed to him that the firing was getting more distinct, that musket shots could be heard cutting through the din of cannon. He told himself that it couldn't be. It was about ten miles from Spuyten Duyvil to Kip's Bay. Anyhow, Spencer at Kips had Prescott's Bunker Hill regiment and strong militia bodies. They ought to be able to beat off any water-borne attack. Couriers dashed up to the buildings, were met by Heath's aides and dashed off again.

None could give any account of the fighting far down the island.

Ripley tugged his watch out of his pocket as the last aide galloped away. Five minutes more. He said between his teeth: "Five minutes be damned!" and swung into the saddle.

The first few miles of the Post Road were clear of troops and no sign of activity showed save at the white-pillared Morris house on the bluffs by the Harlem River where men were loading heavy carts. Loading carts at Washington's new headquarters! That could mean a lot or nothing. Ripley rode on wondering why the general had been so slow to evacuate the lower island. If Howe's landing at Kip's were successful he'd not only crush the defenders but drive a wedge between Putnam at the Battery and Washington at Harlem. But he couldn't land. The Kip's defenses were good.

He came over a small rise in the road, then urged his horse on faster. Ahead of him, nearing the last high ground north of Martje David's Vly, thick columns of men were working south along the road. The nearest regiment showed a few brown coats—Reed's Third Massachusetts. He thundered on. Then he caught sight of Glover galloping over fields toward the distant crest, two or three horsemen at his heels. Ripley overtook the group as the brigadier, gingery hair glinting in the sun, swept his arm in a vast arc. "Colonel Johonot. You will move forward at once. Don't wait for the Twenty-sixth. At once."

The fields were filled with swift-moving Marbleheaders obliquing to the right toward the southern crest, company commanders waving their arms to correct the dress of the lines. Ripley reined in beside Glover, who stared at him. "Damn it, is your hour up? Then stay with Johonot. I'll be back by that house with the red roof." His voice boomed on: "That's it, Johonot. Bring them on!"

The Fourteenth had finished its oblique movement

across the field and was forming in a long line three deep. To its left, Loammi Baldwin's Twenty-sixth was hurrying to close in on its flank. Ripley reported to Johonot, was told to give his horse to an orderly and stay by Blackler's company.

He handed over his reins and ran across the trampled grass. A shattering report pitched him to the ground and a heavy ball sailed high overhead. He got to his feet, trembling. The land to the west fell away, showed a small sloop anchored in the Hudson, the British colors flying at the masthead. Another gun flashed and a shot sang away toward some hidden target. "My God!" thought Ripley. "Hitting us from east *and* west! They're firing across the Vly. God above, what *at*?"

Then he was among the slowly advancing ranks of the Fourteenth. Cuyler motioned impatiently to him. "Don't ask me, Rip. No one knows a God-damned thing! Just keep on going! We'll know soon enough."

"Maybe too soon," grunted Ripley, looking at the priming of his fusee. Then he turned his eyes to the last of the slow climb. The sky of the crest turned to a streaky green as the treetops on Claremont Heights across the Vly began to show. Another step and he saw the heights themselves. One more step and he looked down into the Vly, into the Hollow Way, that strange, scooplike depression that ran east from the Hudson to fan out on the Harlem plains.

A low cry, almost a moan, broke from the Marblehead ranks as the ground below spread out before them. Over the Harlem flats, down the slopes from Claremount Heights and the stone farmhouse by the Bloomingdale road; down the Post Road that spilled out on the plain from McGowan's Pass; down the hill from the Vandewater Farm, poured a torrent of men, weaponless and hatless. A few riders, stretching forward in their saddles, plowed on through the broken mass toward the northern heights. The twisting length of the Post Road on the east and the

Bloomingdale road on the west were clogged with flying men who swept on like a tide up a smooth beach. Now and then a section of road cleared, only to be choked with more fugitives from unseen reaches.

"Militia!" snapped Cuyler.

Ripley's voice was strained. "No. Continentals, too. Prescott's men. What in God's name has happened to us? And look!" He pointed to more horses that reared among the racing men. "It's Washington. Using his crop on them!"

Puppet-like figures lifted their arms to shield themselves. Cuyler whinnied: "God, get him out of there! Something'll happen to him." He stumbled and Ripley caught his arm. Eyes fixed on the rout before them, they had not noticed that the steady progress of the Fourteenth had carried them off the heights and down the slope onto the level floor of Martje David's Vly.

Then from the rear a shout split the air. "Johonot! Halt your men. Let Baldwin dress on you!"

The regiment came to a jerky halt as the broken mass plunged on toward it. The running men were closer now, began to divide at the base of a great promontory on the left, the Point of Rocks. Others swarmed on toward the long line of Glover's brigade. Gray faces loomed in front of the ranks. Panting, strangled voices cried: "Let me through!" . . . "Them guns on the boats! Never had a chance!" . . . "Out my way. I'm going home!" Somewhere in front a voice shrieked, a musket butt whirled. "I'll brain any son of a bitch that gets in my way. I'll—"

Ripley whirled about, caught a sign from Johonot, shouted: "Blackler! He says let them through. Don't lose formation. Hans! Joris! Sidestep them to the left." The wrack of broken men began to pour through the gaps between companies. Suddenly a thought formed in Ripley's mind. "They're not running because they're afraid. They're afraid because they're running." He looked again and was sure. Something had struck these men. Instinctively they had run from it and, in running, panic had swept down on them, a spreading quicksilver of terror.

Hoofs pounded along the front of the line and Glover, face crimson, galloped past, waving his hat. "Fall back! In order! Fall back until your colonel halts you."

Still facing to the front, the Fourteenth backed slowly up the slope, the other regiments of the brigade conforming to its movements. Beyond the extreme left, another brigade was coming into sight. The move to the rear was halted. Ripley took off his hat and wiped his forehead as he covertly watched his men. They stood steady but their eyes flicked and shifted, their tongues played over caked lips. One man raised his flat canteen, drank, recorked it, opened it, drank again.

Cuyler's elbow jarred against Ripley. "They're thinning out. Rip—what are they running *from?*"

Ripley rubbed his hand across his wet forehead. "From? From?" His hand dropped limply to his side. From the higher ground to which they had fallen back, stretches of the Post Road on the east were visible nearly down to Turtle Bay. Here and there the track was flecked with moving patches of brown or gray. No other color showed and the air was still save for an occasional boom of the now hidden sloop in the Hudson. He muttered: "They're scared by their own running. Where the hell are the Lobsters?"

"Maybe Iz Putnam's holding them," said Grenda from his post on the right flank.

"With what? His hands? Listen." Ripley jerked his arm toward the silent south. His teeth set as he thought of the rest of the army, of Henry Knox's guns, of the mounds of stores strung out from Kip's Bay down to the Battery. Had Howe swung his men down the island? He stared at the East River but could only make out the glint of water and the mist-blurred Long Island shore.

Cuyler said between set teeth, "My father was going

to start on the apples this morning. The orchards run down toward Kip's." He turned fiercely to Ripley. "What the hell are we doing here? Are we going to spend the whole war standing around watching? I know a way that runs west of the Post Road. I could take the whole brigade right down there. Where's Glover?"

Ripley laid a hand on Cuyler's shoulder. "In command."

Cuyler's mouth tightened. "And I guess any Lobster that tried to meddle with the aged parent'll be buying a firkin of trouble." He grinned nervously and resumed his study of the south.

The Hollow Way, from the mouth of McGowan's Pass to the Hudson, was slowly emptying. The men who spilled out onto the flats were moving more deliberately and every now and then there was some semblance of order. Ripley worried and fretted in the hot air. The hush, the retreat without pursuit, were weird, unnatural. Then on the summit of Point of Rocks a cluster of horsemen appeared, hard against the sky. One, in advance of the others, sat his mount motionless and a slight wind flicked back his cloak to show Virginia blue and buff. A horse's head tossed. Then the summit was vacant again. Something of the tenseness of the lines was broken.

Slow motion along the Bloomingdale road that overlooked the Hudson caught Ripley's eye. He jumped up on a rock. Fresh masses of men, waves of gray and brown and black, were heading north along it. He sprang down, ran to Johonot in the rear. "Just saw them, sir! Putnam's men! They worked up the west shore."

Johonot whipped out his glass, stared at the land beyond Claremont Heights. "Find the colonel. Let him know."

A voice boomed close by: "Save your breath. I've seen it. No orders, Johonot, except stand firm where you are. Not one step forward without my orders, no matter what happens." Glover galloped off, clutching his vast hat.

Ripley ran back to Blackler's, straining his eyes in the hope that he might see rumbling carts or gun teams lurching along the Bloomingdale road. But as far as his eye could reach there was nothing save the hurrying press of men. "What did Glover say?" called Blackler to Ripley.

"Nothing. We're to stand firm. That's all." He watched the masses of men on the west road. "At least, no one's after them. No one—" He stopped.

Brass twinkled along the Post Road that hugged the east side of the central park-like tangle that ran down the island. A ghost of music drifted eerily north and the brown of the Post Road was stained with red and white.

All along the slope that led up from the northern edge of the Hollow Way, men stood frozen as the two columns, one drab and one red, struggled on, hidden from each other by the rocky hills and tree-choked dells that separated them. Slowly the force on the Bloomingdale road forged ahead. Then it was lost to sight in a fold in the ground and the red tide on the Post Road tramped on. Ripley muttered: "God! If they both debouche onto the flats at the same time!"

Grenda shifted uneasily. "Ain't liking the thought of them tangling spars out there."

From the rear of the line, Glover shouted above the thud of hoofs. "Mayne! Lieutenant Mayne!"

Ripley tore his eyes from the slow advance along the parallel roads and doubled back to Glover, who was bending from the saddle talking eagerly to Johonot. "Here, sir," panted Ripley.

Glover shoved a folded paper at him. "Get aboard your horse and find Heath. I'm betting no one's thought to let him know what's happening out there. Get aboard and make knots."

Hand trembling with excitement, Ripley pointed toward the opposite heights. "With all that coming, sir?"

"Damn it, this isn't a rary-show for you to gape at." Then he grinned. "Know how you feel. But Heath's got to know."

Choking back a flood of protest, Ripley stumbled to his waiting horse and rode north from the impending clash. Once he reined in among a drift of frightened, running men as a brisk patter of musketry sprang up in the south. Then he shook his head and trotted on.

The farther he worked toward the rear, the greater the confusion became. The fugitives who had burst through the brigade lines were spreading panic as they rushed north. Men were slipping away from waiting regiments and companies. In a hollow by a big white house, teamsters were quietly unhitching their horses, mounting and riding away toward the King's Bridge and the mainland. Down by the Harlem River a burst of smoke welled up from a pile of stores to which someone had put a torch.

Ripley felt the contagion of blind panic creeping over him, fought it back. He shouted to passing men: "General Heath? Where's General Heath?" Answers were vague, grudging. He thought, "Anyway, I know he's north of us and the island's too small to lose him in."

Suddenly he saw tethered horses in the dooryard of a stone cottage and galloped toward them. An aide in a tattered uniform held up his hand as Ripley reined in. "Have you got word for the general?" His eyes were feverishly bright.

Ripley slid to the ground and waved his paper. "From Colonel Glover. For General Heath."

"Get right in there."

Ripley hurried through the low door. A short, broad-faced man jumped to his feet. "You're from Glover? Give me that!" He snatched the paper from Ripley, and as he read his face sagged in lines of fathomless discouragement. Then he threw back his head. "Wait here!" The stone floor rang under his boots as he ran out into the yard and Ripley could hear him giving orders in a crisp, low voice. Aides began to ride off and General Heath stamped back into the room. "Guess you can't add anything to what your colonel wrote. You agree that our men can't see the British?"

"The same goes for the British. Two columns pushing up the island and I'll swear neither one knows about the other."

Heath sat down slowly. "And they'll both come out onto the Hollow Way at about the same time, you say." He passed his hand over his forehead. "God, if I were twenty years younger! Never mind. We'll give them something solid to fall back on." He looked up sharply as angry voices sounded from an inner room. "What's that, Nelson?"

A bony face, flushed with excitement, peered into the room. "Frenchies, sir. Boatloads of them. Coming in from the Sound. I been telling Miller we're saved. Frenchies'll never fight for the Lobsters. It's us."

Heath's chin set. "French? Here? You're not serious?"

Nelson nodded eagerly. "I seen them through the glass. Boats and boats."

Heath looked keenly at Ripley. "Hear anything about it? By God, if it's true—"

Ripley said dryly, "What'd bring the French here? They aren't at war with England."

Nelson's voice grew shrill. "What they doing here, then?"

Ripley turned to Heath, whose face was a mask of perplexity. "Let me have a look at them, sir. I've seen plenty of French troops."

Heath caught him by the arm. "Go aboard them if you like, only tell me if it's true. This way."

In the next room three officers were leaning out a window that looked past the mouth of the Harlem to the East River. Ripley caught a single glass from the hands of a fat lieutenant and focused it on the water.

Beyond a headland, two small schooners worked south, their spars showing clear in the lens. Nelson croaked: "Look at it! White coats! That's Frenchies and nothing else."

Ripley shut the glass wearily and said to Heath: "British regulations, sir. When troops are afloat they turn their jackets inside out to save staining. We're looking at white linings, not white coats."

Heath shook Ripley's shoulder. "You're sure? This could be damned important."

"Positive, sir. I served in the Royal Marines."

The group at the window was suddenly silent. Heath shrugged. "Guess it's better this way. It's our way anyway—but, God—five trained regiments to send down the island—two!" He wheeled on the dejected officers. "Get out of here! You've got enough to do. Nelson, I sent you to the works on the west cliffs ten minutes ago. Miller, have you got your working parties—" He rattled out orders and the room emptied.

"May I get back to my regiment, sir?" asked Ripley.

Heath sighed. "I'd like to keep you here. You don't get flustered. Yes, get on back. Thank your colonel for his news. It's the first I've had. Tell him I'll back him all I can."

Ripley saluted and went out into the yard where the light was beginning to fade. He mounted and rode south with his head turned to catch any sounds that might drift up from the distant Hollow Way. Progress was difficult along the single road that skirted the high ground to the west. Groups of men were falling in under arms, muttering and shuffling. Twice he had to turn into the fields to avoid gangs that tramped on with picks and shovels over their shoulders.

By an odd outcropping of rock a man caught at his bridle and cursed him fiercely, pointing to lines of tape that stretched away to right and left along the ground. "How the hell am I going to get this redoubt dug with you clodhoppers breaking my lines?" Ripley shook his horse free and made a wide circuit that brought the animal stumbling through fresh-turned earth and the rise and fall of picks.

It was quite dark by the time he recognized the small white house, glimmering in the night, where Glover had set up headquarters earlier in the day. He shouted, but found that the colonel had not been seen for more than an hour. He pressed on, trying to wring news from the stirring darkness. There was no sound of firing, no rustle of drums. What could have happened to the two columns that he had seen earlier? A wholesale surrender? And what about the brigades that had formed on the north slope?

Suddenly a line of light showed clear, to the south, a bright band that seemed to reach from the East River straight across the the Hudson. He reined in, trying to read its meaning. His horse stumbled and an unseen man grunted in pain, then bawled: "Trying to ride that God-damned camel down my throat?"

Ripley cried, "Joris!" and vaulted from the saddle.

Cuyler stopped rubbing his shin and shouted: "Here he is, Hans. For God's sake, Rip, when are rations coming up?"

All about Ripley, dark forms rose from the grass in a storm of questions. Ripley said: "Never mind the rations. What the hell happened here while I was gone?"

Grenda spoke slowly. "Like what you'd call a miracle."

Cuyler echoed: "It was. Rip—they got away clean. They never saw the Lobsters and the Lobsters never saw them until they began coming out onto the flats. Then some of Smallwood's Marylanders got up into McGowan's Pass and held the Lobsters off just long enough. Putnam's men are back of us now. You must have ridden right through them."

Ripley leaned against his horse. "Jesus! They got away! They— Wait a minute. What did Howe do? How about us?"

Grenda pointed to the line of fires across the Hollow

Way. "There's Howe. Like Joris said, he's still got the Bunker Hill vapors. Still scared to attack us head on."

"It was wicked, just watching," grunted Cuyler. "Why the hell didn't that Virginia buck let us go at them! I tell you, all the brigades along here were whickering like a mare in the spring. Listen, Rip, sure you didn't hear anything about rations?"

Ripley rubbed his forehead. "After what you told me, I'm not sure of a damned thing." In his mind he could still see the solid red column hurrying up the east road and the disorganized drab mass to the west. "Where's the old Bull Seal? Got to report to him."

"Take that path. You can feel it with your feet. Follow it along until you hear him bellowing," said Cuyler. "And tell him about rations."

Ripley found Glover and Johonot studying a map in the shelter of a great rock, lantern light playing over the rumpled surface. Glover looked up quickly as Ripley reported Heath's thanks, then folded his map. "He knows all we do, then? You've heard the orders? We stay right where we are. That's all."

"What's the situation, sir?" asked Ripley.

"Isn't any. Here we are and there they are. I don't know why they stay there or we stay here. I don't know a lot of things. I don't know why Washington didn't clear out the lower end of the island the instant he saw the fleet in the East River. I don't know what we'll do for artillery, because Knox had to leave most of his guns down by the Battery. And I don't know why we don't pull out now and get out of reach of the Navy." He thumped his fist on the rock. "I don't know any of those things and it's not important that I should. What I do know is that we're left here with orders to stay and that's enough. Hear anything that'd interest me?"

"Just that the men are beginning to yelp along the line because Washington didn't throw them at Howe."

Glover leaned his chin on his thick fist. "That's a

good sign." He sighed. "By God, I was wishing every second he'd give me the word. Far as I can see, the reason he didn't is that he's got damned few solid regiments left and if we'd gone in there and struck a reef—what would have happened?" He threw out his hands. "Feeling foundered?"

"Not too much."

"I may have something for you to do later. Get some sleep and be where Colonel Johonot can find you." He spread out the map again. "Now, Colonel—"

Ripley went back to the slope where the regiment sprawled in the grass, and found Cuyler and Grenda. Cuyler shouted: "Rations up, Rip. Give him some, Hans. Listen, Rip, did the Bull Seal say why we were staying? We've got to get out of reach of the ships, I tell you. Damn His Majesty's army! We can take a pair of my Aunt Flukicker's mops and whack the bastards right back to Gravesend. Hans caught one of those chaps who was running through here and wrestled with him until he could talk. Honest, he said it wasn't so bad at first—there at Kip's. Even the militia stood up and blasted back at the barges. Then the fleet opened up and most of the men had never seen anything bigger than a slingshot before they had their militia muskets given them. They let out a whoop and busted back through Prescott's crowd. That started things off and they ran into a lot more men, God knows where from, that'd been sent down to reinforce them and the new ones caught the idea of running from them and—well, you saw the rest. Isn't that so, Hans?"

"More so," said Grenda. "It was like a green crew that's lost a mast in a gale. One man hollers, another jumps for a dinghy, another yells that the ship's sinking." He sat up suddenly. "What in God's name's that?"

Off to the south a wailing screech had broken out, soared high above the roaring tones of a big drum. Ripley felt the skin on the back of his neck tingle.

The sound wailed higher, fell away, soared again.

"Bagpipes! That means they've got Highlanders over there. I've heard the pipes at Gibraltar."

"That all it is?" Cuyler sank back in relief. "Let's get back to our rations." Ripley tried to eat cold meat, found that fatigue had taken all desire for food from him. He got up. "Captain Blackler, the colonel may be looking for me. I'm bedding down under that rock."

"I'll tell the guard," said Blackler.

Ripley rolled up in his blanket and fell into a troubled sleep that was broken by the uneasy stir of the lines. Once a squad of men started up in a panic, shouting that the army was running away from them in the dark. When their fears had been quieted and silence had settled over the slope once more, long files of men blundered past as Nixon's regiment moved farther down. A fresh burst of distant bagpipes set the men stirring and moaning in their sleep.

II

RIPLEY awoke with a start, sniffing the clear air that was rolling in off the Hudson. Had someone called his name? He settled back in his blankets, every bone aching, and tried to shut out the night. No one would be looking for him. No one—

"Mayne!" The sound was unmistakable. He groaned, rolled to his elbow. A light was dancing along the grass toward him. A guard cried, "Over there, sir, abaft the big rock."

He got to his feet and Johonot nodded quietly at him in the light of the lantern. "Colonel Glover said he might want you. You went on patrol over in Brooklyn?"

"Yes, sir."

"He wants you to do that same thing here."

Ripley's eyes shot to the dark heights of Claremont,

ghostly with their muted fires. "I—I'm not much good at that, sir. I had a man with me who used to be a ranger and—"

"You went. You came back. You found out a lot."

"I was lucky."

Johonot's face wrinkled in a slow smile. "Maybe you will be again. Take the same number of men—any men you want. Go across the way and see what our neighbors are doing."

Blackler spoke unexpectedly from the darkness. "Nixon's moved out in front of us, sir. He's probably got scouts out."

Johonot snorted. "No one's doing a damned thing tonight unless Washington comes along, tells them what to do, how to do it, and then does it for them. Colonel Glover doesn't want to work that way. And there's another reason. I've been back of the lines. Those macaronis from New York and Pennsylvania and Virginia are talking mighty hard about New England. They blame us for the wreck today. We've got to stop that."

"Where'll I find you when I come back?" said Ripley.

Johonot laughed shortly. "That's good. But don't bother about me. Go right to brigade. The brigadier'll want to hear what you find out. Good luck." He moved off through the dark.

Blackler said, "Who'll you take?"

"Sholes, of course. Grenda, because they may have moved some of the Germans up here. I want Cuyler—"

"Hold hard. That leaves me without an officer."

"Got anyone better for me? Then those are the ones I'll take."

Ripley crept off among the sleeping men. He found Sholes, shook him. The ranger sprang to his feet, a knife glinting. "Oh—you, is it?" He stowed the knife away. "What's it about?"

"Going over to see Howe. Join me by that birch over there."

Ripley roused Grenda and Cuyler, whispered the mission to them. Cuyler's eyes glinted in the dark when he heard the direction that they were taking. Grenda, without a word, picked up his fusee.

They found Sholes by the birch tree, leaning on a long musket. From the gloom beside him, Adam Gragg's gnarled face shot up as though released by a spring. Ripley shook his head. "Not this time, Gragg."

Sholes spat. "Take both or none. Adam and me always works together. This is volunteer, ain't it? Prowls always is. Both or none."

"All right. All right. Take the lead, Nahum."

The five men slipped down the hill, worked their way through Nixon's lines where blinking sentries passed them on. Then the Claremont Heights were in front of them and they stepped out into an unknown, hostile world. Sholes in the lead, they worked on past a marshy pond and began a slow ascent. The old ranger held a steady course through the dark, avoiding such points as might afford shelter for post or picket. Twice the others waited while Sholes cast off in wide circles to the right or left. Returning from his last sally, he whispered: "Can't weasel nothing out of this. We'd ought to a quarreled with three-four outposts before this."

Ripley hesitated. "We can go back and report that only the crest's held. We—" He looked into the night. "A few more rods anyway. Get going."

They topped the crest and wove their way through saplings and underbrush. Lighter patches showed and they skirted a plowed field where buckwheat whispered in the night. Ripley caught a spear and shredded it. There'd be a good harvest. He chewed a coarse grain and somehow the homely flavor took something of the chill uncertainty and fear from the night. His legs moved more easily as he followed the crouching Sholes.

Suddenly Sholes held up his hand, then dropped to the ground. Tilting his head, Ripley could make out a single black figure against the sky, the figure of a big man whose head was topped with an odd, flat cap. The man moved slightly and a kilt swayed. Sholes pressed Ripley's arm and pointed to the left. Fifty yards away a light-infantry skullcap showed in a patch of starlit sky. They were between two regiments, English and Scottish, who were content with a skeleton guard.

Sholes signaled and the little party moved on, heading for a great tangle of rock whose crest was outlined by the dull glow of a fire on its farther side. They were getting into the heart of the advanced troops. Voices sounded, blurred with sleep. Off toward the river a chain of lights danced along as a guard relief marched out to some post. The relief was small and stumbled on listlessly. "Can't understand it," he muttered to Cuyler. "We could have slid the whole regiment up to the fires before we'd have been seen. Come on."

Flat on the ground, they wriggled on after Sholes. How much longer could it last? How— The fire beyond the rocks flared up, harsh and red. A voice, surprisingly close, called: "Anstruther. Didn't I tell you we'd see sport? A bloody fox hunt. That's what it was."

Deeper tones broke in. "Fox hunt be damned. Sometimes a fox'll turn at bay. These bastards! By God, we'll bloody well sweep them up tomorrow. Posted your guard, Carewe?"

A man laughed. "Tucked them in and they're all asleep by now. They'll want their legs for more chasing tomorrow. We form at noon."

Sholes kicked lightly, began to back away. They crept off, hugging the rock until they were well out of reach of the firelight. "We'll start working back now," said Ripley. "How deep into their lines are we?"

" 'Bout a mile. I got an itch to prowl some more."

"We've got to get back. We can report that they're

in no hurry to start, that they're slack and damned confident."

Cuyler growled in disgust. "Fox-hunting! Did you hear that? Couldn't we nip off a picket and change his mind for him?"

"I'd like to. But I don't want to get caught up here by the sun."

Cuyler began to speak in an eager whisper. "Rip—I've got to go on. I know the land here better than I know the inside of my pocket. Let me chase off and work back toward Kip's Bay. The house—I'm kind of worried about it."

"You'll stay, Joris."

"Damn it, Rip. They'll never see me."

"You'll stay here. Joris, I know how you feel, but if you don't get that idea out of your head, I'll put you under arrest."

Cuyler sighed. "Well, all right."

They wriggled forward again, then Sholes signaled a halt, took a cast off to the left by himself, returned puzzled. "Something funny, Rip. Got an idea someone's heading toward us." He suddenly flattened and the others followed his example. A twig snapped. Another. Heavy boots crunched on toward them, came closer, then sheered off to the right. A line of tall men, vast cocked hats set forward on their heads, swung past, sharp against the dark sky. Ripley heard guttural German and tapped Grenda's shoulder. The crackling died away.

Sholes got to his knees, grew tense. "By God, we're in a nest of them. Some coming down there. More off to the left."

Ripley nodded abruptly. Then he said in a low tone: "Scatter. Every man for himself. Report right to Johonot when you get back."

The patrol melted away through the woods. Cuyler caught Ripley's arm. "Woodsmen and sailors. They'll make it all right. Come with me. There's a path I know."

The two slithered cautiously down a ravine, followed the course of a brook. Twice they crouched among big, tumbled rocks as patrols beat their way through the underbrush above them. "Quarter of a mile more, Rip, then we'll come out on Martje David's Vly. We'll—" He stopped as Ripley caught his arm. On the high bank above stood three light infantrymen, their backs to the ravine. It was getting lighter and the white cross belts showed clear and sharp. Cuyler beckoned noiselessly and slid away down among the rocks, Ripley trailing after him, sometimes losing sight of the broad back, sometimes within arm's reach. He waited by a fallen elm while Cuyler worked around the edge of a boulder, then started after him, taking care not to step on a heap of dried branches. He stretched out one foot over the dead wood— The gray ravine spun about him and his head crashed into the soft bank while a heavy weight bore him down, pushing him against jagged rocks and crackling twigs. He struggled, tried to call out, but a hard hand on his collar cut off his breath. His arms were wrenched back and a tough cord bound tightly around them. He broke loose, shouted, "Joris! Keep going." His wind was cut off again and he crashed to the ground. Then he was jerked onto his feet while four grenadiers grinned sardonically at him. A man with a sergeant's knot said: "Don't worry abaht yer mate. 'E'll find Carroll's lads waiting for him, that he will. Bring him along."

Ripley struggled again, but the points of two bayonets pricked his shoulders. Head down, he followed the sergeant up the ravine, eyes darting right and left. Cautiously he flexed his arm muscles to test the cords. They didn't seem too secure to him. Left by himself, he felt sure that he'd wriggle loose somehow. In the meantime he kept his eyes on the windings of the ravine that seemed to twist off toward the river. He was utterly confident that he could escape and make his way back to the men across the Hollow Way.

With a sort of rough good humor, the grenadiers

hauled and shoved him up the side of the ravine. Day was breaking and Ripley recognized the same buckwheat field that he had crossed with the patrol not long before. At the other end of the field a trim stone farmhouse showed dimly in the slowly growing light. Men in red coats and white breeches moved about it, yawning and stretching. Others slept in long rows on the soft ground to the left.

The sergeant looked over his shoulder. "Right in to Captain Bowes, lads."

A tired-faced man with heavy black eyebrows looked up negligently as Ripley was pushed across the threshold. "Ho. Bagged another rabbit have you? Blast my eyes if I know what we'll do with them all." He turned cold eyes on Ripley. "Name, rank, and regiment, and look sharp."

Ripley set his chin. "I'm a prisoner of war. I demand that my arms be freed."

The officer lounged back in a creaky chair by the hearth. "You're a bloody rebel and it'll be a wonder if you don't get bloody well hanged for all this. In arms against the Crown. I said—name, rank, and regiment —if you've still got regiments."

"I stand on my rights as a prisoner of war."

The officer jerked his head to an inner room. "Mr. Bond! Another rabbit in the bag. Take charge of him." He got up and lounged out of the house, brushing dust from the facings of his tailed coat.

From the inner room a fresh-faced lieutenant emerged. "Can't keep track of all you chaps. Well, let's be about it. Dismiss the guard, Sergeant. Have one man wait at the door." The guard clumped out. The lieutenant smiled at Ripley. "Too damned bad about that rope. We'll have it off as soon as Major Blackstock comes back. You're right, you know, about the prisoner business, to my way of thinking. But a lot of people don't hold with it. You don't want to talk? I'll have to search you if you don't. I'd rather not."

Ripley eyed the young face keenly. "I wouldn't

mind answering you. But I'm not going to talk while I'm tied like a felon."

"Right! Right! Don't blame you. When the major—Damn my eyes, what's that confounded din?" The lieutenant jumped to his feet and looked out the small window. Somewhere out in the yard a voice bawled and bellowed in guttural accents. The sergeant came panting in. "A prisoner, sir. The guard can't make him out, they can't. Looks like a Hessian, talks like a Hessian, and dresses like a Yankee. Will I bring him in?"

The door banged again and three sweating grenadiers shoved Cuyler into the room. He stared at Ripley with blank eyes, and then began a voluble torrent of bush Dutch. The lieutenant blinked, began cautiously. "*Was ist dein*—oh, blast this clumsy talk—" He jumped to his feet and shook a finger under Cuyler's nose. "You're a deserter. A bloody Hessian deserter. I've seen you in the Erb Prinz orderly room. I've seen—" He darted to the window, eyes staring as a sudden blast of musketry ripped through the growing dawn. There was a second volley, heavy and steady, a third.

Someone rode into the yard shouting, "You've got prisoners in there. Move them to the rear. At once, I say. At once."

The guard of grenadiers stamped into the room. The lieutenant snatched up a bearskin cap from the mantel, shouted to Ripley: "Isn't this the damnedest luck? A fight on and I've got to chivvy you back to the rear. Both of them, Sergeant."

Ripley and Cuyler were tugged and dragged out and headed south down the Bloomingdale road. The musketry to the rear was growing heavier. Fresh columns of light infantry were swinging north along the road past the guard, the officers whooping and blowing hunting horns. One of them bawled, "Hoick! Hoick! Stole away, sir," blasted on his horn again. "Another bag of Yankee foxes."

The guard prodded Ripley and Cuyler into a trot, the big New Yorker, eyes still vacant, laboring along. Ripley listened to the growing swell of musketry and pride swelled up in him. "By God, *we're* attacking. *Attacking!*" Over and over in his mind the thought ran that the army that had lain shattered on the slopes of the Hollow Way had somehow found strength and spirit to lash out against the force that had driven it from the Battery to the flat stretches of the Harlem plain.

Lieutenant Bond ran along beside the guard, buttoning his long waistcoat. "Sharp, now, Sergeant. No lagging."

One of the guards touched Ripley with the butt of his musket. "Nah then. Ain't you heard wot he said?"

Ripley ran on, listening for some telltale sound from the north. There was a lull in the musketry, then it crashed again, sharper and closer. Drums banged in the fields at the side of the road and a regiment with blue facings on its jackets formed with swift precision and started north at the double. Beyond a fold in the ground a line of cocked hats moved on in the same direction, a mounted officer shouting and waving toward the sound of the firing. From a decaying barn a heavy mass of Hessians in pointed silver helmets thundered out, followed by a long column of quick-stepping Jaegers, amaranth facings on their green jackets.

The smoothness and ease with which the units were rallied and thrown onto the road aroused Ripley's professional admiration. Then he began to swear under his breath as he realized that each of the well-equipped, solid companies was hurrying to meet the tattered, desperate Americans who had somehow found again the will to attack.

The fresh-faced Bond shouted: "That farmhouse, Sergeant. Get them in there." Panting from the exertion of running with bound arms, Ripley and Cuyler clumped into the kitchen of the farmhouse, whose owners seemed to have fled. Bond whipped out a knife. "Here, blast it, off with those cords."

The ropes swished to the floor and Ripley flexed his arms in relief. "Two of you guards stay in the room with the prisoners. Sergeant and one more outside. I'll be back presently!" He ran out to the road and headed north.

Ripley looked about the room, studied the ground that showed outside the window. If the action up the road developed into major proportions, there might be a chance of getting away in the resultant confusion. He strained his ears but could hear nothing save a banging of drums somewhere off to the east, British drums by their tone. The firing seemed to have died away.

Ripley looked across at Cuyler, who had slumped down on a low bench by the fireplace. His broad face was dull and his eyes vacant. Could Joris have had a whack on the head? That would complicate the matter of escape. He eyed him keenly. Cuyler's lips were slightly parted and he breathed heavily through them. Then he raised his head slightly and the left side of his face puckered in a slow wink.

To hide his relief Ripley walked to the window. The nearer guard motioned him roughly away so he joined Cuyler on the bench, his mind busy reconstructing the country that lay about the little Dutch farmhouse.

Outside the sergeant snapped a command. The door banged open and Bond came in, followed by a thickset man in a metal helmet and blue jacket. Bond pointed to Cuyler: "That's the man, Captain."

The Hessian strode across the room, jerked Cuyler's chin up. "No. I do nod know him."

"Talk to him," urged Bond.

The Hessian captain, thick black mustache twitching, barked out: "*Achtung! Sie sind—*" and trailed off into an explosive string of gutturals. Cuyler, lower lips sagging, looked vacantly at him.

The captain turned brusquely on his heel. "He iss nod of ours," he grunted and swung out of the room.

Bond put his hands on his hips and glared at Cuyler. "Now what the devil are you up to? Can't you answer a civil question? I'm about ready to—" He stopped as the musketry broke out, closer this time, scattering shots and regular volley rapping through the calm morning. Bond shook his fist. "Damn it, I'm not going to stay cooped up." He dashed for the door. "Sergeant, I'm going up to join the regiment. You're in charge of the prisoners. Make sure they can't get away but don't tie them." He raced off up the road.

The sergeant tramped into the kitchen, scratching his head. "You're rebels. That's one thing. You're officers and that's another. Wot'll I do with you?" His eyes narrowed. "You'll be best off in the shed. Bring 'em on, Tobey."

A bayonet at each elbow, the two were herded across the yard and locked in a small, windowless hutch with a heavy door. Ripley fumbled around in the dark, found a small barrow and sat on it. From the semi-darkness Cuyler said: "What do you think about it?"

Ripley whispered: "They can hear you."

"Let them. It'll give them something else to worry about."

"You've just been playing for time?"

"What do you think? The more we can keep them wondering about us the less they'll be thinking of what we're up to." He rubbed his arms. "Damn that major back there. He'd have us in shackles if he had his way." He paused. "By God, firing's closer!"

Ripley jumped up from the barrow and began pacing about the shed. "Damn it, if we only knew what was happening. Joris, do you realize that our crowd —*our* crowd's attacking? I couldn't believe it. How did they ever get a force together? Suppose Washington's taken the few brigades we had left and gone at the heights?"

"He's not that much of a gambler. I can't understand it. Listen! There's another regiment coming by. Whatever it is, they've been stirred up proper."

Ripley saw a shaft of light falling into the shed back of a stack of barrels. He pulled one aside and found a narrow crack in the wall. "Hey! We can see something from here. Joris! Some of them are coming back!" He pressed his eye to the crack. On the road close by, a line of bandaged men, British and German, red and blue, were stumbling and limping south. After them two straw-filled carts jolted and rumbled, booted feet trailing over the tailboard.

Cuyler clawed at his shoulder. "Let me see! Damn it, give me an edge of that." Ripley made way for him and they watched the wounded file painfully out of sight, while more German troops in heavy blue coats pushed woodenly north where the firing was still spluttering and snapping.

Ripley went back to the barrow. "No more to see."

"Guess not. How'll we ever find out?"

"Watch the Lobsters. If they move back, we've done the damnedest miracle that ever happened. If they stay where they are we'll still have done a pretty good one. If they move forward—well, we'd better begin practising standing on a scaffold."

"Maybe we'd better anyway."

"Forget it. We're going to get out of this, I tell you. We'll be moved somewhere that'll be better for talking than this shed with the guards just outside. Get your ear to that crack and see what you can hear of the fighting."

The long finger of light that slanted down through the crack crept along the dirt floor of the shed as the two listened to the rise and fall of the musketry. Soon it began to die away, then ceased in a last distant volley. Ripley rubbed the back of his hand nervously. "That's from the Hollow Way by the echo."

Cuyler moaned. "If we'd only gone with Sholes. I thought that ravine'd be safe. About ten men climbed up my back just after I got by that big rock. Jesus, Rip, I—I'm sorry."

"Quiet between decks, you Dutch loon. Sholes couldn't have done any better than you. We just had bad luck. Any more firing?"

The outside world was filled with the sound of marching men. A few drums flickered through intricate beats, but no shots or volleys jarred the air.

At noon the door was opened and two small bowls of stew and a loaf of bread were cautiously pushed in by one of the guard. Cuyler set his aside. "I can't. Honest, I can't. It's all coming back to me now. We could have taken another turn and—"

"Shut up and eat."

"And I was to take the first shift of guard tonight. Now Grenda'll have to—"

Ripley caught up Cuyler's bowl. "You're going to eat that if I have to kill you first and then work your jaws with my hands. We've got to be as full of pepper as a pair of fighting cocks."

Cuyler nodded slowly, then began to eat. The shed gradually darkened. The sliver of light vanished altogether. Ripley paced about again. "Are they going to leave us here all night? I can't hear anything outside. Maybe they've all moved up. Damn it, why did that firing have to stop?" He thought of the few firm units on the north side of the Hollow Way, of the great ruck of disorganization, bewilderment, and near panic that hung over the rest.

The door rattled and a lantern flared. Bond's voice, sharper than usual, snapped, "Bring them to the farm, Sergeant."

As the prisoners stepped out into the early evening, long columns of red infantry were moving *south* down the Bloomingdale road. Off to the left some German companies were filing away to their tents and stacking their arms in the company streets. Ripley nudged Cuyler, who nodded silently. Whatever else had happened, the American army still lay unmolested north of the Hollow Way, might even be slipping off through the night toward the King's Bridge and the rolling stretches of Westchester.

As they came to the door of the house, three officers strode angrily out, arguing hotly. Again Ripley nudged Cuyler. The day's results had not pleased the officers of His Majesty's regiments.

A major and a captain looked up from a little table as the prisoners were pushed into the room. The major, red-faced and wheezing slightly, shouted: "Your people ran away again, you know. Damned if I think it's worth while asking you questions. It'll all be over soon and then there'll be some rare hangings. Know the uniforms, Captain Aubrey?"

The captain, weary eyes set in a narrow face, shook his head. "They'll have papers, Major Weale." His red-rimmed glance turned on Ripley. "Do you want to save us the trouble of searching you? Be easier for you, you know."

The major tugged at the green facings of his coat. "Blast it, Aubrey, we're not fighting this war to make things easier for the rebels! Get on with it."

Ripley and Cuyler exchanged glances and the former gave curt answers to a flood of routine questions, answers that could do no harm to the army across the Hollow Way. When the captain touched on numbers, equipment, spirit, Ripley fell back on repeated "Don't know's."

At last Captain Aubrey snapped his notebook shut. "That's all, unless the major has—"

Major Weale waved a fat hand. "That's enough. Get them across the island to the ferry."

Aubrey raised his eyebrows. "The hulks?"

"No less. Where'd they expect to go? To the governor's house?"

"The fever, sir—" began Aubrey.

"Blast my eyes! Don't argue! A little fever won't do them any harm." He got up and thumped out of the room.

"Hulks it is," said Aubrey, rubbing his eyes. "Damnably overcrowded but orders stand. Ah—of course, I couldn't contradict the major, but perhaps you'd like to know that your people didn't run. Gave us a deuced hard knock. Amazing. Didn't think there'd be much more to this but chivvying you around until you surrendered. You came right back at us like sportsmen, though. Well, Bond, make out a receipt and we'll have the guard march them away."

While Bond was writing, hoofs sounded in the darkness outside. A hoarse voice called: "Captain Bennett in there?"

Aubrey called: "Gone up to the camp of the Forty-second Highlanders. If you'll wait until I start these prisoners for the hulks, I'll show you."

The door creaked. There was a silence. Then the hoarse voice said close to Ripley: "Hulks be damned. That man's mine!" A heavy hand fell on Ripley's shoulder. He spun about as the candle on the mantel shone on the hard, lined face of Lieutenant Felton of the Royal Marines.

Ripley steadied himself while Cuyler muttered under his breath and Captain Aubrey stared incredulously. Felton spoke again. "This man's a deserter from the marines. He and the other man assaulted me in the town of Concord in Massachusetts Province after accepting my hospitality."

Ripley braced himself to meet the unwavering glare of the hard eyes. Aubrey said impatiently, "Can't do that—take our man, I mean."

"Can't I?" snapped Felton. "I've got six marines outside and they'll show you that the junior service can't dictate to His Majesty's Navy."

Again the door wailed on its hinges and Major Weale stamped in. "What's this? What's this? Why haven't those men started for the hulks?"

Aubrey nodded toward Felton. "He wants to take your prisoners, sir."

"Ho! Does he?" He glared at Felton. "How do you lay claim to them?"

"As deserters from the marines, sir," said Felton.

Weale looked fatly pleased. "And you spotted them? Damned sharp eye you've got, Lieutenant. Can't have desertion, can we? Court-martial, of course, and only one verdict." He nodded to Felton. "Take them. Let me know when the court convenes. I'd like to be there."

Ripley forced a smile and said to Cuyler, "I told you the British army was going to the dogs, but I never thought I'd live to see the day when a marine lieutenant could dictate the disposal of prisoners that the army'd captured. Damned if I did."

Cuyler's innocent blue eyes glinted. "Appalling."

"Silence, you two," spluttered Weale, the veins on his neck bulging above his stock. "I say silence, blast it. You—eh? Ah—what was that?" He blinked rapidly. "Damn your impudence! D'you think I'm going to turn you over to another service after the trouble we've been put to to get you? By God, I'd like to put you in irons. That'd teach you respect for His Majesty's Army. Send in a report about that desertion, Lieutenant. The war'll be over before long and when the hulks are emptied, we'll let you have a look at this pair, perhaps."

Felton's mouth was a grim line. "With all respect, sir, I must insist—"

"Hey? What? Damn my soul and eyes! *You* insist to *me*, a full major, that I give up prisoners I've as good as captured with my own hands? Aubrey! You heard him! By God, I took them and they're mine!"

"Deserters from the Royal Marines," said Felton firmly.

Weale's fist pounded on the table. "Don't bandy words with me. Aubrey, don't tell me that *you* were going to give them up."

"No sir." Aubrey masked a slight smile. "I may add,

sir, that the lieutenant suggested use of force to remove the prisoners."

Weale sprang to his feet. "Force? Force? Your name and ship at once, sir."

"Hugh Felton, stationed on His Majesty's ship *Greyhound*."

"You'll need more than a greyhound for the hunt you've started." Weale suddenly broke into a cackle of laughter that mixed weirdly with his petulant scowl. "I've said my last word. Off with you! And if I find you interfering with my men and my prisoners again, I'll take the matter up with General Howe in person! Be off with you now. At once."

Felton saluted stiffly and marched out of the house. Weale stamped up and down the room. "Force, eh? By Jove, I believe those damned marines'd try it. Aubrey, we'll hold these men here for the night. Don't want any chance of the marines nobbling them up in the dark. They'll stay right here and you'll be personally responsible for them. Damn and blast! I'm going right now to see Colonel Porter. Order up a bigger guard." He snatched up his hat and flung out of the house.

Aubrey's red eyes wrinkled. "Don't worry about the navy taking you. Was the lieutenant right, by the way? Just in confidence."

"They don't recruit for marines in America," said Ripley.

"No, they don't. But he seemed damned sure of himself."

"Didn't he!" said Cuyler. "Why, Captain, do you know I'm not even a Massachusetts man. I live right here in New York and—"

Angry voices outside drowned his words. Someone hammered on the door. "Come in," said Aubrey.

The door crashed open and a short, stocky man in the uniform of a major of marines stood looking into the room. "This the place, Felton?" he called over his shoulder. Then he strode across the threshold. "In the name of the Royal Marines, I demand that those two deserters be handed over to me."

An angry roar sounded outside. "Back again? Out of my way, Felton! I'll put a stop to this flummery, damn my wig if I won't." Major Weale burst into the room, his face crimson. He shook his fist under the marine major's nose. "I've bloody well had enough of this bloody interfering. Colonel Porter's at the lines but the second he comes back—"

"He'll find these men gone. The admiral will back me—"

"Ho! Black Dick'll back you, will he? What do you think Sir William'll say?"

"You'll have to drag him away from his bottle and his little whore first and bloody well rated you'll be for your pains." The two glared at each other as Ripley watched them. Weale was puffing and gurgling in his throat like an enraged turkey cock. The marine, his tough face expressionless, stared back at him. Ripley stole a glance at Aubrey and was surprised to find an expression of concern in the tired eyes. Then the captain cleared his throat. "If I may make a suggestion, Major Weale—" he began.

"Hah? Suggestion?"

"There is no way of settling this tonight. Perhaps the officers of His Majesty's Marines would have no objection if the prisoners remained here—"

The marine's chin set. "They come with me."

"I was going to add, sir, remain here but under a guard of both soldiers and marines."

Weale tugged at his underlip. "Well—hah—now that seems—"

"I agree to that," said the marine quickly.

"Good. They stay here. Both of them. Wait a minute, though. That lieutenant of yours only identified one of them."

Felton, from the doorway, said: "I'm *sure* of one.

The other looks familiar. Besides, they were together in Concord."

"But the other—Cuyler, isn't it?—says he's not a New Englander," put in Aubrey.

"God damn it," roared the marine major. "He can be a deserter without being a New Englander. Seems to me I've seen him somewhere. *Cerberus? Antaeus?* Somewhere, I'll stake my wig on it. The more I think of it the less I like leaving them here."

"May I suggest my plan once more?" said Aubrey.

Weale waved his arms. "All right! All right! I thought we'd settled it. Leave a squad for a guard—"

There was a long wrangle over the composition of the guard that was only settled by Aubrey's suggesting that one marine and one soldier remain in the room with the prisoners while a similar pair mounted guard outside, or all four outside if the quarters seemed secure enough. The marine major threw up his hands and went angrily away, saying that he would be back in the morning with authority from the admiral to claim his men.

A marine guard tramped in and Ripley and Cuyler were marched off to a stone vegetable cellar in the rear of the farm. Aubrey, flashing a lantern about inside, decided that it was escape-proof and the heavy door was slammed and locked.

In the dank gloom of the cellar, Ripley sat slowly against the wall. "This is getting awkward, Joris," he managed to say. "My hands are still shaking." He wiped his forehead.

Cuyler squatted beside him. "Bad luck running into Felton," he said. "But there are so few marines around, I suppose it was bound to happen. It's awkward, but damn it all we're gaining time and that's what we've got to do. And we're together—that's important."

Ripley levered himself up. "Anyway, they'll clear you without any trouble. You'll get out. Know any

New York Tories? You may be able to get them stirring for us."

"For us? You don't know the breed down here. They'd stir to have us both strung up by the thumbs off the Battery. That won't do. We'll stay together."

"You damned chuff. The Lobsters are quite capable of shoving this right through and passing sentence on both of us without any investigation. You've got to get clear."

Cuyler was silent for a moment, then burst out: "God's teeth, this is just selfishness on my part. Think I want to get to the hulks? Old bottoms moored in the East River, crowded to the gun'les and fever aboard?" He began to pace up and down the cellar. "I've got to build up a case for myself as a deserter."

Slowly panic began to leave Ripley. "Joris, we'll do that. We'll keep this whole case so jumbled up that they'll fight over us and we'll keep them fighting until we get a chance to slip our cables."

A little later, there was a thump on the door. Keys rattled. Cuyler raised his voice. "No—I never served on the *Amphion*. *Arethusa* and *Formidable*, though. Went over the side of the old *Formidable* at Porto Bello and—"

Ripley kicked him in the dark. "Shut up, you fool!" The door, that had begun to swing, was checked, then opened with a creak. Two grenadiers came in, one carrying bowls of stew and the other mugs of tea. Over their heads a lantern shone on the shoulder knot of a marine sergeant. Ripley took bowl and mug and yawned. "I'm only a landsman, but I can damned well see that the navy's in charge of us tonight. Any regiment of His Majesty's'd leave us a light."

"They'd give us blankets, too," said Cuyler.

The sergeant growled, "Stow that! You're bloody deserters and—"

Ripley snapped: "You're speaking to officers of the American army, Sergeant. We're to go before Sir

William Howe tomorrow noon and he'll have something to say to his brother the admiral when I report our treatment."

"Confounded scandal," said Cuyler, tasting his stew. "By God, they've even forgotten to put salt in this. I'll remember to mention that to Sir William when he begins to talk of exchanging us against those marine officers that Stirling captured at Red Hook."

"And another thing, Sergeant," broke in Ripley. "The guard is not supposed to address commissioned prisoners except in strict line of duty." He turned to Cuyler. "Afraid it's only our duty to report all this."

Cuyler drank tea noisily, spat it out on the floor. "Tastes like the dregs of a tanning vat. What? Report? Oh—I don't know. Howe'll just think: 'It was only the navy.' We'll get better care when the army relief comes on."

The sergeant spoke in a strangled tone: "Please, sir, if you'll rap on the door when you're done eating, the men'll take the bowls and mugs." He saluted. Then he suddenly set his lantern down on the floor and snarled at the two guards to follow him out into the night. Five minutes later a marine private carefully laid four blankets on the stone floor, produced a small packet of salt, and withdrew in silence.

Ripley handed the salt to Cuyler with a grin and tasted the stew eagerly. "The marines ought to sue you for libel. This stew's fine. Give me another pinch of salt and don't knock over my tea." He finished his bowl and set it beside the door. "First thing we've got to do is get rations that we can hide away and carry with us."

"The army guards us next shift. I'll mention to the sergeant that the Royal Navy'd never serve its prisoners on slops."

"That'll help," agreed Ripley. "Now let's take a bearing. What's in our favor?"

"Time—just as long as we can spin it out," said Cuyler.

"To help on that, we've got the old army-navy jealousy. We can play with it like a tennis ball. The guard tonight'll report that you were talking about His Majesty's ships and deserting. Tomorrow, when the army comes on, I think we'd better go in for farming—with dates. Then we'll switch again and give the navy farming and the army a taste of marine reminiscence. Now another thing we've got in our favor is that a lot of officers don't know what to make of us. Are we prisoners of war or rebels? They're honestly puzzled. Then there are others that seem to have a sneaking bent toward us. Take Aubrey. That wasn't all army-navy that he was after. He kept Weale from looking at our papers. He fought off the marines. We'll find others like him. Most of all, we'll think of every kind of plea and appeal. Do you know where we are?"

"Cornelis Spanjaard's farm. But I don't know this part of the island very well."

Ripley got up and felt around the walls. "Damn it, no way of seeing out. Joris, we've got to have a look around here somehow."

Cuyler scratched his head. "But how—" He suddenly doubled up, clutching his belly. "Christ in the Catskills, what a cramp. Guard! Guard!"

Ripley shook him. "What is it?"

Cuyler muttered, "Easy. These cramps'll be worth about six trips to the ajax and— Guard!"

The door creaked. A guard peered warily in, sighed, called the sergeant, and Cuyler, groaning and bent nearly double, was led out into the darkness.

Smiling in satisfaction, Ripley put out the lantern, rolled up in his blankets and awaited Cuyler's return.

At the end of a half hour, the door opened and Cuyler crept in. As he settled down in his blankets he whispered: "Grenadier at one elbow, marine at the other, and the sergeant bringing up the rear. Didn't have much chance to look around. If we could wriggle out of here somehow, there'd be a fine chance to drop down the rocks to the Hudson."

"How about going east?"

"I'll look at that two cramps from now. The sergeant gave me some rum but I don't think it's going to do much good. Next trip I'll see if I can't swing a bit wider and look at a path that goes west. If it's the place I think it is, it leads right down to a beach under the cliffs."

"What's the army doing?"

"More regiments moving up here. One of them's German. I couldn't hear the men talking much but I've got an idea that they're sore as a green ferryman's hands. They seem to think that it all ought to have been over this morning and they'd counted on drinking rum right out of jack boots tonight. I think they're still full of vapors from Bunker Hill." He lay silent for a moment, then said, "Honest, Rip, what do you think of our chances?"

"Play whist?" asked Ripley.

"Blast your brass! Didn't I teach you the finer points?"

"Maybe, but this time the marked cards are in Howe's hands, not yours. Yes, they're marked. He's got the ace, queen, and ten. We hold the king, knave, and nine. If we play them according to Cocker—maybe there's a chance. When's your next cramp?"

"In just about an hour. I'll keep awake."

"Good luck to you—and for God's sake don't let them get a sawbones to look at you."

III

THE NEXT morning Ripley shaved with a borrowed razor and brushed his clothes as well as he could while Cuyler mumbled through a mass of lather that on his last trip out under guard the army still seemed motionless and he had heard no gossip about any moves on the part of the Americans.

Ripley was just struggling into his coat when the door was flung open. Outside stood a mixed guard of marines and light infantry who had relieved the shift of the night before. A sergeant of the Fifth, blue facings sharp on his coat, intoned, "Orders to transfer prisoners to the court."

Ripley and Cuyler fell in between the mixed files. The latter whispered softly, "Court, eh? What does that mean?"

Out of the corner of his mouth Ripley said: "I feel better. It can't mean anything. Court be damned." To himself he thought: "More time gained, perhaps."

In the long kitchen of the farmhouse a table was drawn up in front of the empty hearth. Back of it sat a colonel in the uniform of the Twenty-third. Behind him stood Major Weale and Captain Aubrey, the latter still drawn and spent. At the other end of the table, a sad-faced man sat brooding over papers. The braid on his navy uniform was raveled and tarnished in marked contrast to the spruceness of two junior officers who hovered at his elbow.

The guard halted with a clatter and the officers back of the table looked up. The colonel said: "Ha! These the chaps we've got to try?"

The sad-faced sailor, a captain by his epaulets, shrugged his shoulders and spoke in a slow drone: "I'm not familiar with the case. Most irregular. Something about rape, wasn't it?" One of his aides bent deferentially and whispered. The sad lines of the captain's face deepened. "Oh—not rape. I was hoping—mixed court. Most irregular."

The colonel cleared his throat. "Perhaps one of you gentlemen will tell us just what we're here for."

Weale stepped forward. "These prisoners, Colonel Musgrave. We took them. The navy claims them."

"Ha! Ha!" The colonel's voice sliced the air. "Damn it all, Captain Truesdale, you can't do that."

One of the aides bent and whispered again. The navy captain nodded like a pendulum, droned, "That's it. Saw some damned marines lolling about the door. Hale them in, Lyell."

The blank-faced marine major and Lieutenant Felton were brought in. "Now what is this all?"

The scene of the night before was re-enacted, although its asperities were somewhat softened by the presence of rank. When Felton had finished his story Captain Truesdale looked across at the colonel. "Clear case, I think, Colonel Musgrave."

"Quite. Your man has no claim to them."

Truesdale's watery eyes suffused still more. "I'm not sure that I'd go quite so far as to agree with you." He turned to the marine major. "You've examined these men?"

Colonel Musgrave helped himself to snuff and cut in testily: "That was done by the captors. Thoroughly, I'm assured."

Truesdale turned to his senior aide. "Lyell, take down these questions." He joined his finger tips. "Now precisely where were these men apprehended?"

The aide whispered again and the captain's mouth dropped. "Well—perhaps that's not quite the question I wished to formulate. What I proposed to say was this—um—hah—" He turned to Ripley. "When did you enroll in His Majesty's Marines?"

Ripley answered, "I stand on my rights as prisoner of war. The question does not arise. I so informed Major Weale yesterday."

The full mouth drooped again. "Ah—quite so. Then the next man. The—the—large one. When did you enroll in His Majesty's Marines?"

Cuyler repeated Ripley's answer. The captain looked helplessly about the room. "Were there not—were there not—um—hah—witnesses?"

Felton, hard eyes on Ripley, snapped, "The first prisoner, Mayne's his name, was a marine private on board the *Cumberland.* I recognized him ashore over a year ago. The other—Cuyler—was with him. I did not recognize him but suspect him of being a deserter as well. Both assaulted me while I was wearing His Majesty's uniform."

Colonel Musgrave took snuff again. "Damned slim evidence. Any more?"

"Yes, sir." Felton stepped to the door and beckoned. Two marine privates, rigid and unblinking, stepped into the room. "These men," began Felton, "were on guard last night. They overheard an admission by one of the prisoners that he'd deserted off Porto Bello from the *Formidable.*"

Truesdale leaned forward in his chair. "Ha! Admitted it, did he? Lyell, prepare a deposition, have the fellow swear to it."

"Just a moment," snapped Musgrave. "How about our fellows? Aubrey. Have those damned guards sent in."

Two tall grenadier privates, eyes fixed on the wall over the colonel's head, were examined. One of them was hopelessly confused by his surroundings but the other managed to say that he remembered the prisoners talking about crops. Dates had been mentioned. "The yellow-haired bugger, saving your presence, sir, was saying as how the crops of '73 had been the biggest. Got bloody hot about it, they did. No, sir, they ain't so much as mentioned the sea, sir."

Musgrave threw out his hands. "There you have it, Captain. Right from his guards."

The naval officer flushed. "The—ah—very remark *I* was about to make. We must have—we must have —eh—Lyell—what's the damned thing I want—ah —deposition in due form, that's it, executed before the court. Then—"

Colonel Musgrave rose from his chair. "Aubrey's right. We're bloody well confusing the point. In the first place, these men aren't on trial. They're facing no charges. And this is an informal, unofficial gathering to ascertain facts. We have no competence over these men. What we're trying to do is to vindicate the right of His Majesty's Army to dispose of its prisoners of war as it sees fit. The matter has been referred to me with power so I rule that they shall be sent to the hulks."

Truesdale rose, head shaking. "And *I* have been given power in this matter and *I*, representing the senior service, say that the men shall be handed over to His Majesty's Marines for trial. I may add that I ah—um—resent that my time should be taken up ashore by haggling about these two damned rebels."

The colonel bowed. "May *I* point out to you, Captain, that it becomes at once—eh? How was that, Aubrey? Exactly. It becomes now not a case of the two prisoners. It becomes a case of whether the royal forces ashore may submit to being dictated to—in a most arbitrary way, sir—by the navy which took no part in the action wherein these men were captured. I may say, too, that I consider your officer's identification to be most unsatisfactory. Neither the army nor the navy recruit in the colonies. Thus—how could the man Mayne have been a part of the corps in the first place? As to the man Cuyler—why, damn my wig, just look at him! New York Dutch!" He turned to Cuyler. "Did *you* ever see Lieutenant Felton in Massachusetts?"

"I'm a New Yorker as well as a prisoner of war," said Cuyler.

"And you, sir?" said the colonel to Ripley.

"Few marines come to Concord, Colonel. The only one I ever saw there was considerably disguised in liquor. He could, in fact, barely sit erect in his chair. I presume that an officer of Lieutenant Felton's known standing would never be found in such a condition."

Colonel Musgrave slapped his hands together.

"There you are, Captain! By Jove, sir, those men shall stay with us."

"I believe in Lieutenant Felton. I believe in what the guards overheard," said Truesdale.

"Rubbish! And which guards?" The colonel picked up his hat. "This board or court or office, or whatever you like to call it, was scarcely called into being legally. But I adjourn it legally this very moment. Major Weale—those men are on no account to leave your hands. Damn it, we didn't take enough prisoners yesterday to fill a hand barrow and those we did take aren't going to slip out. Captain Truesdale, I bid you good day."

Truesdale returned the bow stiffly. "You have not heard the last of this, Colonel. I shall comb the ranks of the marines here in New York until I find someone to support Felton's story. Not that he needs anyone on my account. But when people turn damned, blatantly, mulishly obstinate, why—why—eh? What's that, Lyell? Oh, of course. You'll have no objection, I presume, to our maintaining a joint guard over these men? You are very good, I'm sure. Hah—um!" He tucked his hat under his arm and made an angry exit, followed by his staff.

Colonel Musgrave beamed on Ripley and Cuyler. "Done like soldiers! Now you rest easy. No damned tarry-breeks is going to take men out of *my* command. No, gentlemen, I'll have you in the hulks in three days' time. I wish you good day." He strolled out, humming "Over the hills and far away," Major Weale at his heels. Felton and the marine major, after glaring at Ripley, stalked majestically out.

Aubrey lounged over to the pair. "Don't know but what I ought to let Felton have you after all, destroying relations between army and navy that way. Back you go to your hutch until we get word about you." He began to chuckle. "Just wish I knew what you were up to, damme if I don't. Poor Truesdale's wits'll be fuddled for the next two days."

"I hope so," said Ripley. "Likewise Musgrave's. Now I'll thank you, Captain, to escort us back to our quarters."

Aubrey burst out laughing. "Damned if I do. The sergeant'll march you right back there."

"If you please," said Cuyler. "We insist on the shelter of your rank. I'm a symbol of the power of the British army and no marine's going to herd me up like a stray goose and run me down to Truesdale's pens."

Aubrey shrugged. "Maybe I'd better, and lock you in with my own hands. If they got you away from us, Colonel Musgrave'd have me at a drumhead." He shouted for the guard and Ripley and Cuyler were marched away to the old stone cellar whose lock Aubrey fastened behind them.

For three days they were alone, penned in the cellar. Then Ripley sent the guard to get Captain Aubrey and demanded, as prisoner of war, the right to exercise. Aubrey vanished and did not return until late afternoon. There had, he said, been a devil of a row which had ended in grudging permission to walk, under guard, for a half hour on the Hudson shore after sundown.

There was a glow in the west that laid a faint red stain along the heights on the Jersey side as the two were marched down a steep, rocky path to the river's edge below. All about them in the dusk the camp stirred, but there was no sign of coming movement or action. Then Ripley's heart gave a great leap. Off to the north, beyond the last British outpost, beyond the Hollow Way, low clouds shimmered as they threw back the reflection of the fires of Washington's army. "Still there, Joris," he muttered.

Young Bond, in charge of the guard, said, "You know you chaps aren't supposed to talk. It's part of the bargain."

The two fell silent. Then, as they reached the narrow strip of beach below the cliffs, they jogged steadily north a hundred yards, turned, jogged back south while their mixed guard, muskets bobbing, puffed and wheezed along beside them. At last, panting and refreshed, they scaled the path, passed on through the hum of the camps, and were locked up in their cellar. Cuyler wiped his forehead and sat down. "Damned if I've had an idea worth a stiver."

Ripley tossed his hat onto his blankets. "We're on an island. There's a way out. We know the land better than anyone else. It seems to me there's no use trying to go north to the Hollow Way. We've got to get to Long Island or the Jersey side and work our way back. Light the lantern and we'll scratch a map of Horn's Hook and Ward's Island."

Cuyler scrambled up. "You make the map. I want a breath of air. I'm poisoned again." He began to bawl. "Guard! Sergeant of the guard! Cramps! God!"

Wearily the guard shepherded him out into the night. Ripley made sure that the bread and salt meat that he had hidden back of a loose stone were in good condition, then set to work on the map, scoring deep lines in the dirt floor.

He started, wiped them out with his hand as the door rattled. A lantern shone down on him and Felton's voice barked: "Look sharp and tell me where you've seen this man before!" He pushed a marine private in ahead of him.

Like a shattering blow, recognition struck Ripley as light flooded the face of the newcomer. Dancey—that was his name. He'd been with him at Plymouth Dockyard, with him on the *Amphion*, had stood guard with him at Gibraltar. Ripley struggled to compose himself. "What's the matter, Felton?" he asked.

"Look sharp," said Felton again, shoving the lantern forward.

Dancey's broken nose and close-set eyes moved nearer. Ripley held his breath. Then the man spoke slowly. "No, sir, I ain't never seen him afore."

Felton jammed the light closer. "If you're wrong, Dancey—" he began.

Dancey shook his head. "There was a surly bugger on the *Mersey*, sir, saving your presence, that looked som'at like him. But he had a scar, like, and his eyes was like a mouldiwarp's. No sir, this ain't him."

"Sure?"

"I know my duty, sir."

"God help you if you're lying."

"Lying, to save a bloody rebel, sir?"

Felton dimmed his light. "Enough. Get back to your duty." Dancey faced smartly about, waited for Felton to leave, followed him stiffly without a backward glance. But as he turned, the toe of his boot touched Ripley and his hand made a reassuring gesture. Then the door slammed.

Ripley sank back against the wall, trembling. "He knew me—and didn't say a word." He leaned his chin on his hand and began to think. If one marine would shield him, why not two, five, or a dozen? Perhaps others had recognized him already and kept silent.

Voices boomed outside and Cuyler was pushed through the door. Ripley dragged him to the far end of the cellar. "Joris, this may be big. Listen—"

Cuyler clapped a hand over his mouth. "Big? Wait till you hear what I've got to tell."

Ripley freed himself. "But the marine—"

"Damn the marine. Look, Cornelis Spanjaard's come back to his farm. He and his wife are living on the second floor. They're acting loyal as hell to the King, loyal as a whore's shoulders to her mattress. He just wants to save his land. But I got a chance to talk to him out by the ajax." His voice shook with excitement. "We're as good as out right now. Look at this." He dove at the wall and pulled out the loose stone that hid the supplies. "Kneel down here, Rip. This is a dummy wall. Spanjaard's father blocked this up years ago. It's hollow back there. The outside's turf beyond this and the back wall—the real back wall—faces into the hollow that runs down to the Hudson. Cornelis is going to cut it through tomorrow night. It'll be easy because he's got the run of the place and he offered to bury some empty bottles. See what'll happen? He'll cut it through. He'll have two capes, some homespun breeches, and some food."

"Yes?" said Ripley eagerly. "What then?" His mind buzzed with the sudden prospect of freedom.

"Why—then we're out."

"Oh." Disappointment flattened Ripley's tones. "Out—but still on the island. Can't he do any more than that?"

"Than that? Damn it, don't go so fast. That beach isn't patrolled. We know that. And the river isn't, barring the two anchored sloops upstream. Cornelis has got a skiff hidden at the foot of the cliffs. I know the place because I've fished there. If his should be gone, there'd be a dozen more that we can find with a little hunting. Isn't that complete? A clear run across to the Jersey side"

Ripley nodded slowly. "Yes—it looks watertight. Now see here—what we've got to do is this—keep right on doing what we've been doing. Forget all about Spanjaard—no, wait a minute. Forget about him *until he comes*. Then we'll take each step in order and take it cool as a bull in a shady pasture. We'll keep right on playing the buffoon for the guards and anyone else who comes around. Oh, damn it, why isn't it tonight? Tomorrow may be too late—"

"Why too late?" said Cuyler in surprise.

Ripley told him rapidly about Dancey. "But you see, it shows that they're hunting up marines already. They may dig one out tomorrow who won't do what Dancey did. We'll keep right on planning and if we get a chance to cast off before Spanjaard starts work, we'll take it."

Cuyler, sprawled on the floor, began to wriggle. "This damned waiting. I'd forgotten about it. I've got a whole brigade of ants crawling up and down my spine and my legs."

"That's another reason for keeping busy. Let's get back to our map and do some studying on it." He began to scratch fresh lines on the floor.

They talked and argued and wrangled until they were exhausted. Then they rolled up in their blankets and struggled for sleep, each mind busy with thoughts of Spanjaard and his plan.

Morning brought no change in the disposition of their guard. Captain Aubrey dropped in after the noon rations and brought them rum which they drank sparingly. "Purely unofficial and damned irregular," he said, filling Cuyler's mug. "Can't help thinking about you chaps, though." He turned to Ripley. "Felton's goggling his eyes like a damned sea turtle over some blasted nonsense his guards reported to him."

"If he wants to listen to muffin-brained gossip, that's his concern," said Ripley.

Aubrey's lean face broke into a grin. "He's snapping around the admiral's heels to find out if any officers here have served in the Moluccas. Someone seems to have told him a tale about deserting from an Indiaman and shipping north to Japan."

Ripley laughed. "Be damned to that. Only the Dutch can go to Japan and—" He winced as Cuyler kicked him suddenly.

Aubrey leaned forward. "Ho! The Dutch, eh? So a man with a good old Saxon name like Joris Cuyler could never have—" He shook his fist at the two. "Blast your eyes. I'll not play in this pixie game of yours." He burst out laughing. "Do what you like to Felton's men, but if I find you addling the wits of my grenadiers, I'll come forward and identify you as smugglers and deserters with a hint of murder to boot. Know what Truesdale did night before last? Sat up till sunrise going over navy lists to see if there ever was an Ensign Watchmaker."

"Let him," said Ripley yawning.

"Let him! Blast your teeth, you *made* him. One of the guards brought back a tale of desertion off Caracas, involving the murder of one Ensign William Watchmaker. Can't imagine where he got the yarn, can you?"

"Can't imagine anything in here," said Cuyler. "Any news from the lines?"

"Devil a bit. Most of us think that Howe's just waiting for your people to fall to pieces."

"Think he'd get a little tired of that. He tried it in Boston and the only falling to pieces that we saw was—" Ripley hesitated. "Anyway, it was not done by the army of the United States."

Aubrey frowned. "What really did happen there? I was in England. We heard so many stories."

"Howe felt that a summer in Boston'd be too hot. So he went to Halifax," said Cuyler.

"I know, I know," said Aubrey impatiently. "But what *made* him?"

"A Boston bookseller," said Ripley.

Cuyler nodded solemnly. "That's right. He sold him a map and Howe said, 'Damn my wig, if I can't sail right to Halifax. Why didn't I think of that before?'"

Aubrey looked puzzled. Ripley waved Cuyler away. "Henry Knox was a bookseller. He's in command of our artillery. He went to Ticonderoga and brought the guns overland to Boston."

"In *winter*? That be damned for a shave," said Aubrey.

"It's true," said Ripley. "Cuyler and I helped, along with some of the best seamen who ever spliced a cable. And when the guns got to Boston the only thing Howe could do was get out. No, I think he's had enough of waiting for us to fall to pieces."

"But that was different," said Aubrey. "This time you've had setbacks. Some of your men have run. We've rounded up more prisoners than we can count. I don't see how you can hope to keep going."

Ripley leaned forward. "Listen, Captain—the day

we were taken, our army made a counterattack. You yourself said you were surprised."

"I was. I might even add that *we* were. But that doesn't mean—"

"It means just this. It's what's been happening right along. Time and again our army's seemed to melt away, but every time it was about to die it picked up strength, weathered whatever was ahead, and kept on going. We've fought among ourselves. We've had cowardice to fight, misunderstandings, inexperience, supply troubles, jealousies, lack of arms and powder. And fighting those things is harder than fighting you. But each time we've won. We're going to keep on winning."

"But suppose we attack Washington and chase him off the island?"

"Then you will have attacked him and chased him off the island. That's all. When you get to the mainland, you'll still find him there with his army, not to mention Glover's brigade and Glover's regiment. Maybe you'll beat him there. But that will be all. You'll just beat him and have it to do all over again and all the time we'll be learning and growing stronger. I tell you, I'd rather see a defeat or two for us than an easy victory that we might owe to your mistakes rather than to our own skill and solidness. You see one thing that a lot of you chaps don't see is that we're damnably in earnest about this."

Aubrey tilted his fur cap over one ear. "That's one thing that's kept me wondering—why are you?"

Ripley said, "It's very simple. The night I came—I mean I heard my father say once, when a Tory neighbor asked him that same question, 'We're used to governing ourselves. We're going to keep on doing it.' We claim the rights of freeborn Englishmen and when they're taken away from us and when everything that's done in London seems to be trying to turn us into trading posts—why, naturally, we'll fight for those rights."

Aubrey waved his mug. "Of course, of course. But you've got more rights than a lot of Englishmen have."

"That's not our problem. If Englishmen in England give up the rights that are theirs to the Crown, it's their business. Maybe what we're doing here'll wake them up. We're going to win this, and when we do, it'll be the greatest event not only in our history but in England's. You *talk* about freeborn Britons. We're *fighting* too for them as well as for every American. If we *should* lose—which we're not going to—you'll find plaguy little difference between England and Prussia."

Aubrey laughed uncertainly. "I can't say you convince me—but damned if I can help respecting it. You're *wrong*. Utterly wrong. It won't do to go against the Crown. But as I say, I respect what you said." He got up, straightened his belts. "I'm for duty. Keep the rest of the rum. And—uh—bloody well hope none of the marines make trouble for you. Although—" he shrugged—"you'd be little better off in the hulks. We've got a damned provost named Cunningham who's a black disgrace. Can't see how they tolerate him. Wish you luck." He raised his hand to his fur busby and left the cellar.

"He's a pretty good chap," said Cuyler.

"Agreed. But I keep wondering if he had instructions to see to it that our minds weren't distracted by things outside during the time he was here. Notice he left pretty suddenly."

"Don't be so damned suspicious. And he left us the rest of the rum."

"Hoping we'd muddle ourselves, perhaps." Ripley whistled softly to himself, then said, "Time for you to have a cramp. Keep a good lookout and we'll talk about what you see when you come back."

Cuyler looked wistfully at the rum and got to his feet. "I'm nothing but a damned slave to duty." He was escorted out. An hour passed, two hours, and still he did not come back. Ripley began to pace nervously about the cellar. What could have happened to him? Had the authorities decided to separate them? Or—or had Cuyler escaped by himself? He pushed away the thought. Cuyler would have been incapable of such an act. And yet—time was creeping on.

He turned as voices sounded outside. The heavy door swung and Cuyler, pale but grinning to himself, stumbled in and sat down on his blankets. Ripley caught his shoulder. "Where the devil have you been? Two hours and a half!"

Cuyler waved his hand. His voice was rather feeble. "It's all right. One of the damned guards began to feel sorry for me. So sorry that he told the sergeant and the sergeant told that thickheaded clunch of an ensign and he—rot his guts—told the surgeon and the surgeon gave me the God-damnedest clyster that was ever administered on the island of Manhattan." He sank back on the blankets. "Get out some rations. I'll swoon if you don't. God damn that surgeon." He gnawed at bread and salt meat. "Saw one thing, though. Cornelis Spanjaard was at the front stoop and winked at me when I was coming back. He'll be around for us just the way he said. And it's clouding up."

The sun went down, threw blazing pencils of light through the cracks in the door. Later the guards brought in the evening meal—thick roast beef, greens, and bread. The two ate hungrily, Cuyler crooning over the red slices while Ripley shook his head in doubt. "I can't see it. Aubrey makes a formal call on us and brings us rum. Now we get the best rations we've had since we left Cambridge." He smiled grimly. "Fattening us up for slaughter."

"Maybe the surgeon ordered this for me."

"And maybe King George did." Ripley finished the last of his food, drank from the earthenware pitcher in the corner. "Sure Spanjaard's going to be all right?"

"Don't worry. Now I'm going to set a trap for some sleep." He rolled up in his blankets and soon was snoring gently. Ripley stretched out, envying Cuyler's ability to drop off like a kitten. He himself was tense and nervous, his ears ringing with the effort of listening to the night sounds that drifted through the door from the dark world outside.

The hours slid by. The guard was changed and Ripley could hear the new relief settling into their posts, coughing and grunting. He crept to the door but there was nothing in their sparing words that told him anything of doings in the army.

Suddenly he sat up in his blankets. Through the rough stones of the wall he could hear a faint clink and scrape. He tapped Cuyler's shoulder. The New Yorker sat up with a start. "Cornelis," he whispered. "And on time."

"No noise now," muttered Ripley and began to fumble in the dark for his few possessions that he had arranged earlier.

The clinking and scraping went on. Ripley froze with fear as a harsh voice called to a guard: "Who's back there?" Then relief flooded him as the guard answered: "Bloody Dutchy from t' farm. Buryin' bottles that the colonel has drank."

"Told you Spanjaard'd do this up well," said Cuyler. "He'll begin to break glass when he's chopped away enough for us to get through."

Again Ripley's ears sang with the effort of listening. Any second might bring the sound of breaking glass that would usher them out to the free world.

He cocked his head. "Hey!" he whispered. "What's that?"

The freshening wind from the south was suddenly filled with the sweeping clang and boom of bells, deep-toned and throaty. "Down in the city," said Cuyler. "Maybe it's a fire."

"Or an attack!"

"Not likely. Whatever it is, it's best for us. Damn it, I'd like a good earthquake and a hurricane to add to this. The more mixed up they are—"

"I know. I know." Ripley spoke irritably. The bronze

tones, riding high on the night wind, might drown out the signal for escape. He leaned his ear against the dank rocks, trying to shut out the insistence of the alarm. He stiffened. Drums began to beat off toward the Hudson and hoofs drummed on soft ground. A voice wailed: "Derby! Derby! You're to send word to bring on the Erb Prinz Regiment. Sir William's orders!"

Ripley caught Cuyler's hand in the dark. "What in the name of the devil?"

"Never mind it. Listen for Cornelis. Listen— Ha! By God, there it goes." Through the din of the bells and drums, glass shattered smartly beyond the rear wall. Ripley began to worry at one of the stones.

Then sudden lantern light flooded into the cellar as the door swung open and Felton stepped in, the guard behind him. He spoke quickly. "Get your traps together. We're moving you. Hurry, damn it."

Ripley's heel clinked against the loosened stone, setting it back into place. "Whose orders? I demand to know whose orders."

Felton snarled. "This is according to Cocker. You'll have your precious bloody double guard. Move, now!"

Through a cloud of sickening disappointment Ripley saw three guards shuffle into the cellar, bayonets glinting in the lantern light. Cursing, he picked up his bundle and, with Cuyler, moved out into the crisp air of the night. "This way!" snapped Felton. "Sergeant Carfrae, you'll take the flank and I'll be at the rear. Orders are to shoot at the least attempt. You understand."

The sergeant grunted and the double file of men that hedged Ripley and Cuyler moved off past the Spanjaard house where orderlies were dismounting from frothing horses.

Ripley thought: "What does it matter? It's all over. We'll never have a chance like this again. We'll—" He set his shoulders. "Damned if we won't. We'll force a chance. Now—what's happening?" He looked south through the night and his eyes widened. The low-hanging clouds were ablaze with long sheets of flame that leaped up from the city a bare two miles away. And to the clouds was joined a thickening billow of smoke, vast as the lower island, a solid billow that rose in lazy, oily coils to join with the lowering sky. "My God," he said.

Cuyler croaked. "Look! Down by Whitehall! By Coenties!"

"The prisoners will maintain silence," barked Felton.

Cuyler disregarded him. "It's the whole city!"

Felton raged. "God damn it, don't draw attention to yourselves! Your own people set that and the army's calling for retaliation. The men are calling for it. Keep quiet or I can't answer for your safety."

"*We* set it!" exclaimed Cuyler. "How could we have done that from the Hollow Way?"

"You've got your damned spies in here. They did it. Now silence!"

The column struck east across the island, following a worn footpath. Sometimes, as the path dipped and sank, only the fiery clouds to the south could be seen. Then from a rise they would blink at the sea of flame that surged around Manhattan's lower rim. Boats began to push out into the East River that was a lake of molten light. A small sloop, its masts and spars outlined in flame, staggered drunkenly out into the stream. And all the while the bells boomed and clanged.

As they crossed the Post Road, a long string of laden carts, military and civilian, worked north. Old people sat bent and motionless on high seats and children cried in terror from the shaky loads. Lost dogs ran cringing and barking through the unbroken procession.

At last they came out onto a narrow wharf north of Murray Hill where Ripley and Cuyler, a bayonet at each elbow, were forced into a barge manned by sailors of the Royal Navy. Cuyler watched the marines and grenadiers clamber over the side after them. "I tell you, Rip, it'd do some of these men good to serve with the old Fourteenth. Of course—" he waved expansively—"as it is their feet look like legs of mutton and they're clumsy as a fat girl learning to milk a cow."

"Keep a civil tongue in your head when you talk about His Majesty's Marines," said Felton shortly.

The boat pushed off across the East River and oars rose and fell with magnificent precision. Near the mouth of Newtown Creek on the Long Island shore the bow grated. "Your new home—for a while," said Felton grimly. "I trust you gentlemen will enjoy it."

The guard disembarked awkwardly, formed up, and marched the pair away to a comfortable stone cottage that looked west to Manhattan. Torches and lanterns flared on a stone façade. A door was pushed open and swallowed up the shadowy men. Installed in a second-floor room, Ripley ran to the window and looked out. South a half mile was the wide expanse of Newtown Creek. West was the East River, while north there stretched a belt of moor and marshland rough, empty, and treeless. And over the whole scene, faint in the north, bright in the south, spread the glow of the great fire. Cuyler, looking over Ripley's shoulder, suddenly pointed. North of the burning city, two dots of light shone clear and steady. There was a catch in his voice. "The—the aged parent. Holding the fort. Those lights are from the river room. And—and where have those hell-spawned guards put our blankets?"

Ripley muttered: "Never mind the blankets. We've got to start all over again with our plans. We don't know Long Island the way we do Manhattan. Shut your eyes and try to think of everything you remember about this shore and the back country. What's north of here? Whose house is this? Where does Newtown Creek rise?"

IV

NEXT morning, lower Manhattan was still masked in a pall of smoke. Ripley studied the East River and the old manor house on Blackwell's Island in the channel. "That's a short span over there, Joris. What could we do if we got to Blackwell's?"

"Nothing. Even the fleas are Tory. And the current's enough to knock your teeth down your throat if you tried to swim." He looked around suddenly. The stairs echoed to the tramp of feet, to Felton's shout. "This is most irregular. I shall protest to Captain Truesdale. The admiral shall hear of it!"

Aubrey's weary voice said: "But the papers are signed by *both* the Howes."

A dart of hope shot through Ripley. Those were signatures that Felton did not like. He thought: "It may be parole! It may be—"

The door swung open and Felton and Aubrey stood on the threshold. They stepped aside. Into the room, his long queue jutting out like a scabbard, strode the elder Cuyler. He stood still for a second, eyes on his son. Then he whirled about, waved his stick. "I thank you, gentlemen. You've searched me thoroughly and can give bond that I've no coach and four in my pockets. My pass gives me ten minutes alone with my son."

"But it's so irregular," repeated Felton stubbornly.

"Irregularity, young man, is something denied only to subordinates. A superior may be as damned irregular as he pleases. No. I wish to hear no more about it. The admiral, in other days, has dined at my house and I may assure you that he holds me in some esteem to this day. And may I point out that in addition to being obstinate, you're plagued ill-mannered in keeping Captain Aubrey waiting."

Felton withdrew grumbling. Old Cuyler turned on his son. "Now what devil's caldron have you two managed to get into?" His voice dropped. "This won't do."

Joris, blinking rapidly, said: "How'd you get here? How'd you find out where we were?"

"That's a fine question." Old Cuyler turned to Ripley. "I'm sure that you'd be able to reason that you were recognized—or rather Joris was—crossing the Post Road last night. Damn it, every stews-keeper on Manhattan knows Joris. Dirck Hoogezeele came and told me. I went to the general and the admiral and demanded to be allowed to see you. They wanted to know my politics and I informed them that as they both had dined at my house in the old days, such questions were an impertinence. So here I am. Of course, I'll have you out on parole quicker than you can haul up a well bucket. Parole! You'll stay at the house under my oath, that you will. And if anyone tries to bother you, I'll make those two damned Howes mount guard on my own front step." He thumped his stick on the floor.

Ripley began to chuckle involuntarily. His shoulders shook with relief, with joy. Joris's broad face beamed and he rubbed his hands together. "Hyah, hyah, hyah. And Master Felton shall carry my belongings home for me. On his shoulder. Hyah, hyah, hyah. And we'll bring Aubrey in for a drink. Sound chap, Aubrey."

"We'll drown him in geneva straight from Rotterdam," chortled old Cuyler.

Ripley slapped Joris's back. "We'll—" His elation dropped heavily from him. "We'll stay right here," he said in a flat voice, eyes on the floor.

"Stay?" Joris stared.

"You've lost your head," said his father, pushing his big hat back on his forehead.

Ripley shoved his hands in his pockets and began to pace up and down the room. "No. You see, that idea of parole is mighty tempting. But if we give our words, we're tied here until they exchange us—and no one's going to bother about two lieutenants very much, especially when the damned Lobsters have so many more prisoners than we have. High officers, too."

"But you'll be free," spluttered old Cuyler.

Ripley turned on him. "That's just what we won't be. We won't be free to escape and get back to the army. That's where we belong. As long as we're alive and in jail—"

Joris's big head bobbed slowly. "Rip's right. We stay."

The old man waved his stick again. "Right? Right? What kind of reasoning's that? Get you out of here. I had a hint that there might be trouble for young Mayne on an old score. Just a hint. But that hint'd die if you came home—on parole."

"We stay," said his son.

"Stay? This is disobedience! This is madness! By God, it's against all law! It's against the Bible. By God, I'd break my stick right over your backs if I weren't so damned proud of you both!" He caught their hands, gave them a brisk, dry shake, whirled about, waved his stick. "Damned if I'm not the proudest father in Manhattan! Escape? Of course you will. And until then, I'll see to it that you don't lack for a thing." He went to the east window with birdlike steps. "Ha! Like being neighbors. I can see my own windows blinking in the sun. H'm. Clear view. I shan't forget it." He tugged out an enormous watch. "Must keep my part of the bargain. My time's up." He threw an arm about his son's broad shoulders. "Keep your wits and your eyes about you. That's all I've got to say. Just keep— Ha! H'm!" He whipped out a vast handkerchief and blew his nose a fierce blast. He caught Ripley's hand, gave it another shake, and marched out of the door.

The two leaned on the sill and watched the little old man, queue bobbing briskly, walk down to the landing between two marines. He seemed to be delivering some sort of lecture to them for his arms waved and his stick flourished. Joris said huskily, "Cantankerous old idiot. He'll end by taking over command of both the Howes. God, it did me good to see him!"

That evening, two marines brought in a great hamper containing Rhenish wine, Holland gin, a pair of gigantic roast geese, fresh bread, and apples from the Cuyler orchard. One of the men, as he straightened up, said in a low voice, "Thank ye kindly, sir," and showed the rim of a gold piece between his fingers. His mate touched his cap respectfully.

When they had gone, Cuyler plunged into the hamper. "The aged parent moves in a mysterious way. See those gold pieces?"

"He'll never bribe those men," said Ripley.

"He knows that as well as you do. But he sees that our job'll be easier. Let's get Aubrey up here and stuff him."

Aubrey came up, accepted a glass of Rhenish, and sniffed wistfully at the geese. "Wish I could. I've got to go over to the city. The fire's about out and I'm in charge of work. Young Bond's taking my place until tomorrow. You remember him?"

"You'll come next time, then. Send Bond up by all means. We'll make a neat packet of bones for Felton. Any news about us?"

Aubrey finished his glass. "Not a thing. Both the Howes are on the flagship with their staffs, trying to decide what the Duke of Marlborough would have done in this case. I'm afraid no one'll give you a thought for a few days."

Ripley flung himself into one of the chairs that the guard had brought up. "Damn it! I can't see why the army just doesn't say: 'The whole case is ridiculous. Hands off.' I swear I don't."

"Navy's just chivvying us about," grumbled Cuyler. "Why, in our army, General Washington'd settle a case like this while he was fitting in his false teeth. Damned if he wouldn't." He sighed patiently. "Sorry you can't join us. Send Bond along."

When Aubrey had gone, Ripley raised his eyebrows. "No one'll give us a thought for a few days, eh?"

"No one," agreed Cuyler. "Except the estimable Felton and the guard."

There was a knock at the door. Fresh-faced and diffident young Bond entered, stammering his appreciation of the invitation. Cuyler waved royally. "Rough fare, Lieutenant. But it's wartime. Many's the night we've had to scrape along with nothing but this. Haven't we, Rip?"

Ripley laughed bitterly. "Remember the night when the silver service from the sergeant's mess went astray? That was when we nearly ran out of Burgundy for the privates. Whew! Damned grueling, but —Go ahead and carve, Joris. Mr. Bond, your health."

Warmed by wine, Bond began to talk more freely, to ask questions about the country. "Deuced odd, getting used to things—and well, uh, people over here. Is it true that there isn't much fox-hunting?" He laid down a well-picked drumstick.

Ripley and Cuyler exchanged glances.

Ripley looked at his plate in embarrassment. "Ah—fox-hunting you said? To be sure. No-no—I don't know that we do much of what you'd call fox-hunting."

"Scarcely," murmured Cuyler, busy with a cork.

"Amazing," said Bond. "Why, at home we have great meets, you know. Tiptop horses, all the best people riding out. Maybe the Lord Lieutenant of the County side by side with an archbishop. Nailing fine hounds. I thought that here, with so much game, you'd have some prime packs."

"No," said Cuyler absently.

Bond's well-bred amazement was patent. "No sport? Really—"

Ripley smiled tolerantly. "What my friend Cuyler means is—ah—why yes, foxes *are* hunted. But *we* don't hunt them."

"Quite so," said Joris, eyes on the ceiling.

"You see, Mr. Bond—really, this is awkward, Joris—but anyway it's only the peasants here who hunt foxes. *Autres pays, autres moeurs,* the French say." He laughed indulgently. "It's a pretty sight—in a way—to see the good people prancing over the fields on their horses, tooting horns and shouting to the dogs. Doubtless it's different in England, but frankly I can't fancy you, for example, blowing a brass horn in a fox's ear—"

Bond breathed: "Extraordinary! But I was told—and on very good authority, that Mr.—I mean General Washington is reckoned a fine hard man to hounds. That's one of the reasons that Sir William thought he might treat with him."

Ripley blew out his cheeks. "Oh—to be sure. That's different. In the South—"

"Symbolic," said Cuyler. "Mr. Bond, our general holds many offices. Through one of them—a sinecure, of course—he is compelled to go out once a year, just before Monongahela-tide—"

"Middle of Susquehanna-term, I think, Joris, when the court rises—"

"Of course. Then, you see, he opens the meet in his robes of office. The peasants expect it, you know. But sport! Ha! We have *our* sport. When the war is over, I'll be happy to take you up into the Catskills after bear. Bear! You bowl along in a coach and four with outriders. The bear is routed out. The coachman and the outriders play him like a trout, and at the exact moment you yourself lean from the window of the coach and drive home your spear. Of course, you've got to be close enough to catch hold of an ear and drive the spear into his throat."

"We use a lance in Massachusetts, Mr. Bond," said Ripley. "I grant you that it's old-fashioned, but we look upon it as the true weapon of chivalry. One man, on foot, armed with a lance, pitted against the noblest animal of the north woods—the moose. We go out—

But enough of this, Joris, we're boring our guest. Tell us something about England, Mr. Bond. It seems a faraway country to us over here."

It was eleven o'clock before Bond left, perfectly steady and murmuring well-bred thanks. As the door closed behind him, Ripley sank into a chair, laughing silently. "We'll be examined again in a few days, Joris. We'll have to think up something else."

Cuyler grinned. "We'll have to get Felton talking about cricket."

Ripley shook his head. "No. Not Felton. I'm going to give you a little lecture on the British services. They're the tools we've got to work with and the more we understand them the better for all of us. Merit doesn't count, as a general rule. The best officer we've met so far's Felton, but he's got no family and no influence. Hence he holds the same rank as young Bond, who's ten years his junior. But Bond's been brought up in a county family. I doubt if he'd ever been off the estates until his father bought him a commission. Probably his uncle's a bishop and his aunt's married to a colonel. He'll get along. Aubrey's pretty much the same, but with less family and less influence, hence he isn't a major yet. His father, I'd say, has a good living somewhere, a sinecure parish, and dines with the right people. Quotes Latin tags and knows port."

Cuyler frowned. "I suppose that's damned clever but what does it do for us?"

"Just this. Impressions are going to count for a lot. Now Bond'll go back to his mess bubbling over with tales of gentry sport in America. A man who hunts bear in a coach and four is *never* going to be suspect as a deserter. Maybe Bond's got an uncle right here who's a colonel. Or an old friend of his father is in charge of this or that. Word will drift up where we want it to drift. It won't save us, I grant you, but it'll give us time."

Cuyler nodded. "I see. Solid and workmanlike with the Feltons. Sporting squires with the Bonds and the

Aubreys. By God, it'll work. I've stormed at the British for not knowing more about their colonies. We'll use their ignorance."

"Deftly, though. There are plenty who have served here and know the country as well as we do. Howe, for example, would have pulled your nose over your bear hunt. But the details'll never get to him. Just that old Bond's son reports that the prisoners are keen as mustard on sport. It'll place us in the army mind. I think we'll try Aubrey out on—h'm—how's your Latin?"

"Pretty fair. The aged parent and I used to read Tacitus aloud to each other."

"We'll find out if that touches a spring in Aubrey." He yawned. "Hated to daddle Bond that way. He's a nice chap. But—" His face grew somber. "Don't ever forget that each one of these men may be the one who commands my firing squad or marches you off to the hulks. There wouldn't be much choice. The fever's worse than ever in the hulks and they take out a boatload of dead every day. Now let's get some sleep."

PART SIX

REMEMBRANCE

Washington at last fell back into Westchester County on the mainland of New York. Barring Fort Washington and its garrison of some two thousand on upper Manhattan, he had given up the whole island. Slowly Howe followed by land and by sea. Close by Pell's Point, British and Hessians streamed ashore in a move to hit the extended flank of the American army. In open country they were met by the furious attack of Glover's brigade, faltered, came on again, broke in actual rout. Glover skillfully disengaged his brigade and fell back on the main army, whose right was now secure.

Howe came on again by land, drove Washington from the hills about White Plains; and the Americans, shaken but not broken, moved closer to the Hudson. They were losing battles but winning invaluable experience. They lay in hilly country as Howe studied them. Then he gave up the chase, moved swiftly for once and struck at Fort Washington, which surrendered after a hard fight. He became cautious again, waited.

Following the loss of the last fort on Manhattan, the American army seemed ready to melt away. Regiments fell in two hundred strong at sunrise, twenty strong at sunset. Washington, fearing a move against the Jerseys and Philadelphia, crossed the Hudson with most of his army. Howe followed, took Fort Lee across from Fort Washington, and plunged south on the trail of the retreating Washington, whose entire force at times numbered less than fifteen hundred men. British generals began packing their trunks and reserving passage for England. They'd spend the winter at home.

I

THE September days, soft and smoky with haze, dragged interminably on. South, the charred city showed, distant spires and rafters sticking up into the sky like jagged teeth. North, the Harlem Heights were hidden by the high ground between them and Long Island, and no news of their army came for Ripley and Cuyler.

The double guard was strengthened, but no officers, other than those in charge of the prisoners, came to the little house above Newtown Creek. Once, near the first of October, the two were spirited away at night, rowed down toward Wallabout Bay, and locked up in a small cabin on a frigate. The next night they were brought silently back to the stone house, none the wiser for the mysterious move.

Across on Manhattan the trees began to turn yellow and gold and red, soft mellow colors that seemed pale and washed-out to Ripley's eyes, that remembered wooded bastions blazing with scarlet flame toward the New Hampshire border. There would be bright orange and crimson, too, on the ridge where Concord nestled, far off in Massachusetts. Golden elms and blood-colored maples would be dropping their leaves all about Nashawtuc Hill, to drift down the Assabet or the Sudbury to the Concord River. The Berkshire Hills would be fortresses of raging glory. Ripley sighed. Remembrance, tall and slim, would be walking under torch-like trees in Great Barrington. The toss of her dark head and the sway of her hips came to him with painful clarity. What would she be thinking about on this day and at this hour? He had never found time to write in the last turmoil on Manhattan, before his capture. She would have had his account of the crossing of the Hudson, the rescue of the shaken army; since that, nothing. She might hear of the Kip's Bay rout and slowly tell herself that he had become a casualty. Or she might assume that distance had dulled his interest. If there were only some way of getting word to her. The elder Cuyler was under oath not to take letters from the captives or to write on their behalf. Ripley knew the explosive little man well enough to realize that he would cling to his word. He leaned disconsolately on the window sill and tried to reconstruct each of his meetings with Remembrance.

One midday toward the end of October, Felton came into the room. "You'll have to delay your noon rations. Two officers have come across from headquarters to settle this case."

Cuyler inclined his head gravely. "Duty is duty, Mr. Felton. We're at your orders."

Felton nodded shortly, but there was a grudging respect in his eyes as he motioned to the guard to enter the room. "Mr. Cuyler, you'll take the lead," he said.

Ripley said crisply, "If the point weren't important, Mr. Felton, I'd not mention it. But my commission in the Continental Army antedates by one day that of Mr. Cuyler."

Felton looked at him sharply. "That is correct. Mr. Mayne will go first. Guard—escort the prisoners below."

Ripley composed his mind to meet those of the vague Truesdale and the explosive Musgrave as he went down the stairs. The door was thrown open. "The prisoners will enter," barked Felton.

Ripley tried to mask a start of surprise. By the window there lounged a tall, lean major of marines. Ripley noted the languid eyes, the supercilious mouth. Here were birth and influence, well attested by the beautifully cut uniform, the London boots, and the glossy beaver pot-hat with its brushlike cockade. Birth and influence to which Ripley added mentally a taste for adventure, else why should such a man choose the marines over the smarter Guards, which must have been well within his reach?

At a table beyond the marine sat a major of the King's Own, as immaculate as the marine, with spotless white facings on his uniform. He had a blond, clean-cut handsomeness and an air of alertness that contrasted with the marine's bored languor.

Felton saluted the marine. "Major Lutterell, sir." Then the infantry officer. "Major Peyton, sir."

Lutterell looked up, yawning. "These the chaps?"

Peyton said: "Yes, Major. I've their dossier here."

The marine waved a sleepy hand. "Dossier be shivered." He sat up in his chair, boredom gone. His eyes were keen and hard. "This has been going on bloody well long enough. You colonials think you can dictate to His Majesty's forces just how you shall be treated. Peyton, I'll settle this once for all." He looked at Ripley. "You deny being a deserter?"

"I've nothing to add to previous statements," said Ripley.

"Ho! Standing on your rights, are you? You've got none. You, then—Cuyler, isn't it?"

Cuyler shook his head in silence. Peyton broke in. "Legally, they're in order, Lutterell. *We* can prove that they were captured. *You* can't prove that they've served. They're ours."

The marine seemed to lose interest in the proceedings. He took snuff lazily and his eyes became sleepy again. "Very likely," he drawled. "Just like to see one thing, though."

"What's that?"

"Their backs." He stifled a yawn. "No objections, I presume?"

The room swam about Ripley. His mouth went stiff and his knees failed to answer his will to step back. Dimly the voice of Peyton came to him. "Damned unusual, but I can't say no."

Ripley saw Cuyler pushed forward. The marines stripped his coat and shirt from his back. Then strong arms pinned Ripley. He felt his jacket wrenched from him, then knew dully that cold air was on his bare back. As he struggled, Lutterell said in a weary drone, "Two causes for desertion. Bad food and flogging. Look at those weals, Peyton. Two, maybe three years old. Yes, I'll take—ah, Mayne—right with me. The other, we'll continue to hold jointly. His back's smooth as a baby's bottom."

Vague shapes that must have been marines closed about Ripley. Felton, with grim satisfaction, said: "Guard, about face!"

Peyton's voice cut through the haze. "Just a moment, Lutterell. I'm not so sure your identification's enough."

"It'll be enough for the admiral," said Lutterell languidly.

"But not enough for Sir William," snapped Peyton. "Let me look closer."

Ripley felt strong fingers playing over the old weals and welts. "No! No, by God! This is never a military flogging," cried Peyton. "Looks more—looks more—damn my eyes, more like a bloody good birching."

He pinched Ripley's arm gently. "Been to school, haven't you?"

A ray of hope flickered through Ripley's mind. "Yes, Major."

"Birched a bit, did they? Where was it?"

"Boston Latin School and Harvard College, Major."

Lutterell's lazy laugh coiled out into the room. "Blast me if the idea of a college in the forests isn't enough to make an Oxford don smile. But he can't prove it."

"His word's enough for me," said Peyton. "*Both* school and college, eh? That's it, newer weals over older ones. Lutterell, I've got you. Can you imagine a man from a college, even a Yankee college—serving as a private of marines?"

Lutterell waved lazily. "Imagine any kind of a Yankee doing about anything." He raised his hand slightly to Ripley. "Say you've been at a college, do you? Which one? How long's it been going?"

Ripley concentrated on the question. "Harvard. It's been going a hundred and forty years."

The majors looked about inquiringly. Felton spoke up. "I'm bound to say that's true, sir. I've seen the place. Of course, he only *says* he's been there."

Again Lutterell waved. "This inquiry is not being conducted by junior officers." He cocked a leg over the arm of his chair, looked through lowered lids at Ripley. "Know Latin?"

"I took honors."

The marine leaned forward. "Can you cap this:—

> *"Hoc ego versiculos feci, tulit alter honores;*
> *Sic vos non vobis, fertis aratua boves;"*

Ripley closed his eyes. "*Sic vos non vobis.*" Who? Who had written that? His mind cleared. The incomplete verses that Vergil had written to disprove Bathyllus's claim to a Vergilian distich in praise of Caesar. He cleared his throat:—

> *"Sic vos non vobis, mellificatis apes;*
> *Sic vos non vobis, vellera fertis oves;*
> *Sic vos, non vobis, nidificatis aves."*

He paused, then said: "May I call your attention, Major, to an error in the first line that you quoted? Not '*Hoc ego*' but '*Hos ego.*' It makes the passage rather clearer."

Lutterell murmured: "I'll be bloody well blowed. Dash my wig if he hasn't done it!"

Peyton shouted with laughter. "Told you I had him, Lutterell!" He slapped his palms together. "I'll report to Sir Billy that the case is settled."

"Report and be damned to you. That back tells me more than his verse capping. And I don't give up my claim to the other, either. Come, now, Peyton, really it's absurd. We're keeping the whole damned staff at swords' points over this pair."

Peyton sat down resolutely. "I'll give them to you. And I'll let you have any of the four thousand others we took. Why not? One's as fair as the other. You marines are so bloody jealous—"

Lutterell got up slowly. "As you please. Keep them—as before. I'm to see the admiral tonight." He saluted lazily and lounged out of the room.

Peyton laughed softly. "This won't take much longer. *I'll* see Sir William at once. Mr. Felton—return the prisoners to their quarters."

Alone in their room, Ripley and Cuyler stared at each other. Ripley said: "We're getting closer to the fire. Joris, we've *got* to do something quick."

Cuyler shook his head miserably. "But, damn it, I've covered all the ground around here they'd let me, between going to the ajax and taking exercise. There's not a soul around, barring the army. They've moved some Germans in—the Alt Lossberg regiment, just east of us."

Ripley looked out of the window. It was getting close to dusk and lights were beginning to shine across on Manhattan. Unconsciously he picked out the glow from the Cuyler house. Why hadn't the old gentleman been over to see them lately? Had he lost favor with the Howes?

He suddenly realized that he was very hungry and shouted to the guard to have their rations sent up at once, doubled to make up for the loss of the noon meal.

Half an hour later, while Cuyler was lighting the lamp, the door swung slowly open and a marine guard came in, carrying two steaming kettles and a basket. Ripley picked up the lantern and turned it on the guard. Then he set it down quietly. The guard was the marine Dancey. While small pots were being brought out of the basket, Ripley whispered the name to Cuyler, who nodded. "Maybe he's going to change his mind," thought Ripley.

Dancey put out the basket on the table and arranged dishes. Without looking up he muttered: "There's to be a skiff to the second water north."

Ripley stiffened, then snapped, "Don't be so damned clumsy. Look sharp there."

Dancey went on, "It'll have two marine uniforms. It'll have food."

"When?" Cuyler moved close beside the marine.

"You're to watch your father's window, sir. The night you'll see the lights wobble, like. It'll be then." He jerked his thumb toward Ripley: "He saved me from a flogging off Trinidad, sir. He nussed me when I was took of a fever. I ain't forgot."

"How do we get to the creek—the water, that is?"

Dancey shook his head. "That I couldn't say, sir. I've seed to the uniforms that'll fit sprack enough. They'll be in the skiff. Your father's done the rest."

Ripley thought rapidly. "Can you smuggle two musket barrels to us? Just barrels and I don't care how old and rusty they are."

Dancey nodded. "They'll be here, sir."

"Come with us," said Ripley. "I guarantee you the best regiment and the best colonel—"

Dancey stiffened. "That'd be against my King, sir. This I'm doing for you, being as how I ain't forgot what you done for me."

"Right," said Ripley. Dancey withdrew in silence.

Ripley sat down. "God—I do believe we're getting another chance. But how'll we get away?"

Cuyler drew up a chair and began to eat. "Night, of course. That's when the signal'll be. I know what the aged parent'll do. He's got some old ship's lanterns on chains and he'll hang them in the river room. They can't be seen from Manhattan and no one'll be looking for them over here."

Ripley jumped up. "The second water, he called it. That's less than half a mile from here." He stared out the window into the night. "Can't see anything, but I know the place perfectly. It's got overhanging banks." He threw himself back in his chair. "But how'll we get there?" He ate, scarcely aware of his act. "I've got it. We've had chances here before, but no place to go to. We'll have to plan this carefully." Then he frowned. "Wonder if there's anyone on the island to tell Lutterell that they don't flog at Harvard."

II

Two days slipped away while Ripley and Cuyler stared at the lights on Manhattan until their eyes blurred. On the evening of the third day, Dancey again brought mess. His eyes darted cautiously about the room. "Ain't seen nothing yet, sir?" He dropped his voice still lower. "Ain't wanting to frighten you, but it better be quick. Sergeant Bent and some of the lads from the *Amphion* came in on the last frigate and Lutterell, he's got word on 'em." He laid out the mess and withdrew in silence.

Ripley smacked his hand against the wall in impotence. "The *Amphion* men! By God, Joris, Bent'd sell his mother's body for the tallow in it! Some of the others are—"

Cuyler sprang at him, clapped a hand over his mouth and pointed out the window. The lights in the distant Cuyler house shone clear and steady. Slowly at first, then more swiftly, the lights began to sway back and forth. Their motion was easy and natural. They might have been lights swinging at the tail of a cart off there on Manhattan.

Ripley pounded Cuyler's back softly, then turned to the table. "Take on cargo, damn it. Joris, we'll leave at nine, sharp."

They ate quickly, then pushed the table away. Ripley inspected his boots. They looked worn, but they ought to do. He had drawn them the day before the regiment had gone across to bring back the army, and Cuyler's were still newer. He leaned back in his chair and closed his eyes.

The time dragged interminably. Then from some uncharred steeple across on Manhattan a bell tolled, deep-toned and ominous. Ripley sprang up. From the chimney he dragged down the musket barrels that Dancey had smuggled in to them. They had been taken from short carbines and would be easy to handle. He slipped his in the waistband of his breeches, securing the upper end close by his arm, then helped Cuyler to dispose of his.

They looked at one another, shook hands silently. Ripley stepped back, hammered on the door. A guard clumped up the stairs, blinked, and escorted them below.

The wizened marine sergeant in charge of the night's duty scratched his head. "Ain't said nawthin' 'bout two on yer goin'. S'welp me 'e ain't."

"We went out together last night. Damn it all, man, it doesn't matter if Mr. Bond isn't here. We're only going as far as the ajax. Send your guard along. What do you think we want to do? Run into the Alt Lossberg lot and have them pick us up? We've got enough armies fighting over us now."

The sergeant got up reluctantly and picked up his

lantern. "It's a dight further, sir. They've digged a new one, they have. So, if you please, sir—"

Lantern swinging ahead of them in the sergeant's hand, Joris and Ripley, a marine at each elbow, stepped out into the night.

The way led over a slippery path that ran parallel to the river and then curved inland. Ripley rubbed his eyes, tried to get his bearings. The second water north. Now the path led toward the river again and the bulk of a canvas shelter showed dimly.

Ripley drew a deep breath and began to whistle: "Why, soldiers, why—" Beside him, Cuyler coughed. Ripley stumbled, recovered himself. "Bad footing, Sergeant."

The sergeant grunted a reply, held his lantern lower over the path. Ripley shouted: "Now!" His foot shot out and the lantern vanished in a crash of broken glass. He caught the sergeant from behind, drove his knee into his back, jamming his head forward at the same time. One of the guards shouted and Cuyler's carbine barrel whistled through the air. The second soldier bawled: "Sergeant of the guard!" and raised his musket. Ripley's barrel came down on his brass-fronted cap and the man dropped.

Ripley snapped: "Now for it. Keep your barrel."

He raced away toward the river. Shouts rang out and from the path a musket crashed. The sergeant's voice, thin and weak, croaked: "'Alt, in the King's name."

The water of the second creek was ahead of them. Ripley looked back over his shoulder at Cuyler, who was close behind. The two dove into the creek. Another musket shot rang out and shouts drew nearer. Ripley caught Cuyler's wet sleeve. "Under the bank. Steady. Here they come." He clapped one end of the barrel in his mouth, slowly and carefully submerged. Even with the deep-cut bank above his head, it was hard to keep under water. He fumbled in the mud with his free hand and found a slimy root. Cautiously he opened his eyes to the sting of the water, then closed them hurriedly as the glare of lanterns flickered down to him. The muscles of his mouth began to ache with the effort to keep water from seeping along the sides of the barrel. Then the bank under which he lay jarred to the tread of heavy feet. Voices strangely muffled filtered down to him and the glow of lanterns lit up the water again.

He felt the root slowly easing out of his grasp and his legs thrashed involuntarily in the mud and water. Damp air, drawn straight into his throat, produced an agonizing dryness. He wanted desperately to cough. Each second was sheer agony. Suddenly into his brain came the voice of Nahum Sholes: "Now Rip, if so you was ever taken like that and get under water, just flop softer'n a feather bed and you'll be all right. Fighting's going to get you killed. Soft and easy—"

He relaxed his muscles, felt himself rise. Then he sank and his body rocked gently to the touch of the creek. His breath came more freely. The sense of pressure that had been filling him to bursting point slackened.

He opened his eyes again and saw that the surface of the water was dark. Cautiously he forced himself up until he felt a scrape of cold mud against his cheek and drew clean, pure air in through his nostrils. The water rippled behind him and Cuyler's big head broke the surface. They both waited until their breathing became more normal. Then Ripley whispered: "Hear anything?"

Cuyler's breath was warm on his ear. "Quiet's a Quaker church."

Ripley pulled himself shoulder-high above the bank. Lights still burned brightly in the distant stone house and off to the east lanterns flickered and danced like fireflies. "They're off the scent, but they'll be coming back. Now to find that damned boat." Half swimming, half pulling himself by projections on the bank, he worked carefully toward the mouth of the creek. Dancey had said the boat would be hidden by a deep undercut a few yards in. He threw a glance back toward the winking lights and pushed ahead. Suddenly his feet were swept out ahead of him. He caught at the bank and struggled to get back. His last push had carried him clear of the creek and out into the current of the East River. He caught at the bank and struggled back.

Cuyler panted, "They're still on the other side of the path."

Through his teeth Ripley said: "Hope to God they spend the rest of the night there. Where's that blasted boat? My God, Joris, Dancey couldn't have been diddling us, could he?" He lashed out to swim farther into the creek. There was a muffled boom as his foot hit against something. "Found it!"

The skiff had worked loose from under the bank and its bow was rocking in the free current. Ripley caught the rough wood. "Tow it out into the river. Then we'll climb aboard. First—God—what's that?"

On the bank above the skiff, a dark shape huddled. Cuyler whispered: "Swim for it!"

"Wait," said Ripley.

He drew himself half out of the water. "A grenadier! Dead!"

"Sure he's dead?"

"Certain. Must have been hit by the guards' fire." Ripley fumbled in the dark. "It's that bull-necked private who brought our rations this morning."

"Damn," said Cuyler. "He was a good chap, too."

Ripley tore at the skiff. "He *was* a good chap. *Fuit!* I want to keep on saying *sum*, not *fui!* Catch the stern." He clung to the port side of the skiff while Cuyler clambered in over the starboard, then pulled himself in and seized the oars.

Back on the shore more lights showed and shouts were carried to them on the night wind. "Tear your lungs out with my compliments," grunted Ripley as he pulled on the oars.

From the stern Cuyler muttered, "Here's rations and the uniforms. Bend those oars, Rip. Make them groan!"

Ripley pulled slowly past Blackwell's Island, keeping well inshore to avoid the tide. On the island, someone was singing in a high, melancholy voice, lost and yearning.

By the end of the island, Ripley headed north and west to avoid the swirling menace of Hell Gate. It was better to risk possible detection by posts on Ward's or Randall's Islands than to face destruction in that current. Lights burned dully in bivouacs on the two islands but no one challenged. "Keeping poor watch," muttered Cuyler.

"Best I ever saw—for us. Pick out that light dead ahead and be sure I'm making for it. It'll take us right into the Harlem River. And I'm going away up it to get well back of our lines."

The smooth water lapped about the skiff. Randall's was left astern and Ripley began to relax as each stroke brought safety nearer. He hummed under his breath. Cuyler, in a joyous whisper, chuckled: "First thing we do is report to the old Bull Seal!"

"Then Johonot," said Ripley. "We'll see Hans Grenda and Pedrick and Sholes and that ape of a Gragg." He looked over his shoulder. "We're close. Look at those lights! Our lights! I'm pulling for that clump of rocks right there!" He filled his lungs for a great shout. Then he brought the boat to a silent halt and dropped his voice. "Something's wrong. Get out those uniforms! Quick! Jackets and caps only."

Cuyler moved quickly, handed Ripley a red coat, a cap marked with the foul anchor. Then he equipped himself. Ripley carefully backed water, drawing out from the shore that was less than ten yards away.

Lights burned brighter on the black shore. A figure was silhouetted against the glow. "Who's there?"

Ripley, trying to shape his voice to the accents of his guards, called: "Marine patrol, sir. Seems as 'ow the Yankees was out in a sloop, abaft Randall's."

"Who's with you?"

"Sergeant Blackstock, off the *Amphion*, sir. We've a barge and a pettiauger tother side the islands, a-keeping watch. Beggin' yer pardon, but you ain't Captain Andrews?"

"No. And tell your officer there can't be Yankees about. Damn it, they're all off the island, except those we've penned in Fort Washington up yonder. Where are you going now?"

"Orders was to go up until I seed a big white house on the port bank, sir."

"Pull in closer. I'll go with you. Then you can row me across to Randall's."

Ripley heard Cuyler's feet work on the boards of the skiff. He shouted: "Beggin' your pardon again, sir, we'll be coming right back this way. We'll come alongside and take you wherever you want to go."

There was a silence. Then the officer called: "Back inside of a half hour? Right. Draw in and hail me. I'll be waiting."

"Right, sir." Ripley tried to turn his voice into a cheery acknowledgment. He pulled out into the deeper shadows.

When they were well away, Cuyler's breath hissed in a great blast of relief. "By God, that was close. Where do we go now?"

Ripley rested on his oars. "Ask me what Howe had for dinner. We've got to think. Look here. Our army's left New York except for the garrison at Fort Washington. That means both sides of the Harlem'll be bad for us. That means Lobsters right up to Westchester County, maybe well into it."

"God," said Cuyler. "Start those oars going, quick."

"Wait a minute. There's another thing. We're in a mess of Lobsters. If we're taken—well, just being in their uniform means that we'll be shot without an inquiry. Martial law. Wait, I told you," he went on as Cuyler started ripping at his jacket. "If we're seen by lantern light or daylight, the Lobsters may not bother to question us. If we're in our proper clothes, they'll snap us up."

"But if they do question us?"

"Then we'll have to lot on glibness to pull us out, the same way we diddled that officer back there."

Cuyler began to protest, then said: "Hell, it's a chance, but what isn't? Get going."

For an hour Ripley sculled carefully back of Randall's Island, then headed the skiff into the Sound. At last he rested on his oars and felt the craft move smoothly on. "Wind and tide with us, Joris. Better get into the whole marine kit. Waistcoat and breeches. Go on. It's safer."

They changed as Cuyler grumbled, "God damn, the Bull Seal'd yowl so's you could hear him down to the Kill van Kull if he saw us in these damned monkey trappings."

The skiff moved steadily. As they came near the mouth of Flushing Bay, Cuyler took the oars and Ripley, from the bow, studied the night ahead. North and south the shores were dark and showed no trace of life. Cuyler muttered: "If the wind and tide hold, we'll make the west shore of Great Neck before light. There'll be cover to hide us there."

Ripley ran his finger along his chin. "Sure we won't run into Lobsters?"

"Remember what Bond told us yesterday?"

Ripley grinned. "Probably about the run the pack had the day they drew the coverts at Snickling Haithe near Little Snoring. What of it?"

"Maybe you weren't listening, but he said that the army wouldn't move up to the North Shore," said Cuyler. "He was put out about it, because he'd heard there was prime shooting."

"And there's a prime lot of Tories. Joris, it seems to me that there's trouble for us everywhere except in our own lines. God help me, I thought we were clear as soon as we got into the Harlem."

Wind and tide held. When the first streaks of dawn showed over the hummocky shore, they had cleared Great Neck and the narrow mouth of Manhasset Bay. Ripley picked out a line of dunes that were thick with coarse grasses. Cuyler beached the skiff and the two dragged it up into a dense growth, then took shelter under it. They broke open the box of rations that held bread and salt meat and dried apples and tapped the water cask. As they ate and drank, Cuyler shook his head dubiously. "We don't deserve the luck we've had. It all rested on the marine who dug the ajax so far from the house. Bet he'll get his ears well clipped for it."

"Forget him," said Ripley. "Here we are and that's enough. Now get some sleep. I'll take the first watch." He huddled among dry shrubs and studied the Sound. They were, he thought, just about opposite New Rochelle. It would be best to delay departure until after nightfall so they could see if the north beaches showed campfires. With the growing day, a thin haze came down limiting his vision to less than half a mile.

Toward noon, he roused Cuyler and promptly fell asleep. It was nearly dark when the New Yorker woke him, and the mist had lifted a little. There was no sign of life directly across the water, but west, toward Pelham, lights burned in dim clusters. Ripley eyed them. "Damned if I can make anything out."

The musket shot came with crashing suddenness. Ripley threw himself flat on the sand.

The beach was still, save for the screeches of belated gulls that dipped into the water beyond the low breakers. Then boots crunched in the sand. A lean, hawk-faced man with hot fanatic's eyes moved cautiously through the high grasses, an old musket held out in front of him. Ripley said to Cuyler: "Up on your knees and your arms high. Quick! I've loaded again."

Side by side they knelt facing the lean man whose rusty black clothes were rough with sandburs. Ripley called: "We're not armed! Are you for the King?"

The man's face contracted. "Aye—for the King of Men—for the Prince of Peace and the Thirteen States, ye murdering bastards."

Ripley struggled to his feet. "We're—"

"You're keeping your hands up and staying quiet. What are you doing here? Deserting? Lost?"

Ripley said: "Look under our skiff. You'll find our real colors."

The man, musket still poised, kicked gingerly under the skiff, hooked out a blue coat and white breeches with his foot. "Spies! Sneaking over to get into our lines. The soldiers have a law for that."

He came close and examined the two. Ripley said: "We escaped. We were captured at Harlem Heights." He added their names and their regiment.

The man nodded grimly. "The Fourteenth. That ain't from around here. You done well to choose it. Who's to say you nay?"

"Do you know New York City?" said Cuyler.

"Some," was the reply.

"Ever hear the name Cuyler as Tory? It's mine."

The man stared in unbelief. Then he began a careful cross-examination. At last he lowered his musket. "Maybe you're all right. What are you aiming for? To get back to the army? I'll help." He held out his hand. "I'm Joshua Cross."

"Live here?" asked Cuyler.

"Flatbush. When the British landed my neighbors turned on me. I lit out and came to a friend's house over the dunes. They burned mine for me. They'd have rid me on a rail could they have caught me. You'd best hide with me while I get news. There's many King's people about and I walk delicate."

He helped them bury the skiff in a tangle of seaweed and led the way over the dunes to a low cabin whose shingles had turned a soft silver gray through years of storm and sunshine. He pointed to a shed. "There's nets hung in there, nets and lobster pots. Get in there. I'll leave the musket with you in case of visitors."

The two passed through the creaky door which closed behind them. In the dark interior that smelled of tar and salt water and hemp and seaweed, Ripley rubbed his head. "This is about our last card, Joris. Maybe we trusted him too quick."

"I think he's all right. Anyway, we've got the musket. I'm going back to sleep. Your watch."

For an uncounted time Ripley sat, tense, in the blackness of the shed. He was beyond wondering or planning. He just waited. When the door creaked, he jumped up, musket poised. Joshua Cross said: "Me. Put it down."

He closed the door back of him and a rich, mellow odor filled the shack. "Chowder. Fresh-caught fish. Bread. Brandy. Wake up your friend."

The hot food, rich with fish and potatoes and cream, almost unnerved them. Cross watched them eat by the light of a shaded candle. He grunted in approval. "Now I've been out after the kind of news that'll help you. When was you took? September 16th. And you ain't heard much since? Well, here it is, such as it is. October 16th, Washington pulled off Manhattan except for the big fort. On the eighteenth, the Lobsters tried to land yonder at Pell's Point and hit him in the flank. So say those that's learned in soldiering. They got punished bad. Course, they made their landing, but they got held off so long that Washington got out of danger."

"What did we lose? Did you hear that?" asked Ripley.

"Now I did hear we ain't done badly. Some mighty smart man was leading our men there. Name of—

name of Gorton—Gloucester—no, that ain't it. Let me think—"

Ripley sprang to his feet, overturning his mug of brandy. He caught at Cross's shoulders. "Glover?"

Cross smacked his thigh. "Glover. The name I was hunting for. Yes, he threw a brigade, they called it, at the Lobsters and—"

But Ripley and Cuyler were dancing about the cramped shed whooping and pounding each other's backs. "By God, Rip, the old Bull Seal. He did it! His brigade and his regiment." Joris thumped Ripley again, turned to Cross. "Hear about Blackler's company?"

But Cross could give no other details. "Just held them off and then when it was time this Glover went and joined Washington somewhere around Mile Square. Heard something else, too. Glover's men come down to the shore in the night and stole a mort of British supplies. Now Washington and the whole army's back White Plains way. You can get to him if you cross and make a big swing north and then south."

Ripley grew serious. "How'll we know where it's safe to go over?"

Cross held up a lean hand. "I been lay-preaching west Long Island for fifteen years and they ain't many souls I don't know. A neighbor east of here's going to look around for you. When he's found out how far east on the mainland Howe's gone, he'll sail you beyond him."

Ripley said slowly, "Mr. Cross, you've done more for us than a man has a right to expect. You've made it possible—"

Cross said shortly, "Ain't done it for you. Done it for what I believe in."

"And that's the same thing we believe in. We're grateful. Now, what do you want us to do until it's time to start?"

"Some would pray. But not all folks is prayers. Go

to sleep. I'll read out the Book till you snore. Then I'll stand watch." He drew a fat Bible from a pile of nets and held it close to the candle. With the opening words the nasal snarl went from his voice which suddenly became rich and musical.

"'. . . Will lift up an ensign to the nations from far, and will hiss unto them from the end of the earth: and, behold, they shall come with speed swiftly: None shall be weary nor stumble among them; none shall slumber not sleep; neither shall the girdle of their loins be loosed . . . Whose arrows are sharp, and all their bows bent, their horses' hoofs shall be counted like flint, and their wheels like a whirlwind: . . . And in that day they shall roar against them like the roaring of the sea.'" He paused, closed the book, and lowered his head. "Father, thou hast lifted up an ensign to the nations from far. As one nation, in Thy name they come, the nations, the free nations that Thou hast called. Father, they answer unto Thee—New Hampshire, Massachusetts, Rhode Island—on they come to Thy call. Connecticut, New York, New Jersey, Pennsylvania. Their horses' hoofs shall be counted like flint, as Scripture says. Maryland, Delaware, Virginia, North Carolina and South, Georgia. Lord God of Hosts, they have answered Thy call. 'And none shall be weary.' Amen."

Struggling against sleep, Ripley murmured: "Amen."

III

EARLY the next morning, Joshua Cross brought more chowder and hot coffee. He was going, he said, to talk to neighbor Dorsey and might be gone the whole day. In the meantime, there was cold food and they were on no account to venture out of the shack. The door closed on his lean, bent form and hot eyes. Ripley and Cuyler, sprawling on piled nets, fretted and fumed the day away.

It was long after sundown when Cross returned. The candle lighted up the somber lines of his face as he looked down at the pair. "Hello!" cried Ripley. "Anything wrong?"

"That's as may be. There's some news that's bad, according to neighbor Dorsey, who was across the Sound. Washington made a stand at White Plains and had to fall back again, maybe as far as North Castle up on the Hudson."

"That's bad," muttered Ripley.

"Might be worse. He ain't broke up."

"By God, that's what I told Aubrey," shouted Ripley. "They may win battles but they can't destroy that army, because it's made of something that just won't be destroyed. Any details?"

Again, Cross had none. Dorsey had reported rumors of British patrols as far as Greenwich in Connecticut. Someone else had mentioned Stamford, even, well to the east of Greenwich.

"What does that mean for us?" asked Cuyler, chafing his broad hands.

"Now that I may not say, not knowing. Dorsey opined that, come you was willing to risk it, he'd set you down east of Stamford."

Ripley got to his feet briskly. "We'll lot on it, as Nahum'd say, Joris. When do we start?"

"Now," said Cross. "I counseled with myself and found that'd be what you'd answer. We'll feed up, then I'll take you to Dorsey."

Full of the eternal chowder that had begun to pall even on Cuyler, the three set out through a sharp mist that made Ripley's teeth chatter. A half mile along the beach, Ripley made out a small sailboat rocking and dipping beyond the low breakers. Cross whistled softly and a gnarled man arose from the shelter of a pile of driftwood. "Neighbor Dorsey?"

"You ain't wrong."

"The friends I was telling you about."

"Get going," said Dorsey and shambled to the water's edge where a dory turned its sharp prow to the shore.

Ripley said to Cross, "I don't know how to thank you."

"By getting back and fighting." His sunken eyes looked hard at Joris. "There's Cuylers to a house near Murray Hill. Kin of yourn?"

"My father."

"I'll look by." Without another word he drifted off through the thickening mist.

Dorsey called hoarsely from the water's edge. "Dawdling ain't doing," he announced.

Ripley and Cuyler ran over the crisping sand and clambered into the craft. Dorsey bent to his oars and brought the dory up beside the small sailboat, which was partially decked over forward. "Get in," he said. "Cross dried your uniforms. They're in the cuddy. Now get out from under my feet."

The two crept into the dark blackness of the decked space and huddled against the chill. "God's teeth," muttered Cuyler. "It's cold as a witch's bottom!"

"All questions concerning witches are respectfully referred to Salem. What'd you expect? This is November first."

"The devil it is! Well, well, how time does fly when you're on a holiday. What's our plan, Rip?"

Ripley pushed back his hat. "This is the best *I* can think of. We'll go ashore wherever Dorsey beaches the craft. Then we'll gather news and work inland. I'd say we might have to work as much as thirty miles inland before it'll be safe to hit west. Then we'll swing toward the Hudson."

"It'll have to do, but there's a lot about it I don't like."

"There's more that I don't. I talked to Cross while

you were sleeping that time. Westchester and west Connecticut are stiff with Tories. Now that Washington's had to fall back, maybe to the Hudson, and Howe's on the spot, a lot of weak-knees'll suddenly find that they were Tories all along. I heard a story of a mounted company that goes through the country hitting both sides—murder, plunder, and so on. It won't be easy."

"You startle me, Mr. Mayne. 'Pon my word you do."

"I'll startle you a devil of a lot more before we've berthed from this cruise."

"How about uniforms?"

Ripley bit his lip. "We can be right so many ways and wrong so many ways no matter how we plan. I haven't figured that out yet."

Cuyler dove into the cuddy and came up with two neat bundles which he opened. The uniforms of the Fourteenth had been carefully dried and scraped. Inside the coats, Cuyler found two pairs of long, loose homespun trousers. He began stripping off his marine uniform. "I've got it. The homespuns over the whites. The blue coats don't look too military. We'll be inconspicuous and can talk our way out of anything that we meet."

"Right enough. I'm going out to see Dorsey, now that we've pushed off."

The sailboat was bucking and rolling through a slow swell over which the fog hung heavier and heavier. Dorsey sat in the stern, the tiller under his arm. "How long will it take us?" asked Ripley.

"Plenty."

"Aren't making many knots, are we?"

"Don't dare clap on more sail. Not in this soup. Might poke my sprit through a frigate. Might go on a rock."

"Would you say another hour, two hours?"

"Wouldn't say nothing. Sound's only so wide. You start across it. You get there sometime."

"What'd happen to you if some Lobsters caught you ferrying us?"

"I ain't asked. If any Tory bastard finds me, my woman'll be looking for a new man to keep the house in fish."

"They'd—"

"They'd do anything 'cept chatter to a man that's trying to set a course through this fog."

Ripley grinned to himself and rejoined Cuyler in the cabinlike space forward. "Learn anything, Rip?"

"Only that I was in the way."

"It's a pity."

They plunged into a maze of plans and speculations that lasted until they heard the boom creak. Dorsey barked: "Over the side. Shoal water."

Ripley and Cuyler scrambled out of the cabin. The fog was thick as ever but there was a new smell in the air that told of land close by. They slung their boots about their necks. Cuyler said: "I guess Mr. Cross told you about our empty pockets. But if you get into New York, go and see my father."

"If he talks as much as you do, I won't want to. There's the shore. It'll wait for you, but the boat won't."

He grunted unintelligibly to their thanks as they slipped over the side into thigh-deep water.

Over rocks that were bristling with mussels and periwinkles, they made their way through a hundred yards of shallow water and at last stood on the beach. Ripley drew a long breath. "By God, here we are."

"We've always been able to say that," grumbled Cuyler, rubbing his chafed feet. "What I want to be able to say is: 'By God, there *they* are.'"

They pulled on stockings and boots, then followed the beach cautiously until they hit on a dirt track that led inland past a narrow tidal river that was pungent with salt and seaweed. From time to time they stopped to listen but the shore was silent and inscrutable.

A mile from the beaches, their road struck into a highway that ran east and west. Ripley scuffed his boot on the surface. "We'll follow it until it hits a cross road that'll carry us north."

"Might as well," said Cuyler. "All we know is that we're somewhere between Greenwich and Stamford, unless Dorsey told you more than he did me."

"Not Dorsey," said Ripley. "Come on. The command is forward."

IV

As LONG as the fog held, they pressed north, leaving the flat reaches of the Sound country behind them and catching glimpses of rolling hills and deep valleys. During their third halt, a thin rain began to fall and the curtains of mist coiled away toward the lowering clouds. Cuyler clambered stiffly onto a high rock and studied the points of the compass. "Sail ho?" asked Ripley.

"Not a damned thing. We're getting into the hills. There's a roof off to the west but it's stove in and there's no smoke from the chimney. Want to get back to the main road down there?"

"Not yet. We'll stick to the path here as long as it heads the right way. Come on." He got up and stepped out, limping slightly.

"Foot gone bad?" asked Cuyler.

"It's all right. I raised a devil of a blister on my heel last year when I took French leave of the marines. It started up twice since then and the other night when we found the skiff I whacked the same heel against the bottom. Just sort of a bruise. It'll work out."

The muddy path climbed a long north-south ridge that looked down on empty country on either hand.

As the afternoon wore on, Ripley said: "Down on the main road. There's a cart. Not military."

"What about it?" Cuyler looked down two hundred feet to the narrow valley where a single cart crawled north beside a white-streaked river.

"We'd agreed to keep to the hills, but I've got to give this damned heel a rest. There's only one man in the cart. If he makes trouble, we'll manage to soothe him. Come on."

The steep slope was treacherous with hidden mud and half-buried stones. Ripley set his teeth. At each step, the water-soaked boot dug at his heel. He caught Cuyler's arm and the two skidded and slipped down side by side.

A decrepit horse and cart lurched into view. On the seat a short, fat man perched, his hat held on by a red handkerchief. Ripley limped out onto the road and held up his hand. "Bound north?" he hailed.

"Ain't saying no," said the driver.

"Take us along?"

"Ain't saying yes." The man reached under the seat and drew out an ancient, long-barreled pistol. "Am saying, get them hands up."

Rain trickling down his cuffs, Ripley said, "If you're a King's man, you've only got one shot there. You might miss. Even if you didn't, whoever's left'd pull you apart like an overboiled haddock."

The man shoved the pistol under the seat and clambered down. He stripped off his coat. "Now ain't that God-damned interesting! Which was going to start the pulling?" He knotted big fists and began to move about in a slow circle.

Ripley laughed. "Take your choice, but wait until we get to the end of the ride." He dropped his hands. "We're from Glover's regiment. We got taken and escaped. We're trying to get back to the army."

The driver was back on his seat in one surprisingly agile bound. "Get in. Arden's the name, Jake Arden, and cousin to Francis down to New York, him that owned Molyneux, the fighter. Trained old Mol for every fight, I did. Yep. Get your war over and come back here and I'll flatten you both in ten seconds apiece."

"Ho!" shouted Cuyler as he and Ripley clambered into the tail of the cart. "Old Mol? Used to fight as Pete Arden. The aged parent and I must have won a hundred pounds each, first and last, betting on him. Remember the night he fought the Bristol Gamecock down by Coenties? That was my father who jumped into the ring and caned Molyneux for not trying harder. Always said he was fighting a cross."

Arden rubbed his chin. "Not Mol. He ain't never fought a cross. Remember the time, though. Old gentleman 'bout as big as sheep tick. Happened just after the Gamecock tapped Mol's claret and—"

Ripley cried, "For God's sake, I should have sent young Bond along in my place and he could have showed you how Glorious Jemmy thrashed the Dublin Bruiser at Cardiff back in 1765." He stretched out on the soaking board of the cart. "Any Lobsters around this way? How far north do we have to go to be safe to swing west again? How about Tories?"

"News is funny," said Arden. "Now I heard of Lobsters far east as New Haven and far north as Danbury. But I been both places and ain't seen none. Hear they're thick as pickpockets at a cocking-main along the New York border, but that I ain't seen neither."

"How would you go if you were in our place?" asked Cuyler.

"Me, I'd head up past Danbury, past the Candlewood Lakes and up to Kent or maybe Kent Furnace. Then I'd go west to the river and down it. Heard Washington's clear to Northcastle, but you can't tell."

"You think we can take that route without worrying?"

"Ain't never heard of a route you could take 'thout

worrying. Specially now. Been some stories I ain't liked. Barns burn down and cattle just ain't seen again. Old Mrs. Bryant back Redding way got found with her throat cut and her hens gone. Barlow Bemis went out to bring home his herd and him nor herd ain't been seen since."

Ripley sat up. "Who does all that? Lobsters?"

"Ain't heard. Now I'm heading west of Danbury, say five mile west and north. I'll set you down there."

There was no more news to be had from Arden, who hunched on his seat and droned on endlessly of prize fights and fighters to Cuyler. Ripley loosened his right boot to rest his foot as much as possible. Odd, darting pains ran up the Achilles' tendon, subsided, darted again.

In the pitch darkness, Arden set them down by a white farmhouse in a valley that was loud with the roar of a hidden waterfall. "Bed with me, if you like," he said. "But was I you, I'd walk till I dropped and sleep where I fell. Better take this with you." He handed the long pistol to Cuyler, gave Ripley a leather pouch of powder and ball. "Ain't nothing for you to say. I got a nephew, same name as me, with Ritzema's New York regiment. Do him a turn if so you see him."

The rain poured down harder and Ripley hunched his shoulders to it as he followed Cuyler up the path to which Arden had pointed. "Maybe we're just damned fools, Joris. It's a hundred to one that we could hit right west now and never see a Lobster. But—that one chance—"

"Uhuh. But," said Cuyler. "And I'd put the odds nearer five to one than a hundred. Jesus, this mud's like rotten sauerkraut."

They spent the night under overhanging rocks on a hilltop and woke to see a fine drizzle through which trailed long wisps of mist. Ripley groaned as he pulled his boots on. "That damned heel of mine. Aches and stabs all the time. Had sort of a fever last night, too, and my head feels heavy."

"That's nothing new. I've got a fire going here. Break out the salt beef we got from Arden."

All through the day they kept on north, with the Candlewood Lakes at their left. Ripley's fever increased and his whole foot became a burning torment. When night fell, Cuyler saw a fire on a hill and headed for it, dragging Ripley with him. Through waves of fever, Ripley looked dully at a dozen ragged men, some in fragments of Continental uniforms, some in shabby country clothes, who were cooking fresh beef at a slow fire. Behind them, horses stamped and the firelight fell on stacked muskets. Dimly he heard Cuyler claiming a share of food on the ground of being a deserter. He propped himself against a fire-warmed rock. His hands seemed heavy and useless, so Cuyler fed him while carrying on an animated conversation with the band of stragglers. They called themselves "Skinners" and were planning the next night to ride thirty miles south and raid a Tory farm near the Aspetuck. They cursed the war, cursed Washington, cursed the British, but above all they cursed a band they called the "Cowboys," who had begun to raid patriot farms along the New York border.

When Ripley fell into a broken sleep, Cuyler questioned the leader of the Skinners, a tall powerful man in the uniform of Prescott's Massachusetts regiment. How, Cuyler wanted to know, was the best way to travel so as to avoid both armies? He wanted to get his sick friend to safety, after which he would come back and join the Skinners. The leader, who never smiled, counseled a northern or eastern course. By no means west. "Heard from other Skinners down south that Howe'd sent dragoons forty miles north of the King's Bridge."

Cuyler nodded. "That'd be the Seventeenth. Big helmets with crests."

"That's it. And they say that bastard Englishman, Charles Lee, him that's with Washington, has mounted some of Hand's riflemen and they're patrolling too. No, north and east. You'll pick up my trail when you come back by keeping your eyes open."

In the morning, Skinners and horses were gone. So, too, was Ripley's watch, and Cuyler's, together with their blankets. Ripley tried to stand up, but his head swam and he felt as though his right foot had been plunged into molten iron.

Cuyler looked sharply at him. "No better?"

"It'll be all right."

Cuyler put his hands on his hips. "You've been saying that since we started. Get that damned boot off and let me have a look at it."

"It's all right, I say."

Cuyler's broad chin set. "Rip, I swear I'm going to have a look at that if I have to knock you down to do it, and you're so weak with fever that if a cat kicked you, you'd roll down the mountain."

Ripley sank back against the rock. Cuyler carefully removed the boot. His breath went out in a long whistle. "Christ in the Catskills!" The skin of the heel was unbroken, but underneath a hard reddish lump sent faint rays of color toward the foot and the calf. He sniffed strongly. "No gangrene whiff that I can catch, but—" He scratched his head, then said suddenly, "You're going to stay here. Don't argue. I'll build the fire up and wrap you in my coat."

"No," said Ripley in a thick voice.

"Yes," said Cuyler. "I'm going to get help if I have to make for New York and bring Felton up here. Take the pistol. It's loaded. I'll stack brushwood along the path so thick that you could hear a mouse crawling over it on tiptoe."

Ripley tried to protest but waves of fever swept over him. He mumbled, "How happen they didn't take pistol?"

"Hid it," said Cuyler. "Don't ask where." He

grinned. "I'll just tell you this, that if I'd been a wench they'd have found it quick enough. Be back as soon as I can."

Ripley heard him thrash away through underbrush. Then he tried to keep awake, finger on the trigger of the pistol, but the high trees above him began to rock and dance.

The drizzle had stopped when Cuyler shook his shoulder. "Found a safe place. Good people and they haven't seen Lobsters or Skinners or Cowboys yet." He heaved Ripley to his feet, threw an arm about him and guided him down a path that ran east.

The pain had lessened and walking, with Cuyler's help, was not too hard. Then he felt his left boot slipping and sliding under his sole. The back seam had split and with every step his heel came out of the shoe, had to be worked carefully back, only to slip out again. Weakly, he began to curse. The shoes should have lasted months longer. Now poor leather, rotten thread, and hasty workmanship began to show. He said aloud: "Damn swindling contractors."

"What?" said Cuyler.

"Boots. They buy them for the army." He scuffed along, leaning more heavily on Cuyler. Then he noticed that his companion was moving with the same shuffling gait and saw gaping seams from which wool-clad heels slued.

"It'll be the whole army," said Ripley. "Gragg's boots and Brimblecome's and Sholes's and Cash's. How much farther, Joris?"

"Right over there." Cuyler hailed a low, unpainted house in a maple grove by a swift stream. A gentle-faced old woman ran out, her bent husband behind her. "Bring him right in by the fire." She caught Ripley's free hand and ducked her head under his arm. "You ain't heavy. Jared, hold that door wide."

A tortoise-shell cat, whiskers alert and tail high, rubbed and purred about Ripley's ankles as Joris and the old woman eased him into a chair by a stone fireplace. The cat jumped into his lap and watched with round-eyed intensity while a bucket of hot water was set on the hearth and Ripley's foot plunged into it. The old woman spoke soothingly. "That'll feel a sight better. A yarb tea's brewing in the little pot."

The injured foot burned fiercely at first. Then heat began to play on the sore flesh. The cat purred on, its mottled paws kneading the rough cloth of the breeches.

Cuyler said anxiously: "What do you think of it, Mrs. Yates?"

She shook her gray head. "'Twill ease, but 'twon't cure."

Mr. Yates said: "Were Abner to home, he'd put it to rights. He's got the healer's touch. But he and Ben are off with Silliman and never a word we hear."

"Knew you weren't King's people, soon as I saw you," said Cuyler.

"But we are. We're for the King, us and the boys, but we agreed the King'd got to be taught a lesson. What he'd done wa'n't fitting. Abbie, the brew's ready."

Eyes half closed, Ripley sipped a bitter pungent brew. "That's for the fever," explained Mrs. Yates. "Jared, dish out the succotash and the cold joint." She shook her head severely at Ripley. "'Tain't for you, not till the yarb tea's all gone."

Ripley finished the last drop and felt his head clearing. "Where are we?"

"Ten mile north of Kent," said the old man. "Brew gone?" He gave Ripley a steaming bowl in which cold meat lay across golden succotash.

"Kent? *Kent?*" Ripley forgot the food. "Joris, here's where we hit west. Two days more and we'll—"

"Not safe yet," said Cuyler, exchanging glances with the old couple. "Guess we'll keep going a few more miles before we turn."

"I say, now!" urged Ripley. "Soon's we get to the

regiment, Ike Spofford'll look at my foot and have me running races in a day's time."

"Of course he will. But we don't want to get nobbled by Cowboys or Lobsters, do we? I heard more about the dragoons before I found this house."

Ripley began to eat. His head felt clearer and the magic of the hot water was still about his foot. If only he felt stronger. He turned to the old man. "What's our best way of getting north?"

The old woman spread out her wide black skirts. "Well, now, Jared and me we was talking that over, waiting for you. My nieces have got to go to Lime Rock with my sister. You'd be glad of the ride and they'd be glad of escort—not that we've had bad people about here, but—"

Ripley set down his bowl. "See here, Joris, you said it wasn't safe—"

"Mrs. Yates said they hadn't been *seen* about here. They've been heard of though and if they've been heard of, maybe we'll be the ones to *see* them. North we go, and if we have to go clear to Canada, to Canada we go, and then we'll come down Champlain and the Hudson and start yelling: 'John Glover, here we are!' "

Ripley nodded. His foot had begun to throb again and his weakness seemed to grow with each breath. He closed his eyes and dozed while Jared Yates brought out awl and waxed cord and mended their broken boots, muttering and fuming over the workmanship. Ripley was given more herb tea and as soon as the boots had been dried as well as possible, they set out under the guidance of the old man. The new stitches held for the first few yards, but Ripley soon became aware of a slackening of the pressure about his ankle and his boots slowly opened and condemned him to the shuffling slide that had so wearied him coming down the ridge. "Got to lean on you more, Joris. What if boots came to pieces on the march or during an attack?"

Cuyler muttered in sympathy as his own boots grew slacker and slacker. Old Yates halted them in the road and vanished down a path that led toward the stream. In a few moments he was back, hoofs and wheels clacking behind him. Through returning waves of fever, Ripley opened his eyes wide. On the sagging seat, a stern-faced woman held the reins between masterful fingers. In the body of the cart, jolting on a plank, two extremely pretty girls gathered hooded cloaks about them. The woman stood up as she halted the cart. "These the men, Jared?" She turned keen eyes on Ripley and Cuyler. "He says you're all right. God help you if you're not. I'm Samantha Sherman. My daughters, Jane and Patience." She studied the draggled men with a keen eye. Then she pointed to Cuyler. "Young man, you'll sit right up here with me. Help your friend into the back of the cart and get up here."

The girls turned and smiled as Cuyler boosted Ripley up. He sighed wistfully. "Maybe, Mrs. Sherman, I'd best sit here and hold Rip up. He's liable to—"

"And you're liable to get yourself up on this seat this instant. And don't turn those innocent eyes on me. I know them."

Ripley caught the side of the cart and worked forward to the plank seat. Two pairs of eyes, one round and blue, the other almond-shaped and dark, smiled at him. "Move over, Patty," said the blue-eyed girl. She gathered her cape about her. "Sit right in here between us. Rest your foot on those sacks."

She tugged the damp cloth under Ripley's foot. "Just sit there. You've been with the army? Did you ever meet a Josiah Ingles?"

Ripley's head felt heavier than ever and his forehead was dappled with sweat. He said unsteadily, "Won't I be in your way?" He heard Mr. Yates call from the road and the cart rocked slowly north into the dusk. On either side of Ripley, the two girls began to ask about the army, then, seeing his sagging head, fell silent.

The grind of the wheels sounded soothing in Ripley's ears. From the front seat he caught an occasional cackle of laughter from Mrs. Sherman, punctuating the rise and fall of Cuyler's words. His eyes closed and there was darkness about him, a darkness that grew soft and warm. Once he was aroused by a quick laugh from the girl called Patience, who said: "But my name isn't Remembrance!"

He started, found that the girls had their arms about him, realized vaguely that his head rested on a soft shoulder. He said: "I'm afraid I'm a trouble to you. Better—" He dozed off again.

Later he jerked up his head. Hoofs were pounding down the dark road toward the cart. He rallied himself. "Pistol, Joris. I gave it back to you."

Mrs. Sherman called: "Nothing but a horse that's broke out. They will do it." The animal thundered past them. "Jodab Cusp's, likely."

"Likely," said one of the girls as Ripley's head dropped again.

The blaze of fire caught them unaware. Off to the right, flames burst through a barn roof. Cattle ran about bellowing and men moved in torchlight. "God help us," said Mrs. Sherman reining in. "Cowboys. There's a red coat. The—the—oh! The house has caught! Where's Cusp?"

She reined in quickly as Cuyler snatched the reins from her hands. "I'll turn him, quick!"

Ripley dragged himself back to full consciousness. "Too late! We're seen!" The girls sat rigid on either side of him. Ripley glanced quickly at them, then at the front seat. His hand shot out and caught Cuyler's arm. "Get back here quick! Mrs. Sherman, we've got to be quick or we're all lost. Will you trust me no matter what I do? It's our only chance."

There was a pause. Her voice was dry and steady. "Guess I ain't wanting."

Ripley, weakness forgotten, shoved Cuyler onto the seat beside Patience. "You heard what I said? Right. Here they come. Remember it's our only chance."

Down the road, torches and lanterns flared, drew nearer. Ripley threw his arm about Jane, pulled her face roughly around. "Hi—you Dutch block! Make the old slut keep the cart going."

Joris began to bellow in his Dutch patois and swung Patience clear of the seat as the lights drew nearer. "Steady, all hands," said Ripley. He laughed loudly and kissed Jane as the lanterns flared in his eyes. To his relief and amazement, she turned quickly and threw her arms about his neck, holding him close.

A harsh voice in the road shouted: "Get out that cart! Jemmy, they got doxies with 'em!"

"Yeeah!" shouted Ripley. "A sight more dahn the road! Me and the bloody Dutchy, we're making the old slut—"

By a torch, another voice joined in. "Wot's dahn the road? Women?"

"Abaht 'alf a mile," shouted Ripley. Jane lay close against him, trembling. In the dark he touched her shoulder reassuringly. "In Mother Brine's house," he added.

The lantern lifted higher. "Let's 'ave a look at yer. Ain't seed you afore."

"Charley Blount's troop. Lay on the hill back of Kent last night and got chased by bloody Skinners."

"Where you from?"

"Royal Marines."

"Who's the Dutchy?"

"Just a bloody Dutchy. Lossberg's regiment, he says. Bloody Dutchy, that's all!"

There was a shrill squeal and Patience slapped Cuyler playfully. "He ain't neither. He's a real man, he is. Ain't you, Dutchy?"

"*Ach! Ja!*" The rest of Cuyler's words were smothered.

The man in the road said, "We're more'n you are. Give us t' doxies."

"Nah yer don't," said Ripley. "Cowboys ain't taking each other's rum nor women. Come Blount got word—"

"Who the bloody 'ell's Blount?"

"You'll learn. Raided the Seventeenth Dragoons and brought a string of horses up through Westchester."

" 'Struth," muttered the man. He leaned closer. " 'Ow many doxies yonder?"

"Enough for you," said Ripley. "Down to the bridge, then cross it."

A fourth man came up and the others began talking to him in low tones. Then they put out their lights and stole away.

Ahead, mounted men, bulging bags tied to their saddles, were herding up frantic cattle and milling them onto the road. The cattle swayed, then shuffled slowly north, men on foot shouting at their heels.

Jane freed herself from Ripley. He said, "You're sportsmen, both of you."

"And we're alive and unharmed," said Mrs. Sherman. "We won't forget this. But if you two don't, I'll haunt you until I'm a hundred years in my grave." She gathered the reins. "Be safe to start now, I guess."

Cuyler slid off the board seat and perched at the tail of the cart, his pistol across his knees. "You girls keep watch on Rip. I'll stay back here until the road's clear. Ha! Here come lanterns! They didn't find the bridge or Mother Brine's! Mrs. Sherman, better talk to that horse a little."

The cart bowled on through the dark, slackened at a winding crossroad that led west, and then picked up speed again. Mrs. Sherman said, "How's that man, Jane?"

Patience answered: "He's fainted. Just now."

Cuyler sprang back to the seat. "Rip! Rip!"

But Ripley's head was sagging on his chest and his arms and legs were limp as a straw-stuffed doll's. Suddenly he shook violently. He moaned and began to slide off the seat. Cuyler caught him and stretched him out along the boards. "Shaking like ague. Got to get him warm." He lay beside Ripley and held him close. Without a word Jane left the seat and lay on the other side. She was crying quietly. Cuyler said: "Damn it, hold him tighter! I've seen people slip away in a chill like this. . . . You'll have—I'm sorry. But we've got to keep Rip's head up." His ear caught her broken breathing. "Not hurt are you?"

She shook her head. "It's—it's just everything." Almost to herself she said: "Josiah'd understand. I know he would."

"That's it! Course he would. If he wouldn't he just doesn't deserve a girl like you. Here, push this sacking under your head."

The cart jolted on.

V

FEVER came and went, came on again. Ripley, in conscious moments, was aware of one thing clearly, the burning pain of his foot. As a background to the constant torment his mind dumbly accepted scattered pictures. A farmhouse where he slept uneasily in hay; another jolting cart; a camp by a swift-running stream; and always Cuyler's steady voice, comforting and amazingly gentle. Then there was another cart that wound down steep hills in a chill dusk, a white village that looked vaguely familiar to him as he lay on the floorboards. He tried to get up and banged his foot against the side of the cart and the village faded from his consciousness.

Brandy stinging his lips and throat, he opened his eyes, then closed them quickly. "God, this is getting worse." Slowly he opened them again.

He lay on a small sofa in a room that was mellow

with mahogany and old oak. Cuyler stood looking down anxiously at him. A tall, thin man was pouring something into a glass. And on a cricket, close by the sofa, sat Remembrance Morse.

She said: "Joris—he's revived."

Her father turned his sad, dark face toward Ripley. "That's better. Drink this and don't ask me what's in it. Don't talk."

Eyes on Remembrance, Ripley drank slowly. Her dark glance was soft and troubled and her slim white hands were tightly clasped on her knees. He said feebly, "Where's the red ribbon you used to run through your hair?"

Cuyler shouted with laughter and began to swing his arms. "By God, he *is* better. You were talking about that ribbon back Konkapot way, Rip. You said—" He stopped, flushing and embarrassed. Then he said defiantly, "It's true. He said he liked it."

Remembrance took the glass from Ripley. "I've been saving it. Feel easier?"

"Some," said Ripley. He blinked rapidly. "How'd I get here?"

Cuyler shook his fist at him. "I brought you. Made up my mind I'd do it the day I went to the Yates place. They said I couldn't find a doctor in fifty miles. I knew where there was one in twenty. So we came here."

"Nothing but prison fever," said Morse. "Not unusual, seeing that all of you have made yourselves prisoners to this confounded war. You'll be up in a day."

Cuyler frowned at Morse. "How can you say that? You haven't even looked at his foot."

"Foot?" said Morse, puzzled lines showing on his face.

"I told you about it as soon as we got in."

"The devil you did. The army's wooled your wits, such as they are. You were shouting to Remembrance and asking me for rum and thanking the farmer who brought you here all in one breath. Foot, eh? Nothing broken?" With deft gentleness he stripped off the remains of Ripley's boot, unwound the wrappings that held a poultice in place.

"The Sherman girls did that, Rip. You wouldn't remember," said Cuyler.

"Remember them? I'll never forget them."

Remembrance raised her eyebrows. "Someone you met?" Then she sprang to her feet as her father uttered a stifled oath. "What is it?"

Dr. Morse said to Cuyler, "Turn him over on his face. Now! Remembrance, put hot water to boil. Heat some wine in the deep pan. Then go out and get Hall. Tell him I want him this instant. Cuyler, you hold him right there."

Morse left the room in long strides, then came back with a mahogany case which he set on the table. "What's the matter?" asked Ripley, his eyes following Remembrance, who was bringing two pans on a wooden tray.

"You'll find out. Ah—thanks for coming, Hall. I'll need you. Set the pot of water right here, daughter, and get me the big sponge."

Ripley heard the lid of the box creak. Cuyler eyed its glittering contents in awe. Morse said: "Now, Mayne, swallow all the brandy you can hold. I ought to wait until your fever's gone, but I don't dare. Cuyler, didn't anyone try to set this right?"

"No one I'd trust. There was a surgeon barber in Ashley Falls, but I wouldn't trust him to take a sliver out of a Lobster's rump, he was that bad."

"Might have been better if he'd looked. More brandy for Mayne and if you take a drop yourself I'll slice your ears off. Remembrance! Stay here. We'll need you." He carefully wiped the heel with hot water. "Joe Hall, you sit right across the back of his knees. Cuyler, you and Remembrance keep his arms still. Sit on him if you have to. More brandy for him. Mayne—can you hear me?"

Ripley grunted thickly.

"Then bite on these."

Ripley felt a chill shoot through him as the doctor pressed two small bullets into his mouth. He clamped his teeth on the lead pellets and shut his eyes. He tried to control a shudder as the unknown Hall's weight settled across his knees. Cuyler dragged his arms behind his back and held them tightly. A softer touch closed about his hands. He thought: "I won't let out a sound. By God, I won't—"

Through the gathering haze of brandy he felt white heat burn his heel. The weight over his knees pressed harder. Remembrance's voice, steady and level, reached out to him: "It won't take long." He heard Cuyler say: "He won't care if it does. The Fourteenth's tough."

The searing pain ran along his heel, burned deeper and deeper. Ripley knew that he was struggling, tried to lie still and struggled harder. The world seemed a vast infinity of black and red that swirled on and on —red pain and black pain. Through it all he could hear Dr. Morse talking calmly to Cuyler and Hall. "See what's happened. Deep blister here once that left the flesh sensitive. Got knocked about and started to fester right under the skin. Got to cut out all this rotten flesh, just the way you'd cut a spot out of an apple. Daughter, hold those arms tighter. There—we're down to the clear flesh. See the muscle move, Cuyler? That muscle's one of the best pieces of work the Lord ever did. Watch as I cut and see how it fits to the bone."

Floundering in the helpless torture of his searing world, Ripley knew that he had shouted. The knife bit deeper and his arm, lashing out, sent Remembrance halfway across the room. Then her hands, surprisingly strong, pinned his again while Cuyler pressed down hard on his shoulders.

Suddenly pain ceased to dart along his leg and settled down like a bed of glowing coals. "Done?" said Hall.

"This much. Stay right where you are. Remembrance, give him more brandy." Dr. Morse drew up a chair and climbed onto it, his gray head nearly brushing the high ceiling. In his hand he had a big sponge that he dipped into the pan of hot, sweetened wine.

Ripley started violently, forced back a moan. Then he shouted aloud. Drop by drop, the hot wine fell onto the exposed flesh. The pain was unbearable. It was red pain, scarlet pain, that fell in slow, merciless stabs.

Then it stopped. Ripley braced himself for the next drop, his jaws aching from the endless pressure on the bullets. "That's all," said Morse. Weight lifted from Ripley's knees, from his shoulders. Slowly the agony died away in his leg and foot, was replaced by a steady, burning ache. He knew that his face was wet with sweat, that his heart was pounding violently, that his breathing was broken and jerky. He kept his face pressed into the sofa. He had failed. He had cried out. His hot brain pictured Remembrance's soft mouth curling in faint contempt. Cuyler, he knew, was looking at him with surprised disdain. He steadied his breath as best he could. "Get on with the other foot, Doctor. I'm just getting the swing of this."

He felt a hand suddenly tighten on his and heard Cuyler give a short barking laugh. Morse said: "One's enough for now. That bandage too tight? Turn him a little, Cuyler."

Strong hands faced him toward the room. He began to cough feebly. Cuyler clapped a handkerchief over his mouth. "Sick?"

Ripley shook his head, lifted a weak hand to the handkerchief. Cuyler took it away and stared at it. From Ripley's mouth had come two plates of lead, very thin and dented. "The bullets," said Cuyler, wonder in his voice.

"I'll take those," said Morse. "How do you feel, Mayne?"

Ripley forced a grin that wavered away from his lips. "I'd like to rest a little before we start out again." He closed his eyes. "Hope—hope I didn't bellow too much." The room began to steady. He saw that Cuyler was kneeling beside the sofa, patting his back gently. Remembrance was on the cricket, one of his hands in hers. Morse said, throwing a red-stained cloth into a basin, "I've heard people yell worse. A lot worse. In fact I wish that colonel of yours had been here to see. Or your father." He held out the lead plates. "Those go into my bag. When I have cutting to do, I'm going to show them to my patient and tell him about you. It'll help him." He picked up the basin and went out of the room.

"Where's the other man?" asked Ripley feebly.

"Gone. Ran like a rabbit as soon as it was over," said Cuyler. His voice was thick and his eyes were curiously bright.

Remembrance tightened her grip on Ripley's hand. "Don't try to talk. Joris'll tell me everything about how he got you here." Her voice dropped. "I'm glad—so glad he did. We heard of the awful defeats. I was worried."

Cuyler cleared his throat. "Couldn't ever have done it with anyone but Rip. Oh, what I'll have to tell the old Bull Seal when we get back."

Morse strode back into the room. "Oh, yes, you'll go back, I suppose. It'll be some time before that heals enough for you to walk on, though. Now here's a sleeping draught. You're going to stay right here because it'll be easier for me to look after you. Cuyler, we'll find a corner for you or you can go to the inn. Mayne, drink this."

The draught was bitter, but Ripley managed to choke it down. Gradually the pain seemed to ease. His eyelids fell. The room faded from his consciousness. His last memory was a low husky voice close by him and the voice of Morse, rising in anger: "Hell and death! Soldiers in *my* hospital? Earthworks on the grounds? Cannon? What fool said that man was a reasoning animal?"

* * *

Early sun was creeping into the room when Ripley awoke. His foot throbbed heavily and a hot cord seemed stretched from his heel to his calf. His head ached and he felt desperately weak. He stirred and found that during the night he had been undressed and the sofa made up as a bed. The door creaked and Remorse Morse, fantastically tall in a gray bed-gown and tasseled nightcap, looked in. "Stirring, are you? In five minutes you'll be cursing me and vowing that you feel worse than yesterday."

"Not quite—at least, so far," said Ripley.

"Wait and see." Morse pulled back the curtains. "Now for a look at your hoof. The bandages will stick but I'm going to keep right on tugging just the same. It's the best way."

Ripley winced as the wrappings were stripped off. Morse bent over the foot, grunting and clucking to himself. "Clean, anyway. You'll shake this off in time. Now about the fever." He talked on, poking and prodding. At last he said: "Fever's broken. You've got a good constitution. The army, I suppose. That life does seem to make people healthy. Of course, it's all body. You're probably growing stupid as a half-witted ewe. If you weren't stupid, you wouldn't be where you are. You'll have breakfast presently. I'll be back soon."

He left the room and Cuyler thumped in. "If you looked any better, they'd have to kill you. How'd you sleep?"

"Fine," said Ripley. "How was the inn?"

"Great! There's a man down there who can take a glass of rum and pour it down his throat. Doesn't drink it—just pours. It's a fine place."

"Must be," grinned Ripley. Then he said: "Look

here, I've been trying to piece out the last few days. What happened to the Shermans?"

"Left them at Lime Rock." Cuyler was silent for a moment and then broke out: "Women can be wonderful." He dropped his voice. "This one is, let me tell you. She's—"

A light step sounded in the corridor. "May I come in?" said Remembrance.

Cuyler pushed up the cricket for her. Tall and slim in soft blue that was partially covered by a long apron, she looked gravely down at Ripley, then smiled. "You're better. Joris, turn him over." Her strong hands closed about his wrists. Cuyler locked Ripley's arms behind his back. Another step sounded. Ripley smelled the reek of hot wine and heard a chair creak. The covers were turned back from his foot, and the slow beat of the drops drilled down onto the raw flesh. He was weak and shaken when the torment was over. Morse said grimly: "Be ready for another treatment this evening."

"My God," moaned Ripley. "Again?"

"Again? You'll have this twice a day until I see the signs I'm looking for."

Cuyler waved his arms. "Can't you do something else? I'll go mad watching Rip—"

"I can do nothing else. Of course, if you'd rather have Hall come in again, he can hold Mayne down and you can run off to the inn and guzzle away what brains you may have. I'm not sure that you'd miss them hugely."

"I'll be here," said Cuyler gruffly.

"Then we'll put Mayne back to sleep. That's what he needs. Lift up, sir, and take your potion."

In the late afternoon, Ripley opened his eyes. Remembrance was in her familiar place on the cricket. She smiled. "You've had a fine sleep. Father'll be pleased."

"I wish I hadn't. I'd rather have been awake all the

time you were here. Don't say you just came in. The sun's shining in your eyes. It wasn't when you first sat down. You didn't want to move for fear of waking me. Isn't that true?"

She colored lightly. "You're too weak to contradict. And Father wouldn't like you to talk so much."

"He's overruled—by me. I've waited since January for a chance to talk to you, and I'm not going to miss any time now. I used to talk to you, you know, through a lot of those nights when the Lobsters had us. And then I'd begin wondering what you'd think with all those weeks going by and no word from me."

She touched his hand gently. "I wondered a lot, Rip. I'd come to look for your letters. Then I began to get frightened. We had awful news from the army. And things that happened to it could have happened to you."

He raised himself on his elbow. "You never thought I'd just gotten careless and not written?"

She lowered her eyes. "It could have been that. But I didn't think so."

He smiled. "You were right. You're much too real a girl to be forgotten. At the oddest times I'd remember the way you walked or the way your lips curl up at the corners when you smile or the way you hold your head when you're puzzling over something." Light was fading in the room and her rounded figure was silhouetted against the dim window. He took her hand. "I could tell you a lot more things about you that I remembered. Things you said—things you did."

She freed her hand, slowly. "We'd better talk about something else, Rip."

He said eagerly: "Then I could tell you about things you didn't say. Things you didn't do—and maybe you might have. When I picked you up in the snow—"

She rose abruptly and stepped to the window. Then she cried, "Oh—here comes Joris down the street with a face as long as a goose's neck."

"Damn Joris," thought Ripley. "They're probably out of rum at the inn."

Remembrance rapped on the small pane. The door slammed and Cuyler clumped wearily into the room. He dropped into a chair. "Got some news—things that happened while we were coming up the Housatonic, I guess. Wish I hadn't heard it."

Ripley sat upright. Remembrance crossed the room and gently forced him back. Her hand lay on his shoulder. Cuyler went on: "A lot of the shaves we heard coming up through Connecticut were true. Last month Howe beat Washington at White Plains. Then Howe swung south, back onto Manhattan. He took Fort Washington and about two thousand prisoners. Washington's had to go into the Jerseys with most of the army and Howe's getting ready to follow."

Ripley narrowed his eyes. "Where's the Fourteenth?"

"Northcastle, on the east bank. They're under Lee. People say that Washington's sent for Lee to join him, but the damned chuff won't move. They say he wants Washington to get beaten and then take his place." He rumpled his blond hair. "I don't see how it could be much worse. Lost some of our best men at Fort Washington, lost stores and baggage and powder and guns." His head sagged dismally.

Ripley said quietly, "It doesn't matter."

Remembrance and Cuyler looked at him in surprise. He went on: "Not a bit. Joris, this goes right back to what we told Aubrey. It goes right back to what I wrote Remembrance about the army. Howe's won a couple of battles. But he hasn't won the war and I'm still saying he won't. He can't."

Cuyler slapped his knee angrily. "But the stores—the guns we lost. Whole regiments broken up. Most of Knowlton's old rangers were there at the fort."

"We've lost all that before—and gone on. We'll lose them again—and go on. Joris, you'd better hit out and join the old Bull Seal."

"Not without you," said Cuyler.

"He'll need you. He'll need every man."

"Lee's not doing anything. Just sitting with his regiments at Northcastle. No more arguing. You and I take the road together or I'll desert and join Minnegerode's Hessian grenadiers." He appealed to Remembrance. "You approve, don't you?"

She smiled down at Ripley. "When you go, you'll need someone with you. Now you've got to go to sleep again." She smoothed his forehead lightly. "You've got more hot wine coming to you later."

"And to think I used to drink the stuff," moaned Ripley. . . .

Some days later, Ripley lay tossing on the sofa. The pain was gone from his heel and he felt restless and uneasy. Joris and Remembrance had gone out for a walk, leaving him to his afternoon nap, but he could not sleep. He had tried to read *Joseph Andrews* but the book had failed to hold him and he had ended by scaling it across the room. The afternoon faded into twilight. Ripley fumed: "Someone might at least look in. Maybe my bandage has slipped. Maybe—"

Dr. Morse's voice sounded in the corridor. "Time for our customary bowl of wine, I believe, Mr. Mayne." Tall and lank, the doctor walked into the room, bearing the deep pan and the sponge that Ripley dreaded. The doctor went on: "Since you've stopped squalling and don't have to be nailed down, we can do this alone. Just the two of us." He placed the sponge on the table and reached into the pan. "Your health, Mayne." His long hand drew out a glass full of dark wine which he gave Ripley. Then he produced another for himself.

Ripley stared.

"Confound it, have your wits quite addled? I'm trying to tell you that from now on this is the only way you'll take wine—unless you really want me to cut you open again and go back to the sponge." He raised his glass. "As I remarked before—your health."

"And yours." Ripley set down his empty glass. "This seems to be a red-letter day for me."

"Why do you think that Cuyler and I put you back into those outlandish and obscene clothes of yours this morning?" He whipped off the light blanket that covered the sofa. "Get up. I say—get up. Walk. Walk from here to the door."

Ripley marveled: "I can't believe it!" He slid his feet to the floor and stood, swaying slightly.

"Dizzy, of course," said Morse. "Bound to be. Now go over to the door."

The whole leg felt weak and stiff. Ripley took two steps, a third. He reached the door, turned, and walked back to the sofa. "How does it feel?" asked Morse.

"Burns like the devil and my calf's cramping," said Ripley.

Morse rubbed his hands. "Admirable! Splendid! Cramps are strong, are they? That's fine! Keep walking."

Little by little leg and ankle lost some of their stiffness. Ripley tried army facings, raised himself on his toes, rocked back on his heels, while Morse's sad eyes regarded him as though he were some special creation of his own. "How soon can I go?" asked Ripley.

"Not for a week, anyway," said Morse. "Keep stepping and I'll have a look at it morning and night."

Each day the incision in Ripley's heel grew smaller. His muscles lost their stiffness and he began to take careful walks, sometimes with Cuyler, more often with Remembrance. On the windy hilltop from which they had first sighted Knox's guns nearly a year ago, he confided to her his anxiety about the army. As he talked, she stood on the old rock and the wind blew back her cape to reveal her splendid figure, tall and slim with high, rounded breasts. He recalled how he had thought of her once, facing a gale in the bow of a boat.

When he had finished, she looked down at him,

eyes bright in the clear air. "But I thought you were so confident. You certainly sounded that way when we went to the falls yesterday."

He said grimly, "Sometimes I am. But look at the news from Jersey. Washington's still falling back and they say he's got less than fifteen hundred men with him. Then there's that Englishman, Lee. I never liked him in the first place. He's holding a lot of men, Glover's with them, on the east bank of the Hudson and won't obey Washington's orders to cross and join him. Arnold seems to have kept Carleton from coming down Champlain, but it's my guess that the weather bothered Carleton more than Arnold did. Enlistments run out at the end of the year and how many men will join up again after such a run of bad news?"

Remembrance jumped down from the rock. "Ripley Mayne! You've always said that they'd been through so much that nothing could break them. It's true, I tell you. And I'm not going to have you talking that way about my country and my army." Her slim hands fell on his. "They'll win out and you know it."

He laughed reluctantly, eyes on her serious, eager face. "Yes, I guess they will. When I get the black dog on my back, I'll rant to you and you'll chase it away. And now—"

"And now—" She gently freed her hands. "Now it's time to be getting back. Father wants a look at you before he goes to see old Mrs. Gremp."

Ripley sighed and followed her, keenly aware of the lift of her white throat as she raised her face to the wind.

VI

In the dim little ell room where Ripley had been moved a few days before, he carefully packed his scant possessions in an old game bag of the doctor's: his old boots, mended as well as possible; underwear and shirts from the local Committee; his shaving tackle. A strange dejection filled him as he mechanically debated the choice of stowing his stockings inside his boots or laying them on top of everything to swell out the bag compactly.

His heart leaped at a low cry from the door where Remembrance stood, her eyes big and luminous in the faint light. She said uncertainly: "I didn't know you were here. I thought you'd gone to the inn for Joris." She held out heavy folds of cloth. "I was just bringing this."

The stockings fell from Ripley's hand unheeded. "You thought I'd just get Joris and pick up my bag as we went by?"

She smiled. "Of course not. I meant— It's only an old cape of Father's that I mended for you." She came quickly into the room. "I'll stow it away." She folded the cape neatly. "I'll put it right across the top of the bag. You won't need it today, it'll be so warm walking. And if you do, it'll be right on top."

Ripley said, "Remembrance, I wanted to tell you—"

She fumbled with the strap, then suddenly dropped the bag and ran toward the door.

Ripley crossed the room in a great stride. "Remembrance!"

She lowered her head and caught at the latch of the partly closed door. Ripley caught her, drew her hands from the latch. "Remembrance! Look up at me." Deep joy filled him. "Remembrance! I love you!"

She turned suddenly in his arms. "I love you, Rip. I've been trying all along to think I didn't." She was crying quietly in his arms, one hand against his cheek. "When I touched that bag—I knew you'd take that bag and go away over the hill and you wouldn't be coming back."

He smoothed her hair. "But I am coming back." He caught her closer. "I've got to."

Her face turned up to him, eyes closed and lips slightly parted. "You'll come back, Rip," she whispered. "I'm so happy." For a brief moment there was nothing for them but a soft stillness.

Then Ripley said: "You're not a tenth as happy as I am. We're going to be the most admirable couple in the Americas."

Her arms tightened. "I just want to be part of you and care for what matters to you."

He stroked her cheek. "This war won't last forever."

Her breath went in brokenly. "But we've got to win it first, Rip. She suddenly clung to him desperately and her cheeks were wet again.

"Not afraid?" he whispered.

"Hugely. You've got to go away. I shan't see you. I shan't know anything about you. I wouldn't have you anywhere else than where you're going. I'm telling myself that, over and over." Her voice shook a little. "I'm such a coward about you, Rip."

He raised her chin gently. "Such a brave little coward. I'll think of this room and you in my arms. I'll think of you bending over the sofa downstairs, watching my fever. I'll see the firelight play on your hair and on your face the way it did when you were making soup for the men. I'll remember how your eyelashes flick against my cheek the way they're doing now." He bent and kissed the hollow at the base of her throat.

Eyes half shut she listened, fingers straying through his hair. Then she gently freed one arm and her hand grasped the strap of the bag. He caught her close once more. Arms about each other, they walked in silence down the stairs, the strap of the bag clicking against the steps.

PART SEVEN

ATTACK

Washington was falling back through New Jersey. The Hackensack was crossed, then the Passaic and the Raritan. Enlistments were running out and few fresh men were to be found anywhere. At the Delaware, the skeleton regiments swept the left bank, gathered up every boat that could be found, and crossed over.

Rich in transport, supplies, men, and leisure, Howe followed the retreat. It is possible that he was still rich in memories of the ghastly slopes of Breed's Hill and Bunker's, now a year and a half behind him. Or perhaps he counted on Washington's force falling to pieces through the effects of constant reverses and the absence of rational hope in the future.

On the left bank of the Hudson, Charles Lee waited with a large force. He had plans of his own that did not fit in with Washington's urgent orders to join him. At last he moved and went down through the Jersey counties where he seized on seven New England regiments which had been sent down from Ticonderoga to join Washington. They would be better employed thus than wasted in Washington's unskilled hands, reasoned Lee the adventurer.

Then fortune smiled bleakly on the American army. Lee was captured by British dragoons and Sullivan, next in command, hurried the force to Washington's aid. At the same time, lethargic William Howe decided to go into winter quarters and let further campaigning wait on more clement weather. In the meantime, he would hold New Jersey with a chain of posts stretching from the Amboys right through Princeton and Trenton to the Delaware.

I

It took Ripley and Cuyler more than two days to reach the Hudson, where one of the coins that Dr. Morse had insisted on their taking got them the use of a boat. Past the high, snowy banks of the Hudson they went, shivering in the December air. They touched at Esopus and learned that Heath had broken camp at Poughkeepsie. At Newburgh an innkeeper told them that Lee had at last roused himself and brought his troops across the river. He was, judged the man, making for Morristown.

Ripley, sipping rum, nodded at Cuyler. "Then, if his intention's for Jersey, so is ours. We stay on the west bank."

At Nyack they struck inland, through a thin drift of snow that blew vaguely from the west. Many of the farms they passed were gutted and people muttered of the vicious, pillaging raids of the Hessians, their cruel abuse of the old and the weak. Cuyler snorted angrily at these tales. "Thank God I'm an honest Dutchman! Hanging a pregnant woman up by the heels and leaving her!"

Ripley said nothing, but his eyes took on a cold glitter and his chin set ominously.

The track of Heath's army was not hard to follow. Abandoned equipment, dead horses, scars of old camps marked it for them. Then they began to get news of Lee's passage and hurried on, hoping to strike his trail. They slept in little towns, on wooded hills. Once they were penned on a cliff for a whole day while they watched in bitter helplessness a hundred green-coated horsemen that Cuyler said were mounted Jaegers. Ripleys heart turned sick as he saw flames creep up through roofs, saw a dark line of people making for thick woods beyond the range of the riders.

Then, on a glittering morning they saw the heights loom in the west. "Morrison," said Ripley tersely.

"Glover!" shouted Cuyler.

By noon they had come to a cupola'd courthouse, its shingled sides glinting under a coating of ice. A few people moved through the silent streets whose trampled snow bore witness to the passage of hundreds of troops. Ripley hailed an old man who was dragging a wood-laden hand sled. "Isn't Lee's division here?"

The old man tweaked at the handkerchief that bound his hat to his head. "General Lee? You ain't heard? The general, he got took."

"Captured?" snapped Ripley. "Was there a fight?"

"No. And won't be, less'n the Britainers try to make us take him back. Sullivan's took his place."

"Where's Glover's brigade?"

"A lot'd like to know that, young man. The whole division up and left a day ago. Heard tell they went downriver, but I ain't sure."

Cuyler leaned on a heavy staff. "That would be the Delaware?"

"Seems like it would. They've passed the Raritan."

Ripley said: "Is it safe, down on the plains?"

"Might be, long's you cling close to the river. But

you got to watch the folk down there. A sight has taken the oath to the King to keep from getting looted."

"So your advice is to go south and west? Come on, Joris, we'll pick up the trail."

They bought provisions with the last of their money and set out, bearing west and south. Cuyler huddled his borrowed cape about him. "Lucky we got these new boots. The first thing I do is see the quartermaster and wheedle a new uniform out of him."

"Mine's all right," said Ripley.

"Ha!" said Cuyler. "You hate to give up the old clothes with Remembrance's stitches in them! So do I. I'll wear the new one and keep this as a holy relic." He sighed. "Rip, you're a damned lucky man."

Ripley thought of dark eyes looking into his among the pines at the top of the hill, back by Great Barrington. "The sooner we get this fighting over, the sooner I'll get back to her," he muttered between his teeth. "Step out more, can't you?"

Early the following evening they came to the broad river. A heavy thaw had broken up the ice and they stood in silence watching the great cakes spin slowly as the current took them south and east to the sea. The next day they crossed on an ice jam and began working their way east. Sometime past noon, Cuyler gave a sudden whoop and pointed to a row of fires a mile south of the river. Ripley shouted, "The army! It's still here."

A ragged picket stopped the pair at a small cluster of houses.

"What regiment?" said Ripley.

"Reed's Virginians." The picket shuffled his ragbound feet in the slush.

"Where's the main camp?"

"Reckon you'd find it two-three mile inland."

"Know where Glover's brigade is?"

"Yankees?" The man spat. "Hell, no!"

Cuyler's voice soared: "Hell, no, is it? By God, I'll—"

Ripley caught his sleeve. "Don't waste time. It'll be here somewhere."

They followed a winding track that led away from the river.

Tents and huts grew thicker. Ripley hailed, found that he was passing Haslet's Delaware men, then Chester's, Webb's from Connecticut. A park of orderly guns and limbers marked the camp of Henry Knox's Massachusetts gunners which lay beyond Loammi Baldwin's men from Middlesex County.

"What lot's that?" shouted Cuyler, pointing to a thick column that splashed on through the slush toward the river.

"I'd say militia, if they didn't march too well for that. Hard to tell from here but I think some of the men are wearing blankets for breeches."

"Look like scarecrows in a Mohawk cornfield. I'll lay a pound they—"

But Ripley had started to run after the column whose head was disappearing over a slight rise toward the river. "What the hell?" roared Cuyler, setting out in pursuit.

Ripley was shouting: "General Glover! General John Glover!"

A short man, who marched on beside a dark-faced officer, whirled in his tracks, a big cape flaring out with the motion. "Who the devil—"

Ripley ran up panting. "Lieutenants Mayne and Cuyler reporting, sir."

Glover's blue eyes bulged. He pushed his hat back on his gingery hair, and stared. Then both hands shot out and he caught Cuyler and Ripley. "You—you damned scamps! You—" His face wrinkled in a wide grin. "Lee! Lee! They've come back." He shook them violently while the tall major nodded gravely. Glover went on. "You fell overboard and by God you've made shore at last. You're just in time to hear me chart a course that'd make old Dimond of Marblehead seasick." He hooked an arm through Ripley's, caught

Cuyler by the elbow. "You got caught? We guessed that. And got away? I'll want to hear every step you took later. Cuyler, clap on all sail and lay a course for Blackler's company. You'll be welcome as a run of cod. Mayne, you stay with me and Lee." Cuyler splashed off through the slush.

Glover turned to Ripley. "You get all spare tackle stowed away in your mind because I'll want to hear everything you've seen that'll help the army. I'll send a report on to General Washington. Ha! You missed Pell's Point. The brigade hit the Lobsters and the Hessians. We were wild as a bull seal in mating time. The Fourteenth stood like Caesar's Tenth Legion. We—God Almighty, what's this?"

Down the column stormed a stocky figure, long arms waving and musket bobbing. "Rip!" yelled Sholes. "Rip, by God, you done it!" Sholes utterly disregarded Glover and Lee and pounded Ripley's back. "It's me, Mutton-lip. Look!" He whipped off a disgraceful fur cap and slapped his thigh with it. "Me, back in ranger clothes 'cause soldier suits is all gone." His hands thumped Ripley's shoulders. "Where you been? How'd you get here? By God, you had me and the brigadier worried!"

Ripley shook the wide shoulders. "'Remembered what you told me every time we got in trouble, Mutton-lip. That's the only thing that saved us. We'll give you the whole story later. Just now I've got some things to tell the brigadier about the Lobsters."

Sholes nodded violently. "Sure. Sure. When you've scouted a trail you got to tell 'bout the signs you picked up." He thrust an arm through Ripley's and trudged on through the slush as though he were Glover's second in command.

Glover started to speak. Then he smothered a smile. "Go ahead, Mayne. About the Lobsters."

Ripley began: "Of course, it was in the late fall that we got away and things may have changed, but—" He spoke of the odd mixture of extreme overconfidence and overcaution, the latter possibly bred by the slaughter on the Charlestown peninsula the year before, which seemed to hamper the British; there was bad feeling between the British and the Germans, he thought; both he and Cuyler had commented on the fact that many regiments seemed to have their best officers in the lower ranks, the field officers being apparently chosen by influence rather than merit. There were other points. . . .

As he talked on, to an accompaniment of short nods from Glover, his eyes were on the steady-moving files ahead. A few of the old blue coats and white breeches had survived, but most of the men were in nondescript rags. Many boots had split, or had been discarded for carefully wound rags. But heads were high and the ranks swung on as smoothly as they had in the march to the Sound the past summer.

Then they topped the crest. Ripley's ears filled with the dull roar and grind of the ice. Another sound, a menacing undertone, joined in, a steady boom-thud-boom. Upstream, stretching away for a good half mile, a long line of boats was moored close by the shore.

A low murmur of surprise swept up from the companies, marching at ease. "Jesus! Look at the damned things!" . . . "Them Jersey boatmen ain't nothing but froaches. Boats'll be stove to kindling." . . . "Why'n't they beach 'em—that ain't no way to treat a boat!"

Then a warning command wailed down the column and it shifted into line, came to a smooth halt. Sholes scuttered back to his company. Glover said to Ripley: "Stay by me! I'll have something particular for you later."

Glover faced the regiment, fifty yards from the endless voice of the river, grinned as he saw Blackler's company where a dozen men were mauling Cuyler's broad back, shouting gleefully and profanely. He held up his hand and there was silence.

"Two fish got out of our nets last fall. We've got them back. Most of you've seen Mr. Cuyler already.

Here's Mr. Mayne at my elbow. When I've done talking, you can all surge athwart them as much as you please. But we've got another net out now and I had you marched out by the river to hear about it." His quick eyes swept along the line. Ripley felt his spine tingle as the familiar, staccato tones rapped out. "Now this isn't military and it isn't in any book—no more than our fight at Pell's Point was. But there's something we Marbleheaders have got to talk over and I figured this was the best way to do it." He turned, scraped snow from a high rock, and perched on it, small feet swinging. "Break ranks and moor in a semicircle around me."

The regiment moved forward. Ripley saw a dozen remembered faces—Brimblecome's and Cash's and Trefry's. Grenda, with his stoop shoulders and tight face; Blackler, dark and hard-mouthed; Isaac Spofford the surgeon; the gnomelike Adam Gragg; Bond, Pedrick, Moses Brown.

Glover's voice brought him back. "I'm going to stay perched up here like a gull. Think anyone's going to try to get over that river and tie up alongside us?"

Captain Courtis spoke up. "Not till it freezes or the ice clears."

"What do you think, Blackler?"

"Courtis is right. No crossing. Either way."

Glover's small feet swung faster. "That's what *I* thought." He twisted about, looked at the flood, spun back. "I'm going to tell you two things. They're important to you as part of the army and as Marbleheaders. First, General Washington wants to ferry the whole command over there as soon as it's possible. Second, he wants us to do it."

"When?" asked a voice from the ranks.

Glover sprang from his rock. "He wants to cross—*tonight!*"

The circle about Glover stopped its swaying and shuffling. An amazed voice said: "Tonight? Well, he just ain't a boatman, that's all."

"No." Glover's arms swung. "He isn't. But *we are!* He asked if it could be done. I said my boys could do it." He shook his fist at them. "Damn it, we've *got* to do it. At dark, the army's coming down here. We're going to pile them into the boats up yonder. We're going to land them on the other bank. We're going to fight darkness and cold and ice. *We're going to get the army across.* We're the only regiment on the continent that can do it. We'll fight a hard current and there'll be no waiting for a change in tide. There's no tide. We're going to fight ice cakes as big as the nose of Cape Ann, cakes that'll sink the toughest rig afloat. We're going to embark men that'll be scared of every drop of water that slaps the thwarts. We're going to manhandle guns and horses aboard. You'll use no lanterns on shore or afloat. You'll muffle your oars."

Someone said: "It's impossible."

Glover's arms waved. "Of course it's impossible. And we're going to do it."

A man in Courtis's company shifted his bound feet. "Maybe it won't be so bad. Just getting boats 'cross a strip of water."

"That's it! That's it!" Glover kicked at the thin snow. "Now scatter and have a look at the craft. Cast off! Get the smell of the timbers into your noses. There'll be some Jersey boatmen to help you if you need them."

The regiment broke toward the boats, shouting and whooping. "To hell with the Jerseymen!" . . . "Joe! Look at the nose of that barge." . . . "Lem, get into that flat bottom. She'd ride over a reef on a drop of water." . . . "Let me get my hands on them oars!" . . . "Poles! Got to have poles to fend off the ice. Tear up that fence!" The boats rocked and pitched as the men of the Fourteenth stormed into them.

Glover drew a long breath. "The boys hadn't been feeling good, Mayne. It's been a bad time. Now look at them." He blew out his cheeks. "Don't mind telling you I haven't been feeling good either. No replacements. No supplies. Johonot's sick. Now this order of

Washington's for crossing." He shook Ripley's arm. "We've got to embark the whole damned army. It'll be easier now that you and Cuyler are back. You'll know how to handle the landsmen."

"We'll try, sir," said Ripley. "Do you know what we're going to do?"

"Barring the crossing, no. And I don't want to—yet. All I do know is that the British have got a chain of posts stretching from the coast right up to Trenton. That's ten-mile downstream and it's full of Hessians. Now you get along and look at the boats. Then see the quartermaster and draw anything he can give you. Be back here by sundown, ready to do the job."

By the boats, old friends closed about Ripley. Sholes came roaring up the bank. "By God, I been telling the boys you'd done it. Got clean away, ain't he? Same as I did the first time I got to be called Mutton-lip. 'Twas up by Crown Point and—Hey! Adam Gragg! Get over here and lay your sights on Rip." Then Blackler was punching his ribs, Moses Brown, Courtis, Bond, Speakman, shouted about him. Brimblecome and the others who had gone with him for the guns crowded up.

They were all thin and worn and desperately ragged, but their eyes were steady and their mouths firm.

Ripley drew a deep breath. He was back with his own, his own that roared out an unstinted welcome and pounded him without mercy. Down by the river, among the crews, a small man raced up and down the bank like a blue squirrel, scrambling into a barge, helping to unship a useless mast, hurrying the work along. Ripley caught Cuyler's eye. "Damned old Bull Seal," said Cuyler blinking.

"Just what I was thinking," said Ripley. Then in a lower tone he added, "I ought to have known better than to worry. Joris, the army's here. It's going to attack. I wish Remembrance knew."

* * *

At dusk, Ripley and Cuyler came back to the river. They had had a scant meal and the quartermaster had no equipment for them, barring two rather battered fusees and ammunition. "You look like a duke in your new uniform," gibed Ripley.

"Duke? I'm dressed like a king—King of the Beggars. Where are you going to stand?"

"See those buildings? That's McKonkey's Ferry." Ripley turned his back to the wind that was cutting diagonally across the river. Men scrambled about, worked heavy barges into the current, drove them back to the shore as they tested the butt and heave of the water. Out in midstream arose a continuous grinding and muttering. Close by the banks, great cakes of ice swirled and banged against the boats, setting up an incessant din that echoed above any warning cry or shout. To the south and east, stretching far into Pennsylvania, a low-hanging cloud glowed dull orange—the campfires of Washington's army.

"How'll we higgle them around?" asked Cuyler.

"We'll stay by this platform. When the first lot comes along I'll take them down to the boats. You hold up the next lot until I get back, then march them off. Glover says they've got to go aboard as smooth as fish pouring out of a bucket."

They waited until the first dark mass of men moved up from the south. Ripley jumped to the platform and waved his arm to the Marbleheaders by the bank. The first blunt-nosed barge swung into the current, was backed into the shore again. The footsteps in the dark grew louder. Cuyler held up both arms and shouted: "Hoy!"

A voice called: "Who's there?"

Ripley ran down the road crying: "In charge of embarkation! Who are you?"

The marching shapes were closer in the dark. A hoarse voice said: "Pennsylvania militia. Attached to Mercer's brigade."

"Good. Follow me!" The militia regiment, barely a

hundred strong, tramped on behind Ripley, the men shaking their heads nervously as the roar and grind of the ice swelled in their ears. Ripley shouted: "Captain Courtis's boats! Captain Bond's!" Figures scurried along the bank. "This way! First company, head this way!" Ripley waved the miltia on and waited until he heard a shout: "Barge loaded! Shove off!"

The first barge, black among the tearing ice cakes, nosed out into the stream. There was a thundering sound as a great mass of ice butted against it. The boat shuddered, reeled. Oars whipped the water, slid off whirling cakes, bit into the current again. Foot by foot and yard by yard, the Marbleheaders drove slowly and inexorably for the Jersey shore. Another barge put out, a third.

Ripley ran back to Cuyler, who was holding up a long, shivering column. "Take them on, Joris."

Through the night, the army trudged on in the slush, was guided, section by section, to the barges. New names answered Ripley's hail or Cuyler's shout. Now they were Sterling's men, now Hand's, now Poor's. Sometimes the banks were thick with men who huddled torn clothes about them and stared mutely at the creamy froth through which the barges worked back to the south bank. Sometimes the whole river front was alive with marching files of men who, heads down, tramped onto the craft that had come back for another load.

Near ten o'clock, Knox's field pieces jolted into sight, were steered off far upstream. Then came Greene's men, Stark's, Patterson's. The wind stiffened. Sleet needles drove down the Delaware. Ripley shouted through it. "Next—next—bring them on." With lowered heads and stumbling feet, with muskets clutched in raw red hands, they pressed on. They shivered, huddled numb arms against empty bellies, stared at the reddish blotches in the snow. But not a man fell out, not a man slipped away into the dark blast that swept down from the west.

In a pause when long lines of men hunched their shoulders and waited for the barges to work back from the other side, Cuyler splashed up to Ripley and threw a wet arm about his shoulder. "My hinny's frozen, backing into that gale! Christ, they're taking a long time to get back this trip!"

Ripley shook water from his hat and looked anxiously out at the heave and toss of the vast ice cakes. "Must have stopped for a hand of loo. Hell, guts, and molasses! We'll never get across by daybreak at this rate!"

A small form whirled out of the sleet, wedged in between the two. "Any man who says that again'll get drowned—and by my own hands!" Glover shook his fist. "You're doing a seaman's job, both of you. Cuyler, how'd you ever straighten out Haslet's men?"

Cuyler disregarded the question. "How's it going?"

"Going?" Glover exploded. "I told the general we'd be across by midnight. We won't, because it's the toughest rowing a Marbleheader ever faced, and that's tougher than anything the devil ever thought up on a rainy Sunday. But the army'll be on the march long before daybreak."

Someone called from the dark: "Glover! I want John Glover!"

The little man dashed off toward the ferry buildings where a tall form loomed. Ripley said: "So Washington's down at last, is he?"

"Down at last? He's been over and back already! He's counted every pebble on the bank. Some of Webb's men didn't like the way a boat tossed and damned if he didn't get right out in the bow. Never said a word. Just got there. Then he came back and the boys tramped on like sheep."

Ripley watched the tall figure swinging away into the dark. Someone near by said pleasantly, "Big bastard, ain't he?"

Glover stormed back. "Cuyler—you're going to do the whole job here—alone. Mayne, the general wants you to go up and help load Knox's guns and horses. I told him that a seagoing farmer like you could do it blindfold. Get on with you. And if you lose a horse overboard or spill a single gun, down you go and haul it in with your teeth!"

Ripley slapped Cuyler's back. "Keep your queue dry!" He ran off over ground that was rutted and trampled with the passage of uncounted men. As he rounded a clump of willows, a heavy shape loomed in front of him. He called: "I'm looking for General Knox's guns."

There was a chuckle. "So? Better rein in or you'll dive down a muzzle."

"Who's in charge?" snapped Ripley.

"Hold up! I know your voice. Great Barrington and the guns! Shades of Livy and Tacitus! I'm General Knox. Isn't this a fine night for a fat Boston bookseller to be out? You'll take charge. Now! Here come the barges!"

Ripley darted off among the shivering gun teams and the slush-caked wheels of piece and limber. "Unhitch those teams. Manhandle the guns right out." He sprang into the first barge as it touched the shore. "Guns to the bow. Throw up that coil of rope. Muzzles point forward, trails astern!" He raised his voice as the iron-shod wheels of the first piece thundered onto the planks of the barge. "You, sergeant. Watch me. Reeve through this way. Fast on your side! Bring on that limber. Run it right up the trail! Poles astern. Who's that officer there? Lieutenant Treadwell? Watch this. Then get your guns rolling to the next barge." He lashed ropes, guided heavy wheels, slued the muzzles of guns about as the sleet sang a thin music against the brass barrels.

Knox's gunners, captains and majors shoving and hauling with privates, trundled guns and limbers down to a second barge. Ripley sprang from craft to craft, tested knots, shouted criticism and encouragement. Then he dashed ashore, crying, "Bring on the horses."

The heavy-shouldered farm animals stood tossing their heads to the dagger drive of the sleet, snorted and strained away from the water. Ripley called: "You drivers! Stand to their heads." Then he ran behind the first pair, jammed his shoulders hard against their haunches, pressing close to avoid any chance of a kick. The horses stirred, pawed the ground, moved cautiously forward. Their hoofs rang on the bottom of the barge.

"Next pair!" roared Ripley.

The work went on. Barges pushed into the stream, were met with thundering avalanches of ice. Empty craft took their places. The heavier guns were harder to handle and called for expert use of rope and tackle. A big twenty-four canted dangerously over the water and held up a barge for nearly half an hour before it was righted. On all sides, frightened horses balked and stamped. Twice Ripley had to blindfold a jerking head, coax, shove, haul until the animal was on board.

When a stumpy twelve-pounder had been lashed to a light barge that pushed out quickly, Ripley shouted, "Bring on the next guns!"

Knox's laugh boomed from the stinging darkness. "Hear that, General? Wants more guns. Shall I make them for him?"

A tall, cloaked figure moved away through the storm. "The loading was satisfactory," was all the big Virginian said, and yet Ripley felt a sudden glow. The commander in chief had been watching silently in the dark, intent only on the job. He had seen it done properly, said so, then moved on to the next task.

The fields where the guns had been drawn up were empty and only deep ruts and dark hoof marks showed in the night. Someone called from the water's edge: "Get aboard, Rip."

Ripley scrambled in between the shivering gunners in the stern and the black strip between barge and shore began to widen. He said: "Who's here?"

Cuyler answered. "Hans and I are in charge. God, Rip, I've been across once and I tell you it's enough to make the devil's own mother miscarry! Take this and come up forward." He shoved a rough pole into Ripley's hands.

Grenda, beyond the frightened horses, said tersely, "I'll take midships."

Up by the forward oarsmen Ripley braced himself to the shiver and lurch of the boat. The current grew swifter as they moved from the shelter of the bank. Slabs of ice, twenty and thirty feet across, spun on the surface of the river whose water showed in narrow lanes that closed and widened to the drive of the cakes.

Hands numb, Ripley lunged, pushed, lunged, pushed. A crunching mass, broad as a threshing floor, swung lazily away, shot out of sight downstream. Again, a great slab, tilting, was shoved aside only to make way for a heavier one that nosed up out of the water. But always the oars churned on, drove the boat ahead.

Resting while the boat slapped on through a clear stretch, Cuyler leaned on his pole and looked downstream. "There he is again, Rip."

Ripley turned his head. Thirty feet away another barge beat through the current, the commander in chief sitting alone in the stern, silent and motionless, his eyes on the hidden left bank. "By God, Joris, I don't think he even knows it's storming. All he's thinking about is getting across and what we'll do when we get there."

Cuyler grunted. "Yes—and what'll *that* be?"

"We'll find out," said Ripley, grimly. "The Hessians are only nine miles downstream. They—"

Grenda shouted through the storm. "Port! Rip! Joris! Port!"

Ripley turned quickly, lunged. A jagged strip of ice was lifting from the water, sleet hissing on its pitted surface. His pole engaged, slid off, nearly throwing him among the cakes. He recovered, lunged again, saw the white mass rising higher and higher like the upper jaw of some great river monster. The edge was high above his head. The horses, frantic with terror, stamped and kicked. The port side of the boat began to tilt slowly downward and water slopped over the gunwale. Other poles and splintered oars joined his.

He ducked his head, drove harder, and felt the pole slipping through his torn hands. Then the point jerked downward. The great cake was edging to the left, beginning to settle as some mysterious pressure on its sunken rim was eased. The jagged lip was level with Ripley's eyes, with his shoulders. There was a sudden sucking sound. The whitish mass settled back into the river, spun and drifted on past the bow of the boat.

Grenda barked, "Lay to your oars."

The oars bit and the boat gained headway. Ripley shook off fatigue, shouted for a gunner to take his place, and moved among the horses, talking and whistling to them. A ewe-necked gray had scraped its cannon bone in the panic. Ripley tore a piece from his undershirt, fashioned a pad to protect the scrape. Suddenly he pitched forward on his knees. The boat had brought up against the left bank and dark shapes were running toward it. Grenda and his men threw a ramp ashore and began stripping ropes from wheel and trail.

Ripley and Cuyler jumped ashore. "Know where we fall in?" said Ripley.

"By the ferry shed on the river road."

They found the Fourteenth falling in by the shed, its ranks depleted by details for boat guards. Glover materialized out of the sleet, told Ripley to stay close by Major Lee, vanished again.

Ripley found the major. "Any news, sir?"

"Some," said Lee. "We wait here. They're sorting out the rest of the troops along the road. We stand firm until the regiment on our left moves off. That's Read. Stark's beyond him."

"Follow Read? That means—by God, that means Trenton!"

"So I take it. What I want you to do is to see that we don't lose touch with Read in the dark. And keep a weather eye out for Glover." Lee turned to the regiment where roll was being called. When the captains had reported he stretched out his long neck. "This is the first part of the cruise. We haven't made port yet. We're going on to hit Trenton. The order is that any man who straggles—will be shot. Stand at ease until further orders. Mayne, stay by the head of Blackler's."

The men were murmuring as Ripley splashed up to join Cuyler and Blackler. "Ain't we never going to light our galley fires?" . . . "Christ, I'm so tired I could go to sleep in front of a bowl of chowder." . . . "Hardest night's boating I ever done. Hands is fit for lobster bait and no more." . . . "What he have to say that about jumping ship for? Think we're militia that'll run soon's they land? We ain't fought a river all night just to do that, by the powers." Then their voices died away and they huddled in their dripping clothes, fussed and fretted over rags bound about their feet or carefully rearranged the wrappings of their musket-locks.

"What do you hear from Lee?" asked Blackler.

"Nothing. My idea is that we'll make a quick raid toward the outposts and then get back to our boats and across the river."

"Like Harlem Heights," said Cuyler. "It won't mean much, but it'll get the boys thinking about rum and wenches again."

Blackler nodded slowly. "Attack, stand, fall back. That's it. The general can't be thinking about anything else—yet."

A mounted aide clopped up through the sleet that was beginning to thin out. "Orders from General

Washington. No smoking. No talking. Keep your musket locks wrapped."

"Talk?" said Blackler. "Who'd talk in a gale that'd rip the masts out of a three-decker."

Lee, along the flank of the regiment, wailed: "Attention!"

There was a stir in the dark and Read's men trailed off downstream. Glover's Marbleheaders took up the sodden road after them. Ripley marched beside Cuyler and ran his eye along the weary swing of the Fourteenth. Shoulders sagged and heads were down to the blast, but there was a steady push-push to the aching legs. In places, the snow was bloody and many of the footprints were shapeless blobs that were never made by leather. Soaked boots began to split and men shuffled on, stiff-kneed as they tried to keep their broken soles in place. But nowhere, as yard and rod and mile were trodden underfoot, was a straggler seen, nowhere was equipment thrown aside as it had been by the army on Long Island, on Manhattan, and in Westchester. There was a relentless beat to the column, a grim set to half-seen jaws. The attacking men drove ahead in a silence that was broken only by the steady squelch of feet and the grind of the ice-choked river.

Slowly the sky turned to a dirty, lowering gray. Objects began to stand out in the landscape—a fire-gutted house, a broken wagon in the fields. Motion far across the snow to the left caught Ripley's eye. He fell back and pointed it out to the major. Lee nodded. "Main body. Under Nat Greene and Washington. We keep on with Sullivan and hit the town from the south. Heard any firing? No more have I. Wonder where their pickets are?"

Ripley smiled wryly. "This is Christmas morning. People make a lot of it in England and I guess in Germany. Christmas Eve—that's last night—they probably took on all the rum and wine they could."

"Christmas? Oh yes." Lee whistled softly. "That's

why the big skipper chose today, is it? He's cold as a berg, but we'll all have to dip our colors to him. Get back to Blackler."

Ripley nodded reassuringly to Blackler and Cuyler and tramped on with them. The sky was still lighter and streamed with an icy rain. A big stone house by the river showed hard and cold. Beyond it—

Far to the left, distant musketry pattered, a light field piece slammed. Someone shouted: "Quick-time! March!"

A single roaring cheer went up from Read's, was echoed by the Fourteenth. Bruised and bleeding feet slogged faster through the slush. The Marbleheaders swept up a slight rise. Ripley flicked the cloth from the lock of his fusee, snapped up the frizzen and saw a pasty cake. Useless! About him, men were muttering angrily as they flicked wet powder from their pans. Cuyler roared: "Never mind the damned locks. You've got bayonets, haven't you?"

The rise was topped and away to the left a gray stone village showed, running off from the river in a great V. Beyond it, a smaller stream flowed down to the Delaware. By the first houses a spray of men who had kept their pans dry were firing on a retreating line of blue coats and shiny conical helmets. Commands snapped out, sodden drums fluttered, and the Marbleheaders swung toward the river, Lee waving them on toward the big stone barracks out of which ran blue figures, bright with metal, heading for the center of the town.

There was a little musketry from the left. Cannon shot bellowed through the rain somewhere behind the stone walls. The streets ahead of the Fourteenth were packed with blue and brass. Ripley stumbled, looked down on a big man who lay on his face, white breeches stained with red. Three grenadiers rose from behind a low fence, and ran toward the barracks.

Lee roared: "All hands! At 'em, all hands!"

There was almost no firing now and the Fourteenth moved on through a ghastly silence that was broken only by the splash of boots and the clank of steel. Off to the right front, more units of the brigade, anonymous in the sleet, were slanting off toward the high ground beyond the barracks.

Ripley, at the flank of Blackler's company, saw something green and red rise up in front of him. He lunged with his bayonet, felt his fusee almost wrenched from his hands as the Jaeger reeled backwards. Ripley freed the blade and pounded on. To his left he saw Cuyler, amazingly lithe, slide under a vicious lunge and bring his butt down on an unshaven chin that seemed to burst in a red froth. Farther on, Grenda was yelling in German as he thrust at another Jaeger and sent him crashing to the ground. Sholes glided up beside Ripley, poised, swung an arm. A streak of light shot through the air. A flying figure threw up his hands and fell flat, a knife hilt quivering between his shoulder blades.

From behind came a shout, "Clap on all sail! Stand by to board!" Glover, gingery hair glinting with sleet, raced between the companies and thundered with a musket butt at the white door of the barracks. The wood splintered, gave way. Glover roared to unseen men to his left: "Loammi Baldwin! Set a course for the high ground." Then he dove through the door.

The right companies jammed through after Glover. Blackler swung his men along the left wall. There was no time to stop. Blackler's company, Speakman's, Bond's, crashed into a line of staring men, grenadiers, and Jaegers mixed, who were shuffling into formation. A wiry sergeant, black mustaches unkempt, whirled up his butt. Ripley parried the blow and tripped. The sergeant crashed to the ground with Gragg's hands at his throat.

Ripley recovered his footing. When he had tripped, the three-sided court into which the companies had blundered had been a whirl of fighting, stabbing men, the Germans shouting and the hard-bitten boatmen driving on in a tough silence. Now grenadiers and Jaegers were lined against one wall, muskets at their feet. Lee wiped his sword blade and snapped: "Moses Brown's men for prisoner guard. The rest—out to the street."

Grenda caught a Jaeger by his red collar and shouted in German. Then he thrust him roughly back into line. "This way for King Street, Major," he called.

Ripley was out in the cobbled road between stone houses. At the upper end more Hessians were falling back in disorder. Others in silver helmets were making for the open fields and orchards beyond the town. The boatmen began to roar—"Lay on the oars. All hands!"

Ripley caught a glimpse of Glover up a side street. The little man waved: "Tell Lee to hit them with everything from boat hooks to carronades."

Ripley caught up with Lee and gave the order. The leading companies of the Fourteenth crashed into the disordered mass of Hessians. A thickset officer grappled Cuyler and was sent spinning against a wall. Brimblecome and Gragg and Cash and Trefry cut off a solid knot of green-coated Jaegers and drove in among them. Ripley's bayonet snapped as he tried to free it from the body of a grenadier. He gave a tug, whirled the fusee by the muzzle, then checked himself. All about him, Hessians were throwing down their muskets, dropping to their knees and bleating "*Kamerad!*"

Grenda moved swiftly among them, telling them to stack their arms. Suddenly footbeats sounded down a side street. The companies re-formed, then dropped the points of their bayonets as a column of Virginia infantry trotted into view. A Virginian snarled: "Now why'd it have to be you-all!" as the two bodies stared at each other in disgust.

Lee met the leader of the new troops and talked rapidly with him. The Virginian pointed to regular blue lines that had formed stiffly in the fields at the end of the street, muskets on the ground.

A single hushed voice came from the Marbleheaders. "Boys, we've made port!"

Lee went in search of Glover, returned with the news that the Hessians had surrendered, that the fighting was over. Wearily the companies filed back to the captured barracks. Ripley dropped onto a bench beside Cuyler. "All right, Joris?"

Cuyler mumbled, "Knees are gone." Then he began to sniff. A door opened and two Hessians, smiling uncertainly, came in carrying a vast kettle. At their heels, Sholes waved his arms. "Look at this, Rip! Lots more out there. These fellers had looked at the bottoms of so many bottles last night that they ain't figured on scraping the fuzz off their tongues till noon. Get the bowls that's stacked in the corner and help them eat their breakfasts."

Men began to file up to the kettle. Ripley and Cuyler joined them, bowls in hand. Cuyler tasted his cautiously, then his face broke in a look of wonder. "Beef! Fresh beef!" Ripley nodded in silence as the full flavor of the stew swept through him.

Blackler, his face scored by a cut, joined them and ate hungrily. "They've got Grenda out there talking to the Dutchies," he said between mouthfuls. "Says we've got eight hundred prisoners at least. Rall, Lossberg, and Knyphausen regiments." He shook his head. "These damned Germans are like nothing that ever came out of the sea. Some of them fought pretty good. Now they're wrangling among themselves to see who'll *wait* on us. They want to feed us, clean our boots, clean our muskets and God knows what else."

Cuyler grunted. "Look at that pair by the kettle. Scraping like God-damned lackeys. Christ, give me a good, sullen Lobster. You can wound him or kill him or capture him and he'll curse you and keep on fighting."

Ripley filled his bowl a second time, then grinned as he looked about the room. Many of the Marbleheaders had been foraging for themselves and had found a store of salt fish. Now they wandered happily about, gnawing at great slabs. Adam Gragg, pop-eyes expressionless, stood in front of a Hessian sergeant and stared at him over the top of a dried cod which he chewed almost reverently.

A drum tapped outside. Blackler got to his feet. "Moving. Swallow all you can, boys."

"Moving where?" asked Cuyler, scooping up a last bowlful.

"Back. The Hessians take the road first. We follow." He dropped his voice. "We're all right here—only lost a man or two. But the plan hasn't worked. Ewing and Cadwalader were supposed to cross to the south and meet us here. Seems they found the river kind of full of ice and couldn't put out from shore."

The drum beat again. The Fourteenth assembled in the court, took its place in the brigade, and started off for the boats.

The sleet had stopped and the air had turned almost warm. The men staggered with fatigue but plodded doggedly on.

"Hope Remembrance'll hear about today," said Ripley. "If the army could do that after all it's suffered through—it'll do anything. She knew it. This proves it. And here's another thing, Joris. We did it all with the bayonet. That's where we're supposed to be weakest and where they're supposed to be strongest. We couldn't have managed that, six months ago."

Cuyler nodded solemnly. Far ahead on the wet road, a blue column wound and twisted, a fringe of ragged guards along its flanks. Then followed the striking force of the American army, heading for the boats and McKonkey's Ferry. Its tread was weary but there was assurance in the set of every head—New England, New York, New Jersey, Pennsylvania, Virginia, Maryland, Delaware. They were escorting victory back to the cheerless camps by the right bank of the river.

II

CUYLER poked his head through the door of the rough shack where Major Lee had set up headquarters. "Busy, Rip?" he asked.

Ripley carefully folded a sheet of paper. "Just finished a letter to Remembrance and another to my father."

"Then come with me. I want you to look in at the company quarters." Ripley picked up his cape and hat. Cuyler went on: "There's something I don't like in all the companies. Ever since we got back from Trenton they've been moping."

A few heads looked up as they entered the hut that housed Blackler's company. Men were patching their coats and breeches, mending what was left of their boots. Along one wall lay a neat row of packs. Cuyler was right. There was a different tone to the shack and to the men in it. In times past, Ripley had gone among them, as among the other companies, with the disregard of rank that characterized the Fourteenth off duty. He and Cuyler now squatted by an earthen fireplace and tried to start a conversation. They were answered in brief monosyllables, cold and final, the men scarcely looking up from their work.

Ripley tried to hide his uneasiness and told them of a report that had come down from headquarters about Trenton: how the Hessians had been taken utterly by surprise; how the officers refused to believe that the army had been ferried across the river and claimed that it had come down overland from Morristown.

There was a sharp rap at the door. A booming voice called, "Coming aboard, boys!" A gust of wind seemed to blow Glover into the hut in a great swirl of patched cape. Someone stirred up the smoldering fire. An empty keg was up-ended and Glover perched on it, rubbing his knees. "I thought you boys'd like to hear what Washington said about what you did, day before yesterday. He told me this afternoon he'd have been proud of you if you'd done nothing but fight. But when he thinks of the job you did on the boats before you started taking reefs in the Hessians, he has to stick cod hooks into himself to be sure he's not dreaming. Of course, he didn't say it just like that, but it's what he meant."

There was a grudging murmur in the shack.

"And I'll tell you what the rest of the army's saying. They say we'd have done double the job if Ewing and Cadwalader had been able to get across." He rubbed his knees again. "Then Mercer said it was the same river that you fought and you got across." He sighed. "Guess Washington's going to miss you the next time he's got water in front of him."

Brimblecome raised himself on his elbow. "Ain't January first yet."

"It's close." Glover stretched his hands to the embers. "This is the twenty-seventh. Now I do hear we're going to move again, but I guess you'll let the Jersey boatmen take the army over."

Trefry rasped, "Them Jersey bastards—"

"Don't you see? You might be in your boats when your time ran out. You might be right smack in a run of Lobsters or Hessians. It wouldn't be worth your while."

Cash growled, "No Marbleheader ever quit in the middle of a cruise."

Glover whirled suddenly, pointed to the packs that lay along the wall. His voice crackled. "Then what have you got those things whipped up for? Why do you mount guard with your feet in rags and your boots wrapped up here?"

A man growled, "We've served the time we said we would. It's up midnight the thirty-first."

"Time's up, is it? Look here. You own your own

boat. You've signed crews on it. What'd you do to a crew that crawled down out of the rigging with a storm blowing and you heading for a reef, to a crew that'd go to the fo'c'sle just because their time was up?"

Brimblecome said, "That'd be mutiny, pretty near."

"Near?" Glover jumped to his feet. "You're all seamen and you know how close it would be to mutiny. If you don't then by God you're not fit to be called Marbleheaders. You act like a lot of ferrymen that have never crossed more than twenty rod of smooth water." He paced up and down the shed, his quick steps throwing up little clots from the dirt floor. "You signed for a cruise and the cruise isn't over. How long did you sign for? For one year—*or until* the thing that started you out was settled once for all. That part wasn't on paper, but it was right in your hearts and there isn't a man here that can look me in the eye and say it wasn't."

Cash growled, "That ain't no way to put it. That—"

Glover waved his arm. "When a ship's aground off Tinker's Island, what do you do? Do you get your boats out, and send up a rocket—and then go home because you figure you've done enough?"

Trefry said, "Time's up and they ain't a soul that can make us stay."

"There is," snapped Glover. "And that's yourself—if you're a real Marbleheader."

"That's easy to say," rumbled Cash. "I got a family. I got boats. I ain't like some folks that talks big about staying with the army when all the time they're turning a penny out of it."

Glover's cloak fell to the floor with a swish. His eyes blazed. "I'll waive all rank and fight the man that says I've made a farthing out of it."

There was no answer. Glover slowly picked up his cloak and sat down on the keg. Ripley watched the faces of the men—sullen, angry, resentful, uncertain. He'd seen Glover flare up *for* his men, but never at them. He felt that a mistake had been made, that the men were slipping away from Glover.

Then Glover began to talk again, almost in soliloquy. "Yes—and the new enlistments—if you enlist Continental—are three years or the full cruise. That's the way it ought to have been at the start. What are we giving that Virginian to fight with? A few regiments that have held together. Smallwood's, Haslet's, Baldwin's. For the rest he's had to count on militia that's been raised for a few weeks, men that come in, draw supplies, eat up rations, and then run out on the tide when trouble starts."

He spun suddenly on his keg. "At New Year's, men'll be going home by the hundreds. Washington's got more regiments coming in from all over the country. But—they're not here yet. How'd you like to be Howe over in Jersey, knowing that if he waits a few more days, there'll just be Washington and a few others? Be nice, wouldn't it? But I don't figure any of us left home to keep Howe happy as a clam on a sand bar. Here's what I'm asking. Forget about the three years or duration. Washington's got authority to reenlist men for six weeks. Take the oath that way and see what happens. Give him a chance to fight—because he's fighting for all of us. Give him a chance to get his new crews aboard."

Someone mumbled: "I've writ I was coming home."

Glover's thick finger pointed. "And maybe if you and enough others do, you won't have any homes to go to. How'd you like to see those Hessians quartered along our coast?"

There was a silence. Brimblecome said in a low voice, "Well—six weeks—" The man beyond him began to unroll his pack. Glover jumped to his feet. "I knew you'd do it. I know every company in the Fourteenth will. And I can tell you that that Virginian's going to be pleased as a fiddler crab when I report to him." He strode toward the door. As he went out he called over his shoulder, "Forgot to tell you Congress gives ten dollars, hard money, to every man that takes the six weeks' oath." The door banged behind him.

Ripley looked across at Cuyler. The evil that the first of the year might bring was averted, so far as Glover's men were concerned. Talk suddenly became natural and spontaneous. Brimblecome said: "Rip, I was telling the boys about that hitch Gragg rigged on the long hill. Ain't it like this?" He began to scratch on the dirt floor. Cuyler heard a flutter of cards and slid over to join a group of players. Dice rattled softly across a blanket. Ripley drew a deep breath. All would be well with the Fourteenth. It would be well in most of the other regiments.

III

THE army was across the Delaware again, peering through the night at the British campfires on the opposite bank of Assanpink Creek below Trenton. Through a welter of slush Ripley made his way toward the flickering bivouac of the Fourteenth and called: "Blackler's ahoy!"

Shapes moved about a blaze and Cuyler cried: "Over here! What did you find out?"

Ripley perched on a log between Grenda and Cuyler. "Stay here and keep the fires going. Maybe Blackler'll know more when he comes back."

"Tells us a lot," grunted Grenda. "What was all that firing we heard when we were coming up from the river?"

Ripley dropped his voice. "Lobsters tried to cross the Creek. They got hit pretty hard, Lee says. He thinks they're waiting for daylight to have another try."

"And we're going to sit here and wait for them?" asked Cuyler in disgust.

"Looks like it," said Ripley, pointing to the glow of other bivouacs on the American side of the Creek. "And listen." He held up his hand as the clink of pick and shovel drifted back from the high ground to the north. "We're digging breastworks," he said dryly.

Cuyler groaned. "Moored fast. It's got me worried."

Ripley rubbed his numb hands. "It's not like Washington to wait like a frozen partridge for Cornwallis to come over and cook him for breakfast. All the same, it'd be a tough job to move without having the Lobsters starting a quarrel with us."

"Only one place to go if we did break off," said Cuyler glumly. "That's downstream. We couldn't get over the Delaware again with the Lobsters clawing at our hinnies. Even the Bull Seal'd admit that."

The three plunged into gloomy speculation as a colder wind sprang up from the northeast. Then a voice close by whispered: "Get the company into formation. No talking in ranks."

They got to their feet as Blackler moved into the circle of light. Cuyler asked: "We moving?"

"Don't know," said Blackler. "Hurry up and keep them quiet."

With a subdued rustle the company and the rest of the Fourteenth formed in the wavering light. Hoofs plopped in the slush and two of Knox's guns rolled past the front of the regiment, axles muffled. The drivers were dismounted and the cannoneers walked by the teams holding the trace chains in their bare hands to deaden the clink of metal.

Ripley muttered to Cuyler: "I knew Washington wouldn't stay here. Look—there's another regiment moving off in front of us."

Through set teeth Cuyler said: "He's a gambler. Down the river to the sea *and* the Lobster prison ships. We'll— Here's Lee."

The company commanders joined the major, then doubled back to their units. Blackler said in a low voice, "Wheel to the right. March."

The regiment swung into column, slanted away from its blazing fires and struck downstream. The wind that had sprung up earlier was slowly turning the slush into hard ruts and Ripley heard the squelching steps change to crisp, dry beats. The march went on for an hour or more before word was passed down that talking was permitted.

Cuyler exhaled noisily. "Must mean we're safe now."

"Maybe," said Ripley. "I've had my head pulled in like a turtle's, expecting a Lobster bullet in my back. Wonder how far we've come." He sniffed. "Am I crazy? I can't get a whiff of the Delaware. I can't— By God, I've got it! Joris, we're heading *inland!*"

Cuyler growled: "Can't be."

"We are. We're heading inland under the biggest gambler in the country. He's left his fires burning to diddle Cornwallis and, sure as corn sprouts, we're setting a course dead along the Lobsters' lines of communication."

Grenda, marching behind Ripley, said: "Right. Heading smack into his harbor with our gun ports open."

Cuyler pushed back his hat. "So help me, I've been cursing Washington for making us retreat! Wait till the rest of the boys find out."

"They knew it before I did," said Ripley. "I'd been wondering what was making them step out like a school of horse mackerel." He shook himself. "Come on. No halts."

The march went on through the night, into the first glow from the east. Then, as a hard, cold dawn broke, Ripley cocked his head at a sudden spatter of musketry that sounded out of sight to the left flank. "Beyond that ridge," he said to Cuyler.

"Skirmishers," said Grenda.

"Maybe," said Ripley. "All I know's what I see—and that's Hitchcock's Rhode Islanders just behind us. We're getting close to Princeton, Joris. Like to get a chance to look at the college there."

"Rip thinks he's on a tour, Hans. One day you'll see a book called: 'Travels into the Interior Parts of New Jersey,' by R. Mayne, Esq. He'll dedicate it to— Ho! That's closer."

Over the crunch of feet, musketry sounded louder. A twelve-pounder slammed. "Skirmishers, hell," said Grenda. "Sounds more like a surf off Cape Ann."

Ripley looked to the left but all that part of the countryside was cut off by rising ground and by the frost-coated trees that lifted stark boughs to the sky. Then, from the rear, hoofbeats drummed. Glover, eyes staring, raced up the column, pulled in and spoke briefly to Lee, tore on. Lee shouted: "Wheel to the left! By companies! Guide on Baldwin's to your right!"

The regiment swung into line and plunged into the wooded fields. Cuyler shouted: "Now it's coming!"

Down a glade to the left, where Hitchock's men were deploying, two six-pounders jolted off toward the hidden din, the drivers lashing at their horses. Captains were shouting: "Guide right! Guide right!"

Ripley dodged and wove among the trees, cursing the frosted ground that seemed to slide his feet out from under him. Men stumbled and slipped. Cuyler tripped on a rock and crashed to the ground. Cash, close behind him, helped him to his feet.

The wooded rise sloped up in front of Ripley. He fought and pulled his way forward, catching at branches and trunks. Suddenly he stopped as he reached the crest.

Down in the shallow valley, nearly a mile away, the tragedy of Kip's Bay was being played out again. Through a welter of smoke, Continental troops and militia were caught up in a wild panic, were running to the rear, throwing away their arms. At the far end of the valley, a British field piece slammed and a hard, compact body of red infantry drove on after the fugitives. By Ripley's side Cuyler croaked: "No! No!"

It was Kip's Bay. Among the frantic, running men a

single horseman raged and stormed, laying about right and left with the flat of his sword. The tide flowed away from him and left him alone to face the oncoming light infantry. Grenda howled: "They'll get him. It's Washington! He's adrift alone!"

Then from hidden land beyond the valley's edge, a solid brown column rolled out onto the field, lapped about the single horseman who waved them on, standing in his stirrups. Lee, at the head of Glover's men, pointed: "It's Pennsylvania! Double time!"

As he spoke, a second column broke into sight and Hitchcock's Rhode Islanders, bayonets aslant, drove on at right angles to the advancing Pennsylvanians. Smoke welled and billowed up. Climbing a rail fence with Blackler's men yelling behind him, Ripley saw the two American columns hit the British. He roared: "Clap on all sail!" Through the smoke, less than half a mile away now, the brass light-infantry caps glinted, the bayonets of the Rhode Islanders gleamed with each lunge and parry. Then the light infantry halted, wavered, and the red column slowly began to fray out at the rear like an old rope. One red dot, two, ten, twenty, they began to run.

"By God, it's a rout!" yelled Cuyler.

Blackler shouted, "Keep those feet moving. We want to be in on this!" Other captains were bellowing — "At 'em, all hands!"

Ripley's throat ached with the effort of shouting and his eyes stared in incredulous joy as the tattered red retreat swept past a big house, eddied about a barn. He shook his fusee. "We've got them! We've got them!"

A horseman burst from the woods at the left and thundered on past Ripley. "Major Lee! Orders from Brigade." He bent from the saddle, shouting, then pelted on. Lee roared, "Oblique to the right!"

The Fourteenth, stunned, swung away from the melee in the ringing valley. Cuyler thumped his fusee butt on the ground. "God in heaven! Why? Why don't we go down there?" Others took up his cry.

Blackler stormed at his cursing men. "Orders. Setting a new course. Eyes in the boat!"

The Fourteenth moved away, saw Baldwin's men beyond them marching sullenly toward a rocky hollow. Then Glover plunged down on his big horse, waving his hat toward the hollow. "More Lobsters in there, just coming up. Loammi Baldwin! Dress to your right on Shepherd!"

Lee cupped his hands. "Any more orders?"

Glover made a wild gesture. "Fresh troops! In with the bayonet!" As he whirled away, the hollow became suddenly alive with stabs of flame and oily smoke.

Ripley ducked his head as Lee ordered quick time. There were trees and rocks close in front of him. He fired at a light infantryman, saw Cuyler drive hard with his bayonet at a big grenadier. The hollow echoed with shots, cries, and the incessant grinding of feet.

Then Ripley was across the hollow and details of Glover's men were hustling captured grenadiers and light infantry to the rear. Cuyler was panting beside him and Grenda, tight-lipped and silent, wrapped a cloth about a hand that spurted blood. There were more redcoats in the open field and the Marbleheaders drove hard in among them yelling: "Lay to the oars! All hands! All hands!"

The scattered knots of red gave way sullenly, then broke. There was a church off to the left and beyond it a brick building with a cupola. Men were pouring through the doors under the direction of a big grenadier officer. Ripley stumbled through the churchyard, hurdled a gravestone, and vaulted a flat-topped wall. From the extreme left a shouting mass of men, some of them in ragged brown and red jackets, swept across the front of the Fourteenth and slammed at the closed doors of the church. Lee waved them on to the building with the cupola. "Never mind the church!" he roared: "Get aboard the college!"

Men from the other regiments were already thundering at the doors of the college with logs, and Henry Knox's frantic gunners were trundling a six-pounder over the rough ground. Lee made a wild motion to the rear of the building and the leading companies of the Fourteenth whirled on in his wake. Lee roared again: "Stand by to board!"

Ripley caught at a high window ledge and swung himself up. The butt of his fusee, swinging loose on his back, smashed against the glass. He got one leg into the room, shouted, "Boarders ahoy!" A door at the far end of the room banged open, a long barrel blasted smoke and fire, and Ripley's hat whirled from his head. His face white and his mouth dry, he yelled: "Watch your aim, you froach!"

The shirted Marylander in the doorway scowled at him. "Keep your head where it belongs, then. Supposed to be Lobsters in here!"

Other Marbleheaders were clambering astride the sills as the Marylander slipped away from the door. Beyond him in the corridor, files of men in red coats were tramping in surly silence toward the gaping doors. Their hands, held high above their heads, were empty.

Ripley said: "Done it," and made way for Lee, who scrambled up beside him, leaped into the room, and vanished among the prisoners in the hall. Someone began to laugh thickly. Cuyler, panting and flushed, waved to Ripley from the next sill. "Hey! Guess we've knocked down all the pins on this bowling green! Speakman and Courtis hit beyond us and sent two companies of Lobsters spinning." He swung his legs back out of the window. "Come on. Blackler's bawling for us to fall in!"

The drop to the ground burned Ripley's feet. He bent over to rub an ankle, pausing among the men of the company who jostled past him. A musket slammed somewhere from beyond the college and Ripley clapped his hand to the back of his neck. Then he stared at his reddened fingers. "What clumsy bastard did that?" he shouted. "Half an inch lower and—"

Three more shots rang out. Brimblecome crashed against the wall, holding his hands over a spouting hole in his abdomen. A stray man from Bond's company spun about and went down, swearing dully as he clutched at a shattered knee. Grenda shouted: "Captain Blackler! Half company! Aft those bushes!" Then he slipped to the ground, just a tangle of old clothes. His face was turned toward the east, a face that showed chips of bone and tooth in the red wreckage.

Without command, the rest of the company formed into line and swung toward the bushes. Ripley ran to his place on the flank, dimly aware that Sholes was waving to the men near him to fan out. Another figure dropped close to Ripley as musketry broke out again and the company roared and quickened its pace.

Suddenly the bushes were close to Ripley and he saw a cloud of light infantrymen rise from a kneeling position and form a rough square, back to back, their bayonet points steady. A white face loomed in front of him, was jammed against his as he parried a vicious lunge. The light infantryman struggled in silence, trying to free his piece. Ripley gave ground, then swung for the man's groin with the butt of his fusee. His blow was met with a strong parry and his enemy closed with him again. Ripley's breath came faster and faster. He disengaged, lunged and missed, was saved only by the advantage that his lighter fusee gave him over the other's clumsy musket. He looked into the eyes close to his to read their intent, but the man's gaze was riveted on Ripley's feet. Obviously, he was an expert fencer. Twice Ripley's coat was pierced by the bayonet's point. Once his fusee slid over the musket barrel and he shouted in triumph, only to see his thrust spoiled by a deft movement of his opponent's body.

Sweat was blinding him and a tight band seemed clamped about his lungs. The light infantryman began to press him harder. Suddenly the musket clattered to the ground and the man threw up a bleeding hand in an unconscious gesture. Ripley thrust his point against his pulsing throat: "Give over?"

The soldier's face began to work. "Lucky Yankee bastard!" He waved the bloody hand. "Soon's this heals, so 'elp me bleeding Christ, I'll fight you man to man, musket against musket." He began to sob with rage and the pain of his wound. Ripley stepped on the fallen musket. "Get back to the rear. Our surgeon'll see to your wound." He drew a long breath and looked about among the trampled bushes. A scowling knot of light infantrymen were being herded back toward the college. A dozen others lay stretched on the ground, mingled with the bodies of some of Blackler's men.

Ripley wiped his forehead with a shaky hand. The fight was over. He would have to find Glover and report this last flare-up. He took two steps, then had to steady himself with his fusee. Some of his men moved past him, drove his wounded opponent along with them. A hand fell on his shoulder and Sholes panted: "Different from fighting with them Germans, ain't it? Me and Adam had to choke four of them silly before they'd give over. You all right, Rip?"

Ripley's face felt stiff as he answered, "Guess so. Got to find Glover."

Sholes shook his head. "Heard Blackler say him and Lee'd dig him out. You better get hold your breath and pull hard for a minute. Have trouble?"

"Lucky. My point caught him in the hand. Where's Joris?"

Sholes jerked a thumb over his shoulder. "Seen him and some others hit down among them rocks. He'll be all right."

Ripley said: "Got to find him. That was a hard fight. Anything could have happened."

Sholes at his side, he ran toward the rocks shouting: "Joris! Joris!" But nowhere did the New Yorker's voice answer. He questioned the men who were tramping back to the college and the rest of the regiment, but no one could tell him anything definite.

Sholes took his arm. "This's been kind of a battle, Rip. Just one more place to look."

Stumbling over the rough ground, Ripley went numbly back to the college with Sholes. The old ranger pushed on through the broad corridor whose floor was splashed with wet, dark stains. "This way," he said and carefully opened a door.

Just over the sill a man squatted, his fists clenched. He barely moved as Ripley and Sholes edged in. He said in a low tone: "Easy, Ike, easy."

Isaac Spofford, the surgeon, grunted. "Doing the best I can, John, without rum to deaden things."

Glover, still squatting, shook his head. "Then easy as you can, Ike."

Ripley saw the surgeon bend over the bare torso of one of the Trefry boys, a torso whose left side was smeared with red from shoulder to hip. The surgeon's knife flashed, Trefry winced and tried to break away from the two men who held him down. The steel deftly laid open the muscle that ran from neck to shoulder, was replaced by a probe. Trefry gave a strangled cry. Spofford grunted and flicked out a bullet that had been lodged in the thick muscle. "No bandage. Got to use his shirt and some tow. See to him!" He nodded to his assistants and passed on to the next man. As Ripley followed him, he saw Glover snatch a strip of dirty linen from the hands of one of the men and begin to bind it deftly about the incision.

The light in the long room was bad and Ripley had to move slowly from straw heap to straw heap. Marylanders and New Jerseymen were mixed in with the wounded from Glover's brigade. Some lay quietly, others writhed and moaned, breathing heavily through slack lips. Suddenly Ripley ran forward. "Joris!"

A big form stirred. "That you, Rip?" Cuyler's voice was thick.

Ripley dropped to his knees. "What's the matter?"

"Leg." Cuyler stirred, then winced.

"Hurt much?"

"Like hell," said Cuyler between his teeth. "Smack in the middle of the thigh."

Sholes, squatting on the other side, nodded. "Ain't no use pretending a gouge ain't hurting. Get the bone?"

"Don't know. It was just as we started after them, about the last round they fired, I guess. My leg buckled and someone carried me in here. Where's Ike Spofford?"

"He'll be along," said Ripley.

"He'd better be." Cuyler's voice rose. "Damn it, I can't stay here. Look at that man next you. Opened up by a bayonet the way you'd open a sack of meal. He was all falling out. I heard him die just a minute ago. And the Virginian across the room's got his jaw shot away and tried to yell with what's left." He paused. "Or maybe he's given up trying."

Sholes caught Ripley's eye in the dim light and laughed. "This ain't nothing, Joris. Mind a time beyond Fort Ti and some wounded was left to a bark shack. No guard. No sawbones. Just left. Come sundown the bark took fire somehow and that was all."

Ripley caught Sholes's eye on him again. "How'd you hear about it if that was all?"

"Me? I could crawl. The others ain't been able to. No, Joris, this is fine, here. Kind of wish I'd got tapped myself. Dry straw, first-class sawbones, good roof, plenty to tend you. Course, you don't feel mighty good just now but that's 'cause a bullet always kind of tickles your innards." Ripley jumped to his feet as Spofford bent over Cuyler. The surgeon snarled, "Don't crowd me," and Ripley and Sholes moved away a few steps.

The examination was rapid. Spofford got to his feet, wiping his hands. "If I had rum, I'd amputate just to be safe. If I was sure there were splinters from the bone I would anyway." He looked down at Cuyler. "Want to take a hazard?"

Ripley, moving nearer, saw Cuyler's mouth tighten. "What are the odds?"

"If there are splinters, you'll get gangrene and that'll be all. All. If there aren't—maybe you'll still get gangrene."

"I'll gamble," said Cuyler.

Spofford turned to Ripley. "Get him to the carts, then. We're moving. I'll make a more thorough probe at the first halt."

"Moving?" said Cuyler as Ripley and Sholes carefully lifted him to his feet.

"We're anchored right in the middle of Howe's army. We're slipping cable for Morristown." Spofford turned away and called: "Where's the next man?"

As Ripley and Sholes, staggering under Cuyler's weight, made their slow passage down the room, they heard a deep voice from the door. "Leave our dead? Marblehead doesn't do that for men that have sailed a fair course and made port. I've General Washington's approval."

A long line of carts was being carefully loaded in front of the college. Ripley made Cuyler as comfortable as possible in deep straw. When the regiment was formed and moved off, Ripley walked along beside the wagon, one hand resting on its side.

As he stumbled on, he thought somberly of the carts ahead and their silent burdens—Hans Grenda and his shattered head; Brimblecome, who had bled to death by the wall of the college; Cash with the bayonet thrust through his throat, and the others who had fallen in the last moments of the fight. There they lay, as the army set out along the hard road that led to the western highlands and the heights of Morristown—Marbleheaders, who would never again sniff the breeze that comes out of the sea at sunrise, who would never again hear the boom of the surf against the rocks of Cape Ann as their boats worked out to meet the long rollers of the North Atlantic.

IV

Cuyler blinked in the sun that was streaming through the window of the cottage beyond Morristown and carefully rubbed his thickly swathed leg. "Call me a damned fool, would you?" He grinned at Ripley. "Where'd I be now if I'd let Ike Spofford saw up my gams down on the plains? I could hear you arguing with him to amputate. I thought at the time you just wanted to get a good steak off me and I still think so."

Ripley shook his head. "I was damned hungry, but any self-respecting cannibal would have turned up his nose at the smell that was coming out of that wound. It was worse than gangrene."

Cuyler yawned and stretched. "At least, you got back at me for what I helped do to you at the Morses' over your heel, so we're even up to that point. If Ike'd only tell me how much longer I've got to stay in bed, I'd feel pretty good."

"He won't tell you. I'm going to. He said to let you know you'd be out on crutches in a week and walking in three. I've got to go along and see the old Bull Seal now. I'll look in tonight with some rum." He waved from the door and stepped out into the January cold.

At Glover's hut the sentries admitted him without question. From a partitioned space, Glover called: "That you, Mayne? Come in and see an old friend."

Ripley pushed past a blanket door, saluted Glover, and then looked in polite wonder at the emaciated man who sat with his back to the oiled-paper window. The man raised a negligent hand. "I warned him in Cambridge, John, that I was a well of garrulity. It may be that still he fears me."

Ripley said: "Febiger! I thought—I mean we heard that you'd been taken prisoner at Quebec. I'm damned glad to see you alive and free."

Febiger rose and took Ripley's outstretched hand. "To being taken, I would not say no. But I have lately been exchanged. So back Old Denmark comes to his own country and its army."

Ripley turned to Glover. "I hope you're getting him for the Fourteenth, sir."

Glover grinned ruefully. "Damn it, so do I. But Washington's got other ideas about Kit."

Febiger seated himself again and filled a long, porcelain pipe. "He is obstinate, that one. For two days I argue with him and he will not be turned aside. Time runs short and I wish to come here and see my old friends, so in the end it is I who give in. I am to command a Virginia regiment."

"Ought to be a brigade," said Ripley.

Febiger chuckled. "A not so long time ago, you would have asked me how I, from Massachusetts, could consider turning soldier of fortune to command a foreign regiment from Virginia."

"Blame yourself if you don't like the change," grinned Ripley.

"Yes, there is much on my shoulders," said the Dane. "For it was through me that you and Cuyler came to serve under John Glover." He tamped the bowl of his pipe. "He has been reading to me from what he calls his log. I find what he reads about you two to be all that there is of the most interesting. Unofficially, he went so far as to tell me that you had not too many entries of a nature unfavorable against your names."

Glover coughed. "Never went so far as that, Kit. Now look here, Mayne, I've got another job I want you to do. Sit down and listen to it."

Ripley brightened as he took a chair. "You're going to let me take those men and see what the last of the Lobsters are doing?"

Glover shook his head. "This is something very different. A dull cruise, but it's got to be done." He sprang up from his chair and began to walk up and down the room. "I want you to go to Marblehead."

Ripley's jaw fell. "Marblehead, sir?"

"That's what I said. You'll be gone a long time."

Ripley shoved his hands into his pockets and set his chin. "You mean I'd be away from the Fourteenth some weeks, sir?"

"Months," said Glover.

Ripley shifted in his chair, then broke out: "Damn it—I mean can you send someone else, sir? I'm not a Marbleheader. You've got plenty of men who'd give an arm to get home."

"That's why I'm sending you. Or rather—why I want you to go. You'll be no good for the job if you don't take it willingly. And I need you for it."

Ripley said coldly, "Of course I'll go—if ordered."

Febiger walked to the mud fireplace and rapped out his pipe. "It might be well, John, to tell him what you told me."

"I'm coming to that, Kit. Get back in your chair, fill up your pipe, and listen. If you think I'm asking too much of Mayne—well, I'd be glad to have your reasons." He turned to Ripley. "Most of the men signed on for six weeks more after Trenton. Time's running out. A lot have signed on for the whole cruise, as you know. But a good many haven't. A good many I'm not letting, for family reasons." He took up his pacing again. "We've got to recruit. I'm authorized to send an officer to do it."

Ripley burst but, "Send *me*, a stranger, not even from the same county, to recruit men in Marblehead?"

Febiger spoke quietly. "An American officer is sent to recruit for an American regiment."

"I know," said Ripley. "But will the Marbleheaders see that?"

Glover whirled on him. "You've got to make them. I could send a dozen men—and they couldn't do the work that you'll be able to do. I don't want a Marbleheader. I want someone who won't think in terms of the Neck and the harbor and Front Street, someone who'll see that he's not drumming up men for a Marblehead regiment but for an American regiment. Tell them what you've seen Virginians do alongside of your own men. Tell them about Haslet's men at Long Island, tell them about Knowlton's rangers at the Hollow Way. Tell them—tell them we're sailing in the biggest ship that was ever launched and that the Fourteenth's only part of the crew. Make them see that hands from other states are playing a seaman's part in this. And for God's sake tell them that the ship's being skippered by a man with the coldest head and the truest heart on the continent."

"They'll have heard all that," said Ripley.

"Not from you." He perched on the edge of his table, feet swinging. "I can see you up there, talking. And I can see people listening—if you'll put your heart into it. I can see every soul in that town listening to you and steering right along in your wake because they haven't known you all their lives. You've been sailing on the same ship with Marblehead boys and you come to tell them what those boys and what that ship's been doing." He suddenly jumped to the floor. "Damn it, are you afraid of the good you can do? Are you afraid to go up there and tell the people that the cruise is a long one, but that we're going to make port sure as shad run in the spring? Are you afraid that you may come trailing back with fifty good recruits for the Fourteenth?" He threw himself back into his chair. "Maybe it is too hard. There's another thing I didn't mention. You'll have competition. Lee's to be made a colonel. He's going back there, too, to recruit a whole *new* regiment of Marbleheaders. Yes, you'd have that to face."

Ripley got up. "I'll face it."

Glover jumped up again and seized Ripley's hand. "Knew I could count on you. And I'm glad you crossed me. Damned glad. If you'd gone too easy I might have had my doubts about your being able to do it. What you say, Kit?"

The Dane blew out a cloud of smoke. "You spoke of the fifty men that Mayne would bring back with him. I will wager this pipe, which I somewhat treasure, against a pair of boots that you shall make for me with your own hands, that he brings seventy-five, Lee or no Lee."

"Done!" said Glover. "Now Mayne, I want you to start as soon as you can. We'll look after Cuyler for you. See the adjutant for your travel papers. He'll know all about it."

"You have been most wise to forget one point up to now, John," said Febiger blandly. "Would it not be well to call it to Mayne's attention before you pack him off to the chills of the east coast?"

Glover pursed up his lips. "A small matter. Very small. Just that—ah—I'm also authorized to give you a three weeks' furlough before you embark on your duties. And you may choose your own route." He snatched up papers from the table. "Now I've got lists and returns to make up. Get started as soon as you can, get the men, and be back here quicker than frosted hell once you've got them. That's all."

A furlough! Free to choose his own route! Ripley tried to stammer out his thanks, was dismissed, and ran out of the hut. The door creaked again as he started out through the camp and Febiger hurried after him. "You will do well in Marblehead," he said as he caught up with Ripley. "I expect to win my new boots and shall think of you with gratitude each time I put them on." He walked lightly on beside Ripley, gaunt and patched, but swinging a stick with all his old nonchalance. "Now you must take me to see that good Cuyler about whom I have often wondered as I have wondered about you." He looked around to watch a file of Pennsylvania infantry swing off toward the town. "It is good. It is good. Often, when a prisoner, I doubted our future. As soon as I was freed and made my way back here, I saw and I listened and I thought. Soon my last doubt had gone. There will be times ahead bad enough to split one, of course."

"And we'll be ready for them," said Ripley. "Here's Cuyler's hut. After you, Colonel Febiger."

V

THROUGH a January thaw that had turned the roads of western Massachusetts into ropes of mud, Ripley spurred his horse over the crest of the last hill. Then he stood erect in the stirrups and looked down into Great Barrington, his whole being taut and breathless with elation. There, far below him beyond the bulk of the Town Hall, beyond the snow-mottled common, the chimneys of the Morse house showed clear in the noon sun.

He slammed his hat against his horse's flank and sent the animal slipping and snorting down the last slope. The road bent and twisted, led on through a tunnel-like cleft and finally shot him out onto the west end of the common. He shouted and waved his hat as he caught sight of the white walls and the green fan-lighted door toward which he had been riding ever since he first started down from the heights of Morristown.

Suddenly he swung his horse off the road and urged him into a gallop as he caught sight of Remembrance on the hillside behind the house. Head thrown back, she was tugging on a rope whose taut end disappeared behind a long woodpile. Ripley leaned forward in the saddle and began to shout: "Remembrance. Get the town clerk. Get the minister! No time to write about it! Hurry!"

The rope slipped from her hands as she turned quickly. Then she began to run toward him in a flutter of scarlet-lined cape. He dropped from the saddle, jumped over a snow-covered rock, and caught her in his arms. Her face was cool and fresh against his and her hands were clenched about his shoulders. At last she said huskily, "Rip! Rip! I can't believe it!"

He laughed and rubbed his cheek against hers. "But you're going to. And you're going to start right now." He laughed again and held her tighter.

Her lips curved gently. "I guess you're right." A sudden bawling broke out from behind the woodpile. Remembrance started. "The calf! I forgot!"

"Calf? Forget about him."

"I had, just now. I was bringing him home from Jodab Bumpus's over the hill. He fought all the way and then tried to run home when we got this far. I'll never catch him now."

"It doesn't matter," said Ripley softly.

"But—" began Remembrance. Then the calf emerged from behind the woodpile, moved slowly down the hill, stopped to sniff at Ripley's horse and ambled on toward an open shed behind the Morse house.

"See?" said Ripley. "Everything's going the way we want it."

She raised her face slightly. "Everything. Everything. No—wait a minute, Rip. You haven't told me anything yet."

"No time. There still isn't. Come on." He slipped his arm about her waist. "This way. The horse will follow. Just remember what I said. Town clerk. Minister. That's all you need to know. The rest's flumadiddles and fiddlefaddles—for the moment. Furlough in Concord. Father's there now from Philadelphia. Rest of the winter and part of the spring in Marblehead. Further details may be obtained from the adjutant's office on proper application."

She laughed and squeezed his arm as they went down the hill. "That's all I want to know for now." She stopped suddenly. "Look!"

Down the broad street below them marched a long column of men, muskets aslant, heading west through the town. Ripleys breath went in sharply. "For Washington," he said.

She nodded. "All through the states men are on the march. They've found an idea that's bigger than all of us."

"Bigger than all of us," said Ripley slowly. "Hans Grenda knew that. Hans Grenda and Brimblecome and Cash knew it." His throat tightened as he watched the steady march.

Along the frozen Mohawk, men were marching. They were coming down from the Catskills, over the Jersey flats, up from the rolling hills and forests of Pennsylvania, from the tidal reaches of Delaware and Maryland and Virginia. They would keep on coming. They would always seem too few. They would always be just enough, driven on to do what must be done by the strength of their birthright and their heritage.

Along the heights of Morristown, Washington's weary, tattered army looked back on the campaign that was just over. Within the space of a week, this force that the British had treated as almost nonexistent had struck two heavy blows that altered the war and men's thoughts about the war. The daring thrust at Trenton, the swift march deep into the British and Hessian lines at Princeton, had stunned Howe. Washington had not been destroyed as by all the rules of war he should have been. He had turned and struck when, by Howe's logic, any reasonable man could have seen that he had no force with which to strike.

Howe was stung into action. The chain of posts that had stretched to the upper reaches of the Delaware was withdrawn and New Jersey was slowly cleared of invaders. In British-held New York, there was whispered speculation on who would succeed Billy Howe, the man who had won so many battles, but never a war.

Little by little, Washington's strength grew. Men reenlisted. New levies were sent to him over the road. Tried men from the wreck of Arnold's Quebec campaign emerged from captivity—Dan Morgan, the rifleman, Febiger the Dane, and others. The perils and disasters of the year 1776 were over. Men turned their faces toward those of 1777. They, too, would be met and surmounted.

ABOUT THE AUTHOR

As an historical novelist, Bruce Lancaster is known both for his authenticity and his storytelling ability. He was born and raised in Worcester, Mass., and graduated from Harvard University. His education was interrupted by service with the U.S. Army in the Mexican Border Campaigns and in France during WWI. Before beginning his writing career at the age of 40, Mr. Lancaster's vocational pursuits included the Foreign Service in Kobe, Japan, football coaching, amateur dramatics, and various sales and administrative positions. His first historical novel was *Wide Sleeve of Kwannon*. It was followed by the best-selling *Guns of Burgoyne*. Other works by Mr. Lancaster include: *For Us the Living, Bright to the Wanderer, Bride of a Thousand Cedars, No Bugles Tonight, Roll Shenandoah, Venture in the East, Night March, Guns on the Forest, The Scarlet Patch*, and the definitive volume, *The American Heritage Book of the Revolution.* Before his death in June of 1963, at the age of sixty-six, Mr. Lancaster had written nineteen books and was at work on another. All were superior examples of writing skill and historical accuracy, which won him wide acclaim from critics and readers alike.